Endless
Change

Also by this Author

Mystery/Suspense:

Looking Over Your Shoulder
Lion Within
Pursued by the Past
In the Tick of Time
Loose the Dogs

Cowritten with D. D. VanDyke
California Corwin P. I. Mystery Series
The Girl in the Morgue (Coming Soon)

Zachary Goldman Mysteries
She Wore Mourning (Coming Soon)

Young Adult Fiction:

Breaking the Pattern:
Deviation
Diversion
By-Pass

Between the Cracks:
Ruby
June and Justin
Michelle
Chloe
Ronnie (Coming in 2018)

Medical Kidnap Files
Mito
EDS
Proxy

Endless Change

P.D. Workman

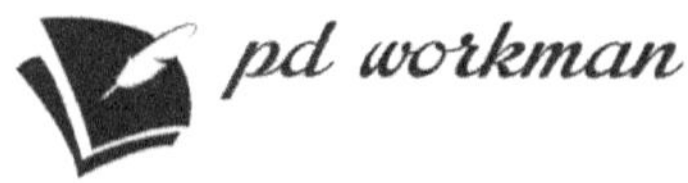 pd workman

Copyright © 2017 P.D. Workman

ISBN: 9781988390611

To those who have lost their childhoods

And those who haven't

Acknowledgments

I wish to personally thank the following people for their contributions and knowledge and other help in creating this book:

Beta readers, Talena Winters, Victoria Schwimley, and Hazel Grusendorf.

Jim Grusendorf for editing.

Chapter One

PARKER HIT HIS BIKE brakes and waited for the light to change. He always got stopped at that light, and it always took forever to change to green. He would just hop across the street during a lull in traffic, but it was a busy time of day and the cars were whizzing by pretty quickly. Not a good time to compete for physical space.

A movement caught his eye and he turned his gaze to watch a woman shuffle into the alleyway. She was short and stout and wore a hoodie, with the hood pulled up over her head. She was looking back and forth and over her shoulder as if she were trying to make sure no one was watching her. But she didn't turn far enough around to look at Parker.

There were lots of homeless people, old and young, in the neighborhood, but this was not a regular that Parker recognized. He couldn't remember ever seeing her before. That wasn't unusual, and she wouldn't even have merited a second glance if he hadn't been bored and waiting at the light.

She disappeared from his view. In a couple more minutes, the light changed, and Parker stood on his pedals to get moving again. As he went by the alleyway, he peered inside to see if the woman were still in sight. She was, not unexpectedly, going through dumpsters. Looking for food or for bottles to cash in for refunds. She turned her head as he rolled by and saw him watching her.

Parker pumped the pedals. He didn't want to get into an altercation with her because she was paranoid about people watching her. And he needed to get to school before the bell rang, which was going to be tight. He got about half a block away before processing the face that had looked back at him.

A broad, round, black face. Not a saggy, wrinkled, broken-toothed old woman like he had expected. The bangs that emerged from her hood were a bright pastel pink. She had on makeup, or at least a shimmery pink lip gloss.

Parker braked and looked back over his shoulder. Had he really seen her clearly, or was his mind just filling in the blanks? A teenager, close to his age, going through the dumpsters. Where was her family? Was she a runaway? He couldn't remember seeing her around the neighborhood before, and the harder he thought about it, the more sure he was that she was a complete stranger. He had never seen her around before. He would have noticed her. She wasn't exactly inconspicuous.

He turned his bike in a slow circle, trying to decide what to do. He knew what his mom would say. Go to school. Don't be late. Take care of the things that you are supposed to do. Be responsible. All of those things that never seemed important when he had a choice to make.

Parker pedaled back toward the alley, avoiding a few pedestrians who seemed intent on getting hit. He looked back down the alley again. She was still there, her back to him once more, her form hidden beneath the shapeless hoodie. Parker stood there on his pedals for a moment, staying balanced on his wheels with just the slightest movement. He watched her. She looked back over her shoulder again, and he saw that his assessment had been correct. She was a little older than he was, maybe fifteen or sixteen. Her eyes glittering and lively, cheeks round, and skin unlined. She saw him watching her.

"Get out of here," she told him crossly. "Leave me alone."

Parker completed a couple of revolutions of his pedals to draw closer to her. "Hi, there."

She frowned at him, thin brows coming down and mouth shut in a straight line. Parker waited for a few moments in silence.

"Hi," she said back finally.

"I'm Parker."

She glanced around. In particular, she looked behind him, seeing if there were anyone else there. A crony or an audience.

"Shouldn't you be at school?"

In the distance, they both heard the school buzzer over the pedestrian traffic and car engines. Parker gave her a little grin. "Uh… yeah, sounds like I missed first bell. Going to be late now."

"You'd better go, then."

"What's your name?"

"You don't ask homeless people their names."

"Why not?"

"Because we're not really people, like you. We're just anonymous. Like the rats." She poked into another garbage bin and pulled out a couple of empty bottles.

"You're a person," Parker pointed out. "Just like me. What's your name?"

She stared at him for a few minutes before going back to her dumpster diving.

"Dakota," she said, not looking back at him.

"Dakota? That's pretty."

"It's a stupid name. It's the name of a state. Who wants to be named after a stinking, dusty state?"

"I think it's pretty. I like it."

"Well, yours is Parker. What kind of judge are you?" Her tone was sharp. "Is Parker your first name or your last name?"

"First. My last name is Jurek."

"What kind of name is that?"

"Polish, apparently."

She snorted, eyeing his white complexion. "That figures."

"You're homeless?"

"Yeah, I'm homeless. What do you think, I just do this for the fun of it?" She gestured to the garbage cans.

"Are you new here? Where did you come from?"

"None of your business."

"Where are you staying? In a shelter?"

"Sometimes." Her tone said 'not very often.' She turned her head to look at him for another moment. When she turned back to the garbage bins, he noticed that her hands were still. She had abandoned her search for the moment, unsure what he was going to do. Parker crept a little closer on his bike.

"You don't go to school?"

"Does it look like I go to school? They wouldn't want me there."

"Why not?"

"I stink," Dakota said explosively. "I stink and I'm… dirty. You wouldn't want me sitting next to you like this, would you?"

He was close enough to see her clothes better, and to smell her. Her clothes were wrinkled and worn, but not stained. Not dirty, like she asserted. And she didn't smell bad. A little sweaty, maybe, but not ripe like some of the bums he passed on the street.

"You don't look so bad."

"Well, I can't go to school like this. And I don't have a shower, so that's not going to change anytime soon."

"Where are your parents? Are you all on your own?"

"I don't have anyone taking care of me."

"What happened to them? Did you run away?"

Dakota turned fully around and faced him with her hands on her hips. "Just who do you think you are? Who made you the big boss around here? I don't have to talk to you."

"No… I was just wondering."

She glared at him steadily. Then she laughed and shook her head. "You are the weirdest little kid."

Who was she to be calling him a little kid? Parker scowled at this. "I was just being nice. I'm not a little kid. You're what…? Sixteen? Fifteen?"

She hesitated, not answering.

"Well, I'm fourteen," Parker snapped. "So you're not that much older than me. I'm not a little kid."

"Okay, sorry." Dakota didn't sound the least bit sorry. She sounded sullen and irritated. She kicked an empty garbage bin, making it clang loudly in the muffled quiet of the alley. "My mom abandoned me a long time ago. I never had a real dad."

"Oh… I'm sorry." Parker bit his lip, thinking of when he lost his dad. He put his feet down on the pavement, bracing himself instead of balancing. "That really sucks."

"Yeah, it does."

"Where were you before you came here? If your mom abandoned you a long time ago, who was taking care of you?"

"None of your beeswax."

Parker blinked at her. "Okay. Fine."

They just looked at each other for a few minutes in silence. Parker couldn't think of what he should say to her. He felt sorry for her and wanted to help her, but he didn't have anything to offer.

"You got money?" Dakota asked, reading his mind.

"No. Sorry, or I'd give you some."

"You got a school lunch program? Or do you bring your own lunch?"

"I bring a couple of sandwiches." Parker reached for his backpack. "You want one?"

She didn't answer, but stood there expectantly. Parker dug down into his backpack for his lunch bag and unrolled the top. He removed one of the two plastic-wrapped sandwiches and held it out toward her.

"You want one?" he repeated, giving it a little shake, like she was a fish that needed a bit of extra encouragement to take the hook.

Dakota took the sandwich from his hand and looked it over carefully, as if there might be something wrong with it.

"What kind is it? Is it meat?"

"It's chicken," Parker confirmed, taking a look at the one he had kept. "It's really good."

"So you say."

"It is."

She picked at the plastic wrap to find the edge. "I should save it for my lunch."

But it was obvious that she was going to do nothing of the kind.

"I can't, though. I'm just too hungry."

Parker felt a little better, watching her unwrap the sandwich and take a big bite of the corner. He had done something to help. It wasn't a lot, but she wouldn't starve. Parker would be hungry all afternoon, but he wouldn't mind, knowing that he had helped to feed someone else who would have been hungrier.

"It is good, isn't it?" Parker prodded.

"You make it?"

"No… my mom."

"It's nice of her to make you something to eat."

"Yeah," Parker admitted. He probably hadn't thanked her for making his lunch in a long time. He usually helped with making their lunches, but sometimes he complained about it and she didn't always ask him. "Yeah, I should tell her that."

The sandwich disappeared in seconds. Dakota threw the plastic wrap on the ground, in spite of the fact that she was standing within an arm's reach of the garbage bins. Parker got off his bike to retrieve it and threw it in the garbage while hanging onto his bike with the other hand.

"Don't you think you'd better be getting to school now?" Dakota prompted.

"Yeah. I guess so. Where will you be later?"

She shrugged. "I don't know. Around."

"Okay… I'll see you around."

She narrowed her eyes at him suspiciously. Parker gave her a smile and got back onto his bike to go to school.

Parker was distracted all through his morning classes, thinking about Dakota and her situation. He knew it wasn't unusual for teens to be homeless, but usually they were couch surfing or staying at a shelter. He didn't like to think of Dakota sleeping on the streets. It was dangerous. And it couldn't be too comfortable. He would be sleeping on his warm, cozy—if a little lumpy—bunk, and she would be on the ground. Maybe sleeping behind one of those dumpsters that she had been searching through.

She had a pretty face. He admired the sparkle in her eyes in spite of the serious situation she was in, and her sarcastic humor when they had spoken. She wasn't beaten down, that was for sure.

There were a few shelters around that she could go to. But a shelter was a temporary solution. A transition between homelessness and finding a real, permanent solution.

Parker would have invited her to stay at his house, but Mona, his mom, would freak out over that. Seriously freak out if he brought a girl home to stay there. She was bad enough when he brought home an injured bird or squirrel. They didn't have any spare beds. The couch would be better than sleeping on the street, but in their small house the living room was the hub of the family, and it was rarely empty. There would be little opportunity for Dakota to have any privacy or to sleep. There had to be some better solution.

"Mr. Jurek? Parker!"

Parker startled, realizing that the teacher was trying to get his attention. He straightened up quickly and looked at Mr. Bonne.

"Uh, sorry," Parker apologized quickly. "I wasn't listening."

"You're not going to be able to do this work if you don't listen."

"Yeah. Sorry. I was just thinking about—" Parker bit off the end of his sentence. Mr. Bonne didn't need to know what it was that he had been thinking about. He wasn't asking. And Dakota wasn't in his purview. "Sorry. I'm listening now."

Mr. Bonne looked at him for a moment longer, then went on with the math lesson. Algebra. Something that Parker was falling further and further behind in. He stared at the board, trying to make sense of what Mr. Bonne had written.

Parker sat with his friends at lunch, trying to focus on their chatter instead of on the Dakota problem. He didn't tell them about her. Chris and Adrian would tease him mercilessly if he said that he had stopped to talk to a girl, given her half of his lunch, and couldn't get her off his mind. And she wasn't someone who would fit their definition of 'hot,' a requirement if he were going to moon around about a girl. She wasn't ugly, but she was overweight, homeless, and smelled of sweat and garbage. Not the kind of girl Parker could bring up with his friends.

"Parker, done already?" Mr. Bonne asked, looking at the empty space on the table in front of Parker.

Parker looked at the table. His stomach was not satisfied with one measly sandwich. But he had known he would go hungry when he had given the other to Dakota.

"Yeah. All done."

Adrian looked over, his brows drawing down. "You're done?" he repeated. "You didn't have anything."

"I had a sandwich."

Mr. Bonne looked at Parker. "Just a sandwich?"

"Yeah." Parker shrugged. He didn't want to make a big deal of it. He didn't want to answer questions as to where the other sandwich had gone or why he didn't have anything else.

"You need more than that," Mr. Bonne said. "You want to grab something from the lunch program?" He gestured to the counter against the opposite wall of the cafeteria. "Another sandwich or an apple?"

Parker felt his face get warm. "I'm not signed up for the lunch program," he said. "It's okay. I'm fine."

"The school lunch program is for whoever needs it. I'm not going to stop you from having something because you didn't anticipate that you'd need to sign up for it. What do you want?"

"Nothing. Really."

Parker's stomach let out a loud growl of protest. Casey, across the table from him, cracked up and slapped his hand on the table several times in applause.

"I know all about teenage boys and the amount of food they eat," Mr. Bonne said with a smile. He walked over to the counter and picked up a sandwich and an apple, which he brought back and placed before Parker without another word. Then he walked away, continuing his supervision of the lunch room.

That was Mr. Bonne. No big deal. He didn't bring a bunch of attention down on Parker or make him sign the forms or talk to his guidance counselor about the food shortage. He just made sure Parker had what he needed and went on.

He was a good guy. Older, starting to go gray, but he moved like a young man and wore a polo and blue jeans. He talked to his students like they were people, not taking on the superior tone of an adult who had more knowledge and experience than they did. And he didn't pretend to get down to their level, trying to look cool and talk like a teenager. He was just Mr. Bonne. Genuine.

Parker glanced around at his friends. They were all looking away from him and talking to each other, making sure not to make a big deal of the fact that Parker had needed extra food. Parker, who always had enough.

He unwrapped the sandwich. It looked like PBJ, but had to be one of those nut butter substitutes. Soy or sunflower seeds or something other than the highly allergenic peanut. He gave it a tentative sniff, and then took a big bite. It was not PB, but it tasted good and would stick to his ribs. Parker ate in silence, listening to the other boys and thinking about Mr. Bonne and Dakota.

After school, he lingered in the classroom. Mr. Bonne looked up from his ledger, sensing that there was still someone in his room after everyone else had dismissed. He gave Parker a friendly smile.

"How's it going, Parker?"

"Good. Everything's good."

"You seem distracted today. And you were short on lunch. Everything okay at home?"

Parker couldn't complain about his home life. He was one of the lucky ones. They might be crowded and poor, but his mom didn't drink or do drugs. She worked hard every day and always found a way to stretch the money between paychecks so that the kids all had what they needed. He didn't go home to family members or housemates who were drunk and abusive

"Yeah. Yeah, home is good."

But he still didn't make any move to leave. He packed his backpack slowly, like that was the reason he was still in the classroom. Just to pack his bag.

"What do you need to do to go to school?" he asked Mr. Bonne.

Mr. Bonne sat on the edge of one of the other desks, and frowned. "You already go to school," he pointed out.

"Yeah, I know that. I mean… like if you just moved here, and you needed to start going to school, what would you need to do?"

"Oh. Well, you'd go to the office and fill out registration forms. The school would requisition records from your previous school. Get copies of your ID. Nothing very complicated."

"Do you need to have a home? Or could someone come who… didn't?"

"You'd need some kind of address. Would this person… be living at a shelter?"

Parker shook his head. "No."

Mr. Bonne rubbed his bristly chin, considering. "I don't know all of the administrative details," he said. "You would need some kind of address."

"What about parents? What if you didn't have parents?"

"As long as you had some kind of guardian…"

Parker shook his head.

"What are we talking about here, Parker? Are you considering running away from home? There are programs that can help, if you are having problems."

"No," Parker shook his head adamantly. "It's not me. It's… a friend."

He knew that Mr. Bonne heard his hesitation in referring to Dakota—someone he had barely met—as a friend, and knew he would take it the wrong way. Mr. Bonne would be even more sure that Parker was talking about himself.

"I'm sure we'd be able to work something out," Mr. Bonne said. "Education is important, and so is the safety of our students. If there was some reason you couldn't be at home, we'd find a way that you could still continue your education."

Parker nodded. He felt himself blushing. One of the dangers of his fair complexion. "It's not me," he repeated. "Nothing is happening with me."

He zipped his bag up quickly. A quick nod to say goodbye to Mr. Bonne, and he hurried out of the room.

Parker was not sure about his course of action. He rode up and down the streets looking for Dakota, and found her sitting with a paper cup, begging for change, on the sidewalk below an overpass. She sat in the shadow of the bridge, sheltered from the full heat of the sun. She had shed her hoodie, so he could see the extra-large *My Little Pony* t-shirt she was wearing and her brilliant pink hair in all of its glory.

When she saw him roll up on his bike, she didn't look like she knew how to react. She nodded a greeting, but didn't smile at him.

"Hey," Parker greeted. "Dakota, right?" Like he hadn't been thinking about her all day and hadn't been looking for her since he got out of school.

"Yeah. And you're Parkinson."

Parker opened his mouth to object. She snorted in amusement at her own joke.

"Parker," he corrected weakly.

"Oh, yeah. Parkinson."

Parker shook his head. He glanced around. There were a few coins in her cup, but it didn't look like she had been able to make very much sitting there. Parker didn't have anything to put in it. Not even food this time. "So… how's it going?"

"I'm having a ball."

"Yeah, I mean… I know you're not in a good place. I'm just making sure… you're okay."

She sighed, relaxing just a little. Her lips curled into the barest hint of a smile. "Yeah, I'm fine."

"Do you want to go to school?"

The way that Dakota looked at him made Parker realize that he had blurted it out without any introduction. Just diving right into the middle of the conversation without any small talk, like his mom always accused him of doing.

"I mean…" He couldn't think of anything else to say. Anything else to lead up to it or explain why he was asking. "Well… do you?"

Dakota didn't look at him. She shrugged her rounded shoulders. "Yeah, maybe."

"My teacher, Mr. Bonne, I think he would help get you signed up. So you could."

"They always need a ton of paperwork," Dakota said. "I don't have anything."

"He said he'd help."

"You told him about me?" Dakota's eyes widened. She looked up and down the street as if she thought someone might be after her. "What did you tell him about me for?"

"I didn't. I just said I had a friend who might want to register."

"You can't tell anyone about me."

"Well…" Parker readjusted his position on the bike, suddenly uncomfortable.

"Who else did you tell?"

"No one. I'm just thinking… you'll need an address, and I might know someone who could help you out."

"Who?"

"A lady I know… I haven't told her anything about you yet. I haven't seen her. I just thought… you could use her address and Mr. Bonne would help you to get signed up. Then if you wanted to, you could go to school."

Dakota considered this. "They got a free lunch program?"

"Yes."

"What about breakfast?"

Parker nodded. "Yeah, sure. That too."

"And showers in the girls' locker room?"

"I guess so. There's showers in the boys' room."

Parker watched Dakota mull it over. He mentally ticked off the advantages as she considered it. If she registered for school, she could get two square meals a day and a shower. Maybe she could use a locker in the locker room as well to hold the rest of her possessions so she didn't have to carry them around the school with her.

Dakota scratched her head. "I suppose… if you wanted to talk to this friend of yours. See if she'd let me use her address."

Parker grinned. "Great! I will. And you'll be… here?"

She looked at her paper cup and clinked around the change in the bottom. "I'll go get a muffin or something. I'll come back here after."

"Okay. I'll see you later, then."

He jumped onto his pedals and hurried away. He wasn't sure yet how everything was going to come together. But so far, his plans were working out. And Dakota wasn't being quite as terse with him as she had been in the morning. Maybe she understood now that he was just trying to help her out. He thought she could use every bit of help she could get.

Chapter Two

H E TOOK A DEEP breath before knocking on Jade Gable's door. While Jade was a good woman, she could be a bit overwhelming at times. Parker hoped that the similarities between Jade and Dakota would help to smooth the way so that things would work out as he had planned. They were both big-boned black women. Neither one was afraid to say what she thought. Both seemed to have a sense of humor and a biting wit.

Parker knew that while Jade could come off as angry or overbearing, she had a heart of gold. Hers was the one house that he always knew he could go to if he had a sick or injured animal that needed watching. Or if he were doing a fundraiser for one of the kids' groups that were sporadically organized in the neighborhood in an effort to keep youth off the street and engaged in something constructive. None of them ever lasted, but Parker had taken part in a few of them, and Jade could always be counted on to put a little something in the kitty. Even if it were only a dollar or two.

"I'm coming, I'm coming," Jade shouted from inside the house, as she neared her door. Parker had only knocked once, but she made it sound like he was beating the door down in his impatience.

The door burst open, and Jade stood there, towering over him. Parker was slim, a good height for his age, but she stood several inches taller than he did, and was at least twice his weight. She was wearing a bright red blazer over a colorful blouse and black slacks, and had huge gold hoop earrings. She put her hands on her hips, as if wondering what trouble Parker had gotten himself into this time.

"Well, then? What is it?" she demanded.

"Uh… hi, Mrs. Gable."

"You know you can call me Jade. Haven't you known me since you were in the cradle? You could call me auntie, if you wanted to."

"Uh…" Parker sidestepped the name issue. His mother always insisted that he use mister and missus, and never call an adult by their first name. Even the teachers at school who allowed the students to use their first name. Mona would boil Parker in oil if she ever caught him being so disrespectful. "I wondered if you could help out a friend of mine."

"Is this a friend with fur, or with feathers?"

Parker laughed. "No, neither one! She has hair. Pink hair."

He looked at Jade's close-cropped curly black hair. What would she think of Dakota? Would she look at her and decide that Dakota was a lost cause? That she was too rebellious to bother with helping?

"Pink hair," Jade repeated. "Parker, do you have a girlfriend?"

"No! She's not my girlfriend. She's just a girl that I met. And she needs some help. I thought maybe…"

"That Auntie Jade was a soft touch and would help you out?"

Parker nodded wordlessly.

"Come in, come in. No need to be standing on my doorstep like a little lost puppy." She motioned him inside and then followed Parker into the living room, where he sat down on the couch and tried to figure out how to explain what he had in mind.

"Now then," Jade said, settling herself into her favorite armchair. "Tell me about your friend with the pink hair."

"I don't know very much about her. Like I said, I just met her. Just today…"

"What kind of help does she need?"

"She's homeless and she doesn't have any parents or anyone else to help her. She wants to go to school. But when I talked to Mr. Bonne about it today, he said that she'll need an address to register. She's not even staying at a shelter, so she doesn't have an address to use."

"I see. Who is she and where did she come from?"

"Her name is Dakota… I don't know where she came from. Not from around here, I haven't ever seen her before."

"She is your age?"

"Yes. Maybe a little older. She didn't exactly tell me."

Jade rubbed her hands together briskly. "Wanting to go to school is a good sign. Tells me she probably isn't a junkie or worse. You know I'm a sucker where helpless critters are involved…"

Parker waited for her decision. "It's just your address," he encouraged. "She just needs an address to use."

"Why don't you use your address?"

Parker opened his mouth and closed it again, trying to think up a good excuse. Jade laughed long, loud peals of laughter. "You don't want your mother to know about this girl?"

"No, it isn't that." Parker felt his face flame up. "I just don't want to bother her with this… she's got enough on her hands already."

"Yes, she has enough to worry about," Jade agreed. She, more than anyone, knew what the family had been through. She pressed her hands to her thighs and stood up. "Where is this Dakota? I'm going to need to meet her."

Parker had expected as much. "I can take you. She was going to see if she could get something to eat, and then she was going to go back to wait…"

He knew Jade didn't need all the details. But sometimes he just couldn't shut the words off. Especially when he was nervous or embarrassed. Outside, he walked his bike beside Jade, taking her back to the spot on the sidewalk where he expected to find Dakota again. It took a lot longer to get there by foot, and Jade was puffing and sweating when they were only halfway there. She wiped her forehead and looked at him.

"Sorry… I was on my bike… it's farther than I thought."

"How much farther?"

He told her the intersection. Jade shook her head. "Next time, you bring your injured bird to me," she told him.

"Yes, ma'am. I'm sorry."

Eventually, they reached the spot where Dakota should be waiting. There was no sign of her. Parker looked around. He was really going to hear it if he had dragged Jade all the way across the neighborhood for no reason. Parker looked over the nearest store fronts, trying to figure out where she would have gone.

"She was right here. She said she was going to come back here."

Jade pulled a wadded-up tissue from her purse and dabbed at her sweaty face. She didn't blow up, but looked around. There was a police car in front of a convenience store a block away. She motioned to it. "Let's try there."

Parker and Jade made their way over and looked in the front window glass. The first thing Parker saw was the flash of Dakota's pink hair. Then he made out the policeman who was standing beside her, his hand on her wrists, which were both pulled behind her back.

"Uh-oh."

They walked into the store. Dakota's voice was angry, self-righteous. "I have the money in my pocket. I don't need to steal anything. I wasn't stealing."

"She did!" the shop owner insisted. "I can show you the surveillance video. She was just going to walk right out of here without paying."

"I was just looking out the window. I thought I saw my friend there. He was coming to meet me. I was just looking out the window, I wasn't leaving." As she jerked her head toward the front door and window, she saw Parker and Jade coming in. "See, there they are. This is my friend, Parker. I was just looking out the window to see if he was here yet. I wasn't going to leave the store without paying."

"Hey, Dakota," Parker forced himself to greet her cheerfully, and put on a confused expression. "What's going on here? Did you get your muffin?"

"You'd better show me the video," the cop told the store owner.

They all waited while the store owner worked over the monitor of his surveillance system to cue up the segment that he wanted to watch. He let it play for the cop. Parker couldn't see it clearly from where he was. But he could see Dakota walking up to the door and put her hand on the crossbar as if to push it open and leave. That was when the figure of the store owner hurried over and grabbed her, pushing her back and corralling her there while he called for the police.

The police officer watched it several times, and finally shook his head. "She didn't leave the store," he said finally. "It's too hard to tell from the video whether she would have or not, but she didn't set foot outside the store. I can't arrest her for theft when she didn't leave the store with the merchandise. It's in her hand, not hidden out of sight. She could have been intending to pay for it."

"Where's her money?"

The cop looked at Dakota. "You have money?"

Dakota wiggled her hands, cuffed behind her back. "Let me go and I'll show you."

He unlocked the cuffs. Two sets of handcuffs that had been chained in series in order to span her girth. Dakota rubbed her shoulders, her lips in a pout.

"Let's see, then," the cop ordered.

Dakota started pulling money out of her pockets. A few coins out of this one, and a few out of another. She laid them on the counter in front of the shop owner, counting them painstakingly. She was short, and kept going through her hoodie and pant pockets, looking for more coins.

"She didn't have enough," the owner pointed out triumphantly. "She didn't have enough to pay."

"She didn't leave the store. She might have thought she had enough, she's close."

"You keep your money," Jade ordered, motioning Dakota to pick her money back up. She put a five-dollar bill on the counter.

"That will cover it. Do you need anything else? Maybe a drink?" Jade suggested.

Dakota stared at her. She turned her head to look at Parker, obviously wondering who the hell the stranger was. She forced a friendly smile. "Uh, yeah, a drink would be nice."

When she went to the refrigerated case that held pop, Jade shook her head. "You are not getting that poison. Some juice? Or maybe some milk?"

Dakota scowled. She looked up and down the glass doors. "Milk then. Grab me one, would ya, Parker?"

Parker opened the case at his elbow and put his hand out. "What kind?"

"Vanilla." Dakota looked at Jade challengingly. "Is that okay? Or is that poison too?"

"Vanilla is fine," Jade agreed. "Go ahead."

Parker looked over the various bottles and cartons. The words blended in with the backgrounds on the labels and he had a hard time making them out.

"The blue ones," Dakota said impatiently.

Parker continued to search, his hand hovering over the selections.

"To your right. The blue ones," Dakota said again. Parker moved his hand to the right, searching for them. He finally saw the picture of an ice cream scoop splashing into a glass of milk. He picked up a bottle, double-checking the words on the label.

Dakota was at his side and snatched it out of his hand. "Are you blind?" she demanded.

Parker swallowed and didn't answer, his face getting hot. Dakota put her milk on the counter and looked at Jade, waiting for her to supply the last couple of dollars to cover the drink. She looked from Jade to Parker and back again.

"What?" she demanded. "What's wrong with everyone?"

"I'm color-blind," Parker explained, rubbing his forehead to hide his tomato-red face behind his hand.

"Well, that explains *a lot*," Dakota said. When neither of them said anything, she looked back at Parker. "*Sorry*," she said in a tone that was more annoyed than apologetic. "So you couldn't tell which ones were blue? Really?"

Parker shrugged. "I can differentiate some colors. But blue is one of the ones I have trouble with."

"Oh. Well, sorry."

Jade gave the shop owner the rest of the money to cover the purchase. He rang it up and handed her a few coins in change.

"I'm sorry, Mrs. Gable," he said. "I didn't know she was with you."

Jade nodded her acknowledgment, but didn't let him off the hook. The shop owner shrugged at the policeman. "Sorry to bother you," he said. "I guess I was wrong."

The cop shrugged. "People make mistakes." With a respectful nod at Jade, he left the store and went back out to his car. Parker watched him for a moment, tapping something into his onboard computer.

Jade motioned to Dakota. "Let's go on out."

Parker trailed the two women out of the store. Dakota opened her milk and took a few swallows.

"So… you're the lady Parkinson said would help me?"

"Parkinson?" Jade repeated. She looked at him. "You mean Parker?"

"Parker, Parkinson, whatever. He said you'd help. With the school registration."

"I said she might," Parker clarified, worried Jade would think he was being presumptuous. "I hadn't asked her yet."

Dakota tipped the milk bottle back again, then wiped her lips with the back of her hand. "So… will you?"

Jade took her time in answering. "I'm not sure that is the thing that you need the most," she said finally.

Dakota shot a glance at Parker. Did that mean that Jade wasn't going to help out? That Dakota couldn't use her address?

"What is it you think I need?" Dakota challenged.

"I think the thing you need the most is a home."

Dakota's jaw tightened. Her mouth was a flat, angry line. She shook her head at Parker. He felt awful for getting Jade involved, only to have her drop the ball. *Dakota didn't know that she needed a home? She hadn't done everything she could already to provide for herself? Dakota didn't need someone else telling her what she should do with her life.*

"How about it?" Jade asked. "Don't you think you need that more than just an address for school?"

"I don't have a place to stay," Dakota said. "That's why I need to use someone's address!"

Jade laughed. "I don't think you're understanding me, little bird."

Dakota was more confused than ever. "Little bird? Lady, you're insane. It's no wonder I can't understand you!"

"She's calling you that because sometimes I take her animals that need help," Parker jumped in with the explanation. "She's calling you my latest… little bird."

Even as Dakota was rolling her eyes, Jade put her hand on the girl's arm. "I'm asking you if you would like to come live with me."

Dakota's eyes popped. "What? You just met me! Shoplifting! And you want me to come stay with you?"

"There would be rules," Jade said. "Just like there would be for any other child. And at the top of the list would be 'no shoplifting.'"

Dakota laughed in disbelief. She looked over at Parker. "Is she for real?"

"Yes. If she offers, she means it."

Dakota handed Parker her milk to hold while she unwrapped her muffin. "I'm starving," she said. "Sorry."

Parker and Jade watched her pull the plastic wrap away from the blueberry muffin. She took a couple of big bites, puffing out her cheeks while she chewed it. Dakota darted little glances at Parker and Jade, evaluating them, trying to figure them out without being caught staring at them.

"It's just me and my husband right now," Jade said. "All of my kids are grown and gone. And the animals, of course." She gave Parker an affectionate look. "Somehow I always seem to be picking up strays."

"Cats and birds aren't enough for you?" Dakota challenged. "You thought you'd pick up another person?"

Jade shrugged. "It wouldn't be the first time. I've helped with other kids before. I'm not new at this."

"You don't know anything about me." Dakota took her milk back from Parker and washed down a few gulps. "How do you know I'm not going to murder you in your bed?"

"Well, you probably wouldn't ask if you were planning it." Jade looked at Dakota's face, her hair, her tight pony t-shirt. She touched Dakota's arm again. "I see more than you think."

"What do you think you see?"

"I see… a girl who's all alone. On her own. Still in need of adult direction. Supervision. Someone who would like to go back to school and have another chance at just being a kid."

Dakota chewed on her lip. "You see all that?"

"Yes. Am I wrong?"

"No," Dakota gave a little shake of her head. Some of her shimmery pink lipstick had transferred to her teeth. "I've had a lot of different homes. Been moved to one place after another until I lost track. I'm… not easy to live with. How do I know you wouldn't just kick me out after a week?"

"I can't promise you anything. There will be rules, and if you're going to break the rules, you will get kicked out. But if you're honest with me and you try your hardest, I think we can work things out. If the time comes…" Jade shrugged. "I can't promise anything. But I'll give it my best shot. Is that good enough?"

Dakota gave Jade and Parker a shy, girlish smile. It was the first time that Parker felt like she had let down her guard, just a little bit.

"Okay," Dakota said. She giggled nervously. "I'll give anything a try once."

It was getting dark when Parker pedaled up to the house, cool air whipping past his face. He quickly took his bike to the back of the house and locked it up, then went inside.

"Parker's home," Link shouted as Parker walked in. Link barely looked up from the TV and didn't bother to say hello. He didn't see Parker's glare in response to the shout.

Mona entered the living room from the opposite side. Her expression told Parker that he wasn't in her good books. "Where have you been?"

"Mrs. Gable's."

Mona was brought up short in her complaint that he shouldn't be hanging out wasting time with his friends and not coming home to take care of his responsibilities. She opened her mouth and looked at him, considering.

"What were you doing at Jade's?"

"I was…" Parker looked for a way to describe what was going on without letting on that it was all his doing in the first place. "I was helping her get a room ready for a girl that's going to stay with her."

A piece of the truth was better than an outright lie. Mona considered the information.

"You should have called me to let me know where you were and what was going on."

Parker shrugged. "I didn't think you'd mind."

"I don't mind. But I like to know what you're up to. You can call and let me know."

"Yeah, okay."

Parker headed for the kitchen. He had had a small bite to eat at Jade's house, but that was just a snack. He was a growing boy and needed something more substantial. Mona followed him to the fridge and watched him rifle through the leftovers, looking for something appealing.

"Who is this girl that's going to be staying with Jade? Is she a relative?"

"No, I don't think they're related. Just somebody she's helping out."

"What's her name? Is it a little girl?"

"Dakota Phillips. Uh, no… she's not little." Not in age, and not in size. Parker resisted the twitch of a smile, trying to keep his face blank, giving nothing away. He opened a bowl of macaroni and decided it would do. "She's... I don't know. A teenager. Bit older than me, maybe. Fifteen or sixteen."

"Oh. How do they know each other?"

Parker shrugged, putting his bowl in the microwave, and didn't answer.

"How long is she staying there?"

"I didn't ask, Mom. It's not really any of my business. I was just helping move furniture and get the room ready."

"Did you meet her? Was she there, or were you just getting the room ready?"

"Yeah, I met her."

Mona waited for more information. She didn't want to look like she was prying into someone else's business, but she wanted all of the details.

When Parker took his macaroni out of the microwave, he squirted it with ketchup and ground pepper over it.

"She'll be going to your school, then," Mona observed. "Jade's in the school district."

Parker shoveled a big spoonful of macaroni into his mouth. "I guess," he said around it.

"Don't talk with your mouth full," Mona remonstrated. "That's disgusting!"

Parker made a big shrug at her, as if it were her own fault for talking to him while he was eating. Taking the bowl of macaroni with him, he headed for his bedroom.

"Eat at the table!" Mona called after him.

"Got homework to do," Parker yelled back at her, not turning around. He went into his room and shut the door.

He could hear all of her usual arguments in his head, even though she didn't follow him into his room again. There was no desk in his room, he would just be spreading his books out on his bunk. It wasn't good for his body to be hunched over them, and if he stretched out, he'd end up falling asleep on top of his books. It would make more sense for him to eat at the kitchen table and to do his homework there.

But Parker didn't want to be out at the kitchen table, with the TV distracting him and Mona hanging over him to make sure he was doing what he was supposed to be and seeing if he needed any help. Even though she was no better at the algebra than he was, she always wanted to help, and ended up getting him more tangled up than he was to start with.

Jessup was stretched out on the bottom bunk, but he was playing a handheld game, not doing homework. He muttered under his breath, keeping up a running monologue about it. Parker knew there was no point in telling him to shut up. Jessup would fall silent for a minute or two, and then he would start again, as if he had no control over his own mouth. Parker fished his earbuds out of his pocket and started some music playing. He started on the macaroni and pulled his books out of his backpack, checking to see what there was that he couldn't get away with leaving for another day.

Chapter Three

I T WAS A COUPLE of days before Dakota showed up at school. Parker supposed it took time for her to get settled in at Jade's and get her registration done. Even though he was sure she was older than he was, she had been put into Mr. Bonne's homeroom and shared a bunch of classes with Parker.

She showed up wearing a classy blouse that was probably Jade's, which fit her figure better than the t-shirt and hoodie that Parker had seen her in before. She was pretty. Not too dressy for school, but she didn't look homeless. She wore a headband that pushed the pink hair back from her round face, and she smiled when people spoke to her, instead of scowling and snapping sarcastic comments.

She saw Parker across the classroom, but she gave no sign of recognizing him or wanting to speak to him. He supposed she was probably embarrassed that he knew her secret and didn't want him letting anything slip that would give her away. Parker smiled at her, trying to communicate that he wouldn't let out anything that was private. She didn't smile back, but looked away from him and said something to one of the other girls.

Later, when the class was working on their math problems, Mr. Bonne approached Parker to see if he needed any help. He gave a small nod in Dakota's direction.

"I take it you were the one who helped get her here?"

"I told you I wasn't talking about myself!"

"Well, I'm glad," Mr. Bonne said with a crooked smile. "I was worried about what might be going on at home."

"Nothing going on," Parker reiterated, his face burning. "Everything is good at home."

"Good to hear. Now, how are you doing on this?" Mr. Bonne indicated Parker's notebook, which was a mess of scribbles and erasures. Parker looked it over in dismay, unable to make heads or tails of it all.

"Why don't we start on a fresh page?" Mr. Bonne suggested. "Which question do you want to do together?"

Parker made an effort to meet up with Dakota after school. He grabbed his bike to catch up with her, then coasted along beside her as she strode away from the school. She looked at him and didn't seem to know what to say.

"How was the first day of school?" Parker inquired politely.

She shrugged. "It was okay. It was… it was good," she amended. She gave a nod and a slight smile. "It's been a long time since I went to school regularly, but it felt good."

"How long… have you been… on your own?"

Dakota shifted her book bag. The shoulder strap sank deep into her shoulder. She looked behind her and looked around to make sure they couldn't be overheard.

"It's been a little while," she said obliquely. What was a little while? A few days? Weeks? Months? "And before that… I moved around a lot. I haven't been somewhere stable in a long time."

"I hope it works out with Jade. Mrs. Gable."

"She said I could call her Jade."

Parker nodded. "Yeah. My mom, though, she won't let me call adults by their first names."

Dakota blinked at him. "Whatever."

"Mrs. Gable is really nice. I'm glad she offered you a place to live."

"Me too."

"You think it will work out there?"

"How do I know?" Dakota challenged. "I don't usually stay anywhere for very long. People promise to take care of me… and then they don't."

Parker had a hard time wrapping his mind around that. He knew Jade. She wouldn't make empty promises. She wouldn't make any promises she didn't plan to keep. But not everyone was like Jade. The people Dakota had stayed with before probably hadn't been trustworthy. He couldn't understand how anyone could just kick a teenager out into the street. But people did. They did it all the time. Even their own kids. With someone like Dakota, who didn't even have parents around, it would be easier for people to just kick her out.

"Jade's good. She always takes care of the animals I take her. She's really nice."

"Maybe." Dakota ran her fingers through her pink hair. "I wish there was somebody who would. Just take care of me."

Parker was quiet, pushing his bike along beside her. He knew he was lucky. He didn't have to worry about not having enough to eat or any clean clothes. Despite how many of them were crowded into the house, they all got along pretty well. Parker didn't have to worry about going home to a beating even if he were late and hadn't called to tell Mona what was going on. He realized that for Dakota, that kind of life was a fairy tale. Something that was so far from reality that it seemed impossible. Like Aladdin's Lamp on TV, fun to imagine and dream about, but not something that would ever actually happen to her.

He didn't know what to say to her.

"I suppose I should thank you," Dakota said. Parker was surprised by the resentment in her voice. Was she angry with him for helping? For getting her out of the dumpsters in the alley and into clean clothes and a friendly classroom?

"No, it's okay," he said. "It was just the right thing to do. Anyone would have."

"Anyone would have? You're crazy. You want to know how many people have walked past me and just pretended I was invisible? How would you like it if everywhere you went, people pretended you didn't even exist? Almost three hundred pounds of me, and people just walk right by like I wasn't even there."

"I… I don't know. I've always tried to help… I don't like seeing people—or animals—suffering."

"There's all kinds of homeless people around here," Dakota pointed out. "More than they can fit into shelters or soup kitchens." She turned her head to look him fully in the face. "What made you decide to help me, out of everyone out here?"

Parker looked around, thinking about it. She was right. There were homeless people or others who were down on their luck all around him. Every street he walked or rode down. So what had made him single out Dakota? What had made him think about her all day long and to go to Mrs. Gable for help?

"I dunno. I hadn't seen you around before. You're a teenager, like me. I just… felt like you needed help. And maybe you'd accept it."

"You think I'm taking charity?" Dakota challenged.

"No. No, I don't think that. Just… a lot of the homeless people I know…" Parker look at the old man panhandling at the corner. The vet down the block with his dog at his side and a new cardboard sign every day. "A lot of them won't take any help. They don't want anyone to get involved. If you try to do something to help, instead of just giving them money or food… they don't want anything to do with you. It's like you've offended them."

Dakota didn't say anything, pondering. She nodded slowly. "Yeah. A lot of them are like that," she admitted.

"But I felt like… I could help you and it would work out." It was the same with the animals. If he knew he could do something for them, then he did, even if it meant getting clawed or bitten in the process.

"Well, I guess you were right."

Parker gave Dakota a grin. She looked away, but there was a small smile on her face. "You want to come over?" she offered. "See how my room looks now?"

He had helped Jade move furniture in and out of the room and had seen what he thought was the final arrangement before going home, but if Dakota wanted to show him how it had all turned out, he was happy to see it. At least she wasn't acting mad or aloof. Her mood changes were a little dizzying.

"Yeah, I'd love to."

Dakota gave him a broad smile, briefly letting the wall down. "Okay. Come see."

They didn't have much discussion the rest of the way to Jade's house. When they got there, Dakota produced a key, showing it off to Parker proudly. "I even have my own key!"

It turned out that the door was unlocked and Jade was home, so Dakota didn't need her key. She put it back away.

"I'm home," she called out.

"Hi, Dakota, how was school?" Jade entered the living room from the opposite direction. "Oh, hello, Parker."

"I wanted to show him my room," Dakota said. She turned her face up toward Jade. "Is that okay?"

"You can show him, but if you're going to visit, come back out here. Boys in bedrooms is not a good idea. My kids were never allowed to have members of the opposite sex in their rooms."

Dakota rolled her eyes, but she didn't argue. She grabbed Parker's hand for a minute to pull him toward the bedrooms, then she let it go again. Parker knew the way to the bedroom. He'd been in the house more times than she had.

The furniture arrangement was the same as when he had left the house last. But she had a fancy coverlet on the bed, a couple of posters on the wall, make up on the top of the dresser, and bits of clothes escaping from the drawers. It looked like she had been living there for weeks or months, instead of just a couple of days.

"It looks great," Parker told Dakota. He tried to imagine what it would feel like to have his own room after being homeless or after bouncing from home to home over the past few years, always having to share and never actually having anything of her own.

"Thanks." Dakota was grinning broadly, looking around the room as if she'd never been happier.

"Have you ever had your own room before?" Parker asked. "I've always had to share. As long as I can remember, anyway."

Link was a year younger, so Parker supposed he had had his own bedroom for his first year, but not in his memory.

"No, I usually have to share," Dakota said. "I don't really remember, I guess I've had my own once or twice." Her expression darkened. "But never for long."

"Sorry. I didn't mean…"

Dakota walked around the room, readjusting each little thing by a hair's breadth. Straightening the coverlet, tucking clothes back into drawers. Lining up the makeup bottles. "It's nice, isn't it?"

"Yes, it is."

Dakota sat down on the bed. She slid herself so that her back was against the wall, and patted the bed next to her, inviting Parker to sit down.

"I shouldn't," Parker said. Jade had just said that he wasn't to stay in the bedroom to visit. He didn't want to cross her. He didn't want to be on Jade Gable's bad side. That was a bad place to be. Especially the next time he decided he needed her help with something. Or someone.

"Oh, come on. The old bat can—"

Jade stepped up behind Parker. She seemed to sense what was going on without being told.

"There are cookies," she said. "Do you want to come to the kitchen and have some?"

"Cookies?" Dakota perked up at the suggestion. "Really? Yeah!"

She bounded off the bed and pushed past them. Jade's mouth quirked up at Parker and she shook her head. They both trailed Dakota to the kitchen, Parker bringing up the rear.

"Oh, wow!" Dakota exclaimed. "These look great! Look, Parker, chocolate chip! Homemade! Like, from scratch? Not frozen dough?" she interrogated Jade.

"Yes, from scratch," Jade agreed.

"These are awesome! And milk? Is there milk?" Dakota went to the fridge and yanked the door open, making everything shake and rattle. She grabbed a carton of milk from the shelf, and showed it to Parker. "Sorry, no vanilla milk. Can you tell what color this is?"

Parker opened his mouth, but she whirled around the kitchen without waiting for an answer.

"I know where everything is," she announced. "I've only been here two days, but I know the whole layout."

She opened one cupboard to retrieve a couple of glasses and another to get luncheon plates. She looked over her shoulder at Jade.

"Did you want some too, Jade? Should I get you a plate and glass?"

"I'll just have one cookie. No milk."

Dakota grabbed another plate. She dealt them around the table like a card shark. The two glasses were handled more delicately and she filled each with milk.

"Come sit down! What are you standing around for?"

Parker obeyed, moving in and sitting in the chair that Dakota indicated. Jade moved more slowly and sat down at the end of the table, moving the plate to where she wanted to sit. Dakota passed the cookies around. The plastic container was warm from the heat of the freshly-baked cookies. The smell in the kitchen was like heaven.

Parker took the first bite and savored the sweet, rich melted chocolate and the perfect cross of crispness and chewiness of the cookie itself. It had oats in it, he thought. They added something over just plain wheat flour.

"Mmm," Parker couldn't think of anywhere he would rather be or anything he would rather be doing at that moment. "These are fantastic. I don't know when my mom made cookies last. We only ever have store bought. If we can afford it. Oh, these are the best."

Dakota took a swig of milk and nodded. She looked thoroughly at home. As if she were one of Jade's own kids and had lived there all her life.

Two days before, she had been going through a dumpster. She'd eaten half of Parker's lunch. Stolen a muffin.

She didn't even look like the same girl.

When they had finished two cookies each, Jade stretched and stood up.

"And now it's time for Parker to be heading home. You both have homework to do. I'm not sure how long it will take for you to get caught up to the class, Miss Dakota. We're going to need to put in some hard work to make sure you're where you need to be."

"Can't I have another cookie?" Dakota whined.

"You've had enough cookies for now. You won't have any appetite for supper."

"One more? Just one more?"

"No. That's enough."

"What if we share one?" Dakota wheedled. "We'll just split one between us."

"That's enough, Dakota," Jade said sharply. "I told you 'no' once already. That's the end of it."

"I'm still hungry!"

"Good. Then you'll be able to eat supper. Now tell Parker goodbye. He has to go."

Parker stood up from the table. He picked up his backpack, getting ready to go. Jade stepped out of the room. Dakota mouthed a nasty name to Parker, nodding in the direction that Jade had gone. She didn't say it out loud. She sat there with her head cocked for a minute, listening to Jade's retreat. Then she grabbed two more cookies and just about swallowed them whole like a python. She gave Parker a wide, triumphant smile.

Parker was embarrassed by the way she was treating Jade. Jade was being nice to Dakota, doing her a favor. A big one. She could at least acknowledge the favor by being on her best behavior. Dakota pushed herself up out of her seat.

"I don't have any homework," she called out to Jade. Which was, of course, a lie. There was homework every night. And Dakota would probably have to do extra studying to get caught up to where they were in the text.

"Don't give me that bull," Jade responded from the other room. "Just go get it done. Goodbye, Parker."

"Bye," Parker called out to her. He didn't follow Dakota back to her bedroom, but headed for the door. "Bye, Dakota."

She looked back at him over her shoulder. "Yeah, bye. See you at school tomorrow."

45

Chapter Four

PARKER LOOKED AROUND THE classroom, but it was obvious Dakota was not there. She was a person who stood out wherever she was. The bright pink hair, stocky body, and her usual loud girl-chatter before class all drew attention to her. She was hard to miss.

He met Marina's eye from a couple of aisles away. "Where's Dakota?"

She gave him a dramatic shrug, as if she didn't know and wouldn't tell him if she did. Parker was a boy, and a boy didn't need to know the comings and goings of one of her girlfriends.

"She texted me she's sick," Charity told Parker, turning around to look at him. "She's staying home today."

"Oh." Parker nodded and sat down at his desk. "Is she okay? What's she got?"

Charity giggled and didn't tell him. The giggle hinted at the fact that Parker should know without asking, and that maybe she wasn't sick after all, but it was just an excuse not to be at school. He got out his books as the start-of-class bell rang. Others moved quickly to sit down and get ready. He looked back up at Charity.

"Is she faking?" he asked. "What's so funny?"

"No, she's not faking," Charity said, still with a suppressed smile that said she knew more than she was telling him. "Just up too late partying."

Parker turned away from Charity to look at the board at the front of the room.

Up too late partying? Where would Dakota be partying? With who? She had gotten to know plenty of people at school, but it wasn't like there were wild drinking parties going on every night. Parker thought that he would have heard if someone that he knew was out late partying with Dakota. And he didn't think that Jade would let her adopted daughter get away with much. She had made it clear from the start that she had rules that Dakota was expected to follow, and Parker didn't like the idea of Dakota breaking them and getting herself kicked out.

She said that she always got kicked out, so why didn't she buckle down and make an effort not to get into trouble?

He hurried over to Jade's after school. He had hoped that Dakota would get to school late, or make it for the afternoon classes. But she hadn't, and he wanted to see for himself whether she was really sick, or whether Charity was right, and it was her own fault.

Parker knocked. It was Jade who came to the door and let him in. She raised her eyebrows at Parker, but she already knew what it was he wanted.

"Is Dakota in?" he asked dutifully.

"She's watching TV. Don't be long, she's supposed to be resting so she can get to school tomorrow."

Parker stood watching the TV for a minute before making himself known to Dakota. She was watching *My Little Pony*. Parker walked in.

"Bored?"

Dakota startled. But rather than looking pleased at his appearance and turning off the TV, as he expected her to, she waved him to silence and watched the show until it broke for commercial.

"Really?" Parker asked. "*My Little Pony*?"

"I like *My Little Pony*," Dakota said.

Parker laughed. "It's a little kids' show. And not even a good one."

"That's your opinion. I like it." She snuggled under a blanket like a little girl at a slumber party.

Parker sat down on the other end of the couch, turned sideways to face her. "You skipping today?"

"I was sick."

"Sick. Charity said you were out partying."

Dakota's eyes slid toward the doorway to make sure that Jade was not close by listening. "What would Charity know?"

Parker took a deep breath, trying to relax the knot in his stomach. "Does that mean you were? What were you doing?"

"I was here. Ask Jade."

"Charity says you were partying. Is she lying?"

"Charity doesn't know everything. I was right here, sleeping in my bed. I just woke up with a bug. That's all."

"The kind of bug you get from drinking too much?"

"What would you know about it? You're just a kid. And you don't party."

"I know what a hangover is. You snuck out? Why would you do that? If you get caught, Mrs. Gable will kick you out. I thought you wanted to stay here and have a room of your own and someone to help take care of you. Why would you do something stupid?"

"I'm not stupid."

"What were you doing? Drinking? Doing drugs?"

"None of your business." Dakota folded her arms across her chest. Closed off. Parker was wondering why he had come. What good was fighting with her about drinking going to do? He had gone to make sure that she was okay, not to get his head bitten off. He turned his attention to the TV and just watched the inane commercials and show for a while. Giving Dakota a chance to unwind and for him to sort out the knot in his insides.

"Sorry," he said finally. "I just wanted to make sure you're okay. I don't want you to be sick or to get in trouble. I missed you at school today."

She looked at the screen, not at Parker. "I used to think skipping was fun. I didn't like school and did whatever I could to get out of it. But today… I guess I don't feel like that anymore. I like the routine of going to school. Seeing my friends. Even doing the work is… I don't know… it's so normal and… soothing."

Parker wasn't sure he'd go that far. But he did feel good when he got a good mark on an assignment. And when he stayed home sick or faking sick, he always got so antsy he was happy to get back to school the next day. So maybe he could understand her attitude.

"So you'll be back tomorrow?"

"Yeah, for sure. It was fun to stay home and watch some TV today, but… my stomach and head were crap, and I didn't get to see anyone. It's no fun just wallowing in how sick you are by yourself."

Parker nodded. "Good."

They watched some more TV. Parker turned back to her during the commercial. "And what about drinking? I want you to take care of yourself."

Dakota rubbed her face. "I don't know. I like to have fun with my friends. I'll try to be more careful, 'cause I hate being hung over. But I need something, sometimes, to get me through the day."

Parker studied her face. Her wide, even features. Clear, smooth skin, full lips, quick eyes. "Why?"

Dakota gave him a long, slow blink. She raked her fingers through her pink hair. "I've had kind of a rough life, Parker. Sometimes… something will remind me. Those old feelings come back, or I can't get a picture out of my mind. I just… feel like I'm drowning, sometimes."

She looked back at the TV. Back at rainbows and talking ponies and a world where the worst that could happen was that a friend might talk behind your back. He didn't know what she had gone through in all of those homes that she went through. But he wasn't completely naive. People could do horrible things, especially to a little girl that didn't even belong to them.

"I'm sorry those things happened to you."

"Yeah. Me too. But they did, and no one can change that. All I can do now is… survive… enjoy what time I have left to be a teenager."

She never had told him how old she really was. He supposed she must have had to put her birthdate on the school registration papers. They had put her in his grade, but that didn't mean she was the same age as he was. That might just have been the last grade that she had attended regularly, and the best place for her to return to.

"At least you've got a couple of years," he ventured, testing to see what her reaction was.

Dakota sighed, not taking her eyes off of the sugar-sweet nonsense on the screen. "Yeah."

Dakota was back at school again the next day. She ignored Parker and gossiped with her friends. She seemed to be doing pretty well with Mr. Bonne's lessons. Parker had figured that she would need extra tutoring or resource room help, but she was picking the information up quickly. She didn't seem like she was behind at all.

Parker wondered how long it had really been since she had attended school last. Had it been a few years or a few weeks? Dakota wasn't giving out many details. Not to Parker.

He'd looked her up on his social media networks when he'd gotten home after talking to her. Lots of selfies, especially showing her paired with her new school friends. Different outfits she had put together. Some popular memes and cute kittens.

Parker took a covert look at his phone before class started. Technically, since the bell hadn't rung yet, he was still in the clear to look at his phone, but the bell would ring any second, and any time he spent looking at it after the sound would mean the risk of detention or confiscation.

Do you know...

There was a list of profiles of possible friends who Parker had not yet connected with. He looked over them before going on to his feed. He didn't recognize any of them, but when he tapped for further details, it was obvious that Dakota was the common link. Since Parker had connected with her, some of the people that she knew who might be in the area or have other mutual friends were starting to pop up on his list. Parker scrolled past them and looked for Dakota's latest post.

It figured.

A couple of selfies with her new friends and a picture quote from *My Little Pony*.

Parker sent Dakota an instant message between classes asking whether they could meet after school. He saw her look up from her screen over at him and then she ducked her head down again quickly. She didn't answer. She probably had other messages to answer as well. Other queries from people she was closer to.

She seemed to connect more easily with the other girls than with Parker. She had a natural bond with them, where her relationship with Parker was strained and more difficult. He supposed it was just a boy-girl thing. Of course Dakota would have an easier time connecting with girls like her. Boys and girls were different. Different personalities, different drives. She was hostile with Parker if he pushed too hard. He had to be careful not to get in her way. Just be around for when she needed him again. And she was bound to need him again.

He was surprised when she messaged him back right before the ending of the final period, agreeing to meet with him at the library.

They could do their homework together. The library was good; it wouldn't feel like a date, so she wouldn't feel pressured and could be relaxed with him. Parker looked up and nodded at Dakota. And when it was safe, ten seconds from the final bell, he messaged her an emoji thumbs-up.

He lost her in the swirl of after-school chaos. Kids getting out of class, meeting with friends in the hall, loading up backpacks from lockers, and running to after-school activities. Rather than trying to find her, Parker just headed for the library. She could get there on her own. There was no need for him to walk her there. She might be his latest injured bird, but she didn't have a broken leg.

Parker spread his books out on the table and started going through what he needed to do. He knew he was getting further and further behind in math, but he didn't know what to do about it. Mr. Bonne always went to Parker's desk at the end of the lesson and helped him run through a couple of the new problems, but it was different when Mr. Bonne was working with him, walking him through each step. When he had to do it for himself, Parker felt like he was losing his mind. He had no idea what to do.

"Algebra?" Dakota was looking over his shoulder.

"Uh… yeah. How are you doing on it?"

Dakota shrugged. "Okay, I guess."

"It's all Greek to me," Parker joked.

She rolled her eyes. "You've got a mistake," she pointed out.

Parker looked down at his page. He was only a couple of steps into the first question, and he had already made a mistake. "Uh… okay. What did I do?"

She pointed to one line. "You can't combine your variables like that."

Parker stared at her.

"You can't add apples and oranges," Dakota tried.

"Why not?"

"Because an apple plus an orange doesn't equal a pear."

"What?"

"You can't say 2x plus 2y equals 4xy. That's multiplying, not adding."

"Two plus two is four."

"Yeah. But two apples plus two pears doesn't make four apple pears."

"Okay." Parker erased it. He stared at the question again. He had no idea where to start. "The Asian market has apple pears," he told Dakota.

"What?"

"They do. They have a fruit called an apple pear. It's round like an apple, but it has a skin like a pear, and inside it's… well, it's like a crisp pear."

"Algebra isn't an Asian market." She sat down beside him, looking at his work. "You really are bad at this, aren't you?"

Parker's face got hot. Dakota hadn't been in school for months and she was ahead of him. Guys were supposed to be better at math than girls. It was supposed to come to them more easily. It didn't come easy to Parker. But for all he knew, Dakota might have already completed the grade before.

Still, it didn't make him feel any better.

"You want me to show you?"

"I dunno. Mr. Bonne has shown me a bunch of times, but I still can't get it right."

"Here." Dakota grabbed the pencil out of Parker's hand and started to write.

Parker watched her hands instead of looking at the characters she wrote. Her skin was dry, cracked in places, and needed a good application of moisturizer cream. Mona's skin got like that, and Parker knew just the stuff that she used to heal them and make them baby-soft again. Dakota's nails were painted pink. It was a pretty color against her rich brown skin.

Parker realized that Dakota had asked him something. He wasn't paying attention to the math question or what she was trying to tell him.

"What?" He tore his eyes away from her fingers and looked at her face. Which wasn't any better, because he immediately focused on her frosty lipstick. It seemed to have glitter embedded in it. "What color is your lipstick?"

She raised her eyebrows. "Are you listening to me at all?"

"Sorry, I got distracted…"

She didn't seem amused or complimented by this. She raised an eyebrow and waited. It was like having a bucket of ice water dashed over his head. Parker dropped his eyes back to his notebook. "Uh, no. I'll listen, I'm sorry."

"I thought you wanted help with your homework."

"Actually… I thought you might need help with yours."

Dakota laughed and shook her head. "I'm okay at school." She inverted the pencil and erased some more of his work. She tapped the page. "How many x's?"

Parker stared at the problem. "Five."

"Where do you get that? What's this?"

"An x."

"And what's this?"

"2x."

"How many is that?"

"Three. Plus two more."

"There's no more x's. Just x plus 2x."

Parker rolled his eyes and pointed. "Right there."

"That's just two. Two ones. Not two x's."

"So what do we do with those?"

"On this step, nothing. We'll get rid of them on the next step." She wrote down the 3x - 2 = 4.

"Then what do we do?" She prompted.

"I don't know."

He caught himself looking at her full lips again, then at her deep brown eyes for some hint of his next step.

"What did I tell you we were going to do on this step?"

"I don't know."

She didn't say anything and he looked back down at the notebook. What else had she said besides adding up the x's?

"Uh… get rid of the two."

"Right." Her lips curved in an approving smile. "How do we get rid of the two?"

Parker swallowed. He should have offered to take her out for ice cream instead of agreeing to meet at the library. His mouth was dry and his face was burning. He could do enough math to get along in real life. He could figure out prices and make change at the store. What did he need algebra for?

"Divide?" he suggested in a bit of a panic. Dakota was looking at him with that same impatience as the resource room teacher did when they forced him to go for extra help. She shook her head.

"If you divide the two, you have to divide everything. We don't want to do that yet. First, we want to get everything onto one side. All of the x's on one side."

"They are."

"But there's a two on that side too. We want everything else on the other side."

"So…"

"How do we get it from one side to the other? We have to do the same thing to both sides."

"Minus it?"

"It's negative two," Dakota pointed out. "What's minus-two minus two?"

"Zero."

"You have a hole two feet deep and dig it another two feet deep."

"Minus four," Parker corrected quickly.

"Yeah. You'd end up with minus four on that side instead of zero. So, what's the opposite of subtracting?"

"Times?"

"No, the opposite of subtracting. If I don't have any cookies, you can't take them away from me. But you could…"

Parker was baffled. "Give you more…?"

"Yeah. So, what is that?"

He scratched his head. "Adding?" That was all that was left.

"Right!" Dakota quickly scribbled the next line of the problem. The two now appeared on the opposite side of the equation.

"Is that done now?" Parker asked.

"Does it look done?"

"No."

"What do we need to do?"

Parker stared at it. "I want to add the two and the four. But you can't do that…?"

"Why not? Of course you can. Two and four is…"

"Six."

"Good. Then what do we do?"

"Now we're done?"

"No. Do you have all of your x's on one side?"

"Yes."

"And everything else on the other?"

"Yes."

"How many x's do you have?"

He looked back down at the problem to make sure that it hadn't changed. "Three."

"And how many ones do we have on the other side?"

He stared at the problem, unsure. Dakota pointed to the number with her pencil.

"Six."

"So if three people have six cookies, then they each have…"

Parker calculated, pressing the pads of his fingers into the table as he counted the last six. "Eighteen."

"No! Not multiplying. Altogether there are six cookies."

"Uh-huh."

"And three people all have the same amount. So how many do they have?"

"Six."

She sighed in exasperation. "I have some cookies, and you have some cookies, and Charity has some cookies. We all have the same amount. And there are six altogether."

"Two each."

"Right!"

Dakota scratched out the answer: x=2. Parker nodded slowly, like he understood everything they had just done.

"That's it," Dakota said. "Get it now?"

"Uh, yeah. I get it now."

"You do the next one, then."

"I… can't." Parker looked at his phone. "I forgot Mom wanted me home to look after the kids. So I got to run."

Dakota watched him pack up his bag. Parker swallowed.

"Thanks for your help."

"Yeah, sure. You sure we can't go out and do something else? Forget about homework?"

He'd already committed himself to going home with the line about looking after the younger kids. Dakota gave him a knowing grin.

"How old are the other kids? They can look after themselves for a while, can't they?"

"Uh… yeah, for a while," he admitted.

"Good. Then let's just go do something else. You can do the rest of your homework later."

Parker knew that if he didn't get the algebra done with Dakota, it wasn't getting done. If he couldn't even do one step right by himself, what was the point in spending an hour struggling and getting it all wrong? Better to get in trouble for slacking off and not getting it done than to look like an idiot who couldn't even add apples and apples.

"Sure, that sounds good. What do you want to do?"

Swinging on swings at the playground hadn't been quite how Parker had imagined spending time with Dakota. She squealed when he pushed her, and wanted to go higher and higher, but Parker could only manage to get her so high. She was a heavy girl, and she didn't seem to be able to pump to maintain her height. Feeling inadequate after the algebra session, Parker shook his head at her. At least *he* knew how to pump on a swing. Dakota gave it a half-hearted effort, but she couldn't seem to figure out the rhythm to keep going. She kept begging him to push her higher.

Then they played a game of grounders on the playground equipment with the little kids. Really little kids. Teenagers like Parker and Dakota didn't play like that. They hung out, texted, smoked, maybe went window shopping at the mall. There were no other teenagers around the playground. But the little kids really seemed to enjoy having the big kids to play with, and begged them to stay when they were ready to go.

"That was fun," Dakota gushed. There was a flush in her dark cheeks and she was sweating. She spun in a circle as they walked away from the park. She held her backpack out in front of her, and spun harder. Like she was going to launch the backpack. Parker backed away, not wanting to get hit.

Dakota stopped spinning and laughed. She swayed on her feet.

"You'd better stop that," Parker warned. "I'm not going to catch you if you fall down."

Dakota dropped the bag, and then intentionally hit the turf herself, catching herself on her hands and then rolling onto her back.

"I don't know when's the last time I had so much fun," she giggled.

"You're crazy."

"Because I'm having fun? Why are you such a spoilsport? Don't you ever play with your little brothers and sisters?"

"Yeah. And then my mom always yells at me to quit roughhousing before somebody gets hurt. Complains about the noise we're making. 'I can't hear myself think!'"

Dakota just smiled at that. "I wish I was part of your family. That sounds like fun."

Parker sat down on the grass next to her. "Do you have brothers and sisters?"

"No." Dakota stared up at the cloudy sky. "I've been in families with other kids. Cousins, or foster brothers, or whatever. But I don't have any of my own."

"That you know of."

She looked at him. "What's that mean?"

"I mean, if your mom abandoned you, and you don't know who your dad is, you could have all kinds of siblings and just not know it. They could both have had more kids after you."

"Huh, I guess so. I never thought of that. I always just felt like I was… alone. Isolated. No one else to take care of me. Never a part of anything. Never had a real family."

"Well, you and Mrs. Gable are like family now. She's happy to adopt you into hers."

"It ain't the same, though. Not as belonging somewhere."

"You belong here now," Parker argued. "It doesn't matter where you've been before or whether you were accepted there or not. You belong here now."

Dakota smiled and put her hand over Parker's for a fleeting instant.

Chapter Five

"PARKER, COME IN HERE. I want to talk to you."
Parker's heart sank. His mother saying that she needed to talk to him was never a good thing. If she just wanted to tell him something, she would do it, just let him know while they were eating or washing up. 'I want to talk to you' meant that it was something serious. That he'd screwed up on something.

He went into the kitchen where she was getting supper prepared. "Yeah, Mom?"

Mona pushed a loose lock of chestnut brown hair away from her face and turned to look at him. A long, appraising look. Like she hadn't seen him in a long time. Hadn't really looked at him lately.

"What's up?" Parker asked, trying to keep it light and casual. What was she upset about? Had the school called her to report how poorly he was doing? Or to report him for cutting a class here and there? She had to know that he was skipping occasionally. Everyone did it.

"Sit down."

Things were getting worse and worse. A sit-down talk? Parker got out a drink of weak, generic drink mix from the fridge. He didn't know what was worse, that it was diluted, or that it didn't have enough sugar in it and was sour. He sat down in Miranda's chair. She would have a fit if she knew he was sitting in her chair.

Parker took a drink. "So…? What?"

"I've been hearing a lot about this girl that Jade took in lately."

"Oh." Parker was relieved to find that it was a talk about someone else, not him. "Yeah. Dakota."

"Dakota. Kind of a boy's name."

"That's her name. There are plenty of girls with names like that."

"Where did she come from?"

"I don't know. She's never said. She's been other places, moving from family to family." Parker was throwing out facts, trying to figure out what it was that she actually wanted to know. "She was homeless, before Mrs. Gable took her in."

"That's what I heard. I also heard that you were the one who arranged for her to stay with Jade."

"Well…" Parker's face was hot, as he examined this piece of information from several angles and tried to spot any traps. "Yeah, I guess I'm the one who suggested it."

"Why would you do that?"

"She needed somewhere to live. I know… sometimes Mrs. Gable takes people in. Helps them out. She doesn't have any kids of her own at home anymore. I thought… maybe she would help Dakota out."

Mona stirred a big pot of red sauce, staring down into it. As if it were a crystal ball that would give her all of the answers she was seeking.

"How did you meet her?"

"I just saw her on my way to school one day."

"You know better than to talk to strangers."

Parker snorted. "Mom, I'm not a little kid! And she isn't an adult. Not someone who's going to try to harm anyone. She's just a teenager. Like me."

"How old is she?"

"I don't know. A year or two older than me. And she's got a job. She's not just a freeloader."

"What job?" Mona's glance flicked toward him.

"She helps out at the restaurant near Mrs. Gable's. Just a couple nights a week. There's nothing wrong with her, Mom. She's just a teenager, out on her own, and needed some help. If I didn't help her, who knows what would have happened?" he pointed out. "She could get into drugs or prostitution or something. But she's not. She just needed a home."

"How much time are you spending with her?"

Parker ground his back teeth, considering his answer. "Not much. She has other friends at school. She's in Mr. Bonne's homeroom, but I can't exactly socialize with her there. Just now and then, in the library or at Mrs. Gable's."

"I don't want you being alone with her. We don't know anything about this girl or what kind of things she may be mixed up in. She's a runaway; she could have been in all kinds of trouble at home. We don't know."

Mona had already put cut-up veggies out on the table. Parker grabbed a carrot and took a bite. He crunched for a few minutes, using his full mouth as an excuse not to talk, thinking about what she had said.

"You haven't even met her. You'd see there's nothing wrong with her. She's just a girl. Just a kid, like me. Or Sophie. If Sophie was in trouble, you'd want someone else to befriend her and help her out, wouldn't you?"

"Of course I would. But I don't want you getting taken in by this girl because you always want to help everyone. You have to understand that sometimes people are going to hurt you."

Parker winced. He knew what it was like to be hurt. And Mona knew it.

"How is she going to hurt me?"

"I don't know." Mona tasted her sauce and added a few grinds of pepper. "Even if she's a perfectly nice girl, I don't think you're ready for a… relationship yet."

"I've had girlfriends before!" Parker's face got hot.

"You've had let's-hang-out-at-the-mall girlfriends before. And they've never lasted for more than a day or two. This girl… well, it's been more than a couple of days, hasn't it?"

"Yes. But we're not doing anything. Just watching TV or doing homework."

"And that's the way I want it to stay. The two of you need to only be together when there are adults around and you can be supervised. Do you understand me, Parker Andrew Jurek?"

Full name. She really was serious.

"Yes, ma'am."

"An older girl, who's been out on the streets… who knows what kind of experience or moral standards she has. You're only fourteen. I don't want to have to worry about child support."

"Child support…" It took a minute for it to click in that Mona was talking about Parker getting Dakota pregnant. "Holy crap, Mom! I said we're not doing anything! Don't you trust me?"

She turned around and gazed at him for a minute. "I know what it's like to be a teenager. And it's that much harder in today's society than it was when I was a kid. So… no… I don't trust that you're going to know the right thing to do or be able to control your impulses without guidance and supervision. Your brain isn't finished developing and your hormones are in full swing. Throwing a girl you feel sorry for and have a crush on into the mix isn't something that fills me with confidence."

Parker wiped his face, swearing. "I can't believe you think I'm just out to—"

"Language, Parker. You're not exactly demonstrating to me that you are thinking logically about this."

"I'm going to my room," Parker growled.

"Parker!"

He got up from the table, ignoring her protests and her efforts to call him back. She was occupied with the meal, so he was pretty sure that she wasn't going to come after him and leave everything to burn. He stomped into his room and slammed the door so loud it rattled the windows.

Link looked up from his book, frowning. He watched Parker climb up the ladder to flop down on his mattress face-first.

"Mom…?" he guessed.

"Yeah. Mom."

Link nodded and went back to his reading.

"Let's go to your place," Dakota suggested as they packed their bags after school. "Jade is all on the war path over me not picking up after myself and everything. Like I need all that extra stress! When did teenagers become slave labor?" She sighed noisily. "I was going to go out with Charity, but then she got stupid detention because she was texting during English. That is so stupid!"

Parker wasn't sure that taking Dakota home was the best idea. Mona had made it clear that she didn't want Parker spending too much time with her.

In all fairness, she hadn't said that he couldn't spend any time with her, just that they had to be properly supervised. If he took her home, then Mona couldn't complain that they weren't being supervised. Not if Mona was there.

And maybe once she saw Dakota, she would relax a little bit. See that Parker didn't see her in a romantic way, just as a friend, just following up to make sure that his latest broken bird was healing properly.

"Well, I guess it would be okay."

"Good. I don't feel like dealing with responsibilities for a while."

Parker nodded understandingly. It had to be harder for her than it was for him. He had a mother to support him, someone to backstop him and make sure that he had everything he needed. For Dakota, it was different. She was out on her own and responsible for taking care of herself. Even though Jade was there, that was only by Dakota's choice, and they weren't actually family. If Dakota screwed up and got herself kicked out, she'd be on the street again.

Parker led the way toward his house.

"Can we watch TV?" Dakota asked.

"Maybe. But the younger kids get home before I do, so they'll already have something on. I doubt it will be anything good."

"I like little kid shows sometimes." Dakota shrugged. "I don't care what they've got on."

"Whatever. And if my mom's home, she's going to expect us to do homework before anything else. She's strict like that."

Dakota made a disgusted noise in the back of her throat. "You should see Jade! Man, she's on my case all the time, about everything. I said I wanted a mom, but she's a bit too much like the real thing!"

Parker snickered. It was good that Jade was keeping Dakota in line. Mona would approve. Between school, work, homework, and whatever other chores Jade assigned Dakota, she wouldn't have any time to be partying or thinking of getting into trouble.

"You know what? You're a jerk," Dakota told him, annoyed by his laughter.

"Yeah, I know."

When they reached the house, Parker felt himself getting warm as Dakota looked over it, her nostrils flaring and her head rising a little. Parker knew how tiny the house was, how dilapidated it looked. But it was their house. Dakota didn't have a house of her own, she was staying with a friend. He wasn't sure where she got her snobbery when two short weeks before, she had been completely homeless.

Dakota caught his look. She turned her face away from him, licking her lips. "Nice little place," she said. "Like the old woman who lived in a shoe."

"Don't you make fun—"

"It was just a joke, Parker. Have a sense of humor."

"My mom works really hard. That's the only way she's been able to keep a roof over our heads. It may not look like much—"

"It looks fine. It was a joke. Ha, ha, Parker. Come on," she couldn't seem to help being snide, "give me the grand tour, why don't you?"

Parker shook his head and led the way in the door. It riled him that she would belittle his home. But he tried to picture her as she was that first day, all alone in the alleyway looking through dumpsters. It was just a defense mechanism. She was just trying to make herself feel better. An animal would bite when it was hurt.

The girls were tumbled together on the couch, giggling and watching their show with bright lively eyes. They quieted for a moment as Parker and Dakota entered, and then started giggling again, louder than ever. Parker gestured at them. "Sophie, Miranda, and Leslie," he introduced.

"Hey," Dakota said. "Nice to meet you."

"Who's your *girlfriend*, Parker?" Sophie demanded, in a sugary tone.

"This is Dakota," Parker said. He didn't bother getting into an argument with her over whether Dakota was his girlfriend or not. That would be too complicated. She was a friend who was a girl. He liked her and was a little attracted to her, but she didn't seem to have any interest in anything other than a friendship. If he launched into an argument that she wasn't a girlfriend, Dakota might take it to mean that he didn't have any interest in her, and he didn't want that.

Instead, he just rolled his eyes a little bit over the impudence of little sisters. They all giggled again. Parker led her across the living room to the kitchen, crossing in front of the TV and making the girls crane their necks to see it as he passed.

Parker had expected to find Mona in the kitchen, but she was not there. Link was at the table, eating a sandwich. He looked at Parker and gave a little nod.

"My brother, Link," Parker introduced. "This is Dakota."

Link nodded, his eyes on Dakota. He had probably heard about her already. Between his mother's complaints, the two of them attending the same school, and neighborhood gossip, he probably knew just about as much about Dakota as Parker did.

"Good to meet you," he said eventually, after emptying his mouth.

Dakota's eyes narrowed at him. She didn't smile and greet him like she had the girls. Parker ducked back out of the room and into the back hallway. He motioned down the hall to the right. "The girls' bedroom there. This one is mine…" He stepped across the hall and opened the door. It was messy. What boys' room wasn't? Even though Jessup was a stickler for everything being properly cleaned and picked up, he couldn't keep everyone's possessions in order. Dakota peered in.

"And this is Jessup," he told Dakota.

Jessup looked up from his handheld game, and then dropped his eyes again, making a little grimace of greeting, but saying nothing. Dakota laughed.

Parker looked toward the master bedroom, wondering whether Mona was home. She might have had to put in an extra shift. He could never keep track of her schedule, and sometimes it changed without much warning. They were all old enough now to look after themselves if the older kids kept track of the younger, so she was more free to pick up extra shifts when she could get them.

"Your parents' room?" Dakota suggested, following his gaze.

"My mom's. Yeah." Parker walked up to the door. He poked his head in; the door was not fully closed, but it wasn't standing wide open, either. A sort of 'I'm here, but don't bother me unless you really need to' position. "Mom?"

Mona was sitting on the bed with her laptop out, her hair hanging in front of her face as she focused on something with a serious expression. She startled at his voice.

"Parker. I didn't hear you come in."

"Are you busy?"

"Well… sort of. What's wrong?"

"Nothing wrong. I was just going to introduce you…"

She looked up from her screen, a frown line between her eyebrows. "Hmm?"

Parker pushed the door open the rest of the way, moving in to allow Dakota to get into the doorway.

"Mom, this is Dakota. My friend from school who's staying at Mrs. Gable's."

"Oh!" Mona looked surprised. She ran her fingers through her hair to push it back away from her face. She looked at Dakota and then around the room. It wasn't much tidier than the boys' room. But at least it wasn't as bad as the girls'. She turned a little pink. "Sorry, I wasn't expecting company." She then attended to her personal appearance, straightening her neckline, sitting up straight instead of hunching over like she got after Parker for doing when he worked on his homework. She smoothed wrinkles in her pants. "I'm a bit of a mess. I haven't changed since work."

Dakota shrugged. "You look nice," she said.

"I'm glad to finally get the chance to meet you, Dakota. I've heard a lot about you."

Dakota's eyes turned questioningly toward Parker. Interrogating him as to *what* he had told his mother about her. Parker shrugged. "Mom and Mrs. Gable are good friends," he pointed out.

"Jade has had some very nice things to say about you," Mona said. "She's very impressed with how well you're getting along at school, and getting yourself a job to try to contribute to the household. She thinks you're a very responsible girl."

Dakota snorted. "When she's not nagging me to pick up after myself or to make supper or do my homework."

Mona smiled faintly. "Those are par for the course for parents. Or those filling the role of parents. It doesn't mean she thinks less of you. She knows you're just a teenager."

Dakota gave a little shrug. "It's nice to meet you, Mrs. Ju—Jur—" she looked at Parker for help.

"Jurek," Mona filled in. "You can call me Mona, if it's easier. It does trip people up a little. Not a common name around here."

"It's Polish, isn't it?" Dakota asked. As if this were something she knew herself, and not because Parker had already told her so.

"Yes." Mona didn't look impressed by this bit of knowledge. She smiled a thin-lipped smile that did not even come close to reaching her eyes. Parker shifted uncomfortably. He couldn't figure out what it was that Mona didn't like about Dakota. She was a cute girl, with a vulnerable air that Jade and most other women her age were drawn to. Parker had seen it in the teachers at school too, who immediately took Dakota under their wings, protecting and encouraging her. But Mona studied Dakota with a definite air of suspicion.

Dakota looked at Parker uncertainly.

"You look busy," Parker said. "We'll just make our own supper and hit the books?"

"Yes. That would be good," Mona agreed.

Parker nodded and headed back out the door again.

"Dakota?" Mona's voice called them back. Dakota looked over her shoulder at Mona.

"Yeah?"

"Where are you from?"

Dakota eased her weight from one leg to the other. "West," she said cagily. "I don't like to talk about the past."

"Were you in trouble?"

Dakota looked back at Parker, but there was nothing he could do to rescue her. "I been in some bad places," she said cautiously. "I left because I didn't want to be abused. Not 'cause I'm a bad person."

Mona held her gaze for a few extra seconds before nodding. Parker breathed out a long, controlled stream of air, and led the way back to the kitchen.

"What've you been telling her about me?" Dakota demanded.

Parker looked at Link, awkward having this discussion before him. Link looked back at him steadily and didn't make any move to leave the room and let them have a private conversation.

"I haven't told her anything. All I ever said was that I helped Jade to move you in. Anything else she heard from Jade or others in the neighborhood. What exactly would I tell her? You've never told me any details about yourself."

She wasn't convinced. "You could have made something up. People tell stories."

"I didn't."

They looked at each other for a few seconds, neither speaking. Then Parker shrugged and opened the fridge door to see what they could make for a supper.

After a thrown-together supper, Dakota had settled in front of the TV with the girls while Parker worked on his homework on the floor of the living room. It wasn't the most comfortable location, but not that different from doing it in his room. Except that there were a lot more distractions and it was hard to stay focused.

"Don't you have homework to do?" he asked Dakota.

"I finished most of mine in class. And Mr. Bonne takes late work, so I can do it on the weekend and get caught back up."

"Don't you have other things you'd rather do on the weekend?"

Dakota stared mesmerized at the TV screen and didn't answer.

The little girls seemed entirely comfortable with Dakota, despite how opposite they were to her in looks. Like Parker, they were all blond and fair-skinned, with thin builds. It's how Mona was built, and Parker's father too had been a tall, thin man. But the physical differences didn't seem to faze the girls at all. Dakota was into the shows that they were watching, so she was one of them despite the barriers of age and race. When Parker looked up from his English essay, Dakota was braiding tiny corn rows into Miranda's hair.

"What was that?" Dakota shouted suddenly, startling everyone out of their TV-induced coma.

They all blinked at her like little owls. "What?" Leslie asked, pushing herself into a sitting position and looking around.

"What was that? Something is flying in here!"

"Flying?" Parker looked around the living room for any sign of a bird or bat.

"Yes!" Dakota's head moved back and forth as she tried to spot it again. Her eyes were wide in panic and she had forgotten all about the TV show and the corn rows. "Something just flew past my face! What's in here?"

Everyone looked around, but couldn't see anything that might be causing Dakota distress. Whatever had flown past her face was gone. Their eyes were all drawn back to the TV screen. Parker had given up on doing his homework, the room had gotten too dark and the girl-talk and TV drivel was too distracting.

Then Dakota shrieked again, louder this time. "There it is! It just flew right in my face!" She let out a squeal that would have rated well in a horror movie.

"What?" Parker tried to follow her gaze and her erratic motions. A moth landed on the flickering TV screen and started crawling over it.

Dakota's continued shouts brought Mona and the boys all out to the living room, sure that someone was being murdered.

"The moth?" Parker asked. "Is that what you're so freaked out about?"

"It flew right in my face! It touched me! I felt it on my face!"

"The moth?" Parker couldn't quite believe that the tiny flying insect was the cause of all of her noise.

"Yes! The moth!"

Parker rolled up a flyer, stepped up to the TV, and flattened the intruder.

"Eeew!" the girls squealed.

"You'll need to clean it up," Mona said.

Parker used his nail to scrape a small spatter off of the screen, and picked up the dead body of the moth that had fallen to the carpet.

"Keep it away from me!" Dakota shouted, when he got closer to show it to her.

"It's dead. It's just a harmless dead bug. What's—"

"Keep it away! Keep it away! Don't get close to me with that!"

Everyone was laughing at Dakota's panic. "Get rid of it!" Dakota insisted. "Throw it in the garbage. Or outside. Or burn it!"

"Chill, it's just a bug," Link said.

The girls squealed as Parker walked by them with the dead bug, but it was obviously dramatized. Even someone who didn't know that they weren't afraid of bugs would be able to tell it was put on.

Parker, the hero, disposed of the tiny corpse and returned to the living room.

"There. All gone. Nothing else to worry about."

Chapter Six

I'LL WALK YOU HOME," Parker offered, as the girls were sent off to bed and Dakota peeled herself up from the couch.

She waved a hand at him. "You don't need to do that. It's not far."

"I will anyway."

Dakota stood there looking at him, hands on hips. "You think I can't protect myself better than a skinny white kid?"

Parker's immediate reaction was to be offended. That was all he was to her? A skinny white kid? She didn't think that he could do anything for her? What he had already done to help her out didn't count for anything? But he kept his mouth closed, keeping himself from lashing out at her. She was far more solidly-built than he was. At least twice his weight, probably more. A veteran of many homes and living alone on the streets, she was probably more experienced and better skilled at protecting herself.

But she was a girl. And he'd been raised to take care of girls. It was the gentlemanly thing to do.

"I'll walk you home," he told her again.

There was a movement from the back hallway, and he saw Mona standing there, listening to the conversation. He grinned at her. "Always walk a girl home, right Mom?"

Dakota turned around and saw Mona standing there. She scowled and didn't argue it any further. Mona didn't agree or disagree, she just withdrew out of sight again.

Darkness had fallen while they were watching TV. Not that the streets were completely dark; there were plenty of streetlights to ensure that the city was never completely dark. There was still foot traffic, people coming and going on the busier streets.

Parker reached over and took Dakota's hand as they walked. She turned her eyes to Parker, startled. For just an instant, she left her hand in his, and then she slid it out.

She didn't say anything and neither did he. She hadn't voiced an objection, which Parker was counting as a good sign. She didn't say that she didn't like him or to leave her alone. He hoped it just meant that she wasn't ready yet. Maybe if he gave her a little more time…

Parker managed a sideways glance at Dakota, trying to evaluate further. Her eyes were wide, like she was scared, and he was suddenly sorry that he had touched her. He hadn't meant to scare her. He knew she'd had bad experiences. There was no telling who had forced their attentions on her in the past. But he didn't apologize, worried that it would just make things worse.

"So… what did you think about my family?" he asked after a period of silence that he worried was growing awkward.

A smile quirked the corner of Dakota's mouth. "Your sisters are very cute," she said. "I had fun with them."

Parker nodded. "They can be bratty sometimes, but I'd never want anything to happen to them."

"You seem like you're a good big brother."

Parker swelled at the compliment. "I try," he agreed.

"Wish I'd had a big brother to look after me. Or at least big brothers that didn't try to torture or take advantage of me."

Parker stared down at the sidewalk in front of him, cracks thrown into sharp relief by the streetlights overhead. Had Dakota had any safe place when she was growing up? Anywhere she could go without fear of being abused? Had there been a couple of nice homes that she had lived in, or had they all been horrible? Had she always lived with strangers who saw her as a burden or target?

"Life's just like that," Dakota blustered, looking at him. "It's tough all over. Be glad your sisters don't have to be out there in the real world, like I did."

"You think it's like that everywhere?"

He could feel her staring at him, even though he didn't turn his head to look at her face.

"I *know* it's like that everywhere."

Parker scowled. "No, it's not! What about at Mrs. Gable's? You know you're safe there and nobody is going to hurt you."

She didn't answer right away. Not until they were almost to the house.

"You don't know Mr. Gable, do you?"

Parker was taken aback. He knew there was a Mr. Gable, but the man was like a ghost. Parker never saw him. Jade mentioned him now and then, as if he really existed and was around from time to time. But he was never there during the day when Parker was around. He worked late, sometimes worked out of town, and was always out of the house by the time Parker was on his way to school or out with his friends.

"No," he admitted. "What's he like?"

Dakota snorted. "Like every other man. Just after one thing. When he isn't in the bottom of a bottle."

Parker's chest tightened. It was suddenly hard to get enough air. "He's bothering you? Did you tell Mrs. Gable?"

"Why would I do that? She's got eyes. She can see what's going on. She knows he'd smack the words right out of her face if she tried to interfere."

"What? He wouldn't hit her."

"Like I said, you don't know Mr. Gable, do you?"

"Well… no… but I didn't think Jade would put up with anything like that. She's so… strong. She doesn't seem like she'd let her husband push her around, or get away with anything."

"Well, he's no hen-pecked husband."

Parker put his hand on Dakota's arm, stopping her. "Wait. Are you okay there? Do you want me to try to find somewhere else? I didn't think… I never knew there were any problems with the Gables. I never heard anyone say anything…"

Dakota slowly removed Parker's hand from her arm. She was shaking her head. Her expression was softer than it had been, the anger leaving it. "Like I said, it's tough all over, Parkinson. It doesn't matter where I go… there's always someone. It's never like they say it's going to be."

"Is there a lock on your door? Can you… are you safe?"

"Don't you worry about me. I'll look after myself. I'm bigger and tougher than you are, white boy."

"Are you sure? Dakota, I thought it was safe there. I really did."

She waved her hand at him. "Forget about it. Nothing you can do. I'll be fine."

They walked the rest of the way in relative silence. Parker saw Dakota to her door. He stood outside for a few minutes, looking at the house. There was no sign that Mr. Gable was home. He worked long hours and Parker assumed he wouldn't be in until late.

The house looked warm and inviting. Just like always.

Parker's house was quiet when he got home. The girls were off to bed, and if they were still awake, were at least whispering to avoid keeping the rest of the house awake. Parker knew it was time for him to get to bed soon too. The TV was off, so Link and Jessup were presumably in bed, reading or relaxing for a few minutes before going to sleep. Mona was waiting for Parker and stepped into the living room to speak to him.

"Hey," Parker greeted in a whisper.

"Hi, handsome." Mona motioned for Parker to sit down. She'd already put out a sandwich and drink of milk for him, indicating that she was waiting for him, planning a sit-down talk for when he returned home.

Parker sat down and looked at the food, not really hungry. He had a sip of the milk.

"It's good of you to walk her home," Mona said.

"I was raised to be a gentleman."

"Yes, you were."

"Mom…"

"Yes…?"

"Do you know anything about Mr. Gable?"

Mona looked surprised at the question. "I've met him before. I don't really know him personally. But of course, Jade talks about him sometimes in passing."

"She's never said… that he hits her, has she?"

"No," Mona frowned and shook her head definitely. "She's never said anything to even hint that he's abusive. And I would know. I've never seen any sign that there's anything wrong between them."

"So you don't think so?"

"No. Is that what Dakota said?"

Parker nodded. He nibbled at the corner of his sandwich. "He's not home very much, is he?"

"No. Rarely. And when he's in town, he's in so late and gone so early, she's practically a widow. If she wants time to see him, she has to schedule it into his calendar. He works all the time."

"And he's not out… messing around with other girls—women—is he? I mean, it's not like he's tired of Jade but out chasing after other…"

"Whatever Dakota has told you… I think you should go to Jade with it. I don't think Dakota's telling you the truth."

"You don't even know her."

"I know what I've heard about her from Jade and around the neighborhood. I've seen her face-to-face now; and I think I've had enough experience to judge some things by sight."

"You don't know her. You can't just go by what other people say about her. People gossip. They tell stories."

"You don't think I can tell the difference between a story and the truth?"

"No… not always."

Mona smiled suddenly, surprising Parker. He had been expecting her to blow up at that. "Okay, not always," she agreed. "But I have heard enough… and I want you to be safe. You can't just trust anything she says. You need to test it out for yourself. See if it feels true, or whether it is a tall tale. See whether the things she tells her friends are true. Check up on her."

"I'm not going to do that to her."

"Then you've got to realize that everything she is telling you could be a lie. You don't know her background, where she came from, who she really is. She's another stray. And just like those cats and birds, you don't have any idea what might have happened to her before she came here. You don't know if she's going to be grateful to you for trying to help her out, or to bite you."

Parker had been bitten by his animal rescues in the past. It always surprised him. Of course it shouldn't, he should understand that feral, injured animals were not going to understand that he was trying to help them.

But it always surprised him when one of them lashed out and hurt him.

Parker watched Dakota as she came into the classroom, giggling and chattering with Addy and Charity. She was always with somebody, always buffering herself from the rest of the world with a gaggle of people around her.

Or maybe she was just a social person and didn't like to be left alone to her own devices. Friendships were important in junior high. Especially with girls.

"When are you going to do something about that?" Adrian asked.

Parker tore his eyes away from Dakota to see what Adrian was talking about. He'd obviously missed part of the conversation, distracted by his thoughts of Dakota.

"What? Do something about what?"

Adrian eyed him knowingly, and jerked his head toward Dakota. "You obviously got the hots for fatso, so when are you going to do something about it?"

His mouth dry, Parker looked for something to say. Deny his interest? Say he didn't know what Adrian was talking about? Punch him in the mouth?

Adrian laughed.

"Yeah, man," Chris joined in. "You're always mooning over her, so why don't you do something? Go talk to her. Ask her out. Take her somewhere… private."

"Like where?" Parker objected. "She doesn't like me. What am I supposed to do?"

He didn't say that he already had done something. That he'd made more than one attempt to get into Dakota's good graces. Just the day before, he'd given her a toy pony. He had no idea whether it was a character she liked, or even if it was a genuine *My Little Pony* or a knock-off, but he had come across it at the thrift store and had to get it for her.

She'd been cute about it. All embarrassed and pleased, turning it over in her hands and holding it up in front of her face. He pictured it in her bedroom, in a special place on her dresser, looking over the rest of the room.

"She likes you," Adrian said.

"She doesn't. We do some stuff together, but she's just… she doesn't like me. Not like that."

"You have to woo her."

Parker had never heard such a word come out of Adrian's mouth. They had watched and rated countless girls together, adding up their good and bad points, talking about who they would get together with and who they wouldn't. Like they were Don Juans, who had their pick of whatever girls they liked. But 'woo' was not in the vocabulary. They were macho guys, urban men who talked about women as objects and never gave any sign of vulnerability.

"Woo her?" Parker waited for both Adrian and Chris to break into hysterical laughter, to admit that it was all just a joke, but they didn't. They both continued to look at him expectantly.

"She likes you," Adrian repeated. "Are you kidding? You're her white knight. If she says she doesn't want to be with you, she's just playing hard to get. I'm telling you man, she's told all her friends she likes you."

"No," Parker objected. He pulled out his phone and brought up the social media stream she posted to the most often. "She's never said nothing about me. Not to anyone."

"She wouldn't post it where you could see," Chris said. "That wouldn't make you work for it. She can hide her posts from you."

"She's on my list."

"Yeah, but she can still keep you from seeing them. Look."

They all took a quick look around as Chris took out his phone as well. It was getting close to bell time, and if they were caught with their phones out when it went, the phones would be confiscated for the day and they might have to serve detention as well.

"Look," Chris repeated softly, sheltering the phone between their bodies so that no one else would be able to see it. He tapped and swiped his way into Dakota's stream, and then angled the phone so that Parker would be able to see it.

Parker saw his own picture. A profile. Candid shot. He didn't even know when she had taken it. He barely caught a glimpse of the hashtags beside it and Dakota's girlish brag, before the bell rang. Chris whipped it away, shoving it into his pocket. He raised his eyebrows at Parker.

"See? She does, man. She wants you. Everybody knows it."

"Everybody except you," Adrian amended.

Mr. Bonne called for everyone's attention and Parker slid into his seat. He considered the development as he sat there, his mind a thousand miles away from Mr. Bonne's daily announcements.

Did Dakota really like him? Or were Adrian and Chris pranking him? There was no guarantee that what Parker had seen was really on Dakota's stream, that it was even her account. It could be a dummy account. A picture one of the boys had taken and was just using now to see if he could get Parker wound up. They had all done it at one time or another. Teased one of the others about the girls they liked. Set up a pretend romance. Encouraged the other to do something stupid so they ended up with egg all over their face. It was what guys did.

Parker glanced across the room at Dakota. What if it really had been her? What if, among those selfies and memes she posted, she posted occasional pictures of Parker? Keeping them private from him so that she could talk to her girlfriends without him knowing about it. Adrian and Chris acted like it was common knowledge that Dakota liked him back.

She'd been so tickled with that pony he had given her. It wasn't even like it was mint-in-package. It had probably been through a dozen babies' mouths before making its way to her, but she didn't seem to care. She loved it anyway.

Not like she'd kissed him thank you. But she had been appreciative. She had not acted like he was being a goof in giving it to her, but like it had really meant something to her.

Charity nudged Dakota, and Dakota turned and looked at Parker, catching his gaze on her. He looked quickly away, blushing to the roots of his blond hair. The curse of fair skin. Why couldn't he be nice and dark like she was, giving nothing about his feelings away to the rest of the world? Dakota giggled and she and Charity whispered together until Mr. Bonne stopped talking and stared at them, waiting for them to realize they were disturbing the class.

One more high giggle escaped from Charity, and then she turned to face Mr. Bonne, arranging her body properly in the desk and looking at Mr. Bonne with a prim and proper expression. "Sorry, Mr. Bonne."

Mr. Bonne went on, continuing with his announcements. Intramural sports, students' council, yearbook photos, it all went over Parker's head. He didn't participate in any of that stuff anyway, but nothing could be further from his mind as he continued to stare at Dakota's face in profile, willing her to look over at him. She did, and then she turned back to face the front again, a little bit of a smile curling the corner of her mouth.

"So what do I do?" Parker demanded of his friends.

Word had spread beyond the intimate triangle of friends formed by Parker, Chris, and Adrian to the rest of the boys in the group. They weren't the best of buddies, but they shared a table in the lunchroom and they talked sports and homework with each other. Girls, when the occasion warranted.

"She doesn't act like she wants to be more than friends. We've done schoolwork together. She's been to my house and I've been to hers. But I don't know what else to do. What does she want?"

"You should tell her friends that you want to go out," Chris suggested. "Then they can tell her, and she can tell them what she wants to do, and they'll tell you—"

"She already knows I like her. It's not news. But when I try to… you know… get closer, she pushes me away."

"She never said anything like that on her timeline," Adrian pointed out, his mouth full as he scrolled down on his phone, presumably looking at Dakota's stream. "If you were making moves and she didn't want anything to do with you, she'd say so. "Ew, this guy…" You know. Saying that you were gross or creepy. But she doesn't. She posts pictures of you. Says how *sweet* you are."

Parker felt the blush rising again. "So, what? I should ask her out? See if she wants to hang out? Go to… where? Movies? A party?"

"She likes to party," Chris advised. "That's your best bet."

She likes to party. Parker turned it over in his mind, trying to act like it didn't make him incredibly uncomfortable. He wasn't the type that went out to parties. He wasn't the type that even got invited to parties. If someone's parents were out of town, leaving the house open for parties, Parker did not head the list of people who would be called to go. In fact, he wouldn't be anywhere on that list. Even if he asked, he wasn't sure if he would be invited. Everyone knew he didn't drink or go out for anything wild. He was like a nerd, except that he wasn't that smart and didn't do well at school. Maybe loser was a better word. No one would normally invite him to anything.

"Ask Charity," Adrian advised, reading Parker's expression. "She'll get you in. She knows Dakota likes you, so she'll make sure."

"I can't ask Charity to get me invited to a party, just so I'll have a chance with Dakota. That's just…" Parker trailed off, unable to think of a word for it. Lame? Loser-ish? Sad?

There was no way he could approach Charity about it.

Chapter

Seven

A s it turned out, word spread quickly that Parker wanted to go to a party with Dakota and he didn't actually have to ask Charity for an invitation.

He met with Dakota after school, ostensibly to do homework and get her help on algebra, but of course, Parker's goal was far different. They spread out their books at the public library—not the school library—in hopes that they wouldn't be interrupted by any of the school kids.

They whispered over their schoolbooks, and Parker actually did one math problem with Dakota, pretending to himself and to her that that was the reason he was really there. As he scratched out the next question from the textbook, Dakota was writing something down in her own notebook. She tore it out and folded it over, then slid it under the edge of Parker's notebook. He looked at the folded note and then at her.

Dakota laughed. "Read it!"

Parker slid the note back out and unfolded it. He looked at the swirls and hearts without comprehension. Dakota waited expectantly. Parker swallowed and tapped the note awkwardly.

"You don't want to?" Dakota was obviously disappointed.

"Uh… I can't read cursive…" Parker said uncomfortably, looking down at the incomprehensible words.

"Oh! I'm so stupid sometimes!" Dakota smacked her forehead.

"We never took it," Parker explained. "My mom was really mad that they don't teach us cursive in school anymore. She tried to

85

teach me at home. But I didn't get it and she really didn't have enough time, so… yeah. I can't read it."

"I know, I know. We took it at one of my schools, and I forget that everyone else doesn't teach it anymore," Dakota said. "Here…"

She pulled out her phone and he waited while she tapped something out. His own phone vibrated, and Parker pulled it over to read her message.

Do u want to prty? Shore Road big pink house Fri night 10:00

Parker gave her a smile. She did want him to go with her. Maybe she did like him a little after all. He texted back an emoji for a 'yes.'

"Oh… can you see pink?" Dakota asked suddenly in realization.

Parker shrugged. "Yeah. It's harder at night, but it's harder for everyone to differentiate colors in the dark. But I figure I'll be able to tell by the loud music and all of the cars parked in front of it."

Dakota laughed. "Yeah, probably," she agreed. "You gonna be able to get away? I know your mom probably doesn't let you go out…"

Parker switched off his phone. "Well, not at ten. But later on, after she's in bed. I should be able to get out then. She sleeps pretty soundly."

"Great. Can you get a ride?"

"I can get there on my bike. I know where Shore Road is." Parker had a sudden thought. "Oh… do you need a ride? I can't exactly pick you up if I'm on my bike."

"No, no," she waved away his concerns. "I'll meet you there. I'll go over with the girls."

"Okay. As long as you're okay with that. I know the guy should pick you up…"

"It's not like you've got a car. Or even a license. It's okay. You don't need to pick me up."

Parker nodded again, letting his breath out. "Okay, good."

Parker lifted his pillow to take another look at the time on his cell phone, and decided it was time to go. He rolled over and quietly slithered out of bed. He could tell by Link's breathing that he was awake and aware of Parker's movements. But Link didn't say anything and Parker didn't think he would squeal. In another year or two, Link would be the one trying to sneak out.

Parker pulled on the clothes that he had laid out under his covers and left the house undetected.

It took half an hour to get out to Shore Road, and as Parker had suspected, it was easy to pick out the house the party was at. Brightly lit, lots of noise, the party had been in full swing for a couple of hours, so there were lots of people there already, in and out of the house. Parker hoped the neighbors wouldn't call the police to get the party shut down.

Parker went up to the door with a knot in his stomach. He felt out of place. Most of the partiers that he saw were several years older than he was. Maybe a few high school students, but most of them were obviously college age. At first, he didn't see anyone he knew. He went in the open front door and looked around. He was less and less comfortable being there. What was he doing? He wasn't a partier and he should just be at home in bed.

"What are you doing here, baby-face?" a college boy jeered at him. "Don't you have a curfew?"

Parker ignored him, wading deeper into the crowd. The lights were strobing, the music was pounding, and people were yelling, laughing, shoving, and smoking around him, everything mixing into one huge, overwhelming sensory deluge.

If he didn't find Dakota in ten minutes, he would be out of there. It would be a relief to get back onto his bike and have the brisk air whipping by his face as his wheels swooshed over the concrete.

"Well, look who made it! Parker!"

Parker tried to home in on the voice and saw Charity on the stairs, waving down at him. He wasn't sure whether to go up, or whether to wait for her to come down. She seemed to be waiting for him and it was less crowded on the stairs, so he made his way over to her.

"Charity. Hi."

"Parker Jurek. Never thought I'd see you here—"

"I'm looking for Dakota."

She gave him a withering look. "I think I know who you're looking for. Last I saw, she was out back." She gestured in the direction of what looked like a porch door.

Parker nodded and headed back down the stairs.

"You'd better get a drink," Charity said. "I wouldn't go out there without a drink in my hand."

Parker thought about that as he went down the stairs. He assumed that she meant Dakota wouldn't want to be drinking alone. She wouldn't want to think that he was all righteous and judging her while she drank and he stayed sober.

The makeshift bar was in the kitchen, which he had to walk through to get to the back. Parker took a quick glance over it and splashed some cola into a plastic cup.

Out back was not just a porch, but a big yard with a swimming pool, some landscaped gardens, and a big pagoda or stage. Parker took a deep breath of the fresh air. He'd only been inside for five minutes, and he'd felt like he was suffocating. He wandered around a bit before he found Dakota and Marina dancing beside the pool, laughing loudly, so unsteady on their feet that Parker wondered how they had managed not to fall into the pool yet.

"Dakota."

She turned slowly and saw him. Marina's eyes lit up. "Well, look who it is! It's your Prince Charming! I thought you said there was no way he'd show up."

Dakota gave a wide shrug. She reached out and grabbed Parker's arm, pulling him closer to her. "Better to say you weren't coming than to make them think I got stood up," she told him in what qualified as a soft voice, with all of the music and rowdiness around them.

"Yeah. Sure. But I didn't stand you up. Here I am." Parker looked around awkwardly. He didn't belong there. But he was there for Dakota. It was what she liked to do, and if he wanted to get closer to her, he needed to show interest on her terms.

Dakota put her hand behind Parker's neck and tugged him closer. Parker thought she was going in for a kiss, but she bumped her forehead against his and they stood there like statues, heads together but bodies apart. She seemed to have forgotten what she wanted to say to him and let him go. Parker stayed close to her, staring into her eyes.

For once, she seemed happy to see him. Eager, even. After being pushed away previously, he was surprised. Dakota's eyes turned to his drink.

"Captain Coke?" she asked, and plucked it out of his hand. She had a sip and made a face. "What're you doing to me, Parkinson?"

She wobbled over to a table serving as the outdoor bar and doctored his drink with a large slug of rum. She tested it, draining the top half of the drink, then handed it back to him.

"*That's* a party drink," she told him sternly.

Parker took an overlarge gulp of the drink, and with a massive effort, managed not to choke or spit it out. He gave her a weak smile. "Yeah, a party," he agreed.

"I gotta introduce you to everyone!" Dakota exclaimed, turning her attention away from his drink. She held onto his arm, and he wasn't sure whether it was to escort him around to meet everyone, or to keep herself from falling down. She had obviously been at the party for a while.

He didn't catch very many of the names as she bounced from one partier to another in random arcs and tangents that made him slightly dizzy. He did notice the shiny shirt she was wearing, which glittered as she moved and it caught the outdoor lights that shone around the pool. It was too dark for him to make out very many colors, but he could see faint patterns across it, and suspected that it was a bright, multicolored blouse. It worked with her figure, showing just enough cleavage and hugging her curves, but cut so that it didn't accent her belly or hips. Dakota touched Parker's chin, steering his head so that he was no longer looking at the undulating shirt, but at the couple she was trying to introduce him to.

"Barry and Tara," she told him with exaggerated pronunciation.

Parker nodded his head in greeting and took another sip of his drink. The lights and the noise were increasing his disorientation.

"He doesn't want to meet everybody," Barry told Dakota. "He wants to spend some quality time with you."

Dakota looked at him for a moment in confusion, then looked back at Parker. "What?"

"Sweetheart," Barry leaned closer to Dakota. "He's not here to socialize with me."

"Oh." Dakota took a long look at Parker and pulled him closer. "I thought you wanted to party," she said.

"I want to be with you."

"Well, you are."

Parker nodded. He was. Right where he wanted to be. Except for the sensory deluge, the alcohol, the danger of a police raid and his mother finding out where he had gone…

Dakota interlaced her fingers with Parker's. "You're so sweet, Parkinson."

Barry was laughing. He pulled his partner away from them. "Let's leave the lovebirds alone together."

Parker wondered how it could be so obvious to an outsider that he was attracted to Dakota, and that he was not there for the party, but just to see her. Maybe she or one of the other girls had told him. Hopefully, it was common knowledge and not written all over his face like a lovesick puppy dog.

"Why don't we just… walk?" he suggested, gesturing toward the green manicured lawn and gardens.

"Yeah, why don't we just walk?" she echoed. They walked together, Parker trying to hold Dakota steady and not lose his own footing. Dakota veered on a detour to the drinks table, pouring dark liquid into a cup for herself and gesturing to Parker to finish his.

"Drink that and we'll get you a refill."

Parker looked down at the rum and Coke remaining in his plastic cup, and with an effort brought it up to his lips to drink it. In a few swallows, it was gone. Dakota helped him to mix another, dictating the proportions of the mixer and the alcohol. The fumes went up Parker's nose when he tried to taste it, making him pull away and sneeze.

Dakota giggled at this display. She grabbed his hand and they kept walking.

"It's a nice night," Parker ventured. *Nice night.* He liked the way the words slid off his tongue.

"A very nice night," Dakota agreed. "I'm glad you came."

"Thanks for inviting me."

"I didn't think you'd come."

"Well… I did."

"Yeah."

They got farther and farther from the noise and the bumping crowds of people. There were couples wandering through the gardens, like they were, or in private nooks off to the side; heavy breathing in the shrubbery.

"Let's sit," Dakota suggested. There was a white stone bench nearby. Cold and uncomfortable, but Dakota gave a long sigh like she'd been on her feet all day. "That's better." She swayed a little bit, then seemed to get her balance again. Parker wasn't sure how close to sit to her. She pulled him closer, their bodies touching each other. Parker nervously took another swallow of his drink and looked around for somewhere to put it. He set it on the pavement beneath the bench. Dakota handed him hers, and he set it down as well. With the amount she had consumed, she would probably take a nose dive if she tried to bend down far enough to put it on the ground.

When he sat back upright, Dakota leaned in to him, and this time it was for a kiss. Parker was distracted by the pounding of his heart and the sweatiness of his hands. He wiped them on his jeans, afraid of touching Dakota with his clammy hands or getting a damp handprint on her shimmery blouse.

She tasted more strongly of alcohol than his drink and was breathing fumes in his face. Parker pulled back to breathe in the cool, crisp air of the garden. "Whew. It really is a nice night, isn't it?"

Dakota gave him a disappointed look. He held her hand, trying to communicate that he wasn't rejecting her. He smiled too brightly. "Is that a fish pond over there? Maybe we could throw pennies and make a wish."

"Not yet."

They kissed again and she pulled him close. She was sweating, the smell of alcohol seeping out of her pores. Parker tried to ignore all of the other distractions and to focus on her. Dakota was the reason he was there. He'd been trying to get close to her, and finally he was. He focused on her grasping hands, her lips, on timing his breaths with hers.

Dakota pulled back suddenly. She put both hands down on the bench to steady herself. Parker looked at her with concern.

"Are you okay…?"

"Sorry… I gotta puke!"

Parker pulled back immediately, giving her a wide berth. Dakota had barely finished saying the words, when she turned to lean over the back of the bench and threw up. Parker got up and walked a little way away, trying to ignore the sounds and smells. It was a beautiful night. They were surrounded by exotic flowers that he had never seen before. He could still hear the music from the party, but it was muted, not so overwhelming. There was a fish pond on just the other side of the pathway, he was sure of it. He checked his pockets to see if he had any change.

Dakota had finished vomiting and sat on the bench breathing heavily. She wiped her mouth with the back of her hand, then dug in her purse and found a wadded-up tissue to wipe and blow her nose with. For a minute, she just sat there, breathing, her stomach jumping occasionally under the fancy shirt.

"Well, that's a mood killer," she said shakily.

Parker shrugged. What was he going to say? Nothing that was going to make her feel any better about it.

"Where's this pond?" Dakota asked, holding the tissue to her mouth as she suppressed a hiccup.

Parker gestured. "Over here. Let's go have a look."

They walked close together, but not touching. Now as well as smelling like sweat and alcohol, Dakota reeked of vomit. They followed the path to the pond. Parker gazed down at the dark surface, looking for the ripples of fish shapes underneath. It was too dark to see them well. The night-time lights in the pond were muted colors. Maybe greens or blues. He saw an occasional white or orange body as the fish moved from one side of the pond to the other.

"Pretty," Dakota said.

Parker patted his pockets again, finding a few pennies. He handed one to Dakota, and looked at the frog with an open mouth in the middle of the pond. It didn't seem like it was that far away, but he wasn't exactly a sharpshooter. He closed his eyes briefly to make a wish, then sailed it out into the water.

The penny landed nowhere near the frog. It splooshed and went down into the water, out of sight. Parker was pretty sure wish frogs only granted wishes if they landed in the stone frog's mouth.

"Lemme try," Dakota said, holding her penny tightly in her fist. "I'm pretty good at throwing at a target in drinking games."

Maybe that was the problem. Parker hadn't played enough drinking games to polish up his skills.

He watched as Dakota waved her hand toward the frog several times. She might be trying to throw the coin, and forgetting to open her hand. Or she might just be aiming or warming up. Or she might have completely forgotten about throwing a penny for a wish and was just completely hammered.

Dakota released the coin suddenly. It bounced off of the frog's lip and into the dark water beneath.

"How about that?" Dakota crowed. "That wasn't too shabby a shot, now, was it? Mama's still got it! Woo!"

Parker rubbed his fingers over his final penny. He didn't hold out much hope that he'd be able to match Dakota's shot, but he had one more try. He rubbed his hands together with the coin between them. He blew on it. He tried to think of what other luck rituals he had seen gamblers use to improve their odds. No rabbits' feet or lucky articles of clothing. He should have worn a fancy shirt like Dakota's. Maybe that would help.

"You blow on it," he offered the coin to her, cupped in both hands.

Dakota blew her foul breath on it.

"Uh, kiss it," Parker suggested.

She obliged, leaving a wet spot on his hand. Parker's stomach twisted. He wiped each hand in turn on his pants. Then he spun in a full circle, closed his eyes, opened his eyes and sighted the frog, and then gave it a little toss.

The penny went right into the frog's mouth. Parker let out a cheer. "I did it! It went in! Did you see that, it went in!"

Dakota was turned away, looking back toward the house. She didn't cheer at his success. She didn't even acknowledge it.

"I got it in the frog's mouth," Parker told her, touching her arm.

"Yeah, great. Let's go back. This is boring. I need another drink."

Parker sighed. He didn't bother to argue that Dakota had already had too much to drink. She was obviously beyond that conversation. What he really needed to do was to figure out how to get her home. He couldn't exactly double her on the back of his bike. Not sober, and certainly not falling-down drunk. Whoever had brought her would have to take her home. Or maybe the rich folks who owned the mansion would pay for a cab to get her home safely.

He followed her back toward the house. Back beside the pool, and to the drinks table again. Dakota unsteadily poured herself a drink, miraculously getting most of the alcohol into the cup. It was a good thing the cups had nice, wide mouths. She didn't pour him another drink. Which was probably good, because he suspected that he was getting a little tipsy himself. Not too drunk to ride his bike home, but just enough to make him worry about saying something silly. He didn't want to make a fool of himself in front of the kids from school who were there. In front of Dakota.

Parker realized that Dakota had stalled beside the drinks table, talking to an older man. He too was black. Taller than Dakota.

Years older. What was he doing at a teenagers' party? Maybe he was one of the owners? Or some kind of vendor or a cabbie who had stopped in and was looking for someone? Parker stepped closer, trying to hear what he was saying.

"Come on," the man said, with his hand on Dakota's arm. "You're here all by yourself, I'm here, why don't you and me keep each other company?"

"Hey!" Parker pushed forward to get to Dakota's side. "Leave her alone!"

The man looked Parker over and snorted. "What do you want here, little boy?"

"Leave Dakota alone! She's not interested in you. She's not here by herself, she's here with me!"

"With you?" the man wrinkled his nose, looking Parker over. "How is a little boy like you going to satisfy a woman like this?"

"I'm not a little boy," Parker growled, slapping the man's hand away from Dakota's arm. "And I told you to leave her alone."

Dakota was swaying back and forth. Parker wasn't sure she had any idea what was going on. What if he hadn't been there to look after her? Would she have just gone off with the man, so blind drunk that she didn't have a clue what she was doing?

"Didn't anybody ever tell you to stay away from minors?" Parker challenged the man. "What are you, a pedo? You want to get arrested?"

"You're no cop," the man said. "And she's no minor. Now, why don't you just scram? I don't have time to babysit the likes of you."

"No." Parker stood his ground. He pushed his way in between Dakota and the man, red rage filling his brain. "You aren't touching her! You just get out of here!"

He was aware that he was attracting attention. The nearby conversations had stopped and everybody was listening to Parker and the man over the noise of the music. There were a few hoots and shouts of 'you tell 'im, kid' or 'fight!' but mostly people just waited to see if anything was going to happen.

Parker gave the man a shove in the chest, feeling strong and confident that he could beat the old man if he needed to. Chances were, the man would just slink away now that he'd been challenged. No one wanted to hang around after being called out like that.

"I said, get out of here."

The man resisted. He grabbed Parker's wrist and twisted it to the side. "You think you're man enough to take me on? You haven't got a clue, kid!"

Parker threw himself into the fight. He lost track of the blows. Blocking the fists flying toward him, trying to get his own jabs in when he could. It wasn't like a boxing match, with blows politely exchanged back and forth, but an out-of-control frenzy, a wolverine and a wild boar snapping at each other in a whirl of claws and teeth.

Then Parker took a crushing blow to the nose, and when he reached up to hold it, was grabbed and thrown to the pavement. He tried to catch himself with one hand, the other still reaching for his nose, and ended up landing in an awkward heap on the ground, his arm doubled underneath him. There was noise like he'd cracked his knuckles, and then a rush of pain.

He wasn't sure what happened next. He never did see what happened to the man. He was there, and then he was gone. Everything was gone. The noise of the party, the crush of people, the strobing lights, the smell of alcohol. It was all gone and the world was gray and quiet. Dakota was still there, hanging over him, speaking in a baby voice, patting his arm and mothering him. There was an ice pack over his nose, but he didn't know who had gotten it for him and where it had come from. He didn't know where he was. He wasn't at the party anymore. He was sitting, sobbing, holding his hurt arm.

They kept talking to him about hospital, but Parker shook his head and refused, telling them to take him home. He was in a car, he realized. A van. Someone at the party was driving him to the hospital, but he didn't want to go.

"Just take me home," he insisted. "Where's Dakota? She'll tell you where it is. Just take me home. It will be okay."

"You can't just go home," someone told him in a slow, exaggerated tone, as if he were speaking to someone who was deaf or a hundred and three. "You have a broken arm. And probably a broken nose. You have to go to the hospital."

"My mom can take me. Just take me home."

"What are you going to tell her?" Dakota demanded. "You can't tell her about the party."

"I won't. I'll just tell her… I fell out of bed. I had a nightmare."

"How is that going to work? You sleep with two other boys in that room!"

"They'll be asleep. I'll sneak back in. No one will know."

"Parkinson, you're crazy! I mean, that's certifiable! You'll never get away with it."

"Take me home!" Parker insisted. He reached for the door handle of the van. "Let me out. I'll ride my bike home. I don't want to go to the hospital!"

Hands restrained him. The pain in his arm was agonizing and Parker let them hold him back, no longer resisting.

"Your bike's not here. You can't jump out of the van. We'll take you home, okay? Just stay put!"

The driver and the others in the car muttered with Dakota, getting directions, finding their way to Parker's home, where they finally pulled into an empty space along the curb.

"You're really going to go back in there and tell them you just fell out of bed?" a man's voice asked.

Parker nodded. They helped him out of the car.

"How are you going to get your shoes off?" Dakota demanded. "You can't tell them you went to bed in your shoes or that you got them on after you broke your arm!"

"Untie them. I'll take them off at the door." Parker was determined not to go with the partygoers to the hospital. They had no idea how much trouble he would be in if Mona figured out that he'd snuck out to an unsupervised party when he was supposed to be in bed.

Dakota was too unstable to help him with his shoes. One of the other partiers untied them. "Now don't trip on the laces…"

Parker shuffled to the door, not lifting his feet. He managed to slide his key into the lock with his left hand and opened the door. He stepped in and, for a few minutes, he just leaned against the closet, trying to get his breath back. Then he pried his shoes off with his toes. Sitting on the floor so he couldn't fall down and injure himself worse, he used his left hand to peel off one sock, and then the other. He shoved the socks between the cushions on the couch and crawled into the back hallway.

Chapter Eight

"Mom? Mom, wake up…" Parker shook Mona with his left hand, trying to rouse her from sleep. Her days were long and she slept hard. "Mom!"

"Mmm…" she rolled over slightly to look at him. "What's wrong? Parker…?"

"Mom, I hurt myself." He let the tears that he had been holding back enter his voice, finally able to stop being tough and be Mona's little boy again.

She propped herself up on her elbow, trying to see him in the dark. "You what…? How did you hurt yourself?"

"I had a dream. I fell out of bed, and I… I really hurt it, Mom."

"Where are you hurt?" She reached over and turned on the lamp on the bedside table to have a look. She stared at him and touched his shoulder. "Parker, what happened?"

Parker touched his swollen nose tenderly. "My arm too," he explained.

"Your arm…?" She squinted in the dimness, but couldn't see much. She sat the rest of the way up. "What did you do to yourself?"

"I don't know. I had a nightmare…"

"You had a nightmare." She frowned at him, shaking her head. "Parker, that's crazy. What's going on here?"

He let tears squeeze out of his eyes. "I think I need to go to the hospital."

His words sounded funny inside his head. His nose sounded clogged up. Mona picked up her phone and unplugged it from the charge cable, then got to her feet and picked up her purse and keys. She rubbed her eyes.

"You go sit on the couch. I need to get dressed."

"Okay." Parker dragged his feet out of the bedroom and made his way slowly back to the living room. It occurred to him that Mona was going to help him with his shoes, and they would be warm from having just worn them. He kicked them into a messy pile with the other shoes, and grabbed a pair of Link's flip flops. He sat down on the couch and slid his feet into them.

He wasn't exactly dressed for having fallen out of bed, but it wasn't too far of a stretch. He wore a black t-shirt and jeans, his usual school uniform. No shimmery dance tops for him. Normally, he wore shorts or sweats to bed, so he might have to come up with an explanation for having gone to bed in his jeans.

Parker could hear Mona going into the boys' room and waking Link to tell him where she was going. Then she was in the living room, pulling on a jacket and doing up the buttons one-handedly.

"Do you want a jacket?" she asked him. "It's a bit cool…"

She would be cool in the middle of the hottest day of the summer. Parker shook his head. "I couldn't get it on…"

"Oh… a blanket, then? We can wrap it around you…?"

"No. I'm okay."

She looked doubtful. "If that arm is broken, you could be shocky. I should be keeping you warm."

"I don't need a blanket," Parker insisted.

"I'll bring one along anyway," Mona decided. She went back down the hall to the linen closet and returned with a superman comforter. "Just in case."

She looked at his feet, and didn't criticize his choice of footwear, even though flip flops usually got an exasperated growl that sandals were for the beach, not for walking around outside in the city. Maybe sandals were okay for going to the hospital too.

"Do you need a hand?" She offered to put her arm around him as they headed for the door. Parker was about to object and say that he didn't need it, but his head was still spinning and the pain was making him tired and nauseated. And he wanted the comfort of his mother's touch, like he was the little boy who had fallen out of a tree after putting a fallen baby bird back in its nest and being dive-bombed by the mama bird. So he accepted her help and shuffled out to the car.

Of course, going to the hospital meant waiting. Parker dozed in an uncomfortable chair while he waited to be treated. They had, at least, given him an ice pack, though they hadn't given him any painkillers. Mona dug a couple of Tylenol pills out of her purse and gave them to him, complaining about the doctors and how slow the emergency room always was. It was pretty quiet, not a lot of other people there ahead of them, no traumas screaming in the door. But still they waited. It was a long time before a doctor finally took them in. After a cursory examination of Parker's arm and nose, he agreed that they were both broken. He ordered x-rays and at last assigned a nurse to insert an IV to start Parker on some real painkillers.

"Mom, I need to talk to Parker in private for a few minutes. Can I get you to wait in the chairs area? I'll get the two of you back together as soon as I can."

Mona didn't like the idea. "I'll stay with him," she asserted.

"We have mandatory questions we need to ask him alone. I'm sure you understand."

There were posters everywhere about domestic abuse and asserting that every patient would be asked about domestic abuse and their personal safety, so Mona couldn't exactly say that she didn't understand the need. Parker imagined how he would respond if he were abused. Had Dakota ever tried to talk to a doctor about what she was going through in her various homes? Or had she been so afraid of ending up in a worse place or with no roof at all over her head that she had just kept quiet and not revealed what was going on? Parker knew it would be very hard to report a loved one for domestic abuse. But certainly all of the people that Dakota had lived with hadn't been loved. From what she had told him, some of them she barely knew.

Mona was gone and the nurse was working on inserting the IV into Parker's left arm while the doctor scribbled notes on his chart.

"You didn't get those injuries falling out of bed," the doctor said, without looking up from his clipboard.

Parker stared at him. "What?"

"I'm not sure your mother believes it either. She may be willing to suspend her disbelief, but I am not." The doctor shifted Parker's hospital robe to display other bruises from the fight with the man at the party. "These are from a fight. Not from falling out of bed. Even a bunk bed."

Parker didn't say anything.

"Did your mother give you these injuries?"

Parker was shocked. "No! My mom would never hurt me! And she's smaller than me."

"Shorter. Probably still in your weight class. But that really doesn't matter. I see men who are beaten by women half their size. They've been taught not to fight back against a girl. They don't know how to handle an abusive relationship. Even to admit that they are being hurt by a girl."

"My mom would never hurt me. She doesn't hit me."

"Look me in the eye."

Parker obeyed. "She doesn't," he repeated, looking the doctor straight in the eye.

"How much have you had to drink tonight?"

"What?"

The doctor put his head to the side. "You heard me. How much?"

Parker glanced aside at the nurse, who didn't appear to be listening to the conversation. He swallowed. "Less than a cup," he admitted. "A couple of rum and Cokes, but I didn't drink even half of either."

"How long ago?"

Parker glanced at the walls for a clock. "Uh…"

The doctor looked at Parker's chart. "You were triaged an hour and a half ago."

"Then maybe… three hours since I had anything…? More than two."

"One or two servings of alcohol two to three hours ago," the doctor summarized.

Parker nodded.

"We should be fine to run Demerol, then," the doctor informed the nurse, who was fiddling with the IV tubes. She nodded and pushed the painkillers. Parker felt a wave of cold rising up his left arm. It hit his chest and suddenly he was woozy, feeling drunk all over again. He suddenly had more sympathy for Dakota, puking her guts out in the middle of the carefully-maintained gardens at the party house.

"Are you okay?" the nurse asked. "Here, lie down."

She helped him to lie back on the gurney, Parker feeling the whole time like he was going to fall right off of it. He clutched at the mattress beneath him to try to keep from going over the edge, and she put up the sides.

"There you go. You're not going to fall."

He gave a small nod of thanks, which sent the world spinning even further out of control.

"How's that feeling?" the doctor asked.

Parker considered, and realized that his arm and nose were not hurting anymore. "Really good!"

"Good. Your blood pressure is already coming down. So we're going to send you down to x-ray to get films of both of those injuries, and then we'll set them. You'll go home almost as good as new."

"Thanks."

"And if I was you, I'd be staying away from the drinking parties. Not a good place for a young man your age to be. Really, not a good place for anyone to be. But at least wait until you're of age before you continue your drinking career. And stay clear of places you're going to get beaten up."

"Yeah."

Parker stayed home the next day, catching up on his sleep and recovering from the hangover caused by both the alcohol and the Demerol at the hospital. The girls had playdates and Link and Jessup had plans for the day, so the house was empty and quiet. Mona checked in on Parker at the beginning and end of the day, but she had to go to work still, so she asked Link to nip home at lunchtime to make sure that Parker was doing okay.

"You can sleep on the couch," she had told Parker when they returned home from the hospital. "I don't want any more falls while you're still dizzy from the Demerol."

And she was probably right. Parker wasn't even sure whether he'd be able to climb up to his bed with his arm in a cast and his head still floaty from the painkillers and lack of sleep.

"Hey. Hey, Parker."

Parker awoke to Link shaking him. He rubbed his eyes.

"Mmm. Hi."

Link sat on the arm on the couch, looking down at Parker. "How are you doing?"

"Just tired. I'm fine."

Link nodded. He brushed back his hair, long and dark, in contrast to Parker's close-cropped blond hair.

"You done being all stupid over this girl?" he asked.

Parker glared at him. "What do you know?"

"I don't have to be Mom to know that Dakota is bad news. If you didn't think so before, you know now."

"Dakota didn't do anything to hurt me." It was incredibly annoying to have his younger brother, not even old enough to shave, telling him he was being stupid about a girl. Link didn't know anything about girls. Not a thing. Wasn't it just last week he'd been complaining about cooties?

"It was nothing to do with her?" Link demanded.

Parker was silent.

"It's all over cyberspace that you were in a fight over her," Link said. "And that's how you got hurt."

"That's just a rumor. You should know better than to listen to rumors."

"You really think she's worth fighting over?" Link shook his head. "She's not even *pretty*."

"Hey!"

"She's okay," Link temporized, "but she's not… I mean, she's not hot or anything. So why…?"

"You think it's okay to abuse her because she's not hot? I should only defend her honor if she meets someone's idea of pretty?"

Link scratched his jaw. "I just think… the more you hang around with her, the more trouble you're going to get in. Is she really worth it?"

Parker shook his head angrily. "You don't know anything, Link. You'd better just leave it alone."

"Or what, you're going to fight me one-handed?"

"I could still sock you in the nose!"

Link grinned. "That worked real well last night, huh?"

"I did okay."

A snort told Parker what he thought of that. "I wouldn't get in too many of those fights, if I was you." Link slid off of the couch and stretched. "You want anything? Food?"

Parker thought about it, trying to evaluate how his body felt. "Well… maybe a drink. And a couple more pills."

Link went into the kitchen and got what Parker wanted and made a sandwich for himself. While he ate, he turned on the TV and sat on the floor in front of the couch, keeping Parker company.

When Parker next awoke, Dakota was leaning over him. She gave him a little smile.

"Hey, sleepyhead."

Parker tried to see the time on the video machine, but the LED was too dim in the light of the room for him to make it out.

"What time is it? I thought you said you were supposed to go to some class Jade had signed you up for." Parker yawned and stretched.

"I skipped all day. Didn't feel good this morning."

Parker rolled his eyes. "I wonder why."

"Hey, you're the one still sleeping. I'm up and around."

"Well…" Parker searched for an excuse that didn't sound lame, and gave up. He pushed off the warm cocoon and slid his feet to the floor. "I'm up…"

"You don't need to get up. I'm just teasing. I came to see you."

"You want to sign my cast?"

Dakota's lips curled a little. "Am I the first?"

"No," Parker looked down at it. "The girls already marked it this morning." He showed Dakota the pictures and scribbles. She laughed.

"That's cute. They really like their big brother, don't they?"

"Yeah." He wasn't sure why that made him blush. "They're good kids."

"So did you get a big lecture last night? Grounded?"

"No… she believed I fell out of the bed."

"Really?" Dakota shook her head. "You sure, or is she saving it up for later?"

"Why would she do that? Mom's never been one to pull her punches."

"I've had some parents who would. Just keep totting them up secretly, and then blam! Blow you out of the water when you least expect it."

Her 'blam!' made Parker jump. He shook his head in irritation. "That's not the way my mom works. She wouldn't do that, she'd just tell me outright."

All the same, her words made his stomach knot. He had been expecting some kind of push-back from Mona. Questions about how he had managed to fall out of bed. Why he wore his blue jeans to bed. Why his falling off the bed hadn't woken his brothers up. She hadn't done much to question the veracity of his story. And the doctor at the hospital had seen right through him. Had he really thrown up a smokescreen for Mona but not for the doctor?

"I'll bet she is," Dakota said, nodding. "That's what they do. I'd rather have one that blew up right away at the first sign of trouble.

The ones who save it all up and hold grudges…" Dakota gave a mock shiver. Even though she spoke about it lightly, Parker could see the worry in her eyes. The voice of experience.

"I think I'm hungry," Parker said, pushing thoughts of other problems to the side. "How about you?"

He stood up and tested his balance for a moment before heading into the kitchen.

"I dunno. You guys don't look like you got much."

"We have enough to share!" Parker insisted. He'd hate to see Mona's reaction if Dakota accused her of not having enough food in the house to take care of her children. She worked hard to make sure that her family was never neglected and that they had enough to share with friends. To be hospitable. "We've always got enough for company." He started opening and closing cupboards. "I could make some pancakes. You want pancakes? Or biscuits?"

"You can make biscuits?" The skepticism was clear in Dakota's voice.

"Sure!" Parker pulled a box out of the cupboard. "They're just from a mix. Really easy."

He scooped out the mix and added milk without having to read the instructions. Dakota sat down in one of the kitchen chairs and watched him proceed to roll the dough, cut out circles, and put them into the pan to bake. It was awkward with the cast, but he'd done it enough times before that he could have done it with one hand tied behind his back. Dakota's eyes were wide.

"You can cook?" she asked incredulously.

"I can make biscuits! That didn't look so hard, did it? It's just a mix."

"I never knew anyone who could make their own biscuits."

Parker laughed. "I'm full of surprises."

"Wow, you are. Are you sure you're not really an old woman in a boy's body? Rescuing animals, baking biscuits… and I don't know what *that* was last night." She nodded to his cast.

"What, protecting you?"

"I didn't need protecting. I can look after myself."

"You think I should have just let that guy paw you and say filthy things to you? That's not how I was raised."

"Yeah? You were raised to sneak out and go to parties, though?"

Parker was confused by her argument. He looked in the fridge to see what else they could eat with the biscuits. While he was happy to eat just biscuits for a meal, he figured he should get out the ham and maybe some kind of veggie to go with them. Mashed potatoes and gravy? That would make a good meal. He didn't think Dakota was going to be satisfied with just a couple of biscuits.

"You invited me to the party."

"Yeah. I didn't think you'd go, but you did. Surprised me."

Parker nodded. "I like being with you," he said. There was no one else in the house, but he still lowered his voice. "I like you. I thought maybe it meant… you liked me too."

Dakota laughed and turned away from him slightly, fanning herself with her hand. "You're such a charmer."

"Does that mean you don't?"

"I didn't say that."

"You didn't say you do."

"Well, what do you expect from me?" Dakota snapped.

"I want you to tell me that you like me too. And to do things with me, and go places with me other than to parties!" The words came pouring out. "I want you to act like you care about me, instead of that you think I'm… some little boy."

Dakota sat there, not saying anything.

"I'm not a little boy," Parker insisted. "So don't treat me like that. You're not that much more mature than I am. I helped you out, and I've been nice to you, and I thought… I thought you'd like me too."

"Parkinson…" her voice started in a wheedle. Then she caught herself and used a more measured tone. "Parker. I do like you. But I have a lot of history. I'm just not sure… how ready I am to jump into anything."

"But you'll jump into it when you're drunk. Or when some other guy tries to pick you up. Is that it?"

"That's different! Don't be so stupid! You don't know what it's like!"

Parker stopped his meal preparations and stood leaning against the front of the warm oven. He tried to meet her gaze and convey how strongly he felt about her and about how he wanted to protect her. But she avoided his eyes.

"Why don't you tell me, then?" Parker asked.

"This isn't one of those times when talking helps," Dakota insisted. "I—I wouldn't even know where to start."

"Maybe just talking like this. Open and honestly."

"I can't. It's just too hard for me, Parker. Too many bad memories."

He was sad to think that she'd had so many bad experiences that she couldn't even think of where to begin. He resumed his dinner preparations, saying nothing.

"Don't be mad at me, Parkinson."

"I'm not mad at you."

"You are. Listen. Going places like that party and getting hammered… it may not be the smartest thing to do. I know everybody says that I could end up really sick… or something… but it's the only way to forget, for a few hours, all of the bad stuff I've been through. And some of the bad stuff I did to end up here. I'm not a bird with a broken wing, Parker. I'm more like a wolf caught in a trap."

Parker envisioned this. He could see it. The animal trapped and snarling. Biting at the hand that tried to free it. Frantic with pain and fear.

Dakota went on, her voice rough and her eyes reflecting deep pools of pain. "The only thing you can do for an animal that wild and that hurt is to put it out of its misery. Just shoot it."

"I don't think so," Parker disagreed. He held her gaze for as long as he could. "I'm good with hurt animals."

Dakota loved the biscuits. She slathered margarine on them and bit into the tender flaky disk, and moaned over how good they were.

"I can't believe you made these. Right in front of me. They're so good!"

"Well, have Jade pick some mix up from the store, and you can make them too. You could have biscuits every day."

"No way." She swiped her biscuit through her gravy. "These are like… food from the gods. They're magical. I don't think just anyone could make them." She smiled at Parker. "It has to be someone the gods have smiled on."

"At least someone is smiling at me."

"I'm smiling. You just can't tell 'cause my mouth is full."

Parker bit into one of the biscuits. He had to admit they were good.

"Do you think there's something we could do together? Something other than going to a party. I'm okay with us going slow. I just… I hate not being able to get anywhere. Being completely shut down."

"I'm not shutting you down."

"No?" Parker looked at her, raising an eyebrow.

Dakota chewed. She wiped her mouth with the back of her hand.

"You're just so young. I don't go with younger guys. I like… older men. More mature."

"So you *are* shutting me down."

"No…" Dakota looked at the chair next to her. "Sit down, okay? I don't like you hovering over me."

Parker sat down. He waited for her to talk to him, to touch his hand or make some kind of move to let him know that she wasn't shutting him out like he had suggested. She just continued to eat her meal without looking at him. But she had asked him to sit by her. Parker turned his attention to his own meal.

Mona was busy, so Parker went to the grocery store to take care of the necessities and make sure that they had what they needed for the upcoming week. Because of his cast, Miranda was elected to go with him to help. Parker wasn't sure what they expected Miranda to be able to do that Parker couldn't, but he didn't fight it. Any time any of the younger kids wanted to help with the grocery responsibilities, he was happy to have them along.

"Can we get Kool-aid instead of the generic stuff?" Miranda asked. "I like purple, and only Kool-aid makes the purple."

Parker glanced at the prices of the flavor packets.

"They're almost twice as much," he pointed out. "We can't do that." Her face fell. "You can get one purple Kool-aid. Then generic for the rest of the week."

Miranda brightened at this and nodded eager agreement. "Okay! That's fair!" She followed his suggestion and added the drink crystals to the cart. They moved through the aisles a little less efficiently than usual, but it was a Sunday and Parker wasn't in a big hurry.

"Oh, Parker!"

Parker turned around at his name, and saw Jade. "Hi, Mrs. Gable."

"I'm glad you're here. I wanted to talk to you."

"Sure," Parker agreed. "What's up?"

She considered Parker, putting her hands on her hips. Parker knew she wasn't doing it because she was mad at him. It was more of a 'thinking' posture for Jade.

"Parker, I wanted to talk to you about Dakota."

He shook his head and sighed. "Not you, too."

"Has someone else expressed concerns...?"

"Only everyone. I don't understand what everyone has against Dakota. You know what kind of life she's coming from. She's had to put up with so much crap at her other homes. Why can't people just be nice and let her alone? She's not an ax murderer. She's just a kid. A homeless kid."

"I'm not trying to be mean when I say this, Parker. I just want you to... be careful. I know what Dakota says about herself and her past. But I'm just not convinced... I think she makes things up..."

Parker gave a shrug. "Everybody makes things up. Nobody sticks to the truth all the time. Even when you mean to be honest, you make mistakes."

"I'm not talking about just neglecting to say something… or embellishing a story a bit for your friends. Or even putting something on your resume that's not exactly true. I'm talking about so much more than that. I'm talking about the person she is," Jade explained.

"What do you want me to get?" Miranda asked, impatient to fill the shopping cart and get home.

"Uh…" Parker looked at the food already in the basket, comparing it to his mental list. "Fries. Why don't you go get frozen french fries for me?"

"Okay!" Miranda skipped off.

Parker turned back to Jade again. She was wearing a long purple dress. Usually she wore a blouse and pants. Maybe she had just come from church or choir.

"What do you mean, she's not the person she is?"

"She isn't the person she pretends to be. A homeless teen from an abusive background… I don't think so. I've had abused teens before. And there's something different about her. I can't explain it. She's hiding something else."

"What?"

"I wish I could tell you, but I can't… she has secrets she doesn't want you to know. Doesn't want any of us to know."

"I'm not going to push her to tell me. I'm just going to be there for her. When she's ready to tell me about it… I'll be there."

"You're a sweet boy, Parker, but I don't think you understand this girl. She's pulling the wool over your eyes."

"What do you know about her? Really know about her?"

"Nothing." Jade shook her head. "I don't know a thing about her for sure."

"If you can't prove that she's lying about anything, then you shouldn't say anything about it. Just leave her alone." Parker clenched his teeth, and could feel his face getting red. He knew that Mona would not be happy with him if he disrespected her friend, so he did his best to put Jade in her place without being offensive. "Isn't that what they always say? If you can't say anything nice…"

Jade sighed. "I'm not trying to malign her. I'm not trying to spread gossip or rumors about her. I just want you to be prepared. I want to protect you. You're going to get hurt if you get too close to her. I don't want that to happen."

Parker stood with his arms folded and shook his head. "Don't try to tell me stories about her when you don't know if they're true."

Miranda returned with two big bags of frozen fries. She threw them into the basket as if she were the last member of a relay race. She gave Parker a big smile. "There! What else?"

"Do we have enough milk? Eggs?"

"Yes, right there."

"I need… umm… Tylenol for my arm. Could you go and get that?"

"Sure!" Miranda was off again.

Parker looked at Jade. "Dakota says that your husband is putting the moves on her. Maybe this is how you're trying to get back at her."

Jade looked staggered. She put her hand on the corner of a shelf unit to steady herself.

"Mr. Gable putting the moves on Dakota? I don't think so! She's barely even seen him. Where does she get off spreading stories like that?"

"She says he's after her," Parker told Jade, encouraged by her reaction. "And she says that he's abusive. Hits you."

"Give me strength! And you believed her? Who else is she telling this to? You know very well it's not true, Parker Jurek. You know my husband doesn't beat me or chase girls."

Parker opened his mouth to disagree; to say that he barely knew Mr. Gable and all of those things could be true. But something stopped him. He'd never seen Jade with bruises or a black eye. He'd never gotten a vibe that she was suffering abuse at her husband's hands. He rarely saw Mr. Gable, and there were certainly no rumors that he was chasing young girls. Rumors spread through the neighborhood like wildfire, so Parker would know if there were any such suspicion. What were the odds that Mr. Gable would remain a perfectly normal, well-behaved member of society for so many years, and then suddenly turn into a drunken, abusive lech the minute Dakota moved into the house?

"Then why would she say that?" he asked. "What was the point in telling me that?"

"I don't know what happened before that. Was she trying to distract you from something? Looking for more attention? Worried about something? I haven't figured out why it is that she lies. What it is she's trying to cover up."

"I don't know." Parker thought back over Dakota's behavior since he had first met her. He had to admit that there were times when she had lied to him. He had caught her at it. But there didn't seem to be any rhyme or reason to it.

"Please be careful," Jade reiterated.

Miranda vaulted back with the Tylenol and threw the bottle into the basket. "Is that it? Are we all done?"

Parker looked at Jade.

"Yeah. We're done here."

Chapter Nine

AFTER THE WEEKEND, IT was back to school. Parker hated to have to get up early for the start of the school day, but on the other hand, he felt like the events of the weekend had squeezed all of the mental energy out of him, and he was happy to be going back to the routine of school. He didn't have to think about Jade or her theories. He didn't have to deal with Dakota drunk or Jade in the grocery store. Everything could go back to normal again.

"How are you going to get your work done?" Mr. Bonne asked Parker, leaning over his shoulder before they got started. "You're right-handed. How are you going to take notes or do your homework?"

Parker looked down at his casted arm and tried to figure out if there were any chance he could still grip a pen in his fingers and move it to the correct angle to write on a piece of paper. It wasn't going to be easy. But writing with his left hand was out of the question. He was nowhere near ambidextrous.

"I'm not sure… maybe…" Parker looked around him for some solution.

"I'll help. I can take notes for Parker and write down what he dictates for his homework."

Parker looked over at Dakota, astounded by her offer. Every time he tried to get close to her, she pushed back, and now she was doing something for him voluntarily?

Mr. Bonne looked from Parker to Dakota, and eventually nodded. "Okay. That's fine with me. But if there are bigger projects required by other teachers where that would be more onerous, we may need to rethink and come up with another solution. It's up to you two to let us know if there is an issue."

"Okay, Mr. Bonne." Dakota gave him a broad smile.

He nodded and moved toward the front of the room to start on the announcements when the bell rang. Parker looked over at Dakota.

"Thanks."

"Sure." She shrugged as if it were nothing to her. "After all you've done for me, I can at least return the favor."

They sat in the school library after classes let out. It seemed like the easiest option. Jade didn't want Parker hanging around in Dakota's bedroom. Mona didn't want Dakota hanging out at Parker's house. They needed somewhere they could spread out their books without worrying about rain or wind or any of the other perils of nature that lurked outside. The school library was the closest and most convenient place to go.

"Okay, tell me what you want for question one," Dakota prompted, after pulling out the social studies textbook. Parker started to dictate his answer. He stopped after a couple of sentences. Dakota looked up to see why he had stopped.

"You're using cursive again," Parker pointed out.

Dakota laughed. "Well, the social teacher should be able to read it, right? It's just you who can't read cursive."

"And the rest of the kids in the school."

"Well, the rest of the school doesn't need to be able to read it. Just the teacher."

"Well… yeah," Parker admitted reluctantly. "But… shouldn't I be able to read my answers?"

"Do you think I'm writing something down that's different than what you're saying?"

"No… I just want to be able to read it."

"Printing takes longer," Dakota said. "Cursive is much faster."

"But I can't read it."

Dakota stared at Parker for a long minute, then gave a sigh of exasperation. "Fine. I'll print for the rest of the questions."

Walking home later, Parker tentatively took Dakota's right hand in his left. She didn't pull away immediately.

"Thanks for all the help with my schoolwork. I guess I'm going to be a pain in the neck for the next few weeks."

"Sure," Dakota shrugged. "No problem. I owe you."

"You don't owe me anything. I never expected anything from you."

"You got me a home to live in. A nice one." Dakota seemed to have forgotten she had told him that Mr. Gable was abusive. "And you want to take care of me and stand up for my honor. Most guys wouldn't do that. Not nowadays."

Parker laughed. "You sound like someone's granny." He put on a shaky granny voice, "'Back in my day, things were different. Nowadays, these young folk…'"

Dakota gave a weak laugh. She pulled her hand away from his. She put both hands in her pockets, as if that were her only reason for pulling away. Parker tried not to dwell on it. At least she had let him hold her hand for a minute. That was progress. And this time, she wasn't drunk. At least as far as he knew. She had seemed perfectly sober at the library and he couldn't smell any alcohol on her.

"What's your best memory?" he asked her. "When you think back to all of the places that you've lived in your life, what was the best time?"

"Oh… I don't know."

They walked together in silence. Parker let her think about it. He didn't need an answer right away.

"I don't remember where I lived," Dakota said after a couple of blocks. "I don't know if it was at an auntie's, or foster home, or even my own mom's. I just remember being all cuddled up on the couch, all warm and cozy and happy, watching an old Gilligan's Island rerun on an ancient black and white TV." She raised an eyebrow at him. "See, nothing special… but I felt so safe and protected there. Everything felt… right with the world."

"A black and white TV?" Parker repeated.

"I told you it was ancient, right?" Anticipating his further question, she jumped ahead. "And I assume it could only play reruns of really old shows, like Gilligan. That's just my memory, okay? Don't knock it."

"No, I'm not," Parker told her quickly. "That's a nice memory."

"Sort of like watching TV with your sisters," Dakota said. "That was nice."

Parker hadn't been expecting anything earth-shattering from her. But he hadn't thought it would be something quite so mundane, either.

"They liked it when you came over. You should do it again."

"Yeah," Dakota agreed with a little sigh. "But sometime when your mom isn't there."

"Mom's not that bad. She's not going to do anything to you."

"She doesn't like me."

Parker looked for a way around denying it. He could tell Dakota that it wasn't true, Mona liked her just fine. But they both would know it was a lie, so why say it?

"She just doesn't know you like I do. If she knew you, the way I know you, she'd love you."

"Love? Nobody loves me. That ain't gonna happen."

Parker took her hand again. He didn't interlace their fingers, but brought her fingertips up to his mouth and kissed them gently. Dakota pulled back away. She shook her head, unable to find the words. But she had a little bit of a smile on her face, the corners of her mouth pulling up just a little, as if she were happy but didn't want anyone to know it.

He wanted to tell her that he loved her, but she wouldn't accept that. She would just say again that no one loved her. And then she would again point out that he was younger than she was, and too young to know what love was. And how she liked older men, not younger ones.

But Parker didn't see any older men taking care of her.

There was just him.

Mr. Bonne let Dakota change desks so that she would be sitting closer to Parker and could help him with any work that required writing. Parker couldn't stop himself from smiling. It was great to have her right next to him for most of the day.

They couldn't text each other during class, but the new arrangement allowed them to whisper together occasionally, as long as they could make it look like it was about their schoolwork. Not in the middle of a lecture. That would just be taking advantage of the situation, and Parker didn't want Mr. Bonne to change his mind about letting them sit together.

At lunchtime, Parker stood in line behind the girls. Charity was complaining about Dakota moving so that she was no longer close enough for Charity to whisper to her. They were only a few desks apart, but too far apart for verbal communication.

"And if I get my phone confiscated again, I'm going to lose it for a week!"

Dakota shook her head. "Well, back before cell phones, they had this thing called passing notes."

"Passing notes?" Charity repeated in disbelief. "What, like across the classroom?"

"Sure. You fold it up and you put the name of the person it is to go to on the outside, and you pass it to the person closest to you, and get them to pass it on."

"How do you do that?"

Dakota laughed. "You say, 'pass it on.'"

"Oh… I don't know if that would work. What if someone doesn't pass it on? Or what if they tell the teacher? The teacher would probably read it out loud, like they do sometimes when you get caught texting during class."

Dakota rolled her eyes. "Yeah. So you don't get caught! Don't pass it to someone who will snitch."

Charity continued to shake her head, frowning. "I don't think that would work. We gotta find another way."

"I don't know how you're ever gonna survive if your phone does get confiscated for a week."

"Well, would you?" Charity challenged. "I can't imagine living without my cell."

"It's possible. I've lived most of my life without cell phones."

Charity boggled at this. "Really? Why? I can't imagine. I got my first cell when I was, like, eight years old. So I could keep in touch with my mom when I was out playing at the park. She could call me if I forgot to let her know what I was doing. Me and my phone have been inseparably connected," Charity showed off the cell phone nestled in her hand. "BFFs."

There were echoes of agreement from Marina and Addy.

Dakota gave a shrug. "If you don't have any money or a place to plug in…"

"Even the bums around here have cell phones," Addy inserted. "They've got enough money and they plug in at the coffee shop. I don't think anyone is so poor they can't have a cell phone anymore. You can spend ten bucks and get a phone at the corner store. So why wouldn't you?"

"What do they got to eat today?" Dakota demanded, squinting at the board listing the day's specials.

"You need glasses?" Marina asked with a giggle.

Dakota looked away from the listing and blinked a few times. "No, I don't need glasses! They just don't write big enough to see it from back here…"

Parker opened his mouth to read it to her, but Marina jumped in. "Pepperoni pizza, mac and cheese, and potato chowder soup."

"You can see that from here? What I'd give to have your eyes! So I guess… pizza. It's included in the lunch program, right?"

"Pizza's always included in the lunch program," Charity said. "Man, what did we do before free lunches?"

Dakota picked up a tray. "Went hungry."

Charity cracked up. Dakota looked at her with a frown. "What? How is that funny?"

"Went hungry," Charity repeated in a mock-solemn tone.

"Well, it's true. And you just try getting through school with no breakfast and no lunch. It's damn hard!"

Parker's muscles were tense, ready to jump to her defense if they laughed at her. Her friends quieted, looking at Dakota and not sure what to say.

"We've got enough to eat," Charity said, looking down at her tray still waiting to be filled up, instead of at Dakota's face. "And even if you're still hungry after breakfast or lunch or you are too late and miss it, Mr. Bonne keeps crackers in his desk. Just in case."

Dakota licked her lips. She slid one of the small pizzas onto her tray, along with a bottle of juice and a package of cut-up carrots. "Really? I didn't know that."

"He's the man if you ever need help," Addy jumped in. "Food or whatever. He's the guy that will do something."

Dakota nodded.

"I thought free lunch was, like, a federal program," Charity said, frowning. "You went to a school that didn't have it?"

"Not every school does," Dakota said.

"But I thought—"

"What do I know?" Dakota snapped. "I don't know how it all works. But I know what it's like to go to school with a hole in my belly!"

That silenced Charity's questions. She muttered 'okay, okay,' under her breath and they finished getting their food in silence.

Chapter Ten

"C AN'T DO HOMEWORK RIGHT after school today," Dakota informed Parker. "I've gotta put in a shift at work. We can do it after that."

"Okay. So what time? Where do you want to meet?"

"Is eight o'clock okay? Just come to the restaurant and we'll go somewhere from there."

Parker nodded. Eight wasn't too bad. Any later would be pushing it with Mona. But she knew he had to get help to get his work done with his arm out of commission.

He'd caught Mona staring at his cast the other day.

"What?" Parker had demanded.

She raised her eyes to his face and shook her head. "Just wondering how you managed to do that, actually. Doesn't seem like you could hurt yourself so badly falling out of bed."

All of Parker's guilt came rushing back. He cleared his throat. "It *is* a bunk bed."

"I know. You fell more than just a foot or two. I get that part. It's just… I've seen you fall out of trees and second-story windows. It doesn't seem like…"

"I guess I just landed wrong. I was asleep, so I didn't have enough time to get my feet down." He could feel that his face was red. Beet red. "I *have* broken bones before."

"Yes, you have," she agreed briskly. "Boys will be boys. And that means bumps and bruises and broken bones."

"Parker… Where are you, Parkinson?"

Parker returned to the present. Dakota stared at him, waiting for his response. He shook off the residual guilt the memory left him with.

"Sorry. Yeah, I'm here. Just got distracted. So, eight o'clock, right? I'll meet you there."

"Yeah. That's what we agreed."

She was still looking at him.

"What did I miss?" Parker scratched at his forehead to hide his embarrassment from her.

"I just wondered whether your mom would be around. Can we go back to your place? Or is she going to be home?"

"I think she's supposed to be home. But one of the other ladies has been sick this week. Mom will pick up an extra shift if she can."

Dakota made a face. "Well, we'll decide when you come to meet me. You'll know by then."

"Yeah. Exactly. We can decide then."

Parker got to the restaurant before Dakota finished her shift. He sat in an empty booth and watched her take orders and enter them into the cash register, a big bright smile on her face as she dealt with the customers. She seemed happy and animated, not brooding like she often was with him.

"Dakota!" A twenty-something young man with deep acne scars and sweaty temples barked at her. "How come you take twice as long to take an order as anyone else? Your line is always backed up!"

There were only a couple of people waiting in Dakota's line. They didn't look impatient like they would if they'd been there for a long time. They looked at the manager in surprise.

Dakota's smile faltered for a minute at his criticism. Then she forced it back again. "Yes, sir, Mr. Taub. I'm sorry, I'll try to go faster."

"I'm not going to keep you on if you can't keep up. I can't have one person pulling the whole team down."

"No, sir. I'll work on it."

"People come here because they want something quick to eat. They don't want to be standing around for twenty minutes because you can't take an order."

"No, sir. I understand that."

"See to it, then. Or you're going to be out of here."

Dakota nodded again. Parker saw just the barest hint of her lip trembling as she tried to control her emotions. She opened her mouth to take the order of the woman who was standing in front of her, patiently waiting for the manager to finish reaming her out. But just as she did, the man had to get one more parting shot in.

"And don't try clocking out early today, either. Your shift goes until eight. Not ten to."

"Yes, sir."

He gave her a long, appraising look and finally decided he was done. He returned to the kitchen, probably to see who else he could yell at.

Dakota forced an even bigger smile and politely took the woman's order. She glanced toward Parker and swallowed as she tapped the order into the cash register.

Parker hated the manager for upsetting her like that. For calling her out when she was being polite and friendly to the customers. The reason she had more people in her line was that people wanted to deal with the pleasant young woman, not because she was so much slower.

Parker wanted to confront the manager, to try to force him to apologize to Dakota; but he knew it wasn't the right thing to do. The guy would never apologize. He would just fire Dakota, and then there would be no chance of Dakota and Parker ever getting together. So Parker held his tongue and played with his phone while Dakota finished her shift.

He noticed she worked a few minutes late, ensuring that she couldn't be accused of clocking out too early. She gave Parker a little wave before going into the back of the restaurant where she would clock out, change out of her apron, and do whatever else she was required to do at the end of her shift.

It was almost half an hour before she was back. Parker looked anxiously at his phone again. Mona wasn't home, but if one of the other children told her that Parker had stayed out after nine, she wouldn't be happy. Dakota put a large order of fries down on the table and a milkshake in front of each of them. She slid into the hard plastic seat with a grimace.

"Sorry for being so long. But as you can see… we have a little management problem…"

Parker laughed. "Yeah. It looks that way. Guy seems to think he's Hitler."

She nodded.

"Is this okay?" Parker asked, pointing to the fries. "You're allowed to take food…?"

"I paid for it. If he checks, I never took a single fry without paying."

"Okay." Reassured, Parker squirted ketchup all over the fries and took a couple. "I don't want to get you in trouble."

"No. Thanks for waiting. You okay being a bit longer…?"

Parker put aside any worries about Mona. If she got home, or if one of the other kids told her that Parker had stayed out late, she would just have to deal with it. He was nearly a grown man, and could make his own decisions about his curfew. He was, after all, the man of the house. And he was there to do his schoolwork.

"No, it's fine."

"You'd think I'd be tired of the food." Dakota put a few fries in her mouth. "But I could honestly eat here every day. I do eat here every day, almost." She chewed. "They say they put lots of stuff that's really bad for you in the food, so that it tastes good and is, like, addictive."

"Well… it *is* good!"

"Exactly. I don't care if I'm eating a lot of chemicals. You only live once. And *you* shouldn't care, you eat really healthy in your family, right?"

"I wouldn't say that, exactly."

"But you cook your own food. You're not having takeout every day. You eat a lot healthier."

Parker shrugged. It wasn't something he wanted to argue with her about. They ate in relative silence for a few minutes. Parker noticed Dakota scowling at something and turned and looked over his shoulder to see what was going on. He saw a father and a daughter sitting, sharing an order of fries. The girl had a junior-size burger and small fountain drink in front of her. The father had a coffee. Parker looked at them for a minute, then turned his gaze back to Dakota.

"What's wrong?"

"What do you mean? Nothing is wrong."

"You look like you're mad at them. What'd they do to you?" Maybe they had been in Dakota's line earlier. Maybe they had complained about her services, and that's why her manager had jumped all over her.

"Nothing. They didn't do anything to me. I'm just wondering…" Dakota trailed off and ate a few more fries.

"What do you mean? Wondering about what?"

Her voice was low, almost a whisper. "Well…" she was breathless. "First of all… is she his? Is he the dad? Or the foster dad? He's old enough he could be a grandpa. Or an uncle."

"What does it matter?"

"Look at how skinny she is. He could be neglecting her. Or could have kidnapped her away from her parents and has had her locked in a room somewhere."

The little girl was chattering away and seemed cheerful to Parker. She didn't look like a little girl that had been locked in a room or otherwise neglected.

"He'd use the food to control her," Dakota explained, as if sensing Parker's argument. "He'd tell her she has to act like everything is fine and pretend she's having a good time. Or she's going back there in that hole again."

"He doesn't seem nervous."

"He wouldn't if he's a psychopath. They don't feel nervous or guilty."

"Oh."

"Or he could be grooming her. Treating her just to get her confidence. To make her like him and trust him."

"He's probably just her dad. Taking her out to eat. He just got her for the weekend and he doesn't cook. They look okay to me."

Dakota didn't stop looking at them. Parker took another quick look. The father had one of the fries, but it was obvious that the food was really the little girl's. The man had his coffee and just picked at a fry or two, leaving the rest for her.

"He's not even eating," Parker told Dakota. "I don't think he had enough money to buy food for them both."

Dakota's look softened slightly. "You think?"

"Yeah. Look how he's dressed. Old blue jeans and t-shirt. No suit or uniform. No leather jacket or sports jersey. He's blue collar. Or worse."

The man's hands were stained with ingrained dirt or grease or welding residue. That was a good sign. At least he had a job.

"You don't think he's abusing her?" Dakota persisted. "Abusive dads… they can look like great guys in public. Put on a real convincing act."

Parker didn't want to keep turning around to look at them. Sooner or later they were going to notice. But he took one more look, turning his head casually while he was drinking his milkshake. Pretending he was looking out the window for a friend they were waiting for.

"Watch her eyes," he told her. "She doesn't look scared. She looks him in the eye. She's not looking around for help or because she's afraid someone is looking."

Dakota rolled her eyes. "When did you become such an expert on child abuse? You got no experience with what it's like. What she'd be feeling and looking like if she was sitting there across from her abuser. You live such a sheltered life; how would you know anything?"

The accusation stung, but Parker tried to keep himself calm. "Okay." He turned back to face Dakota and helped himself to more fries. "I don't know anything. You're the one who knows."

Dakota's mouth dropped open. She looked back over at the father and daughter again. "Maybe it's nothing," she admitted. "Maybe I'm just imagining things. Sometimes I see things… I flash back to stuff I went through…"

"Why don't you tell me what happened to you? Maybe that would help more than imagining it happening to her."

Dakota shook her head. She swirled a clutch of fries in the ketchup that had pooled at the bottom of the cardboard container. "I don't want to talk about all the crap that happened to me."

Parker sighed. "Okay." He sucked the thick milkshake slowly, trying to avoid brain freeze.

"I remember one dad I had. He used to always take me out for fries like that," Dakota said, her eyes on the little girl. "Wanted to make me like him. Told me how special I was. But it was all just… he just wanted to get at me. Wanted to make sure he could do whatever perverted things he wanted without me telling my mom."

Parker swallowed. He kept his eyes down, trying to keep from showing his anger at her words. He didn't want her to misinterpret it as anger or judgment toward her. It was her dad—or foster dad or stand-in dad—that he was angry at, not her.

"They're all like that," Dakota said. Apparently, she no longer believed that the man could be just looking after his little girl, getting her something to eat while he went hungry. That was too far out of her experience.

"You never had any… good dads?"

Dakota shook her head. "There were dads I liked. But they all turn on you sooner or later. They're all just trying to touch you. Or smack you around. Or both."

Parker blinked. His eyes burned, but he wasn't going to let the anger show. "I wouldn't do that. I'd never treat a girl that way."

"You're not a dad."

"But I wouldn't. I wouldn't treat my little sisters that way. I wouldn't treat my daughter that way, if I had one."

"What about your girlfriend?" she challenged.

Parker looked up at her. "I'd never hurt my girlfriend. I'd never hit her and I'd never make her do anything she didn't want to."

She stared him aggressively in the eye. "What would you do, then, if she wouldn't do what you wanted?"

"What have I done to you?"

She considered this, then broke eye contact.

"I won't hurt you, Dakota."

Tears glistened in her eyes. "Everyone does, sooner or later. They all do. Abuse me until they're sick of me, then kick me to the curb."

"I haven't done anything to hurt you. And I'm not going to."

Dakota stood up. She whipped her milkshake in the direction of the garbage can, hitting the side of the opening. The cup popped open and splattered shake across the front of the garbage. Dakota stormed out of the restaurant, slamming the door open with a crash. Then she was gone. Parker watched her stride off down the street. She could move fast when she wanted to.

Parker looked around the restaurant. Everyone was wide-eyed by the disruption. Some of them watched Dakota out the window, as if expecting her to do something else erratic. Others were looking at the milkshake mess or at Parker.

Parker got up, awkward. The little girl was whispering to her dad. Parker threw out his refuse, placing it quietly in the garbage. He attempted to wipe up some of Dakota's milkshake mess with napkins, but didn't do a very good job of it. It needed a washcloth and bucket of soapy water. He threw out the napkins.

"Sorry," he said to a restaurant worker who was watching him.

She shrugged. "It's okay," she said softly. Her eyes went to the window, but Dakota was long out of sight.

Parker headed for home. He wouldn't be getting any help from Dakota with his homework.

Parker was startled to see that Dakota had made it to homeroom ahead of him. She was always later than he was, often arriving just before or just after the bell. Sometimes she missed homeroom altogether, and then Jade got a phone call from the school and imposed some kind of consequence, like making Dakota do extra chores.

Dakota was talking to Mr. Bonne over by his desk in the back corner of the room. Parker couldn't tell for sure what they were talking about, but Dakota kept giggling and pushing her pink hair back from her face. Parker watched her, frowning to himself. When Charity came in, just before the bell, she looked around and spotted Dakota. She gave Parker a 'what the hell?' look as she put her books down on her desk. Parker shrugged at her. He didn't know what was going on either.

Even after the bell rang, Dakota kept talking to Mr. Bonne, one hand on his arm, preventing him from going up to the front to take attendance and make his announcements. He kept trying to politely end the conversation, motioning to the front, trying abortive explanations, and nodding vigorously. None of it worked, and eventually, he plucked Dakota's hand from his arm, turned his back on her, and walked up to the front of the class. Dakota didn't look offended by his behavior. She didn't blow up at him. She just walked over to her desk and sat down, looking over at Parker and giving him a wide smile. She looked at Charity with an expression that Parker couldn't quite interpret, but Charity seemed to read her like a book.

He didn't get any chance to talk to Dakota until the last period break before lunch. He stood beside her desk as she gathered her books back up.

"What was all that about this morning?" he asked.

"What was what?"

"All of that with Mr. Bonne. Were you asking him for help?"

"No." She fluttered her eyelashes at Parker, looking coy. The look sent Parker into a tailspin. He didn't know which way was up. Was she coming on to him all of a sudden?

But as quickly as it had come, the expression was gone and Dakota was just looking at him in amusement.

"Were you talking to him about my homework? About why we didn't get it done?"

"Your homework?" Dakota looked at him blankly. "Didn't we do your homework?"

"No. You were… upset when you left the restaurant. We never did anything. I tried to get Link or Sophie to help with writing some stuff down, but… they had their own schoolwork. Or they were too tired to do it."

"Oh… sorry about that. I guess I forgot all about it."

Parker wondered what she had ended up doing instead. Had she just gone home? Gone out drinking? She didn't look hung over, and she had gotten to school early, so maybe she had just gone home and gone to bed early. Had she really forgotten she was supposed to be helping Parker with his schoolwork, or had she just wanted to punish him for pretending to be a kind, caring person instead of the abusive creep she asserted all men were?

"So…" Parker had gotten sidetracked in the conversation. "What were you talking with Mr. Bonne about?"

"Oh, just random stuff." She shrugged and smiled a secretive smile. "Nothing you need to worry about."

Which probably meant that he really *did* need to be worried. Dakota seemed to operate the exact opposite way from what Parker expected, so 'don't worry' probably meant he should worry. Why would she want to worry or upset him? Was she really that upset with him for saying that he was a good guy and that he'd never hurt her? Was it just so far out of her realm of expected behavior that she thought he was lying to her?

The bell rang and they both sat down quickly to avoid being singled out by the teacher. The dull roar of conversation in the room settled into a few whispers and then silence. Parker looked sideways over at Dakota.

If she could only understand that he did care about her and he would never do anything to hurt her.

Chapter Eleven

D AKOTA TOLD PARKER TO get started on his homework, with whatever reading and studying he needed to do, while she went on one of the public library computers to do a few things. He had done all he could without a scribe, so he went over to see if she were just about done.

"Dakota—" he put his hand on her shoulder.

She whirled around, jumping to her feet while the chair was still spinning. She threw a punch right into the center of his chest. Parker reeled back. He put his hand over the point of impact and coughed, trying to get his breath back.

"Sheesh!" He coughed again. "What the hell was that for?"

Dakota fell back, withdrawing a couple of steps from him. She swore. "I'm sorry, Parker. I didn't mean to do that. You just startled me!"

A uniformed security guard reached them. "What's going on here? The two of you need to pack up your bags and leave!"

"No, no…" Parker held up his hand to stop the man. He coughed again. It hurt his chest. "It's okay. We're not fighting, or horsing around. I just…"

"He scared me," Dakota said. "I hit him before I realized who it was. I'm sorry. It won't happen again. We'll be good."

The guard looked at them. He was not amused. "If I hear one peep out of either of you…"

"No, not a peep," Dakota said meekly.

"You better not."

Dakota nodded. She shuffled over to Parker and took him by the hand, showing that they were friends or a couple, and that they weren't going to cause any trouble. Eventually, the guard nodded and walked away with one more warning of 'not a peep.'

"He's tough," Dakota observed, sighing. "I thought he was going to throw us out anyway."

"I'm glad he didn't. I've got work to do."

Dakota turned back to her computer. "I've still got things I need to get done."

"Can it wait? I need to get my homework done and then I gotta get home and check in on the sibs. Make sure they haven't killed each other yet."

She rolled her eyes, unconcerned about his siblings. "I'll just be a few more minutes," she wheedled. "I'll be… ten minutes. Okay?"

Ten more minutes.

Parker knew it wasn't very much, but he had already been waiting for her for an hour and it was irritating. When he looked at her computer screen, it wasn't on any school research or report, but social networking. Lots of inspirational memes, selfies, and news stories.

"That's not work, Dakota. Just help me out with my writing. I've done everything else."

"You don't know what's work and what's not!" The words came out in a snarl. "Schoolwork isn't going to get you anywhere in life. No company twenty years down the line is going to give a crap about what you wrote an essay on in junior high school! But this stuff…" she made a short gesture toward the screen. "This could save my life."

Save her life? Parker couldn't see anything of importance. Nothing that would have any effect on the rest of her life. Cute kitten videos? Pictures of sunsets?

"I don't know how long I'll be able to stay at Jade's. I don't know how long it will be before she kicks me out." Dakota held up a hand to stop Parker from interrupting. "I know you think she'll let me stay there forever, but that's not the way it works. Nothing is forever, especially a roof over your head. Sooner or later, she'll kick me out. She's already ticked off about all the stuff I do that she says breaks the rules. It's her house, so it's her rules that count, not what I want. Sooner or later, she's going to kick me out. And when she does, one of these people," she gestured to the photos and memes, "one of these people is going to help me out."

Parker looked at the screen. He tried to pick out some of the words on the latest posts, but was standing too far back to see much.

"What is this? Who are these people?"

"People who want to help me. People who have said that they'll give me a home if I get kicked out again. People who care what happens to me."

"What kind of people? People you've met before? Friends?"

Dakota clicked the mouse to minimize the window. "I don't want to talk to you about it. It's private. I… I did a search, to find people who would help. I never want to be on the street again, eating out of a garbage can. If things fall through here—*when* things fall through here—I'm gonna be ready. I'm going to have the next place lined up and ready to move into."

"And… where do these people live? They're all close by? In the neighborhood?"

"No. Who would I find in the neighborhood? Each one is just as poor as the next. There's no one else around here who would help me. I was lucky enough to find Jade."

Parker refrained from pointing out that *he* was the one who had found Jade, not Dakota. He would offer her his house if he could, but he knew that it wasn't big enough and that Mona would never agree to it. However much she thought it was important to be respectful of others and help out who they could, she would not be taking this broken bird in.

"So you're making plans to go… somewhere else? You never planned on staying here?"

"I'm staying here as long as I can!" Dakota's voice was impatient, as if Parker were being willfully stupid and refusing to understand what she was saying. "But it isn't going to last. It never lasts! I have to line up my next home, because I know this one isn't going to last much longer."

Parker moved closer to Dakota. He touched her arm. Lowered his voice. "What does that mean, not much longer? You think Jade is getting ready to kick you out now?"

"Of course she is. She doesn't want a lazy slob like me hanging around the house all the time, making messes and eating her food. Getting into trouble. She's had her kids and kicked them out of the nest already. She doesn't want another snotty teenager around all the time. I try not to spend too much time there, but… well, I've worn out my welcome. Worn it out really good."

"But you can't leave. You can't just go like that."

Dakota motioned to the computer. "We can still keep in touch. Just because I move, that doesn't mean we can't talk or that we'll never see each other again. It just means that… for a while, I'm going to be somewhere else. And sooner or later, you are going to be too. You're not going to stay in your mom's house forever. You'll probably leave home the week you graduate."

"No, I won't," Parker disagreed. "I'm the man of the house. I'll get a job and help my mom out while she's still raising the other kids. She needs someone to help out. Since my dad's gone…"

"Well, even that's not going to last forever. In the meantime… we can keep in touch. It's so easy now with the internet. In just a few seconds, you can send someone a message. Before the internet you had to write letters, mail them off, and wait weeks for a reply. This is simple."

"Before the internet?" Parker repeated.

"Yeah. There *was* a before the internet, you know. It hasn't always been around. I remember—all the stories that I've heard from my moms or aunties about how things used to be. How you couldn't just Google search whatever you wanted to. There weren't any smart phones. Lots of homes didn't have computers or cell phones. It was a whole different world back then."

"Yeah," Parker agreed. "I'm glad I didn't have to live back then."

"All these people who might help me…" Dakota sat down and brought her screen back up again. "I never would have been able to find them like this before. I'd have to… rely on people at church, or try to approach strangers… random stuff. There was no way to reach out to people like this."

Parker sighed. "Okay. So finish your work. I guess… I can wait."

It had been a long week at school. Dealing with his broken arm and still getting his schoolwork done had been a much bigger problem than Parker had expected. He tried not to rely solely on Dakota, as her help was sporadic at best. He got a little help from other friends at school, from the resource room teacher if she could manage to see him after school, and even occasionally from Link or one of the other kids. Most of his teachers were understanding and would forgive work being handed in late, but it had still weighed heavily on Parker and had not been as easy as he would have liked.

So he was the one who had suggested a walk outside to get some fresh air. Even though they were in the middle of the city, there were still some parks and walking trails that were close enough to the house for them to access on foot. Dakota was not much of a walker, but agreed to go for a revitalizing stroll with Parker in one of his favorite greenways.

"It's nice out, isn't it?" Parker pointed out. It was a beautiful day. He understood that she was a city girl, not much of a nature person, but he wasn't sure how she could ignore the green living things around them and the birds chirping cheerily in the trees.

"Yeah. Good weather. At least it's not raining."

"It's a beautiful day."

"You're so chirpy," Dakota complained. "Didn't anyone ever tell you how annoying that is?"

"Sorry." But he wasn't. He was enjoying the walk and he didn't want to be quiet about it or to pretend that walking down the treed paths was just the same as walking down the sidewalks with buildings on either side. It filled him up and he didn't want to just keep quiet about it.

They walked for a while in silence. Dakota walked slowly and they had to stop to rest often.

"Guess I'm not in very good shape," she huffed, bending down to put her hands on her knees.

"It's okay," Parker said. "I can wait."

"You're too much."

Parker wasn't sure what she meant by that, but he shrugged it off. "So… how many families have you been with?" he asked, thinking about some of their conversations.

She swore. "I don't know. I lost count a long time ago. Dozens."

"Dozens. Really? How could there be that many? You're only, what, sixteen? And your mom abandoned you when you were…" he took a stab at it, "five?"

Dakota looked up at him from her bent-over position. "I don't know how old I was."

"So you've been moving around from place to place for ten or eleven years. *Dozens* of families? You'd have to be going somewhere new every few months."

"You did that math all by yourself?" Dakota sneered. "Maybe there's hope for you in algebra after all."

Parker leaned against a tree, waiting for Dakota to straighten out and indicate that they could start walking again.

"You weren't any place more than a few months? Never anywhere they let you stay for a year or two?"

"I don't really want to talk about it. Maybe. Sometimes. But none of it lasted. People figured I could just manage on my own."

"That's crazy. No little kid should have to be on the street, looking after themselves."

"I wasn't a little kid when I was on my own. Older. When I was little… they'd just find someone else to pawn me off on. Whoever wanted me."

"I can't believe they did that to you."

"Well, they did," Dakota snapped. "I'm not making it up!"

"No, I didn't mean I don't believe you. I just mean… it's amazing. It's… disturbing. That no one would take care of you. Just take you in and raise you up."

"People aren't like that. And I wasn't the perfect child, either. I caused plenty of trouble. Who would want me around?"

Parker thought about his young siblings. Sure, they caused trouble. Parker himself caused trouble for his mother; falling out of trees, being hyper at school, breaking her precious things. And stuff she didn't know about, like sneaking out at night. But she would never kick him out for that stuff. Pawn him off on whoever would take him. Jade, or his uncle in Baltimore, or some scruffy guy at the bar down the street. And he would never consider trying to find a new home for one of his siblings because they had broken the house rules or caused him grief. They were his family. He'd never let anything happen to them.

"Is there somewhere around here we could sit down?" Dakota suggested.

Parker looked around. He was close to some of his favorite haunts. Places he could just go and be alone in nature, even if it were in the middle of the city.

"Yeah. Follow me."

Dakota blundered along behind him, cursing at the bushes and undergrowth and sounding like a charging rhino. Parker hadn't appreciated how much larger and more awkward she was at navigating through the bush. Parker slipped through the narrow game trails with barely a sound. Dakota was another story.

But in ten minutes, they were in a green clearing. Thick grass on the ground without brambles or thistles. A green canopy overhead. It was like a fairy house.

Dakota fell to the ground with a grunt. She lay down and closed her eyes. Parker sat beside her and breathed in the sweet, green smell of the place. He had spent many happy hours in the glade, recovering from the stresses of school and the world and just communing with nature.

Dakota's breathing slowed. He looked over at her, wondering if she were going to fall asleep. It would be nice to just sleep in the grass with the warm sun filtering in overhead.

She opened her eyes and looked at him. "What are you staring at?"

"Not staring. Just making sure you're okay." Parker took a chance, and bent down to kiss her on the forehead. Nothing pushy. Just a little peck, far away from her lips. Like he would give a child he was babysitting who fell down and scraped his knee. He sat back up, not lingering close to her face. Giving her some personal space and waiting for her reaction.

Dakota looked up at him, expressionless. Her lids went down to half mast and she just watched him, saying nothing. Parker raised his eyebrows. Wondering how she wanted him to proceed. If it was okay.

She still made no move, and eventually Parker bent down and kissed her on the lips.

There was no alcohol on her breath this time. No loud music or throwing up.

It was just Parker and Dakota in his green space, like Adam and Eve in the Garden of Eden. Dakota reached up, putting her arms around Parker and gently tugging him down to her.

After the day in the park, Dakota withdrew again. Parker was frustrated by his inability to stay close to her. To engage with her like he saw other couples doing. It was one step forward and two steps back. An interminable return to where they had been and another step forward, and then two more back again.

She didn't talk to him about what had happened in the park.

It was like she wanted to pretend that it never happened. Wasn't that the way that guys were supposed to behave, not girls?

Chris and Adrian didn't know about any of the recent developments, but they were full of advice.

"If she's not interested in you, that's her loss. Forget about her and get together with someone else," Chris said.

"Some girls just need more time," Adrian disagreed. "You need to… romance them. Give them time. And presents. Chocolate helps."

"And this has worked for you… when?" Parker laughed. Adrian had had a hopeless crush on little red-headed Alisha Perkins since first grade. Except that little Alisha Perkins was no longer little Alisha Perkins. She was now Luscious Lisha, who had a reputation for having slept with every eligible boy in the grade. Which actually wasn't very many, most of the boys being way too immature for her.

"Some girls take longer," Adrian repeated, red-faced. Maybe someday he would get together with Lisha. Maybe when she was thirty and all worn out, no longer so luscious.

"Dakota!" Parker saw her across the cafeteria and pushed through the crowds to get to her, leaving Chris and Adrian to argue with each other about the best way to woo a girl. "Hey, hi!"

Dakota turned and looked at him. She hesitated before giving him a small 'hi' back.

"Hey, did you watch anything last night?" Parker launched into a neutral topic of discussion immediately. Dakota liked sitting cuddled up watching TV, so he would talk to her about TV. "I watched this old movie, after all of the kids were in bed. It was really corny, but there wasn't anything good on. Did you see it? Back to the Future."

Dakota blinked. "Are you kidding? Watched that on Betamax years ago."

Parker shook his head. "Betamax?"

"Videotape. Like VHS. You know, those things that came before DVDs?"

Parker tried to wrap his brain around this. "I never even heard of Betamax. Where did you watch one of those?"

She licked her lips. "Oh, you know… one of the dads collected old stuff like that. Betamax videos. Eight-track tapes. LPs."

"LPs," Parker repeated the one that he recognized. "Vinyl."

"Yeah. Some people say it has better quality than CDs. That you lose something when you lose the imperfections of the vinyl."

Dakota shrugged. "People collect all kinds of crap, right? And he collected Betamax."

"Sure." Parker nodded. "Makes sense. So… what did you think of it?"

"What?"

"The movie. Back to the Future."

"Oh. It was so many years ago. I don't remember anything about it. That dad… he was nice… liked to buy me presents."

Parker shifted uncomfortably. She had always maintained that none of the dads was good. They had all treated her badly. Had the presents been a prelude? Grooming her? Or a reward or apology after? A bribe to keep her mouth shut? Or had he just been a nice guy, who didn't count when she was totting up all of the nastiness she had been through?

"You want to eat together?" Parker motioned to a table with some empty seats at it.

Dakota looked at him, puzzled for a moment. "You didn't get anything."

Parker held up his lunch bag. "I brought my own. The food here is too expensive."

"Just do the free lunch program."

"I don't need free lunch. I have my own."

She shrugged widely, like he was making a majorly big mistake. But she hadn't objected to sitting with him for lunch, so he led her to a couple of empty seats.

Mr. Bonne was on cafeteria supervision duty and was slowly making his rounds up and down the aisles between tables, settling down the rowdies, talking to the loners and rejects, making sure that everyone had something to eat, and basically just making sure everything was going smoothly. As soon as she saw Mr. Bonne, Dakota's eyes lit up.

"Hi, Mr. Bonne!"

"How's it going, Dakota?" Parker noticed Mr. Bonne didn't look Dakota in the eye, but somewhere past her. His expression was neutral.

"Good. It's going good. Except… I really need some help with that algebra."

Parker just about fell out of his seat. Dakota needed help with algebra? She could probably teach the class. He opened his mouth to dispute it, and Dakota shot him a murderous look. Parker closed his mouth again.

"You seem to be keeping up all right," Mr. Bonne said.

"Parker helps me out with it."

"Parker?" Bonne looked over at him, his mouth quirking up. "I'd be worried if Parker is helping you with your algebra."

Dakota laughed, nodding agreement. "Okay," she said. "Parker's not helping me. But I do need some help, I keep getting mixed up."

"I'm sure we can work something out."

"Could you help me after school today?"

Forgetting again that she was supposed to be helping Parker with his homework after school. She had promised Parker that she would be there this time.

Bonne looked at Dakota. He hesitated. "Do you both need help?"

Dakota waved at Parker to keep him silent. "No, just me. Parker's gotta go home to look after his sisters."

"I don't know if I can do that…"

"Come on," Dakota begged. She grasped Mr. Bonne's arm. Tears glittered in her eyes. "I'm going to get behind, and if I don't keep my marks up, Jade is gonna kick me out! I won't be able to come to school anymore if she kicks me out!"

Mr. Bonne looked worried about this. "You really aren't behind. You've been doing very well."

She clutched him harder, tears dripping down her cheeks. "Please. Just half an hour after school… just to help me get straightened out…"

"Okay." Mr. Bonne pried her hand off his arm. "Just half an hour, okay? I have marking and class prep to do."

Dakota beamed at him. "Thank you so much. I won't keep you long, I promise!"

Mr. Bonne nodded and moved on with his circuit. Parker looked over at Dakota, his brows drawn down.

"What?" Dakota asked, all innocence.

"You don't need any help with algebra."

"Yes, I do. We're doing new stuff and I don't understand it."

Even though Dakota had done her best to shoo Parker away to make sure that he wasn't around while she met with Mr. Bonne, literally pushing him out of the room when the class dismissed, he stuck around to keep an eye on things. He sat down on the floor outside the classroom, a textbook on his lap that he didn't really look at. He strained his ears to hear every word.

"What is it you're having problems with?"

Dakota turned pages in the textbook. Had she even decided yet what she was going to ask Mr. Bonne about?

"Uh, this stuff we were looking at yesterday… I keep getting confused about the order…"

Mr. Bonne's voice was low and soothing as he went over the previous day's lesson. Parker slid over a little so that he could see through the door into the classroom. Mr. Bonne's head and Dakota's were very close together as he went through the explanation.

"I didn't understand that part. Can you go over it again?"

"Which part didn't you understand?"

"I just… that last part again."

As he explained, Dakota was looking at Mr. Bonne's face more than at the text or the example he was writing out for her. Parker's stomach was tight and his heart pounded harder.

She wouldn't show any interest in Parker, but she was openly flirting with Mr. Bonne.

Mr. Bonne was trying to wrap up the discussion. "I think you've got a pretty good grasp of this…"

"Just a little more…"

"I need to get on with other things. I'm sorry, I have to get ready for tomorrow's class."

"Maybe after you do that…" She touched his hand tentatively. "We could meet. You could go over it again… We could have a drink…"

He pulled back from her sharply. "Dakota. This is inappropriate. I can't be socializing with a student."

"Socializing?"

"You know what I'm talking about. We can't meet somewhere else. We can't go out for a drink. You need to stop touching me and making inappropriate comments. We can't be involved with each other."

"You're just playing hard-to-get," she teased.

"No, Dakota." He shut and stacked her books. "We can't meet after school again. I wasn't sure why you were pretending not to understand the work, but I see what's going on now. You need to stop playing these games. Talk to boys your own age."

"I'm not interested in teen boys. They're so immature. I'm interested in a *real man*."

"Then you're going to need to wait for a couple of years. Because it's not legal for an adult to have… a relationship… with an underage girl."

Dakota's lip curled in a pout.

"Don't start the tears again," Mr. Bonne warned. "It's not going to work this time."

"I can't help crying. You're being so mean to me!"

Mr. Bonne shook his head. "You need to go now, Dakota. And I will be filing a report about your behavior and discussing it with staff. So you're not going to pull any other teachers in either."

"I'm not interested in any other teachers. I'm only interested in you! You're the one who is so… kind, and handsome… so caring about all of the students. I'm not interested in anyone else."

Mr. Bonne had moved a couple of steps away from Dakota, putting a cushion of space between them.

"What about Parker?"

It was too late for Parker to pretend that he hadn't heard or to escape before hearing Dakota's answer. He was stuck there, frozen.

A sigh from Dakota. "Parker is a *boy.* He's nice, but he's not a man, like you."

Parker's stomach roiled. He was sick and angry, and stabbed to the core. He had done everything right. He had treated her with respect. He hadn't pushed his attentions on her. He'd waited until she was ready. Now she acted like what they had shared together was nothing. How could she say that he wasn't a man after *that?*

"You need to straighten out, Dakota. You're going to hurt a lot of people with your behavior, but most of all, you're going to hurt yourself. Have some self-respect. Treat yourself like you deserve to be treated, instead of using your body as a weapon."

Dakota got up out of her desk.

"You've got no idea what you're talking about."

She strode for the door. Parker got to his feet as she approached. Dakota and Mr. Bonne both looked at Parker. Neither one seemed surprised to find him there. Parker reached out his hand for Dakota. Her face was a thundercloud. She didn't look cute and happy. A furious scowl twisted her face into an ugly shape.

"Dakota…"

She ignored Parker's outstretched hand and walked past him without a word. Mr. Bonne stepped into the doorway of his classroom.

"Parker." Mr. Bonne actually reached out and shook Parker's hand. "Parker… I'm glad you were here." He didn't ask how much of the conversation Parker had heard. "You be careful. That girl…" he trailed off, searching for words. "She isn't stable."

Parker didn't know what to say to that. He just nodded and turned to follow Dakota. Even mad, she wouldn't get too far ahead of him. She might make a short sprint for the front doors, but she couldn't maintain it. He would catch up.

Chapter Twelve

I T'S TIME FOR US to do something fun."

Parker looked over at Dakota. She had been alternately angry and teary since the episode with Mr. Bonne, and he sensed something darker under the surface. A depression and self-hate that didn't come and go, but was always there.

So her cheerful tone and suggestion took him by surprise. *Something fun.*

"What do you want to do?" he asked.

"I don't know. Go and… do something new. Try out a new restaurant. Have a few drinks. Just… you know… have fun like a normal teenager."

Parker considered the options, ignoring the part about having a few drinks. "What about… there's a new water park that just opened up. It's supposed to be really good. Water slides, wave pool, kiddie stuff. I've got some money put away. We could try that."

"I can't swim…"

"You don't have to be able to swim. Stay out of the deep water; there's supposed to be plenty of shallow stuff. I'm not supposed to get my cast wet anyway. I'll have to put a bag over it."

"It sounds like it could be fun…" Dakota admitted. "I always wanted to go on a waterslide."

"Then that's what we should do! I'll get us passes online. See if I can find some discount coupons. We can spend a day there when you don't have to work."

"I'll call in sick Saturday. Can we go then?"

"You shouldn't call in sick when you really aren't."

She blew a raspberry at him. "It's a mental health day. I need it to stay sane."

"Well, it's your job. It's up to you. I don't want to get you in trouble with your boss or with Jade."

"No one is going to find out."

"Okay, then, Saturday."

When Parker confided about the planned waterpark trip to Link, Link's mind immediately jumped ahead to the obvious.

"That means you get to see her in a swimsuit."

Parker's face burned. "Yeah, I guess," he agreed casually.

Link's nose wrinkled. "She doesn't really have a body, though."

"She has a body!"

"I mean… nice looking. Hot. She's fat."

"Well, but she still has a body. She still has… you know… a figure."

"I'm not sure you're gonna want to see all that hanging out of a bikini. You may think you like the girl, but until you see her body… well, up close and personal…"

Parker hadn't told Link about the day in the park. That was too private. Too personal.

"I've… uh… already seen," he informed Link. "And who says she's going to be wearing a bikini? It could be a one-piece. Or those… whatcha call it… tankinis. There's lots of options."

"Lots meaning three?" Link stared at Parker. "And when did you see her…?"

Parker tried to shrug it off as if it was nothing.

"When?" Link demanded. "The night you broke your arm?"

Parker was glad their first time hadn't been that night. Not when she was drunk, and sick, and maybe wouldn't even remember in the morning. The day in the glade, with the warm sunshine filtering through the green canopy. That had been worth remembering.

"No. It's none of your business."

"Seriously? Why didn't you tell me? I'd think that would be something important you might tell to your brother!"

Parker shook his head. "You're too young," he said. "I shouldn't be telling you at all."

"I'm not that much younger than you. That's going to be me in another year. Maybe sooner!"

Parker didn't like that idea at all. Link was still a kid. He wasn't old enough to have a girlfriend. Or to be *sleeping* with her. The thought was horrifying. Parker was the oldest. As the head of the family, he was more mature. Not like Link. Link was still a baby by comparison.

"You just—you're not old enough," Parker insisted. "Don't be in such a rush. Trust me."

As it turned out, Dakota did not wear a bikini. At least, Parker didn't think she did. She wore a big t-shirt that covered everything up. She did, however, stand looking at Parker for long enough to make him squirm.

"For a skinny guy, you've got a nice body, Parkinson."

He blushed. And being in swimming trunks, they could both see that the blush extended down his neck and past his collarbone. Parker rubbed his face with his hand, as if he were tired and just waking up or he could hide behind his hand or wipe away the blush. He looked around.

"Let's get in the water," he suggested. That would cool his flush in an instant. Dakota looked around the waterpark.

"Where do we start?" She pointed at one of the steeper slides. "I don't think I'm going to be going on anything like that!"

"We can start with some of the easier ones. They're all color coded." Parker pointed to the signs that he had been examining while waiting for her to come out of the change room. "Green is easy, moving up through yellow and orange, and then red for extreme."

"So we can start with the green ones."

"Yeah." Parker shifted his feet. "Maybe you can read the signs," he suggested. "Since color coding isn't really my thing."

"Oh!" Dakota laughed. "Of course! Well, I may not be able to swim, but I can see all the colors of the rainbow!"

"Lead the way. I'd like to try the rafting, if it's not too hard." He could see families with young children reclining across the big inflatable rafts, so he assumed it didn't require any particular skill.

"Let's go see."

They headed across the waterpark, carefully avoiding the little kids who seemed to be underfoot everywhere. They walked across the shallow end of the wave pool while the waves were rolling in, slapping against their legs with a force that almost pushed Parker over a few times. He couldn't imagine what it was like in the deep end, where he could see the stronger swimmers fighting against the current, whooping with excitement. Dakota looked at Parker, shaking her head, her eyes wide.

"Can you swim?" she asked him.

"A little. Not like that. We did some swimming classes at school, but I never went past the first level or two." He looked down at his ribs, visible through his skin. "Apparently, it's easier to float if you have some more fat to make you buoyant."

"Well then, I shouldn't have any problem at all."

They continued to walk.

"Don't call yourself fat," Parker eventually said.

"Can you think of a better word? I'm not afraid to say what I am. And I am fat." Dakota looked down at her round body. She jiggled her belly with her hand. "See? Just look at that."

"I… just… just don't call yourself fat. Please."

He couldn't help looking back at her body when she stopped intentionally jiggling, the waves in her fat slowing like the ripples in a pond after throwing a rock. He wasn't repulsed by her body, like Link and some of the other boys seemed to think he should be. Some girls were skinny and some were fat. No one could deny that she had a mature figure. Even the big t-shirt strained slightly around her chest. Her legs were bare, and he could see the rolls of fat that hung down and the loose, deflated-looking skin around her knees. Parker looked back up at her face, trying to look like he hadn't been distracted by her body and had been listening to her the whole time.

"I haven't been fat my whole life," Dakota said. "It started when I was... I don't know... nine or ten. I wanted to get fat. I wanted to protect myself from the men... it made me feel better to be insulated, protected. And eating makes me feel better. Like a drug."

Parker nodded his understanding. Though he wasn't sure if he really could understand. He could imagine it, but that was a long way from feeling or experiencing it himself.

"I thought that if I was fat, they wouldn't want to touch me anymore. I would be too repulsive, and they just wouldn't want anything to do with me."

"You're not repulsive!"

"Well, since it didn't work, I guess I'm not repulsive enough. Doesn't seem to matter how bad I look, they still want to mess around." Dakota shook her head. "I guess not all guys only go for skinny girls. Some of them actually like fatties better." She gave him a stern look. "Is that what it is for you? You like fatties? It turns you on?"

Parker stood there with his mouth open. He had no idea how to respond to such a question. Getting along with a girl was a lot harder than they made it look on TV. After watching James Bond a hundred times, Parker should have been able to sweep any girl off her feet. But in real life, girls were a lot more complicated.

Dakota laughed at Parker's consternation. "Good answer, Parkinson. Good answer." She grabbed his hand and gave him a little tug. "Weren't we going to go check out the rafting?"

It turned out to be an incredible day. Dakota stayed in a good mood, happy and light, teasing Parker, willing to hold his hand or kiss in the hidden turns of the slide stairways. They took a couple of breaks during the day to eat at the incredibly greasy snack bar that served the waterpark.

Parker kept waiting for Dakota to bring up Mr. Bonne and either how much he had hurt her or what she planned to do next to get his attention, but she didn't mention him once. It was like they were in another universe, where there was no Mr. Bonne. There was only Dakota and Parker. And Dakota didn't complain that Parker was immature, or too skinny, or too cheerful.

She did say that he was too white, a non-sequitur when Parker had started grooving to a hip-hop song played over the waterpark speakers. At her words, Parker stopped and looked at her, and then looked down at his milky-white skin.

Dakota laughed. "It's not like you didn't know that you're white, Parkinson."

Parker turned his hands over and over, looking at them as if shocked. "I just realized something," he told her.

"What?"

"I think I'm color-blind."

Dakota erupted into peals of laughter.

It was a good day.

Chapter Thirteen

I T WAS THE NEXT day that everything changed. Only Parker didn't know it at the time. He wanted to take Dakota for another walk in the park, during which they would be sure to stop in their little clearing for a repeat of their last encounter. Sunshine, a green carpet, and lots of time to get to know each other.

But Dakota said that she was tired after the long day at the waterpark. Parker was tired too, and he wanted to work out his stiff muscles so they wouldn't be even more sore the following day.

"I just want to stay home," Dakota insisted. "I couldn't go out for a walk. I swear. I wouldn't get a block and I'd be a puddle on the ground. I'm not in the same shape as you are."

"Just a short walk," Parker coaxed. "Then we could… sit down and rest…"

"I'm still picking grass out of crevices from the last time we sat down to rest."

Parker's face burned and Dakota laughed, pleased with his reaction.

"Why don't we just sit down and rest here?" Dakota said, motioning to the couch, where she was wrapped up in a blanket watching TV, even though the room was already hot from the sun.

"We can't do anything here," Parker pointed out. "Not with Jade around."

"You could sit down."

"Yeah, but…"

"You could come cuddle under the blanket with me."

Parker sighed. It was way too hot for a blanket, and he didn't want to be stuck in Jade's house. He wanted to be somewhere they could be themselves, without a chaperone hovering over them.

"Why don't we go down to the Rooster?" he suggested. It was a corner store. One of the few that was not a chain. They carried eclectic products that the big franchises didn't. Stuff that was specially ordered from Korea, or a favorite brand that someone had requested, or just something new and exciting that no one else had picked up. Dakota liked to go there to pick up flavored cigarettes or special bottles of herbs that Parker didn't really want to know about.

Her eyes flicked over to him, leaving the TV for the first time since he had arrived and tried to cajole her into a walk. "You want to go to the Rooster?"

"Yeah, sure. You want to?"

"This isn't just some lame plan to get me out of the house and make me walk somewhere else, because 'we're already out here'?"

Parker couldn't help grinning. He certainly would have tried whatever line he figured would get her from the Rooster to a more acceptable rendezvous. "I promise I won't make you go anywhere else."

"You promise?"

"Unless you want to. If you want to go somewhere else, I wouldn't stop you."

"I don't want to go anywhere else."

"You never know. You could feel differently once you get out into the fresh air."

"And people say *I* have a one-track mind."

She got up and left him in the living room watching the drivel on the TV while she fetched her little purse. Parker didn't have any money, especially after the trip to the waterpark. He had paid for as much of the date as he could, but Dakota was the one with a job and she had covered some of the admission, locker, and food costs.

Dakota hitched up her pants, which were riding too low. "Why don't you get a job? Then you could have some spending money too."

"Mom gives me a little for looking after the kids, when she can afford it. But most of the time… it has to go to household expenses."

"Then get a real job."

"Mom needs me to keep an eye on the kids. I couldn't be at work all the time. I need to be home to keep track of things."

"So you get to be a slave? Why do you let her push you around like that? Why don't you just tell her you're not going to do it anymore? You're a big boy. You need to be earning your own money. You kick a bit back in her direction now and then, and I bet she stops complaining about you not looking after the little kids. They're old enough, they don't need you around all the time."

"I want to help out. I'll get a job when they're a bit older."

Dakota gave a wide shrug.

Parker took her hand as they walked down the street to the Rooster. Dakota put up with it for a few minutes, then shook him off. So much for being able to show more physical affection once they were no longer being supervised.

"I just need a bit of space," Dakota said.

"Okay."

At the Rooster, she browsed the shelves for anything new, bought her favorite cigarettes and cookies, and some kind of Chinese snack or cereal that appeared to have a prize inside.

"Here. Try one."

As Parker reached for the box, Dakota pulled it away, and Parker thought that she was teasing him. But then he saw her face and knew that something was wrong. Dakota lowered the hand holding the box, oblivious to Parker's reach. Her eyes were on something down the street.

"What? What's wrong?"

She didn't answer him. She didn't even seem to know that he was there. All of her focus was a block or two down the street. Parker couldn't see anything out of the ordinary. Just people coming and going, walking singly or in groups, going about their usual business.

"No. Oh, no, no, no…"

"What is it, Dakota?"

"Him." Dakota didn't point, and Parker had no idea who she was talking about. "He can't be here. How would he know I was here?"

"Who? What's going on, Dakota?"

Dakota blindly pushed the box into Parker's hand, and fumbled to pull out and light one of the cigarettes. With her dark complexion, Parker couldn't say that she was pale, but her lips seemed suddenly dry and cracked, and sweat was gathering at her temples, mixing with the pastel pink hair to make it lay against her head, dark and moist.

"That guy. Down there. No, don't look. Don't do anything to attract his attention. We have to get out of here. Without him seeing me."

Dakota wasn't exactly hard to spot. Not with her bright pink hair and bulk. She didn't quite blend in with the crowd. Parker couldn't look over his shoulder to see who it was she was referring to. He stood between her and the person she was looking at, blocking her view, but also the view of the man she wanted to avoid. Dakota objected, but then held him where he was, using him as a shield.

"Okay. Yeah, you just stay between us. Just to the corner, and then we'll go around, and we'll take the alleys back to Jade's house. So that he doesn't see me."

Parker nodded, trying to keep her calm and relaxed. "Just walk slowly. I'll stay between you. Don't look back."

"Yeah."

They worked their way along the street in an awkward waltz.

"Who is it?" Parker asked, taking a glance back over his shoulder to see if he could spot anyone suspicious.

"My… ex-boyfriend. Why can't he just accept that it's over and leave me alone?"

Now that Parker knew what he was looking for, he spotted a tall, young black man. Parker studied the man the best he could at that distance. He couldn't see the man's face very clearly, but he studied his clothing, the size and shape of his body, and the way he moved as he made his way down the street, looking around, trying to spot his ex-girlfriend.

"How would he know this is where you are?" Parker asked.

"Come on. We gotta get away from here."

Parker was relieved when they made it around the corner and Dakota relaxed a little.

"That's good. He won't see us now. What's he doing here?"

Parker went with her, working their way through the alleys and back streets to get back to Jade's house.

"How would he find me? I have no idea. I didn't tell anybody where I was going. *I* didn't know where I was going."

"Then somebody here must have told him. Or you posted it on social media or something. Is he on any of your friends lists?"

"No. I started totally new accounts when I moved here. Nobody from my old life was on any of them. I don't know how he could have tracked me down."

Parker had watched a lot of spy movies, and he knew there were a lot of ways to track a person. Social insurance number, employment records, credit cards, mail forwarding… Dakota might have thought that she had avoided everything from her old life, but she had obviously left a clue somewhere.

"Should we call the police? Do you have a restraining order against him?"

"No. No, I don't want to involve them, and I would have to go to court, get him served. Then he'd know where I was for sure. Right now… he's just looking for me. Or he would have come straight to Jade's."

They had reached Jade's front sidewalk. Both of them looked around, making sure that he hadn't magically appeared.

"What are we going to do?"

They went into the house.

"Nothing. We can't do anything to tip him off that I'm here. Just stay quiet and out of the way… he'll give up and go home."

Parker bit his lip. "Are you sure? I think we should tell somebody. If we let people know not to let him know where you are… otherwise, someone might tell him, thinking he's a friend…"

"No! I know how to deal with this, Parker. We can't say anything to anyone. He's looking for someone else. It isn't anything to do with me. Nobody is going to tell him anything."

"What do you mean, he's looking for someone else?"

"A different name. He doesn't know the name I'm using here. He'll never find me."

He could have a picture of her to show to people. He had managed to track her somehow. But Parker kept quiet. Dakota said that she knew what she was doing and the ex wouldn't be able to find her. He had to trust her.

Dakota pushed the living room curtains aside to peer out at the street.

"What's going on?" Jade came into the room and looked at the two of them. Parker realized in retrospect how loudly the two of them had been speaking, panicked by what was going on. Parker looked at Dakota to answer. He wasn't going to even attempt to explain it.

"Nothing is going on," Dakota snapped.

"You seem upset. What's up?"

Dakota faced off against her, both of them standing hands on hips, looking like two roosters about to start a fight.

"Why don't you stay out of my life? Just because I live here, that doesn't mean I can't have my own business? You don't have to know everything that's going on!"

Parker expected an angry reply back from Jade. That's how it always worked in his house when teenage hormones got the better of him, and his moods were all over the place. He snapped at Mona, talked back about something or other, and then she would get angry at him, escalating the argument until one of them stormed out of the room, followed by the slamming of a door. But Jade stood there coolly and didn't yell at Dakota for being such a bratty teenager.

"I care about you, Dakota. If there's something wrong, I'd like to know what it is."

"You're always on my case. You don't care about me. You just want to control me! Make me do all your chores!"

Jade studied Dakota. She cocked her head to the side for a minute.

"I'm going to make some tea."

She turned away and walked into the kitchen. Dakota stared after her. Parker didn't understand what was going on. Was Dakota in trouble? Was Jade just going to let the backtalk go? Dakota's posture slowly relaxed. She folded into herself, her shoulders slumping forward. The fear that had warped into anger evaporated. Dakota looked at Parker, her eyes teary, and then she followed Jade into the kitchen. Parker didn't hear any words pass between them.

"Parker, are you going to join us?" Jade called.

Parker went to the doorway of the kitchen, looking in on them. Dakota was sitting down at the kitchen table, her elbows resting on the table and her face in her hands. Parker wasn't sure whether Dakota would want him there, or if he were intruding. Jade motioned him in and pointed him toward a chair.

"Come on, sit down. We'll all have a hot tea and just relax for a few minutes."

Dakota sniffled, but didn't uncover her face.

Parker sat down in the chair next to hers, sitting rigidly, not sure what to expect next. Dakota's emotions were all over the place, and Parker wasn't so good at the emotional support thing. When Mona or the girls were all weepy and emotional over something, Parker never knew what to do about it. There was no broken wing for him to mend or boo-boo to bandage. Whenever he tried to help, it seemed like they didn't even *want* him to fix anything.

Jade poured them each a cup of hot, strong tea and sat down at the table on Dakota's other side. "Here you go, dearie. You'll feel better once you've had this."

Dakota wiped her face and picked up the cup. Parker's was too hot to sip yet, still boiling hot, but that didn't seem to deter Dakota. She took a couple of large swallows and put it down again.

"Now, doesn't that feel better?" Jade asked.

Dakota nodded, gulping.

"Why don't you tell me what's going on?"

Dakota didn't answer, and Jade looked at Parker, her eyes piercing. He shifted uncomfortably under her stare.

"Dakota saw a guy—" Parker started.

Dakota kicked him under the table. "I saw somebody who reminded me… of a guy I used to know," she said, her voice choked. She sent a warning glare to Parker. But he'd gotten the message and wasn't going to say anything. "A guy who… he wasn't so good to me."

Jade reached out across the table and put her hand over Dakota's. "Oh, honey…"

"It scared me," Dakota said. "I… I just didn't know what to do."

Parker looked at Dakota and didn't know which story to believe. Was the man she had seen really her ex, or was it just a man who reminded her of someone she had known? A boyfriend or one of the fathers in a home she had lived with? Or was it something different altogether?

"This man abused you?" Jade guessed.

Dakota nodded, a tear dripping down her cheek. "He said he loved me, and I really liked him. But he would drink, or he'd lose a bet, and he would get so angry. He would come home, smelling of drink, and he would just beat on me." Dakota gulped and sobbed. "He would say he was sorry. That he didn't mean to act like that. He'd tell me he would never do it again. But there was always another time."

Jade shuffled her chair over slightly and rubbed Dakota's shoulder. "What he did was wrong. He never should have treated you like that. You know that, right? You know it wasn't your fault?"

Dakota shook her head. "I tried so hard to keep him happy. If I took care of him, he wouldn't feel like he needed to drink or to go out and gamble. He only did those things when he was stressed out. If I just kept things at home unstressed…"

Parker frowned at Dakota. It sounded more like something out of the plot of a movie than something that might have happened to Dakota in real life. She might have had an abusive father or boyfriend, but she hadn't been keeping house for anyone. She wasn't someone's wife, cooking dinner for him at the end of the day and fetching his slippers so that he could just relax and wouldn't be inclined to beat on her. The language just wasn't right.

The man that he had seen, the man that Dakota said was looking for her, was a young man. Maybe nineteen or twenty. Older than Parker, but not an established family man. Not a character that fit the story that Dakota was telling.

But Jade didn't seem to notice anything wrong. She just kept nodding and cooing to Dakota.

"My whole life is filled with men like that," Dakota sobbed. "They act like they care, but they really don't. Sooner or later they always hit me. I just can't get away from it."

"You're safe here," Jade soothed. "No one is going to hurt you while you're home with me. I would never let them. This is a safe place."

Parker wanted to say that Jade wouldn't be able to do anything about an angry, abusive man who broke into the house with a gun. If that ever happened, all of her reassurances would be for nothing. If Dakota's ex-boyfriend stalker—if that's what he was—came into the house after her, words would be of no use. Only a bullet to the chest would stop an armed gunman.

But he kept his mouth shut. The look in Jade's eye as she looked across the table at him told him that she knew exactly what he was thinking. What he was remembering. But she didn't tell Dakota that. Dakota reached over and hugged Jade, cuddling up to her so that she was nearly crawling into the older woman's lap.

"You'll keep me safe?" she begged. "You won't let him come and get me? You'll keep me safe, right?"

"Of course I'll keep you safe," Jade soothed. "You never have to worry while you're living with me. I would never let anyone hurt you."

Parker shuffled through his locker contents in a fog. He had thought a lot about Dakota and her stalker and her past life while he was away from her. He tried to understand all that she had gone through in her short life. On the surface, it seemed straightforward enough, but he was no longer sure what the truth was. Mona had warned him. Jade had warned him. Some of the inconsistencies in Dakota's stories sent up red flags. But he had still been convinced of her sincerity.

The flip in the story about her stalker ex-boyfriend made him really stop and examine the stories again. If she could lie that convincingly, how much of what she had told him had been the truth and how much was just made up? Maybe skimmed from movie plots or books she had read?

She was a lot smarter than she pretended to be. She put on her 'street kid' persona, acting like she was a disadvantaged, uneducated, unwanted urchin, when she could whip through algebra or turn out an English paper almost effortlessly. Her knowledge went deeper than just a ghetto-raised, homeless girl's. She sometimes made Parker feel ignorant, talking about stuff he'd never even heard of before.

"Hey, handsome," Dakota teased, startling Parker out of his reverie.

Parker's face flared, wondering if she could have read in his eyes what he had been thinking. He never wanted her to guess that he doubted her. He still loved Dakota and wanted to be closer to her. But he had to admit that she was far from perfect and that much of her life might actually be fiction.

"Oh, hey."

Parker was also distracted by the fact that she didn't normally call him handsome or anything to suggest that she might be interested in him as more than just a casual friend.

"Long day?" she suggested. "You seem spaced out."

"A little. Do you have time… to help me out today?"

He had stopped expecting that she would be available to write out his schoolwork for him every night. In retrospect, it had been selfish and presumptuous to assume that she would just drop all of her responsibilities or needs to cater to him. Just because he had broken his arm in a pathetic attempt to defend her honor.

"Yeah, I could fit it in. You all up on the algebra today?"

Parker ground his teeth, even though he knew that she only meant it as a lighthearted tease. "I'll need your help."

Even knowing how difficult the algebra was for him, he had been unable to attend to the day's lesson, distracted by watching Mr. Bonne and Dakota. Each seemed intent on ignoring the other and not acknowledging that anything had happened between them. Their perfect aloofness was far more distracting to Parker than their arguing or sniping at each other or Dakota continuing to flirt with Mr. Bonne would have been. He kept looking at them, waiting for the fireworks, and they continued to ignore each other and him, as if it were a perfectly normal class and nothing at all had happened.

"Parker. *Parker!*"

"Oh. Sorry, what?"

"Sheesh, you are a space cadet today. What's going on with you?"

"Sorry."

"Where do you want to go do our schoolwork? Somewhere we can have some privacy…?"

Parker swallowed. He wasn't sure if she meant *privacy* or just privacy from stalker ex-boyfriends and curious siblings or parents.

"You want to go to the library?" he suggested.

"No… I was hoping for somewhere more private than that."

The smile twitching at the corners of her mouth suggested the answer to Parker's question. *Privacy.*

"You want to go to the park again?" he suggested. "Are you up for a walk?"

Dakota looked at him for a long minute, her lids half-lowered. He could see that she had applied some kind of shimmery eye shadow, but he wasn't certain of the shade. It made her eyes look bigger and exotic. His heart pounded harder while he waited for her response.

"Maybe," she teased.

"Maybe? Does that mean you want to or not? Yes or no?"

"Patience." She considered. "I don't want to run into… you know who. He wouldn't be able to find us there. No one would know where we were and we could do what we wanted. But…"

Parker was getting really antsy trying to figure out what she was getting at. "But what?"

"Parker… me and you…" she trailed off.

"What?"

"We have to be careful. You know people already look at us. I don't think you get that… people think it's wrong, you and me getting together."

Parker blinked. "People think it's wrong?"

"I know you're color-blind," she teased, "but other people aren't, and they don't like mixed-race couples."

"So what?"

"Maybe you don't know what that kind of hate is like. But I do."

"I can handle it. Anyone who says anything…"

Dakota looked significantly at his cast. "I don't think you're going to be challenging anyone to a fist fight! Look, it's more than that… it's not just the racists…"

Parker waited for further explanation.

"People can't know that the two of us are, uh… getting together. I mean it. You can't be telling your friends, or acting like a couple in public, or letting your mom know. It's important."

"I don't care what people think."

"Then you're stupid. You should care. And I care. Especially about your mom. So please, listen to me. Trust me on this one, because I know. *People can't know.*"

"Okay… people can't know. It's not like I'm going around bragging to everyone; I'm not that kind of guy. If you don't want me to talk about it, I won't."

Link already knew, but Parker trusted him to stay quiet. Link kept to himself. They didn't need to worry that he was going to be broadcasting Parker and Dakota's intimate details over social media. Or telling Mona about it. He was a quiet, serious kid. Kind of nerdy. And he knew to keep his mouth shut. Even when he was a little kid, he'd known how to keep a secret. He wasn't the kind who broadcast it as soon as you told him 'don't tell anyone.'

Dakota nodded. She started walking away. Parker hurriedly got his books out of his locker and raced after her.

When they were outside, Dakota looked around carefully. Parker knew that she was looking for the young black man. Her stalker ex-boyfriend. Parker didn't see the tall, slim young black anywhere.

Dakota blew out her breath. She looked over at him, as if waiting for him to put his arm around her, attempt to kiss her, or some other public display of affection that she had just warned him about. But Parker just stood there, waiting. Dakota gave him a quick smile and nod.

"Okay. Let's go."

He went slowly so that she wouldn't get tired or out of breath. They were both watching for the stalker, trying to be covert about it and not let on that they were. But the tension was there. They both knew. Parker touched Dakota's back as they walked, then remembered and dropped his arm, leaving space around her.

"This guy," he said. "Did you go with him for long? You guys were… serious?"

"Yeah. I left him… but he won't let me go. Keeps trying to hold onto me."

"Did you tell him to just leave you alone? That you weren't interested?"

"I left him, Parker. Packed my stuff and cleared out. You think he didn't understand the message?"

"I'm just saying… maybe he thinks he just has to try harder. Win you back. Maybe if you talked to him, explained that you've moved on and he needs to too…" Parker was thinking about his father. Mona always said afterward that if she had just talked with him—sat down and explained things to him calmly—maybe the outcome would have been different. But they both knew it wouldn't have made any difference.

Dakota shook her head vigorously. "Are you ever naive. I'm never talking to him again. I don't want anything to do with him. I'm not going to sit down and have a nice little chat with him."

"Well, maybe I should, then. I could tell him that you're with someone else now…"

"You? Oh, that would go over well. He would break you in half like a toothpick!"

They walked in silence for a while. Dakota didn't remember the way as they entered the pathways, and Parker redirected her, leading the way to their little patch of paradise.

"I been with so many abusive guys," Dakota said. "I've tried talking. I've talked myself hoarse. I've cried my eyes out. They tell you that everything will change. They talk you into staying. They always tell you they'll stop. And they never do. And S—he wouldn't either. You have to just leave, break it off nice and clean and leave everybody behind. Because otherwise… you just can't ever get out."

"How many guys like that have there been?" Or was she making that up too?

"I don't know. It's like I attract them. They see me, and they know they can hurt me. I don't know."

"I wouldn't ever hurt you. I don't understand how anyone ever could."

Dakota looked at him. They were in the trees, out of sight of any observers. She took his hand briefly and gave it a squeeze.

"I know, Parker. But when you're older… a grown man… that's all going to change."

"You really think I'm going to change that much? That I'm going to turn into a completely different person?"

"No… plenty of guys are still nice on the outside. You can't tell any different. It's just… something changes inside. Addictions… the way their dads hurt them… something changes, Parker. Men are hard inside. They're… explosive."

"Not me."

"No. Not you… not now. Not *yet*."

He didn't know how to convince her otherwise. Did she really think that all men were like that?

Dakota was watching him carefully. "You know what? I never hear you talk about your dad. Like, ever."

Parker stared off into the trees. It was so beautiful and green. He hated the people who left litter beside the pathway. How hard was it to hold onto your garbage until you reached a garbage can? People should care about keeping the environment clean and healthy and nice for everyone else.

"Parker? Did you hear what I said?"

"Yeah. You didn't ask a question."

"Do I gotta?"

"We're just about there."

"Where's your dad?"

Parker eyed the path ahead of him, watching for roots, rocks, or other obstacles. The small branching trail that would lead to their glade was just up ahead.

"My dad's dead."

"Yeah? Do you remember him? You must, 'cause your little sisters wouldn't have been born until you were old enough. Unless they've got a different dad."

"I remember him." Parker took Dakota by the hand to lead her onto the branching pathway, but soon had to let go of her so they could make their way through the growth in single file.

She didn't plonk down on the grass like she had the other day. She stood face-to-face with him in the clearing, putting her hands palm-to-palm with his. She slid her fingers between his, and clasped his hands.

"What was he like, your dad?"

Parker swallowed. Her question made it hard to breathe. "I am not my dad."

"No, but he lives inside of you. That's who you're going to grow up to be like. Some girl crosses you, and that's gonna come out, and you're gonna go off on her just like your dad would have."

"You don't know anything about my dad. And it doesn't matter, because I'm not him." Her words hit too close to his own secret fears. "I don't have to become anyone. I can make my own choices."

"Tell me about him, then."

"No."

"You've heard me talk about my parents, the other folks who took care of me. You won't talk to me about one person?"

"That's not what we're here for." Parker sat down on the ground and opened up his backpack. "Are we going to do this first?"

Dakota looked down at him, her lips pointing down. "What's the big secret? You're afraid to tell me what he was like? That I'm going to think less of you? Or of your mom? I don't blame you for what your dad was like."

No, but she thought Parker would become him. And Parker would never become him. He would never hurt someone he loved. And he would never, ever make them hurt him back.

"Algebra?" Parker pointed to it.

Dakota sat down with a grumble. She shuffled over so that she was sitting against him, their legs touching, while she looked at his schoolwork. Her proximity distracted Parker from the algebra before they even started.

Maybe the plan to do homework in their special spot had been a mistake.

Chapter Fourteen

D AKOTA WAS STANDING OUTSIDE the school doors with her girlfriends when Parker got there. The girls saw him and started to giggle. He shook his head and kept going, but Dakota motioned for him to stop and come over.

Usually, when she was hanging with her friends, she didn't want him bugging her. Parker approached warily. Dakota made a motion to him, holding one of her little cigarettes between two fingers.

"Parkinson, what d'ya say we skip today?"

He looked around for any teachers or supervisors who might overhear, and then looked back at Dakota. While the question was not unwelcome, he was nervous of the girls standing there giggling at him. Was it a set-up? He'd say yes, and then she'd mock him for something in front of her friends? But for what? The girls were on the rebellious side, girls who would skip if they had an excuse to.

Parker raised his brows. "Works for me. What do you want to do?"

"Open to suggestions."

They stood there looking at each other. Charity giggled again. Parker switched his gaze to her.

"What's your problem?"

She gave him a big smile. "I don't have a problem."

"What are you laughing at?"

"Nothing. I'm just happy."

Parker looked back at Dakota again. "Something I should know about?"

She shook her head. "No. I was just saying we had trouble getting algebra homework done. I don't want to tell Mr. Bonne we didn't do it, so maybe we should take the day off today, and get it done."

"Get the algebra done?"

"Yeah. Maybe we could do *that* too."

Parker felt the blood rushing to his face. After she had made such a big deal to him about not telling anyone about their relationship or letting people think they were a couple, she was telling—or at least implying—to her friends what had happened during their aborted homework session in the park.

He strove mightily to keep his voice even and unconcerned. "So you want to go to your house to get that algebra finished? We should get out of here before someone notices us."

Dakota gave a nod to her friends as she stubbed her cigarette out. Charity and Addy both giggled. Parker rolled his eyes. He was supposed to be mature and discreet, but Dakota could be as careless as she liked. And those girls would probably spread everything they knew all over the school.

They had a lazy morning at Jade's house. Jade was apparently gone for a couple of days to visit an out-of-town sister and Dakota had the house to herself. They did eventually put some effort into getting the algebra homework done, and Parker felt less stressed about having something ready to hand in. He did his best to be a good student and didn't like falling behind. Math was getting to be more and more of a struggle for him, but with Dakota's help, he could work his way through it and at least hand in something halfway decent.

"We need drinks," Dakota said, getting up off the couch where they were cuddling and watching kiddie cartoons.

"Actually, we could probably really use some lunch!" Parker said, looking at the time on his phone. He grabbed for his backpack to get out his lunch bag. "You got something you can warm up?"

"No, no. Liquid lunch for me."

"Trying to lose weight?" Parker asked. Then he saw she was getting a bottle of wine, not Slim-Fast. "Oh. That kind of liquid lunch."

"You're so naive sometimes. Parker Parkinson." She was already being silly and hadn't even started drinking yet.

"We don't need that. We're having a good time without it, aren't we?"

Dakota gave him a broad smile. "I know I am," she agreed.

"Then let's not drink. We'll find something else on TV, or go hang out somewhere else if you're too bored here."

"Nah. Let's not."

Parker started to unwrap his first sandwich. He looked down at it. "You remember that first day…?"

"Yeah. Of course I do. Man, I was so hungry. That little sandwich was gone in two bites. I was *so* hungry."

"You want one?" he held it out to her slightly.

"Nope. Don't need one today."

Parker took a bite. It was dry and tasteless. He was angry at her for insisting on drinking and ruining the good time they were having. Wasn't she the one who had been talking about how drinking made people behave? If she knew it could result in abuse and injuries, why would she choose to even get close to the stuff?

"Don't look at me like that," Dakota said defensively. "You don't know what it's like to live my life."

"What, this…?" Parker made a gesture to indicate their surroundings. "I get a pretty good picture. You're not exactly suffering."

"That's what it's like outside. You got no clue what it's like in here." Dakota tapped her head. "What's wrong with a few drinks? Everybody drinks."

"I don't like the way it makes you sick. Or changes your behavior. I know… I've seen what it can do to people. Like you said before, it makes people lose control. Makes them hurt other people."

"Your dad…?" she prodded. She took a long swig directly from the bottle. So much for slowing her down and helping her to think the decision through.

"No, not my dad," Parker lied, not wanting her to bring him back up again. "I've got friends. I've seen what's happened in their families."

"Uh-huh." Dakota's tone was doubtful. He didn't know how she could see through him quite so clearly. He'd never said anything to her about his father, or any issues he might have had. Maybe she was just pulling it out of the air. Or maybe Jade had said something to her. Jade had been in the neighborhood since Parker was a little kid. She knew everything that had happened in the Jurek household. All of the history that Parker would rather forget.

Dakota returned to the couch and snuggled up next to him. Parker worked on his sandwich and watched the TV. Dakota nudged him, holding the mouth of the bottle in front of his face.

"No, it's okay," Parker said, pushing it aside with the back of his hand. "You have it."

She moved it back closer, just about touching his lips. The sweet, fermented odor tickled Parker's nose and brought memories flooding back. He didn't want anything to do with it.

"Just take one little sip," Dakota coaxed. "I'm not saying get buzzed, if you don't want to. Just have a little taste. So I'm not drinking by myself." Dakota smiled invitingly, fluttering her eyelids at him.

Parker hesitated, then shook his head. Dakota leaned back in the couch and raised the bottle up, taking a couple of swallows. She leaned closer, so she was whispering in his ear.

"How about this, then? No more making out unless you take a drink."

Parker looked at her, then back at the TV, pretending to be engrossed by the cartoons that hadn't interested him since he was six years old. Dakota didn't leave him alone for long. She started to tickle his ear and neck, driving him crazy. Parker couldn't ignore it. He laughed and turned toward her, reaching for her. But the bottle was between their faces.

"A drink first."

Frustrated, Parker took the bottle by the neck and put it up to his lips. He took a small sip and let the sweet wine work its way down his throat and into his stomach. It was barely a mouthful. Not enough to affect him. He put the bottle onto the side table and raised his brows at Dakota. He had completed his part of the deal, it was time for hers. Dakota obligingly pulled him in close for a kiss. But in a moment, she was pulling back from him again. Parker looked at her in consternation, wondering if he had done something wrong. Or maybe her phone had vibrated or she had to sneeze.

Dakota nodded to the bottle. "Give me another sip."

He rolled his eyes and handed it to her. She took a couple of swallows and handed it back to him.

"You too," she insisted, when he reached to put it back down without having any himself.

Parker took another quick sip, barely enough to wet his lips, and put it aside again. Dakota smiled, and they continued to exchange kisses for wine.

Parker moved sluggishly, trying to remember where he was and what he was doing there. He couldn't focus on what day of the week it was, or what he was doing there in the strange living room. But it wasn't a strange living room. It was one that was completely familiar. Jade's.

And Jade was standing over him, shaking him and saying something, but she had been drinking and her words were indistinct. Or maybe there was something wrong with Parker's head or his ears. He tried to sit up straight and to rub his eyes. He couldn't get his hand up to his eyes, and it took a few tries before he saw the brightly colored cast that was apparently keeping him from bending his arm properly to rub his eyes. He had to settle for rubbing them with his left hand, which was awkward and not quite as satisfying.

"Parker! Come on, wake up." Jade continued to shake Parker. The movement made his head spin, and he groaned at her to stop.

He could hear Dakota's voice somewhere nearby. Was she singing? Maybe she was just whining about Jade coming home and interrupting them when she was supposed to be visiting with her sister. Or was it the next day already? Parker tried to pin something down in his whirling thoughts. How long had they been at Jade's? Had he gone home to bed? Forgotten to go home? Mona wasn't going to be happy with him if he'd been away all night.

"What time is it?" Parker demanded. "What day?" The words came out all mushy and slurred together.

"Get up off your butt. You need to go home."

"He just fell asleep," Dakota was protesting. "Just give him a minute to wake up, he'll be just fine."

"Are you supposed to have him over here while you're by yourself?" Jade demanded. "You knew that was against the rules. No boys around without a chaperone. I trusted you to follow the rules while I went out of town."

"He just came over after school. For a couple minutes. He was tired from school."

There was a ringing slap that startled Parker, making him go rigid for a minute while he tried to sort out the sensory signals. It took a minute to confirm to himself that he wasn't the one who had been slapped.

"Do you think I can't tell that both of you are drunk? Do you really think you can hide how hammered you are?"

"I'm sorry! I didn't… I didn't mean for that to happen. I just thought we'd have one drink. Get kind of mellowed out…"

"Look at him, Dakota! He's fourteen, and he's less than half your bodyweight. He can't drink like that! And you know you're not supposed to be drinking in this house. We've had *that* discussion before too!"

"I *know* how old he is," Dakota muttered.

"Do you? Do you really? I don't think you realize how much trouble you could be in for something like this!"

"It's nothing. It was just a coupla drinks. I won't do it again." Dakota moved closer to Parker, into the limited range of his foggy, blurred vision. "Come on, Parker. Get your head working and tell her. It wasn't anything. Just a couple of drinks, we were just having a couple of drinks together."

Jade pushed Dakota back. "Stay away from him. You've done more than enough already. You want to be the one to call his mother and let her know?"

"I'm not calling no one," Dakota said sulkily.

"Someone has to call her and tell her what's been going on."

Dakota's arms were crossed over her chest. "Not me."

"Then you'd better go have a shower and get yourself cleaned up. I want you in your jammies and ready for bed at nine-thirty."

Dakota left the room, muttering under her breath about how she wasn't a freaking baby. Jade had stopped shaking Parker, and he just let himself doze a little bit while she made a phone call and busied herself with other jobs around the house. He wasn't awake enough to know what she was doing. The shower went on, and Parker laughed to himself, listening to Dakota banging around the shower, occasionally swearing or shouting some complaint out to Jade.

The front door opened with a whoosh of air. Parker pulled the fuzzy blanket he and Dakota had been sharing farther up to his neck.

It was Mona. Parker sensed her presence even before she started swearing, standing over him, her voice shrill.

"Mona!" Jade hurried into the room. She attempted to give Mona a hug of greeting, but was brushed aside with an angry gesture. "Mona, I'm so sorry! They were supposed to be at school. I didn't know they would skip and come back here to an empty house."

"I got a call," Mona said. "I didn't know where he had gone. I tried his cell, but they're not going to answer when they're cutting classes. I supposed it could just as easily have been at my house."

"But it wasn't, it was mine. I was responsible for making sure that Dakota was behaving herself and that I was here to supervise when she had someone over. I'm so sorry."

Mona wiped at her nose. "Where did they get the alcohol?"

Jade picked up bottles that clinked together. "I'm sorry to say, it was here. I shouldn't have had alcohol in the house. Not when I knew she had a problem…"

Mona shook her head, her face all tight and sour. She nudged Parker. "Parker Andrew Jurek! It's time to go home! Get your butt in the car."

Full name. Alarm bells rang. Parker struggled to sit up, eyes blurry, head spinning. "Mom…?"

"Up. On your feet."

Parker slid the blanket off and rubbed his eyes again with his left hand. He didn't normally drink coffee, but he thought that he could probably use one. His thoughts were slushy and movements slow. He needed to get some sleep or some caffeine. Jade had said that it was bedtime, so maybe he was just tired.

"Where is your shirt?" Mona enunciated each word separately, like each was a sentence by itself.

Parker felt around on the couch. He felt his chest, naked and smooth, with just a peach fuzz of hair starting to come in, only visible with just the right light and angle. He was not wearing a shirt and couldn't remember what had happened to it. Had he been wearing one when he arrived at Jade's? He must have put one on for school in the morning.

Jade moved the blanket around, until she found Parker's shirt and handed it to him. Parker looked for the sleeves and head hole, but couldn't seem to sort out the right direction for each to go in, and was sure something was backward or inside out. Mona snatched it out of his hands. She shoved it down over his head, folding his ears and scraping his right one with one of her rings.

"Ow! Careful, Mom…" Parker complained.

"You're not the one to be telling me to be careful right now," she snapped back. She stretched the shirt around to get Parker's casted arm through one sleeve, and then pulled his other hand through the other sleeve, like she was dressing a toddler.

"There. Now stand up."

He tried a couple of times to rise up off the couch. Then he tried to push himself up. The room kept shifting and his head was too wobbly to find a position where the floor stayed firm under his feet. Mona grabbed his arm and coaxed him to his feet, holding on to him to keep him steady.

"Do up your fly."

Parker was staring off into space, watching the shapes and shadows that shifted with the room.

"Parker!"

"What?"

"Your fly."

He stared at the ceiling, looking for it. "What fly?"

"Pull up your zipper."

Her words gradually sank in. Parker clutched at his pants, fishing for it, but couldn't find the tiny tab with his too thick, numb fingers. Mona let go of his arm briefly to push his fingers out of the way and zip it up herself, then she fastened the button with a quick movement.

"I'm sorry," Jade repeated. "I'm so sorry."

"We'll have to figure out what we're going to do about it later. Right now, I've got to get him home."

"Do you think…"

"What?"

"I wonder if you should take him to the hospital."

Mona shook her head briskly. "He can just sleep it off."

"We don't know how much alcohol he has in his system. He could get alcohol poisoning. And… I don't know if you want to press charges…"

Mona was still for a moment, looking at Jade. Then she shook her head. "No. Just keep her away from him."

She pulled Parker toward the door.

"My schoolwork." Parker looked around for his backpack.

Jade slid Parker's books back into his bag and handed the bag to Mona. She pulled him out of the house and helped him navigate carefully down the front steps, keeping him from falling and re-breaking his nose. Or breaking his other arm.

"Mom…"

"What?"

"Mom… I don't feel good…"

"No, I don't imagine you do."

"I'm gonna hafta puke…"

She stopped. "Well then, you'd better do it here and not in the car."

"Okay."

Parker turned around and woofed into Jade's carefully-maintained rosebushes. He wiped his mouth. Mona waited.

"Are you done?"

"Can I go to sleep now?" The green grass looked soft and inviting.

"No!" Mona yanked on Parker's arm as his knees started to buckle. "Get in the car. Over here. Come on."

Once she had pushed Parker into the car and buckled him in, she went around her own side and started the car.

"No kissing after you throw up," Parker told her. "That's just gross."

Chapter Fifteen

P ARKER WOKE UP ON the couch as Mona got everyone up to get ready for school. His head pounded and pulsed and he felt nauseated, the taste of vomit from the night before still sour in his mouth.

"Hear you had some excitement yesterday," Link commented, giving Parker a nudge.

Parker sat up with his head in his hand, trying to figure out how he was going to get ready for school. He'd already missed one day, so Mona wasn't going to let him miss another. At least his algebra was done. Parker snorted at the thought. Link thought he was gagging.

"Don't be sick out here. Do you need a bowl?"

"No. I'm okay."

"You are gonna be grounded for the rest of your life."

"Yeah," Parker sighed. "Things didn't work out exactly like I had planned."

"Like you planned? What exactly did you plan?" Link laughed.

"I dunno… just to hang out. Miss a class or two. Get my schoolwork done. Nobody would know the difference."

"Well, you blew that all to hell," Link agreed.

"Link," Mona called, seeing that he was talking to Parker instead of getting ready for school. "Leave your brother and get ready, please. I don't want you to be late."

Link waved a hand at her and dashed to the bathroom as Sophie came out. Mona stopped in front of Parker and he was forced to look up at her to see what she wanted. She handed him a couple of aspirin and a glass of water.

"You'll need to drink a lot today to get rehydrated. The more dehydrated you are, the worse you will feel."

Parker swallowed the pills and got down as much of the water as he could before his stomach started to protest at the sloshing.

"And you need to eat something little. Aspirin is bad on an empty stomach."

He wished she had told him that part before giving them to him. He might not have taken them. Food was the last thing he wanted.

"A little food might help the nausea, too. Just a few crackers or a piece of toast."

Parker nodded. "Okay. Thanks, Mom."

"You and I are going to have to have a long talk about this."

"I already know I messed up. Just give me my punishment."

"This is a lot bigger than you think."

"No, I know it is. I'm not going to drink again, Mom. I… I didn't mean to this time. I just… I thought a couple of swallows wouldn't make that much of a difference, and then she'd… I won't do it again. No matter what she says. No matter what anyone says. It's stupid and I feel sick, and I don't want to do that again."

She sat down on the couch next to him. "You need to stay away from Dakota. And I don't just mean don't let me see you with her. I mean *really*. She's bad news. She's not good for you. You're… not mature enough for this kind of a relationship. I know you're growing up and getting interested in girls. But you can't do this. You need to wait until you're older. You stay clear of her."

"We're in the same classes at school."

"I know you can't help that. But you can help what you do before and after school. And while school is going on. If you're in your class in your desk and she's in hers, that's one thing. If you're alone in a hall or empty classroom, or under the bleachers, that's another thing. Do *not* be alone with her. Ever."

"Mom…"

"I know. You think I'm being stupid. That I'm overreacting. But you don't understand the consequences. Either one of you could end up in jail. She could get pregnant. You could get a disease. Something that could be with you for the rest of your life. Things like that change the course of your life forever. One little mistake, and everything you have planned for your future could be gone. Don't take the chance."

"I'll be okay, Mom."

"Don't tell me that. Tell me you'll stay away from her."

"I'll be careful. I'll be okay," Parker said stubbornly. "Nothing is going to happen."

Parker avoided the door that he figured Dakota would be at with her friends, smoking or gossiping. He wondered what she would have told her friends about the previous day. Would she think it was funny? Be proud of herself for getting Parker drunk? Would they all be laughing at him? He didn't want to see Dakota or her friends until things had had a chance to blow over. But of course, that wasn't going to be possible with them in the same class. Parker went in one of the other doors, got his books from his locker, and went into the classroom where his own friends were hanging out and talking.

They went quiet at his approach. Not just Chris and Adrian, but everyone in the room. Parker rolled his eyes toward the ceiling. Obviously, word was out. He hadn't even logged on to his social networks, so he didn't know how bad it was. Compromising pictures? Intimate details? Polls? He suppressed a shudder and slid into his chair, dropping his books onto the desk.

"Hey," Adrian greeted, voice subdued.

"Hey. What's up?"

Adrian shrugged. "Nothing with me. You… feeling okay today?"

Parker's head was pounding, his stomach roiling, and he felt far from fine. But he put on a stoic face and didn't reveal any of that.

"Yeah, fine. What'd I miss yesterday?"

Adrian's face relaxed, and he and Chris pulled out their books to run through the details. Mr. Bonne walked into the room. The bell hadn't rung yet, so the boys ignored him. He stopped and looked at Parker for a minute. He looked as if he weren't sure what to do. He went over to his desk and sat down.

"Parker, can I see you for a moment?"

Parker got up slowly from his desk, looking at the other boys for their sympathies, and went over to Mr. Bonne's desk.

"Yes?"

"You and Dakota missed yesterday. Everything okay?"

"Yeah. We're fine. I'm fine, I mean."

"Do you have a note from the doctor or your mom?"

Parker stared down at Mr. Bonne's pencil jar. "No."

"You don't have a note?"

"My mom wouldn't write one. I… I cut classes."

"I see. You really can't afford to do that, Parker. Not if you're going to keep up with the class. Your marks are already suffering. Especially in math."

"Dakota's helping me with the math. She's really good." Maybe he shouldn't have said that, when she had claimed not so long ago that she was having problems with the math. But Mr. Bonne had seen through that ruse. He knew how well she did on her homework.

"Dakota is not helping you by taking you away from class. I want you to stay after school so we can run through some of the work together. Without her."

"You have to prepare for your classes," Parker pointed out. "Mark assignments."

"I need to help a student who is struggling." He didn't say anything about Parker's relationship with Dakota, but it was all there. It was in his eyes and in the words he carefully avoided saying. How much did he know about what had happened? Surely it hadn't spread to the teachers too.

"Umm, okay," Parker said, as the bell rang and the rest of the students filed into the classroom. "I'll stay after."

"Good. Thank you."

Parker went back to his desk and Mr. Bonne got up to give the day's announcements. Parker avoided looking at Dakota or any of her friends. He got out his agenda and his books for the first class, luckily not math. But while Mr. Bonne made announcements, Parker hid his phone behind a textbook and turned it on.

Checking Dakota's stream, he was glad to see no pictures of himself. Though, of course, she might have blocked them from showing up on his timeline. He'd have to get one of the other boys to check for him later. Or maybe he just didn't want to know. He looked at the other comments in Dakota's timeline. Not just at the cute stuff and selfies that she posted, but also at the comments she had made on other people's posts or timelines. She had told him at the library that she needed to have others in hand who could help her when Jade decided to kick her out. And considering Dakota's behavior, that might not be very far off. Digging into her comments, he could see the women she was grooming.

I wish I had someone I could trust

If I could get away from here, I would come c u

Do you know where a kid can go to get off the street?

Parker followed a few of the women so that he would see the posts that went back and forth between them in his own timeline.

The phone was pulled out of his hand. Parker looked up at Mr. Bonne, swearing weakly.

"Sorry, Mr. Bonne."

"We'll talk about this after school."

Parker ducked his head, blushing furiously. Mr. Bonne dropped Parker's phone into the 'Jail Cell' basket on his desk, and went back up to the front to continue his announcements and begin the day's lessons. Parker got sympathetic glances from his friends. They all knew how crippling it was to be without a phone the whole day. Even if he couldn't use it in class, he could normally still use it between classes, over the lunch hour, and any other non-class time he could carve out.

Parker didn't intend to look over at Dakota. He had been studiously avoiding even looking in her direction to see whether she was there or not. Even though he knew by hearing her voice and her whispers and giggles with the other girls that she was there. He didn't mean to look over at her, but when he did, she shook her head at him, as if shocked that he would use his phone during class. She had on a self-righteous expression like his mother would probably have worn, had she been there. *We are here to learn, not to play on our phones.*

Parker looked back away from her, grinding his teeth.

Normally, Parker sat with his guy friends at lunch and Dakota sat with her girl friends. They didn't socialize with each other or look or act like a couple. That was what Dakota had wanted. So he was more than a little surprised when Dakota came over and sat across from him.

"I know you're supposed to be avoiding me," Dakota said candidly. "Well, this way, you're doing all you can. You can't help it if I come over and sit with you without being invited."

Parker opened his mouth to argue, to tell her to leave. Then he thought better of it. It was probably best just to let her have her own way. As she had said, Mona couldn't fault him for letting her sit with him at lunch. And Parker wasn't supposed to be being romantic with her in public, so what could it hurt?

"Sit where you like," he said curtly. "It's a free country."

"Oh, it's a free country. That's an original line."

For a while, they ate in silence. The conversation that had been flowing between Parker and his friends before Dakota had shown up had shut off. Everyone watched Parker and Dakota awkwardly.

"How are you feeling?" Dakota solicited.

Parker raised his eyes to her. "Like crap."

"Yeah? I have a remedy that could help you…"

He could well imagine what her remedy was. "I'll stick with aspirin. Thanks."

"Aspirin isn't good for you. You know it can make your stomach bleed? And same with Tylenol, it's really bad for your liver."

"Unlike alcohol."

The boys sitting nearby all chuckled.

"Oooh, burn!" one of them intoned.

"Well, I wouldn't want a hole in my stomach or liver problems," Dakota said primly, ignoring his response. "So I stay away from that stuff."

"I don't need anything. Thanks."

She looked at him for a moment, trying to decide how to react. She took a sip of her juice. "You want to trade one sandwich for half a pizza?" she suggested, indicating her own lunch.

Who wouldn't? Parker loved pizza. Especially the salty, greasy, overprocessed crap that the cafeteria sold. But he stubbornly shook his head. He was mad at her, and that meant he wasn't going to share his lunch with her. He couldn't stop her from sitting there, but he could eat his own damn lunch, dry and boring as it was. He shook his head and continued to eat his sandwich.

Dakota snorted and took a big bite of the pizza. "Mmmm. It's just so good! After a morning of stupid schoolwork, there's nothing like a hot pizza for lunch."

Parker ignored this. They ignored each other.

"What happened to your arms?" Chris asked.

Parker looked at his cast, bewildered as to why Chris would ask that when he knew exactly how Parker had broken his arm. Then he realized Chris was looking at Dakota's arms.

Parker had noticed the scars on her arms before. It was pretty hard to miss them, especially in the short-sleeved t-shirts she often wore. But any time he had focused on them or tried to ask her about them, she had simply waved the questions away with, 'That was a long time ago.'

And they did look like old scars, not anything new. Not from the last few years. Maybe she had been in an accident as a child. Or, he hated to consider it, one of the abusive families that she had spoken of had intentionally hurt her.

Dakota looked at Chris over her pizza. She lowered her gaze to her arms, as if she didn't know what he was talking about. It was kind of rude to ask someone you didn't know very well about their scars or personal appearance.

"I used to cut," Dakota said finally. "A long time ago. When I was a t—when I was little."

"Like, self-mutilation?" Chris said, his eyes wide. They were all looking at the scars. Some of them were obviously very deep. Had Dakota really done that herself? It seemed impossible. Maybe it was just another story, and the scars were really from a car accident. Or a fire.

"Yeah. I cut because of all the nasty stuff that was happening to me. To… get away from it and make myself feel better." She shrugged. "Lots of people do it." She took another bite of her pizza. "Now, I like other forms of anesthesia better."

Dakota was waiting for Parker after his detention/tutoring session with Mr. Bonne, just like he had waited for her after hers. Mr. Bonne had had curiously little to say about Dakota or Parker's relationship with her, which suited Parker just fine. He was tired of people trying to interfere with them. They had spent most of the time on math, and only a few brief minutes had been spent on a lecture on not using his phone during class and on trying to get back on track again academically.

Parker saw Dakota when he stepped out of the classroom. He stopped, not sure what to do.

"I'm not supposed to be hanging around with you," he said.

"And I'm supposed to be staying away from you," Dakota said, her full lips pulled up in a smile. "But you know what? No one can stop us from associating with each other."

And since Parker didn't really want to stop seeing Dakota, he found it hard to argue the point. Parker got his books sorted out at his locker and they walked out together.

"Parkinson…" It seemed like a long time since she had called him that last. "I'm sorry about yesterday, okay? I didn't mean for you to get so wasted. I never meant to do that. Just a little tipsy. I just didn't want to drink alone."

"You got me in big-time trouble."

"Yeah. Me too. I'm still holding my breath about whether Jade's gonna kick me out or not. She told me if I couldn't follow the rules, she would… and this is a pretty big mistake…" Dakota swore and shook her head. "You should hear her going on about it. How she should call the police and put me in jail, and how you're the best kid ever and I'm corrupting you. Mona is her best friend and now she probably won't even talk to Jade…"

"Jade wouldn't really call the police, would she?"

"I don't think so. I think she'd just kick me out. Maybe put me on a bus with a one-way ticket. I dunno. Pretty sure she wouldn't put me in jail."

"I'd tell them it was my idea. That you weren't forcing me to do anything."

Dakota gave Parker a long look. She touched his cheek lightly, her fingers vibrating. "How did I get myself into this? This is so wrong, Parker. I never meant to… I never meant us to be anything more than friends. I never meant to hurt you."

He tried to hold her hand, but she pulled away. "You didn't hurt me. I'm just fine. I'm a big boy, and I knew what I was getting into." Although… he hadn't intended to get drunk or get his mom so mad at him. He knew how worried Mona was going to be about him all the time now. He couldn't remember a lot of what had happened when she had come over to pick him up from Jade's, but it was enough to know that she was going to be super pissed at him.

Weren't romantic relationships supposed to be pleasant? Weren't both of them supposed to feel good and be happy together? So far the relationship had brought them little more than trouble. Not Romeo-and-Juliet type trouble. No one was getting killed over it. But Dakota looked miserable and Parker was feeling pretty rotten.

They went down the stairs to the main floor. Parker slowed down, as Dakota was dragging behind.

"Come on," he encouraged, surprising himself with how depressed and defeated his voice sounded.

They got out of the school and stood on the steps for a moment blinking in the bright sunlight. Dakota swore and grabbed Parker's arm, then let go of him like she'd been burned. Parker looked around, worried about Dakota's stalker ex-boyfriend. He hadn't even been thinking about what would happen if the guy came to school looking for Dakota. It would be the logical place to look for her, wouldn't it? Should he call 9-1-1? Fight the older boy with one arm already broken? If it had been TV, he could have used his casted arm as a weapon. But he had a feeling that in real life, that would hurt him more than his assailant.

But it wasn't the angry stalker ex who stood outside of the school watching for them. It was worse. It was Mona. Normally, she wasn't off of work yet, which meant that she had left early in order to meet Parker at the school. And instead of finding that Parker was following the rules and staying away from Dakota, she caught them leaving the deserted school late, nearly arm-in-arm.

Dakota swore again, stepping back. "I didn't touch him!" she shouted. "I haven't done anything, so you just leave me alone!"

Mona gave Parker a glare that made his stomach shrivel up into a small, hard pit, and motioned for him to go to her side. "If you don't stay away from my son, I will have you arrested." Her voice was an even, reasonable tone, but the sounds were so clipped it was obvious she was barely able to keep her fury under control. "Do I need to take out a restraining order to do that?"

"Mom!" Parker was horrified. Dakota was sweating, her eyes wild. "Just leave her alone. She didn't do anything."

"I told you to come straight home. Where should you be right now?"

"I had to stay after. So Mr. Bonne could help me with my math."

She nodded, apparently believing that. "And I told you to stay away from *her*."

"She's my friend and we have the same classes. I'm not going to stay away from her."

"You will stay away from her if you want any privileges. Or maybe I should send you away. To your grandparents."

Mona's parents were both dead and gone. And Parker would never go to his father's family. He would be out on the streets like Dakota before he would go to them. Perhaps Mona saw this rebellious thought in Parker's face, because she didn't carry the threat any further.

"You are grounded until further notice. That means if you have to stay late after school, you have to call me and let me talk to the teacher. Otherwise, you are straight home and you call me from the landline. You are not allowed to go to anyone's house or out wandering the neighborhood. And you are not allowed to have anyone over. And the others *will* keep me informed."

"You're treating me like a criminal! I haven't done anything."

She gave his arm a jerk to get him moving toward the car, turning her back on Dakota and walking away as if she weren't even there.

"You're going to try that line on me?" she challenged. "You didn't do anything?"

Parker's brain whirled, trying to come up with an argument. He knew it was wrong of her to be so strict with him. He had only been following his heart. She had taught him to be compassionate and to treat other people with respect. Not to be racist or judgmental of other people's problems. Walk a mile in their shoes. But he couldn't quite reach the argument that he needed to show her that he had been doing the right thing all along. Even if he had made mistakes on the way, his heart had been in the right place, and he hadn't done anything quite that bad.

"In the car," Mona ordered, motioning. "And I don't want to hear a peep from you. Not one argument."

Chapter Sixteen

HOWEVER MUCH PARKER'S MOM might have wanted to completely get rid of Dakota and her influence, there was nothing she could do to keep them from seeing each other at school unless she decided to report Dakota to the police. And she hadn't pushed it that far. They stayed for a while in a sort of a ceasefire, with Parker doing the best he could to follow the rules and not give Mona any reason to punish him longer than necessary, and with her just watching and waiting for Parker to make his next move.

At school, one of the subjects that Parker hated the most—not because it was hard like math, but because it was easy and worthless and nobody ever failed it—was Career and Life Management. All of the little moral rules that the school or government wanted to communicate to their young people. Anti-drug, anti-bullying, talk it out, plan for the future. Everybody already knew everything they were being taught. They had been taught it in 'Health' or other formats since they started school. It was in public service announcements and after-school programs on the TV. It was at church, and in family discussions, and everywhere else.

But Parker was anticipating the day's class. Previously, Mr. Bonne had walked them all through the instructions for filling out the job skills survey that he had passed out to them in sealed test booklets. They hadn't been allowed to open it until he had finished giving them instructions and told them to begin. Everyone had burned through the questions as quickly as possible, and all of the tests had been scored in the ensuing couple of weeks, so that Mr. Bonne now had a personalized career choice recommendation package for each one of them, filled with suggestions as to what kinds of jobs would suit and fulfill each one of them. Parker was eager to open his and see what it had to say. He was always stumped when people asked him what he wanted to be when he grew up. It was like a trick question that everyone else seemed to know the answer to, but Parker didn't.

But at lunch time, Dakota was on a huge rant about the placement tests. How they were inaccurate, and how she could never get the training or pay for the schooling that she would need to become any of those things. She tore it up in front of everyone. Parker watched the strips and squares of paper go raining down all over the table. She could at least have made her statement over the garbage can, so that everyone around her didn't have to clean up her mess.

"What did it tell you that you should be?" Parker asked, curious about what it might have told her. What it was she was so upset about. She had her whole life ahead of her; maybe she could get a scholarship or grant to study in her recommended areas.

"I told you, it's stupid," Dakota repeated. "These things are worthless. They don't mean anything. You think any of us are going to get anywhere in life? Crawling on our bellies in the ghettos? Who here has the money to go to school after we graduate? Who is even going to bother to graduate at all? One or two, even if you work really hard at it. Pretty much everyone is going to fail. You're going to end up flipping burgers and changing oil and painting the lines down the middle of the road. Whose placement test told them they should become a garbage man? Because *that's* what we're qualified for."

Parker nibbled at his sandwich. He was hungry, but he wanted to make it last for a while. He didn't want his lunch to just be gone in two seconds.

"You know I'm right," Dakota told him explosively.

"So what do you want to do?" Parker asked. If she didn't plan on following her suggested vocational plan, then what was she going to do? What did she have in mind?

"I just want to be a kid forever," Dakota said in a calmer voice. "I don't want to grow up. I just want to be safe and taken care of."

They all looked at each other, shrugging or grimacing. Of course, they would all like that. But life wasn't set up that way. They would each have to figure out a path to follow as adults, right or wrong.

Nobody got to stay a kid forever.

Since Parker was grounded and wasn't allowed to go out anywhere or do anything, he turned to the internet and his online relationships. He had been neglecting his social networks and online forums since meeting Dakota.

He was following her online, but it was a strange relationship, since she would rarely post to him or reply to his queries, and he knew that she was—or had been—posting about him but keeping him out of the circulation. Picking one of the girls from their school class who didn't have much of an online presence, Parker downloaded her pictures and a few facts about her, and set up fake accounts in her name. He followed Dakota and a bunch of the other girls, and most of them followed back within the hour. Using the fake account, Parker could then access all of the posts that Dakota made.

There wasn't anything nasty or over-the-top, but it was a little weird to see things that she had been posting about him when she said she didn't want a relationship and they weren't allowed to look like a couple in public. She had still been posting about him like he was her boyfriend, or at least a crush.

He dug more deeply into the posts that she had been making to older women who were out of town. Women who ran shelters and outreach programs, pastors and pastors' wives, motherly women of one sort or another. She was grooming them or courting them, coaxing them into giving her promises of assistance. Some of them were obviously direct-messaging with her, and it appeared they were sending money to her into an online account.

There were a number of new potential friends in his feed and, looking at them, Parker could see that Dakota and a couple of her friends were the common link. He clicked to look at their profiles, expecting that they would be older sisters or students, but instead found more middle-aged women like the ones Dakota was courting. Looking for ones with public feeds, Parker scrolled through them, looking for any posts by Dakota.

"What'cha doing?" Leslie asked, making Parker jump. He looked up from his phone and breathed heavily, hand to chest.

"Don't sneak up on me like that, Les!"

"I wasn't sneaking."

"Well, you scared the heck out of me. Why are you being so quiet?"

She giggled. "Usually you're telling me I'm too noisy."

"I want you to be quiet. Except when you're sneaking up on me. Then I want to hear about it. You'll give me a heart attack one day, and then who would make you peanut butter sandwiches when Mom is out?"

Her little pink tongue flicked out and licked her lips. "Peanut butter sandwiches?"

Parker slid the phone into his pocket and headed resignedly for the kitchen. Once Leslie had food on the brain, there was only one recourse. He had to feed her or she would drive him crazy all night.

Once Leslie had her sandwich and was again sitting in front of the TV with the others, Parker pulled out his phone again. He scrolled through the posts, trying to remember what he had been looking at.

He'd been looking at potential connections' timelines for any posts by Dakota. Parker spotted a couple. They were the same type of posts as he had seen before. Just to different people.

Then he looked at the poster, and realized that it wasn't Dakota, but someone who looked like she did. He squinted at the small screen, then tapped and enlarged the profile picture. It seemed to be a picture of Dakota, her hair and makeup done a little differently, but the name on the account was not Dakota Phillips.

She had said that she had changed her name from what it was before. She said that her ex would be searching for her using a different name, because she had changed it. So it had to be an old account with old posts. But it wasn't. Not when he looked at the dates. He tapped his way through the fake account's details. Different entries for hometown, birthdate, and other vital statistics. But he was sure that it was Dakota in the profile picture.

Of course, Parker himself had just proven how easy it was to create a fake account in someone else's name, with their face attached to it, without them even knowing about it. Someone else might have set up that account, and Dakota didn't even know about it. There was no indication that she was the one who had set it up. Anyone could have downloaded a selfie she had taken and used it to set up another account.

He continued to look at the suggested friends to see which of them were connected with Dakota's real account, and which were connected to the fake account. His stomach knotted as he realized there were several fake accounts. All had different pictures and different names. And a couple of them were not just courting potential new moms online, but were actually running crowdsource fundraising campaigns. One of the fake accounts claimed to be homeless and needed funding for a mailbox address and work clothes for a new office job that would help her to get herself off the street. The other, a turban-like scarf completely covering her bright pink hair, apparently needed money to cover medical bills as she went through chemo for ovarian cancer.

Parker turned off his phone and slid it into his pocket. He felt sick. He couldn't prove who it was that had set up those accounts, but what were the chances that someone had set up four different accounts with Dakota's face on them and were running similar scams on each? They all seemed to use similar posting styles and abbreviations, and included plenty of selfies. If it weren't Dakota running all of those accounts, someone was putting an awful lot of time and effort into making it look like she was.

Parker and Dakota were out together. Getting soft-serve ice cream, one of Parker's favorite treats.

They had escaped the scrutiny of both moms thanks to the school, which had let out early for a pep rally and apparently not informed the parents. So they had a couple of hours after sneaking out of the pep rally and before checking in at home.

Parker didn't ask Dakota about the fake profiles. He wasn't sure how to even bring it up. Dakota had already explained to him how she had to have an escape plan if things didn't work out at Jade's. *When* things didn't work out at Jade's. She hadn't exactly tried to lie or cover up what it was she was doing.

They both had their cones and stepped out onto the city sidewalk. Dakota froze. Following her gaze, Parker saw the ex-boyfriend stalker standing right across the street. They ducked back into the ice cream store and watched out the window, hanging around until after their ice creams were done, waiting for him to move on.

"Why don't we just call the police?" Parker asked. "They can warn him off. Get rid of him for you. The guy hasn't moved on yet, he seems pretty intent on finding you."

"No." Dakota gripped his arm. "You can't get the police involved. That will make big trouble for me, Parker."

"What kind of trouble? If this guy is harassing you, you need to do something about it."

She didn't offer what kind of trouble she was talking about. Outstanding warrants? Some dispute between Dakota and her ex? Unpaid debts?

"Then let me talk to him."

"No way, he would kill you!"

"I'm not saying I want to fight him, just talk to him. Explain how he should leave you alone…"

"No," Dakota was adamant. "Do not talk to him! Do not approach him. If you see him coming, you go the opposite way."

"I think we could get this straightened out. If he realized that you had a new boyfriend, he'd stop bugging you. He'd realize that you had moved on."

"That's stupid. It would just make him crazy jealous and he would try to kill you!"

Parker knew it was an exaggeration. The young man didn't look like a fighter. He was slim, like Parker, even if he were older and taller. The fact that he hadn't yet found or challenged Dakota made Parker think that he couldn't be trying too hard. What was he waiting for?

"Promise me you won't talk to him," Dakota said, her voice strained. "You promise me you won't do something stupid that's going to get you hurt or killed. You have to leave him alone. Don't confront him."

"Okay, I won't," Parker agreed, holding up his hands to sooth and quiet her. "I won't try to talk to him. I won't do anything."

"And you won't call the cops. I don't want to end up in jail. That's what's going to happen if you call the cops."

Parker swallowed. What had she done that she was so certain they would put her in jail? Had she stolen his car when she left him? Cleared out the bank account? Had a fight in which she injured him?

What exactly had happened between them?

Parker should have known that it was only a matter of time before the stalker caught up with him. Maybe he had known. Maybe Dakota had too and that was why she was so paranoid about it.

Parker wasn't with Dakota when her ex caught up with him. If Parker had been with Dakota, maybe she would have seen the man, and they would have run away again, over and over until he finally caught up with Parker.

Parker was on his way home from school a day or two later. Straight home like a good boy. Still reveling in the fact that they had gotten away with an ice cream date during the pep rally. Not paying much attention to where he was going or what he was doing.

He jumped off his bike in front of the house and pushed it toward the back to put it away.

"You."

Parker stopped and turned around to look for the owner of the voice. The speaker was taller than he expected. And the voice coming out of the young man was much quieter than Parker had envisioned when he had imagined talking to him.

"Oh, boy."

The ex was standing there on the sidewalk in front of Parker's house, staring at him. He looked almost as if he were afraid of what Parker was going to say or do. He certainly didn't look like the jealous stalker Dakota had made him out to be.

"Uh… it's you. You're Parkinson, the one she pretends is her boyfriend."

Saul's eyes went down toward the phone in his hand for a minute, as if he felt like he should check out Parker's picture on it just to be sure. Because of course he had seen Parker's picture in Dakota's social media streams. He had followed her there. He had seen everything.

"She doesn't pretend I'm her boyfriend," Parker said, trying to keep his voice as calm and confident as he could. "I *am* her boyfriend."

"You might think that, but you don't know Dakota."

It gave Parker a little pang of surprise that the ex knew her by the same name as Parker did. Or at least knew what her current name was.

"I know her better than you do," Parker said. "And it's Parker, by the way. Not Parkinson."

"Parker. Right. My name is Saul."

They both just stood there looking at each other. Parker gave a little shrug.

"She never said anything about me?" Saul asked.

"Not really… just that you were an ex-boyfriend. That you were… following her."

"That's not true."

"What's not true? Here you are, looking for her."

"I'm not looking for her. I already found her. I'm looking for you."

Parker frowned. "Why would you be looking for me?" Then he realized. Jealousy, of course. Saul wanted to remove Parker from the picture. Get him out of the way.

"I've already talked to her. Can't get anywhere with her. Of course, I never could. But you… I couldn't leave without explaining things to you. You need to understand. So you know to stay away from her."

"I don't know what you're talking about. I'm not going to stay away from her." Except, of course, when he knew Mona was checking up on him. Once he was no longer grounded…

"Everything she has told you is a lie," Saul said. "Everything you think she is, is a lie."

"She can change her name, but that doesn't change the person she is," Parker said. "I *know* who she is."

"You don't. She's told you she's this poor, homeless girl who's never had a good home or a real family. That everywhere she's been and everyone she's been with has abused her. Isn't that what she tells you?"

Parker shrugged. He'd seen Dakota living homeless on the street. He knew it was the truth, no matter what Saul made up.

"You think she's a teenager," Saul said. "You think she's your age. In your grade."

"No," Parker said cautiously. "A little older than me. Fifteen or Sixteen, maybe."

Saul shook his head. Parker thought about it.

"Maybe she's older. Maybe she's your age. But I don't care how old she is. That doesn't change anything for me."

"Oh, no?" Saul let out a bark of laughter. "You don't think it matters how old she is? What's she said about where she came from?"

"I know where she came from."

"You don't know anything about her."

Parker wheeled his bike up to the house and leaned it against the wall.

"Why don't you go away and just leave us alone? Nobody cares, Saul. Nobody cares how old she is or what name she had before."

"But you will," Saul said. "You say you don't care? Dakota is not my ex-girlfriend, Parker. She's my mother."

Chapter Seventeen

PARKER WASN'T SURE WHAT happened next. His head whirled. He might have thrown a punch at Saul, but he wasn't sure. He found himself sitting on the front steps of the house, head between his knees, hyperventilating.

He was breathing so fast that his chest hurt, but he still couldn't get enough oxygen. His head felt like it was going to explode. The whole world was collapsing inward.

"No!" he told Saul, who had one hand on Parker's shoulder and was trying to calm him down after exploding a nuclear bomb right underneath him. "No, no, no!"

All of the lies. All of the bits that didn't quite fit. All of the warnings that there was something different about Dakota. Something wrong.

All I want is to be a kid forever.

All I want is someone to take care of me.

She had fooled Parker. She had fooled all of them. The school, Jade, her girlfriends, everybody in the neighborhood. They had all been her dupes, just like all of those future mom targets online and those who were sending money to help a teenager who didn't exist.

It had all been a lie, from the moment he had first offered to help her.

"She fools everyone," Saul said. "She has that pretty, round face, and everyone believes she's a teenager. But it's all just a con. So that people will take care of her."

"No," Parker protested. "You're crazy. You're the one trying to scam me."

"I couldn't believe she would have a relationship with a fourteen-year-old," Saul said in a tone of disgust. "She kept trying to brush me off and get rid of me, but I couldn't go until I had talked to you and told you what she was."

Parker tried to take a deeper breath. He gasped a few times, unable to speak without puffing.

"You didn't—want to—be with her? Take her—home?"

"Why would I? I don't want to be with that crazy woman. I had to see her, but I don't want to live with her. She's seriously disturbed!"

"No. She's—damaged…"

"A lot of people are damaged. That's not an excuse for what she's done. She's turned into a monster!"

"No," Parker protested. "She's not a monster. She's—a person. She's your mother."

"Biologically, yeah. But she's never been mature enough to be a parent. She abandoned me when I was five. I've only seen her a few times since then. And each time, she's been… younger."

Parker felt sick. He clutched his stomach and turned away from Saul, worried he was going to throw up. He wished he could throw up. The pain was unbearable. He was being shredded from the inside.

"Nothing was true? Nothing?"

"I don't know what she told you. But she's not the person she pretends to be. She has family. She's always had friends to support her and help her out. But she chooses to continue this… this insanity."

"Her life…" Parker was breathing open-mouthed, still sure he was going to throw up. "Foster homes, abuse, self-harming…?"

"Yes," Saul's tone was conciliatory. "That's all true. She's been through some pretty dark times. Some of the stuff I found out when I was looking for her… well, it was pretty sick. And sometimes done by her own biological family. But that doesn't excuse what she does."

Parker gave a little nod. "Sorry… I hit you."

Saul squeezed Parker's shoulder. "I get it. I deserved it for bringing you this kind of news. But I couldn't let her go on… doing what she was doing."

Parker tried to sort it out in his head. If Dakota was Saul's mother, than she had to be at least Mona's age, maybe even older. And Parker had pursued her like a lost puppy. All of the times that she had turned him down or pushed him away, and he had kept pushing. He should have just left her alone. Let her scam everyone else. He should have just stayed out of the picture. He was the one who had stupidly gotten Jade involved. Gotten Dakota registered for school, where she could play a teen in all her glory.

"She has to be sick. It's some kind of illness," he told Saul.

"I agree she's sick. But that doesn't give her an excuse."

Parker rubbed his eyes and tried to lift his head, still feeling dizzy and faint. He almost *wanted* to faint, and for it to all just be a dream. The horrific nightmare that it seemed to be.

"Maybe she has a brain tumor or something. Maybe there's a medical reason…"

"She doesn't. It's just something she chooses to do. She's a con artist. She puts a ton of effort into conning everyone. It's not just some random hallucination of a schizophrenic. She does it on purpose. Intentionally. She doesn't really think she's a teenager. She's just pretending."

"No." Parker put his head down again, closing his eyes in spite of the spinning sensation it caused. "She's not just pretending…"

Saul stopped touching Parker's shoulder and just stood there, watching him. "I can't imagine what you're feeling like right now. I'm sorry she did this to you."

Parker felt tears flood his eyes at the compassion and regret in Saul's voice.

He could hear voices in the house behind him.

Miranda's voice: "He's home. He's on the steps."

The door opening and Link poking his head out. "Parker? You okay?"

Parker lifted his head to look at Saul. To make it clear by his expression that Saul was to keep his mouth shut and not say anything to the younger children.

"I'm not feeling good, Link. Just give me a minute."

"Okay. But you need to call Mom. You're supposed to check in by now."

Parker pulled out his phone and looked at it without comprehension. Time had ceased to exist. Time no longer made any sense. It had fooled him. Time had duped him, making Dakota look too young.

His fingers found the familiar icons and it rang through to Mona.

She answered, suspicion already in her voice. "Parker? Where are you? You're supposed to be home."

"I am."

"Call me from the house line, then."

"I'm here," Parker insisted. He handed the phone to Link. "Tell her I'm home."

Link looked confused, but took the phone from Parker. "Hi, Mom. Yeah, he's home… he's just on the front steps. He said he's not feeling good."

Link listened. His eyes slid over to Parker. "No… I don't think so."

More listening.

"No, not her. There's somebody else, though… a guy…"

Link nodded at whatever Mona was saying on the phone.

"Mom said you're grounded and aren't allowed to have friends over," he relayed to Parker.

"He's not a friend."

"She says you're not allowed, Parker."

"He's not coming into the house. I just need to talk to him for a minute longer. In private."

Mona could apparently hear enough of their conversation to understand what was going on. Link listened to her instructions.

"Five minutes, and then if he doesn't go away, I'm supposed to call Mom back."

He handed the phone back to Parker, the call already terminated. Parker looked down at it in his hand. It was like something foreign. Just a lump of metal. No connection.

Link gave Parker one last puzzled look, then went back into the house.

"I guess I should go, then," Saul said. "I don't want to get you in trouble with your mom."

Parker looked at him. He hadn't really looked at Saul, studied him closely. He'd always been the stalker at a distance. And then when he had set the bomb off… Parker hadn't been able to see anything.

His earlier impressions of Saul all seemed to be true. A tall, slim, black boy. A young man rather than a kid. Maybe nineteen, maybe in his early twenties. His face, like Dakota's, was smooth and unlined. Parker tried to see her features in Saul's face, but it was hard with his being so much thinner and more masculine. Maybe something around the eyes. Maybe the shape of the lips.

When he thought of Dakota's lips, almost always painted with some shimmery, girlish color, his emotions spun into confusion. Attraction, anger, and confusion all ran together. How could she have lied to him every day? How could he have believed anything about her, knowing how much she lied about other things?

As if his concentration on her face could have conjured Dakota up, she was there. Walking along the city sidewalk toward him. Seeing him hunched on the steps there, looking sick, and then Saul standing beside him.

"Get away from him!" Dakota exploded, moving purposefully toward them at a fast walk. "You get away from Parker and leave him alone!"

Both of them just looked at her.

"Parker, go into the house," Dakota tried. If she couldn't get Saul to leave, maybe she could still get Parker away from him through other means.

"I already told him," Saul said.

"No!" She was furious. "I told you to stay away from him! I told you to leave him out of this. This is between you and me, not anything to do with Parker!"

"Nothing to do with him?"

Dakota was close enough to see her features now. Parker drank them in, as if he might have imagined them before and was only seeing her as she really looked for the first time. Knowing that according to Saul, Dakota was older than Mona, he looked for the signs. No crow's feet around the eyes. No age spots on the skin. No wrinkling or sagging. Her round, girlish face looked nothing like that of an older woman. And with the addition of the bubblegum pink hair, it was impossible to see the truth. If it *was* the truth. Parker's spirits lifted a little. Maybe it was Saul who was trying to con him. Maybe Saul was the one telling lies, pretending Dakota was older than she was. She had jilted Saul. She was together with Parker now, and Saul wanted his revenge. Saul wanted to break them up.

"Is it true?" Parker asked Dakota. He gulped. "Tell me it's not true."

"What?"

"That you're older. That you're Saul's mother."

"I never told you how old I was." She looked over at Saul, lip curling. "And I don't have any son."

Parker breathed out slowly. It wasn't true. It was just Saul trying to make trouble for Dakota. Telling stories to get her in trouble and make people reject her.

"You're pretending to be a teenager, going to school," Saul said hotly. "Tell him how old you really are."

Looking at Saul, Dakota's face was a snarl. She turned to face Parker. "How old do I look?" she demanded. "Do I look like an old woman?"

Parker shook his head. Dakota reached for his hand, but Parker pulled back. For the first time, it was him pulling away from her, still not convinced she was really who he had thought she was. There was still enough doubt in his mind, urging caution.

"I'm calling Mom," Link yelled through the door. "And she's going to call the police!"

Dakota's eyes widened. She snarled at Saul. "Now look at what you've done!"

"I haven't done anything. It's all you, Mama."

She hesitated, then peeled away from them, going around a corner and disappearing out of sight. Saul looked at Parker.

"I guess I'd better go too." His lips pressed together in a line. "Don't believe anything she says."

"Who was that? Someone from school? And what was Dakota doing here? You guys know she's not supposed to be here!"

Parker ignored Link's questions. He walked through the house like a sleepwalker, not stopping to get supper going for the kids or to get his homework out. He didn't sit down in front of the TV to try to understand whatever program was playing. He just went straight to his bunk, climbed up, and lay flat on his face, closing his eyes.

"Are you sick?"

"Leave me alone, Link."

Link huffed. "I'm just asking."

"Lemme alone."

Link stood there for a few minutes longer, then shrugged and walked out of the room. With Parker under the weather, the family responsibilities would fall to Link. He'd take care of everything. He was just about as good at cooking and entertaining the younger kids as Parker.

Parker's phone vibrated. He ignored it. In a couple minutes, it was buzzing again. Not just a reminder buzz, but another series of texts coming in. He tried to ignore the disruption and just mentally swim into a place where he didn't have to think, but the phone kept buzzing wildly like a wound-up toy. Parker pulled it out and turned on the screen. There were a number of notifications scrolling down the screen. He swiped one from Adrian and was taken to a series of unanswered messages from Adrian's account, ending with,

Dude, where r u?

Answer!!!!

Parker looked at it for a minute before tapping in his answer.

What's up?

Adrian's message showed up almost immediately. Parker could hear other messages arriving in the background, each one making the phone vibrate in his hand.

Have u seen what thr saying abt Dakota?

Parker bit his lip. He had been secure in the fact that he was the only one who knew Saul's allegation against Dakota. But obviously something was up. Did everyone know, or was it something else? Some party she had crashed or she got caught shoplifting?

What whose saying?

Adrian's answer flew right back.

Everyone! She is old?

Damn. He switched over to Dakota's timeline using his fake account. It was filling up with confused questions and accusations. Dakota was replying on each post; angry, staccato replies. Defending herself. Saying that an ex was spreading lies about her. That she'd never lied to anyone.

And just as fast, the replies were coming back to her. People who knew that she'd lied. Not about her age, but about other things. Her name, where she had come from, stories she had told that had changed from one telling to the next. Apparently, everyone had known that she was telling stories about herself, but had kept quiet about it.

Parker was afraid to look at his own timeline. Since he was using the fake account, there would not be any notification to his friends that he was online, but he was afraid that they would be posting to his timeline even without him there to defend himself.

He looked anyway. It wasn't as bad as he had feared. There were plenty of 'dude, did you know?' posts, and a couple of classmates had run some of Dakota's selfies through aging photo booth apps so that she looked like she was eighty or a hundred years old and posted them. But overall, it appeared that people were attacking Dakota rather than holding Parker responsible for not figuring out that she was older than she said she was.

Messages had been continuing to come in unheeded, and Parker switched back over to Adrian's message thread.

No way she has a kid that old, Adrian had asserted.

Parker tried to figure out what message to send back to Adrian. Deny it? Say that he didn't know? That he believed it? That he didn't? He didn't know what to think of the whole thing. There was no proof Dakota was old like Saul had said, and there was no proof that she was a teenager like they thought. Parker drummed his fingers on the back of his phone while he thought, before he finally brought up a message window and started typing his message.

School didn't have birth date?

There was a pause while Adrian thought about this and composed his answer. Parker listened to the other messages coming in. He didn't really want to know what everyone was saying. They all must think he was an idiot for being so close to Dakota and not knowing how old she was. Or for not standing up and defending her, saying he knew it was all a lie. No one would be able to understand how he could have been deceived. Adrian's message came in:

They cldn't have had birth cert. She was homeless.

Mr. Bonne had promised to help. He had said that they would need to request her old school records when they registered her, but that must never have happened. Especially with her using another name. Somewhere in the school office, there was a memo, or a task on a to-do list, saying that they were still waiting for proper identification from Dakota. In the meantime, who would stop her from going to school if she wanted to attend? He tapped a message back.

She has job. SSN?

Must have fake ID. Stolen #

Parker's head whirled with all of the possibilities. How had she fooled everyone? How had she come into the neighborhood and just established herself as a teenager, and no one knew her real name or history or who she really was? Was it that easy to con them all?

Adrian's next question popped up. Parker stared at the white text on a colored background. Blue? Green? He didn't want to actually read the words.

Did you know???

He stared at the blinking cursor on the screen. There was no right answer. Parker was gullible and didn't have a clue? He knew and just let her pretend? Whatever he answered, he would be judged. He just sat staring at the LCD screen. His life was effectively over. How long would it take before the whole thing blew over and became last year's news? Maybe in a year. Maybe never. He might be branded for years as the guy who was fooled.

Birdman

Adrian tried to get his attention using his gaming handle. Parker still didn't respond.

Birdman, did you know abt her age?

Parker shut off the screen. Then, thinking better of it, he powered down the entire phone. He would say that he got spammed by so many messages, that his phone had crashed. Or the battery had run down. He just couldn't deal with the questions. He couldn't think of what the consequences were going to be if Dakota really was old. And what the consequences would be if she were innocent and everyone had already shut her out of their circles and refused to have anything to do with her. What if she had been telling the truth the whole time?

I never told you how old I was.

That's what Dakota had said when he asked her. She still hadn't told him her real age. She hadn't defended herself. Just that. She had never told him she was sixteen. That had been his own guess. She hadn't told him that she was older, either. He *had* asked. More than once. He'd been forced to guess and to make decisions based on how she looked and acted.

Chapter Eighteen

IT WAS A LONG night and Parker didn't spend much of it sleeping. When Mona got in late, Parker could hear Link murmuring to her outside the room, filling her in on all of the evening's happenings. Parker couldn't tell what Link told her about him.

Mona tiptoed into the room, quiet so she wouldn't wake up Jessup.

"Parker? Are you awake?"

He considered playing possum. Then he wouldn't have to talk to her until morning. They couldn't really have a discussion while everyone was hurrying around to eat breakfast and get out the door to school, so it would have to wait until the next time they could really sit down and talk about it face-to-face.

But Parker was feeling strangely lonely and in need of mothering.

"Yes."

"Are you sick? Link said you just went straight to bed after school."

Parker sighed and turned his face toward her. "No. Just... just feeling down, I guess. Didn't want to deal with... anything."

She stood beside the bed, looking up at him, her hand on the bunk.

"I'm sorry you're feeling like that. It can't be easy, trying to sort out all of this stuff with Dakota."

For a moment, he thought that she too had heard about what Saul had said. But she wasn't talking about Dakota's age. Just about the other stuff. Drinking and being grounded and being banned from seeing her.

"Link said that she came here after school. After you called me."

"Yeah. Just for a minute. I didn't ask her over. She just came."

"Tell her not to. And if she comes, just come into the house and don't let her in. If she won't leave, that's trespassing."

"I don't want to be rude to her. People are really mean to her sometimes and that's not right."

"If she won't comply with your wishes, then you need to be assertive and take action. If you don't want me to have to call the police or take out a restraining order, you do what you have to. If it's rude… at least you're obeying me and keeping yourself out of trouble."

"I want to be able to see her. Why do you have to be that way?"

"Because she's trouble," Mona said flatly. "I'm sorry. I haven't interfered with any of your other relationships, so you know I'm not just being an unreasonable, paranoid mother. It isn't that. There's something really off about her. She's going to get you in big trouble if you don't stay away from her."

Parker just breathed deeply, trying to keep himself calm and not get drawn into an argument with her. She didn't know what she was talking about. She especially didn't know all of the recent developments. All she was going on were guesses. Being introduced to Dakota once. Whatever she had heard from Jade or around the neighborhood. And just once, Parker drinking a bit too much with her. That had only been once, and it wasn't going to happen again.

"Link said there was another boy here after school too. That surprises me for a couple of reasons."

Parker guessed he was supposed to ask her what the reasons were. But he didn't have the energy. What did it matter why she was surprised to hear that another boy had been there? Parker could have a friend over from school. Usually. When he wasn't grounded. Mona should be happy that there had been someone other than Dakota there. She should be encouraging him to have his guy friends over, if she didn't want Dakota around.

"First, because you're grounded and you're not supposed to be having anyone over." Mona paused, waiting for an argument or inquiry. The silent seconds drew on. "And second… because it's been a long time since you've had any of your friends over. Not for… a long time."

She didn't say how long it had been. They both knew. Parker didn't really have anyone over after his father died. It was too hard for him. He'd made a clean break from his old life with a nuclear family; two parents and all of the kids. His friends' parents wouldn't let them go to the Jurek house after what had happened there, and Parker and the others had cocooned, just spending time with each other, insulating themselves from the outside world.

It had been four years. The younger children had recovered the quickest. Memories faded, people moved away, and the younger children now occasionally had friends over. But usually it was just the Jurek kids, depending on each other.

Parker hadn't had anyone over in the years since his father had been killed. He hadn't realized how isolated he had become.

"I had Dakota over," Parker said. Because there was really nothing else to say. He had tried to expand his circle. He had tried to make a new friend and grow a new relationship. And she had objected and had put a stop to it.

"I'm sorry." It was Mona who sighed this time. She was probably lonely too. She was probably lonelier than he was. He at least went to school every day and saw friends there. He didn't think Mona had very many friends at work.

"It's okay, Mom. I know… you're just trying to look out for me."

She put her small, warm hand on his shoulder for a moment. Then she walked back out of the room.

Parker closed his eyes to sleep. He was still awake when Link finished doing his chores and went to bed. Parker stayed awake listening to the old clock in the living room mark each passing hour with a chime. As much as he wanted to sleep, it just wouldn't come.

And then he had to go back to school. Back where everyone had heard Saul's allegations and would be waiting to pounce, to ask questions about whether he had known Dakota's secret, and how he could not have, and all of the other questions that had been on his timeline that he just couldn't face.

He did log in under his own name, so that he could take a quick look at his private messages. And there were almost as many private as there were public. Everyone wanted the inside scoop. Some of them were bullying about it, rude and aggressive, and others went about it in such a kind, soft way that he could almost fool himself into believing that they really did care.

But everyone just wanted the dirt, however they asked him about it.

Parker logged out of all of his social networks. He shut down each of the apps, and considered whether he could or should delete them so that he wouldn't be tempted to go back into them any time soon. Maybe he could even suspend his accounts. Then everyone would be forced to leave him alone, and he could go back once everything had been quiet for a while.

He biked to school as usual, remembering as he waited impatiently at the intersection that first day he had seen Dakota, going through the garbage bins. It seemed like such a long time ago. And it seemed like hardly any time had passed. He avoided the door where Dakota might be waiting. He grabbed books from his locker without really looking to see what they were. People were watching him. Whispering behind his back.

"Parker!"

Chris and Adrian approached him together. They'd obviously been watching for him. They closed in behind him and stood at his flanks, looking around like bouncers at a rave. Parker would have laughed at them acting as his security detail, ready to fend off anyone asking questions or making fun of him. But it was touching. He wished it would last forever. His friends sheltering him and no one bothering him. He could just go on as if it were any other day and he didn't have anything to worry about. Nothing had changed for him. He was just Parker Jurek, going to school, messing up his algebra and struggling along in his other subjects. Like he had always been. Before Dakota. Before his dad died. Just Parker, and not all of the other baggage.

"How's it going, Birdman?" Adrian asked, looking around the hallway and not turning to face Parker.

"It's fine. Everything is fine. Really."

"What happened last night? You didn't want to talk?"

He had been planning to give excuses about his phone. To say that he wanted to continue the conversation, he just hadn't been able to because of his stupid phone. But instead of making him more tense, Adrian's question relaxed him.

"No. Sorry."

"It's okay. You don't have to."

Chris looked over at Parker, and it was obvious that he was dying to ask questions. But Adrian gave him a stern look, and he resumed the bouncer act, looking for any approaching trouble. It would have been more impressive if they hadn't been three of the skinniest boys in their grade.

Parker swallowed. "Let's go sit down, I guess."

"Yeah, sure."

They walked with him, escorting him between them into Mr. Bonne's homeroom and to his seat. Parker slid into his desk, and they hovered over him, eager as puppies waiting to be thrown a treat.

"I didn't know," Parker told them. "I still don't know. We'll just have to wait and see how it shakes out." He gave a little shake of his head. "I really don't know anything yet."

"Yeah," Chris agreed. "It's just he-said/she-said right now, right? I mean, neither one of them has any proof of anything. She's registered for our grade, so how old could she be?"

Parker nodded his agreement. "I haven't talked to her," he said. The few words that he had exchanged with Dakota over the matter didn't count. He hadn't sat down to go over it with her. They hadn't had a real heart-to-heart. "We haven't heard her side at all."

"Well, you know her side, though, right?" Adrian said. "I mean, if you were watching her timeline yesterday, you could see all of her posts denying the story. Her story is that he's just out to wreck her reputation. He just wants to ruin her."

"Yeah."

"We all know she tells lies," Chris said.

"She… changes her story," Adrian offered diplomatically.

"Yeah," Chris agreed. "She tells lies," he repeated, and grinned.

Students were trickling into the room. The bell hadn't rung yet, so there was no rush. They came in individually or in small groups. Parker saw Charity and Addy come in together. No Dakota. A couple of minutes passed and Marina entered. Still no Dakota.

Maybe she was going to skip. She knew just like Parker did what kind of questions she was going to face if she showed up. So she had decided to skip for a day, have a drink to calm her nerves. Or maybe she had decided it was time to run. She would just hop a bus, go on to one of the potential moms she had been courting in another city, and start a new life. She'd done it before. How hard could it be to do it again?

And would Saul follow her? Would he show up a few weeks or months later and spread his poison again, making her move on yet another time, and start over with yet another family? Would he be happy to stop once he had broken up Dakota and Parker, or would he feel the need to keep following her, and, like some kind of avenging angel, continually wreaking his vengeance on her? How long would she have to suffer before he would be satisfied?

And then, just as the bell rang, Dakota was there. There were dark circles around her eyes that almost made her look goth. She obviously hadn't slept any better than Parker had. She tried to make eye contact with her girl friends, but none of them would look at her. When she bent over to talk to Charity, to share some gossip or tidbit with her, Charity deliberately turned her face away and ignored her. Dakota stood there for a minute, looking shocked. She looked at the other girls, who continued to avoid eye contact.

Dakota widened her gaze to the rest of the classroom. Everyone was watching her. Even Mr. Bonne seemed aware of it, standing at the front of the room and waiting for everyone to get settled before the second bell rang and he could begin to read the daily announcements. Had the news spread to his social media as well? Or had someone emailed him or phoned him up to ask him about his involvement in Dakota's registration?

Everyone looked away when Dakota looked at them. Some were shunning her, and others were just embarrassed to be caught looking at her. But they all looked away.

It was a struggle for Parker to keep his gaze on Dakota and to meet her eyes when she finally, after looking over everyone else in the room, looked at him. He tried to communicate to her that he wasn't judging her. He was waiting for her side of the story. He was not a coward who refused to look her in the eye. She might have betrayed him, but he was going to withhold judgment until all the facts were in.

Dakota's eyes met his for an instant, and then she looked away. There was no moment of communion between them. She couldn't look him in the eye.

Dakota sat down at her desk, and instead of getting her books arranged in front of her, she put her purse on the desk and started to rifle through it. Looking in a tiny mirror and ignoring everything going on in the room around her, she went to work on her face.

There was certainly nothing unusual about that. Dakota and the other girls regularly made themselves up at their desks or wherever they happened to be. And some of the boys too. But Parker was fascinated and couldn't tear his eyes away. He watched her dot concealer on the bags under her eyes, and to use various brushes and potions to hide the circles. When she was done, he could tell if he looked carefully that she was wearing more makeup than usual, but it wasn't obvious that the shimmery color around her eyes was hiding anything. She looked just as bright-eyed and fresh-faced as ever. Parker had an impulse to take a picture of her, but he didn't dare, knowing that she would catch him and that everybody else in the classroom would know. He would have to, instead, imprint that memory on his brain. Keep it as a cherished memory without a digital picture to refresh it.

Parker realized that Mr. Bonne had finished his announcements and moved on to the first lesson of the day. Parker hadn't even opened his books. He eased them open slowly, not wanting to attract Mr. Bonne's attention to him with any sudden movements.

He didn't need any more attention than he was already getting.

He wasn't sure where Dakota went over the lunch hour. She certainly didn't stay at the school and eat the free lunch as usual. She was smarter than Parker, knowing that she would be assailed with questions and comments if she stuck around. Even with Chris and Adrian running interference and doing their bouncer act, Parker couldn't escape the looks, the whistles, and the catcalls. And Chris and Adrian had questions themselves. While they were trying to show him respect by not pestering him, he could see their unvoiced questions in their eyes.

How could he not know?

It was the same question that kept running through Parker's own head, all the more troublesome because he still didn't know. He still couldn't look at Dakota and say that Saul was right, or that he was wrong. Dakota's smooth, ageless face gave nothing away.

When he got back to the classroom after lunch, Mr. Bonne handed Parker a hall pass. "You're supposed to go see your counselor."

Parker looked down at the pink slip. He slid it through his fingers, as if the smooth texture of the paper were something that was important to note. He raised his eyes to Mr. Bonne's face.

"Do I have to?"

Mr. Bonne gave him a little grimace. His eyes were compassionate. Mr. Bonne was always, as Addy had said, a stand-up guy. He was the one to go to if you had a problem. He would deal with problems in the simplest way, cutting through any bureaucratic red tape, and he'd do it in a way that wouldn't embarrass you.

"I think you need to go talk to her," he said.

They both knew what it was about. But Mr. Bonne didn't voice it aloud. Parker shook his head. "What if I don't want to talk about it?"

"That's your right. Just tell her. But I think… it would be a good idea to get some outside help."

Parker shook his head. He didn't know whether to take his books down to the office or not, and eventually just left them on his desk. He wouldn't be that long, and it wasn't like he needed his textbooks or notebook to go talk to his guidance counselor.

He had arguably the best guidance counselor in the school. Mrs. Strauss was a small, pleasant woman with long blond hair that almost reached her waist. While a fairly young woman, younger than Parker's mom, she had sort of a hippie look and attitude, born in the wrong generation. She was into new agey stuff, but she had never seemed flighty to Parker; she seemed well-grounded and solid in her training.

"Parker," she acted surprised to see him, even though she had surely been the one to arrange for the meeting. "It's been a long time since we've had a chance to talk. Come on in and have a chat. Pull the door shut."

Parker hesitated, not sure he wanted the privacy that shutting the door would imply. With the door open, Mrs. Strauss would have to be careful what she said, in case it were overheard. With the door shut, she would feel free to dig deep into things that Parker really didn't want to talk about.

"It's okay, shut the door," she encouraged, seeing his hesitation.

Parker obeyed. There was a big knot in his stomach as he went to the visitor chair and sat down.

"So, tell me how things have been going," Mrs. Strauss suggested. Her tone was calm and neutral. Not conspiratorial or overly breezy. An easy, feel-free-to-confide tone that didn't demand that he spill his guts, but indicated that she wasn't looking for a socially-appropriate 'everything is fine' sort of reply.

Parker just sat there, looking at her.

He had felt free to talk to counselors in the past. He had been young enough when his dad was killed not to understand the social pressure put on boys to just power through any difficulties as if they were unaffected. They had encouraged him to talk through the trauma and had done a lot of listening, and it had helped Parker get through to the other side without too much emotional damage. He hadn't been told to just stuff his feelings, and he appreciated the professionals who had helped him to get through it.

But he was older now. Now he understood the pressure for a man to just deal with his own problems and not have to talk about it with a shrink. Counseling showed weakness. Getting help meant that he couldn't handle things on his own. Real men were tough enough to just get through it.

And it wasn't like when his father had died. Finding out that Dakota might have lied to him and might be older than she said she was wasn't a violent or traumatic experience. It was just words. Feelings. Relationships. All of the stuff that men didn't talk about. Parker wasn't a hurt, scared little boy this time. He was a man. With a man's problems.

If what Saul said was true, then all Parker had to do was say goodbye. Maybe not even that, if Dakota decided to run to avoid dealing with the issue. Maybe she already had.

"I talked to Dakota over lunch," Mrs. Strauss offered, as if she had read his mind. Parker stiffened, sitting up straight and taking notice. "She's having a pretty hard time with these… *rumors*… that are being spread. I wondered how you were handling it."

"What did she say?"

"I'm sure you realize that I can't repeat anything that was said between us. Unless it is to report something to the authorities because I think a child might be in danger."

She sounded like there was more to say. Parker waited.

"I don't think I would be breaking any confidences if I told you that Dakota is having a hard time with this." Mrs. Strauss gathered her striking blond hair together with two hands, and stretched it out, taming it into order between her fingers. Parker was fascinated by the process. She sometimes had it in a braid or a ponytail, but now it hung loose around her face and shoulders, spilling everywhere. She must have to pick long blond hairs out of everything. "It's very hard to have things spread around like this. To have people shun or bully you, and have no defenses. Is that how you feel about it?"

"It's not so bad for me," Parker said. His voice was strangely gravelly. There was no reason he should be hoarse. He wasn't crying. He wasn't at all emotional. He was holding it all together. He just needed to convince her of that fact.

"I would imagine you're probably facing a lot of teasing. Even if your friends stand by you, there are going to be a lot of people who just don't understand how you feel. There are going to be things said that are inappropriate. Even your close friends might unintentionally hurt you and not understand how you feel about these events."

"Mrs. Strauss… I'm okay. Really. You don't need to worry about me."

"Dakota is worried about you."

Parker thought about that. "If she wants to talk to me about it, she can. We don't need you playing go-between."

"No, you're right. Discussing it face-to-face is a much better idea. Something is always lost with an intermediary. But you may be thinking things that… you aren't ready to share with her at the moment."

"I don't need to share them with you."

Mrs. Strauss looked at him. Not like she was upset or offended. Just… thinking.

"Why don't you tell me about Dakota?" she suggested. "She's new here and I think you know her pretty well. Maybe better than anyone else."

"Wouldn't that be… breaking confidences…?"

"No, I don't think so. You don't have a counselor-client relationship with her. And I am *your* counselor, so I can't share it with anyone else. This is ideal, really… you are free to talk it through, and I'm not going to share it with anyone. It's a nonjudgmental environment. You're free to explore your feelings safely."

Parker shook his head. "No. I don't want to talk about Dakota. Or about anything else. Can I go back to my class, now? I don't want to miss any more than I have to. I don't want to fall behind."

"There has already been a decline in your grades…"

"So I need to get back to class. Not to miss more." Parker stood up.

"Is the slump in your grades due to what's been going on with you and Dakota?"

"No. It was before that. I'm just having trouble with some of the work. It's hard."

"Yes. That's understandable."

Parker headed for the door, not waiting to be dismissed.

"I want you to know that you can come and talk to me any time," Mrs. Strauss called as he let himself out.

He didn't make any attempt to respond.

Parker went to his afternoon classes, but he didn't hear anything that was discussed. A couple of times, Mr. Bonne or other teachers attempted to get his attention and get him engaged with the lesson, but Parker just couldn't focus on schoolwork. Not with all of the crazy stuff spinning in his brain. He put his head down on the desk in his folded arms and closed his eyes, trying to shut everything out.

He had thought at first that he could go to school and have a normal day. In spite of his lack of sleep. In spite of the rumors and all of the questions. He thought he could just face the other students, brush it all off as something not worth talking about, and have a normal, routine day.

But of course he couldn't. And it was getting worse the longer the day dragged on. The more he tried to avoid the questions, the harder they pressed in on his brain. But when he tried to focus on the questions, his consciousness disengaged and all he wanted to do was sleep, not to think about those things. He just wanted to sleep. And it would all go away.

Parker wasn't ready to move when a strong hand on his shoulder shook him insistently awake. Parker tried to squirm away.

Groaned and said to just leave him alone. Tried to keep consciousness from seeping back into his brain. Why couldn't they just let him sleep? It was the only thing that worked.

"Parker."

"What?" Parker growled and rubbed his eyes.

"Bell's rung, Parker. You need to get up," a man's voice said.

Parker opened his eyes and peered around the empty classroom. Almost empty. A few students were hanging around curiously, rubbernecking to see what Parker would do next.

Parker sat up and rubbed his stiff neck.

"Where is everyone?"

"Gone home," Mr. Bonne said patiently. "And you need to go too. Go home and get some sleep. You'll feel better tomorrow."

Parker sighed. He started to pack his books up. "You think so?"

"Today was a tough day. It'll get easier."

Parker shook his head. "Doubt it."

Mr. Bonne walked to the classroom door and looked up and down the hall. "I don't see Dakota. I think she's gone."

Parker wasn't sure whether Mr. Bonne expected him to be happy or disappointed about this. Maybe he said it just to see what Parker's reaction would be.

"Okay."

Parker stood up and slung his backpack over his shoulder. He thought he should probably say something to Mr. Bonne. Thank him for being concerned. But he couldn't think of what to say. His brain gears were grinding and binding up. He couldn't get a clear thought free.

Chapter Nineteen

U NEXPECTEDLY, MONA WAS HOME when Parker got in from school. He paused in the living room, looking at her, not sure what to say. She gave him a smile that looked strained.

"Thank you for coming straight home."

He didn't feel all warm and happy at her praise. It just made him sad that he no longer had anywhere else to be. He was adrift. He didn't even want to go to the park to hang out anymore. It was tainted with memories of Dakota. He wouldn't ever be able to go there and not think of her again.

Parker trudged toward his room.

"Dinner's on. Don't get started on anything," Mona warned.

"I'm not hungry."

He dropped his books inside the door and climbed up to his bunk. Mona followed him into the room.

"Parker? What's wrong? Are you sick?"

"Just not hungry."

"You're going to bed?"

He put his face in his pillow and closed his eyes. "Yeah."

"You must be sick, then!"

"Just tired."

"Parker, is there something going on that I should know about?"

He just grunted, waiting for her to give up and leave him alone.

"Do I need to take you to the doctor? You're scaring me, Parker. Talk to me, please!"

"Just… tired and want to go to sleep. That's all."

"Does your stomach hurt?"

"No. My head."

"You have a headache?"

Parker circled his left arm around his head, clasping the cast on the other arm. "I just want to go to sleep," he told her. "Please just let me go to sleep."

"Okay…" Her voice was small. "Call me if you need anything."

Parker shut all of the worries and questions off and sank into a deep sleep. It was the only place he could go to get away from it all. All of the questions, all of the worry, and all of the confusion. There was no Dakota, no Mona or Jade, no school, and no friends. And no school counselor.

But he was wrong. Dakota was there. Even in his sleep, he couldn't get away from her. Or maybe it was the only place that he could go to really be with her. He couldn't talk to her at school, and he couldn't go to Jade's house or have her over to his.

In his dream, Dakota was older. Much older. Her face showed its age. Much thinner, with sagging, unhappy wrinkles, hair that was all gray but for pink tips, and a stoop and a wobbly walk that made him think she must be ninety or more.

"Why didn't you tell me?" Parker demanded. "I wanted to know. Why didn't you tell me how old you were?"

"How could I?" Dakota said, her voice old and shaky, like the nanny-goat song on the kids' singalong CD that Mona used to play in the car, back when the player still worked. "I don't even know myself anymore."

"But look at you! You're ancient! How could you pretend to be a teenager like me? It was all a lie!"

"You didn't used to think I looked so bad."

"You never looked like this! What happened to you?"

She smiled a snaggletoothed, foul-smelling smile. "I just haven't put my makeup on yet. Once I do, I'll be beautiful again. Just like a princess."

"Makeup isn't going to hide all of this!"

"Why would I need makeup?" The scene had suddenly shifted. He was looking at young Dakota again. Her face was no longer wrinkled. She laughed at him, showing even teeth, only slightly yellowed. "Don't you like the way I look, Parkinson?"

"No!" Parker didn't know why he had said that. He *did* like the way she looked. Of course he liked the way she looked. He didn't want the old Dakota back again. He wanted her to stay young forever.

"You don't want me to change, do you?" she teased.

"No. I don't want you to change. Just stay like this."

She turned away from him and stared off into the distance. Parker tried to focus on what she was looking at, but everything seemed a little dark and foggy. He squinted, trying to make out shapes in the fog. Dakota sighed.

"I wish I could always stay like this," she said. "I would stay young and good-looking forever. I don't ever want to get old."

"Never?" Parker thought about all the things he wanted to do when he was older and independent. His own job, car, and house. Finding a wife and having two or three perfect little children. He'd be the dad to them he wished he'd had. Just like he tried to be to his younger siblings. Their real father was gone, but he tried to keep them on track and be a good example and a responsible person, so that they wouldn't miss that influence. He had heard at school how kids who didn't have a father figure were more likely to get involved with gangs and to break the law. He wanted to be that figure for them, even if he were only a few years older. "Don't you want to grow up to have a family? To do all those things you can't do when you're just a kid?"

"I want to stay a teenager forever," Dakota pouted in the dream. "I've tried being an adult, and it's too hard. I just can't do all that stuff."

"All what stuff?" He didn't understand what she meant. Sure, adults had to take care of chores and responsibilities, but that was normal. You had to do your part if you wanted to be treated like a grown-up.

"I had a baby, you know," Dakota said, putting her hand over her big belly. "I thought it would be fun. I wanted to have my own family, my own kin. Not just aunties and cousins and people I really wasn't related to. I wanted my own blood. But it wasn't like I thought it would be."

"Babies are nice," Parker said warmly. He liked taking care of babies just like he liked taking care of animals. Little defenseless things that needed his help. That's where his heart was. He would never take to things like algebra and writing essays the way he took to helping the helpless.

"Babies are awful!" Dakota snapped back. And he saw her, with a baby held carelessly like a toddler would hold a doll, letting it dangle and slip out of her arms. "They keep you awake with all of their crying and complaining. They poop and they puke and they just scream and can't tell you what they need. And it gets worse when they get older. When they tantrum and hit and bite. When they won't do what they're told just because they don't feel like it. They talk back and they are dirty and messy and are not even cute anymore." She gave a shudder, and tossed away the doll she was holding. "I hated it. I felt trapped. I couldn't go anywhere. No one wanted to help." She put on a snide adult voice, "'If you're old enough to make a baby, you're old enough to take care of one.' Everyone was so nasty about it. How is it my fault I got pregnant? And why didn't anyone tell me what it was going to be like? All of the social workers and the special programs. 'We're all here to help,' they said. 'People younger than you raise children successfully. You can do it too. There are lots of programs to help you.' And then where were they? There wasn't anyone there to help when he was puking all over the place. There wasn't anyone there to help when he kept running away in stores."

Parker remembered chasing Jessup in stores. If Parker took his eyes off of Jessup once, he was off and running. It didn't matter if he were buckled into the shopping cart or stroller, the little Houdini would find some way to wriggle out. And he was quick. Parker would have to sprint to catch Jessup, or he would be lost, and they would have to get store security to help secure the doorways and track him down. Parker laughed at the memory.

"What are you supposed to do when they run away?" Dakota demanded. "You smack them and you get all kinds of angry strangers telling you that you can't hit them. You grab their arm or pick them up while they're kicking and screaming, and everybody thinks you're trying to kidnap them or beating on them. And they say those toddler leashes are okay, but you should see how people look at you and get after you if you put a kid in one of those."

"Besides, they can get out of them," Parker chuckled. Jessup could, anyway.

Dakota didn't seem to think it was funny. "So I left him," she said. "I just found someone to look after him and I left him. And I went to being a teenager again. Back to being who I really was."

"How old were you then?" Parker asked.

But she didn't answer him. Maybe because it was a dream and Parker didn't have the answer inside his head. He could understand how she didn't want to be a mom. How she didn't want adult responsibilities. But he didn't know how old she had been when she had left Saul behind. Saul had been five. If Dakota had gotten pregnant as a teen, then she would have been in her early twenties when she abandoned him and went back to being a teenager again.

"And you just stayed a teenager?" Parker asked. "You decided you didn't want to act like an adult, so you just kept pretending to be a teenager?"

"It's not pretending," Dakota said. "Not if you really believe it."

Was that the excuse that she gave for herself? That she really was a teenager inside, so that made it okay?

"But now you wrecked it all." Dakota's voice was older now. Not the old-lady nanny-goat voice, but a mature woman's voice, like Mona's or Jade's. It was angry and hard and not the Dakota that he knew. "You wrecked everything for me. How could you do that to me?"

"I didn't," Parker protested. "I didn't do anything! It was Saul who told everyone, not me. I didn't even know."

"You knew," she insisted. "I told you. Everybody told you. You knew, and you wrecked it for me."

"No. It wasn't me. I'd never do anything to hurt you."

Her words stung. How could she think that he was the one who had started telling everybody the truth? Or the rumor, if it wasn't the truth. But deep down, he knew now that it was the truth. The dream didn't lie.

"Now I have to go," Dakota said sulkily. "Now I have to kill myself off and start over again. I hate it when I have to go somewhere new and start over."

"Then stay here. It doesn't matter if everyone knows. I still want you to stay here."

"I can't, Parkinson. I have to go now."

Parker awoke from the dream with a start. His heart was beating rapidly. His body thought that the dream was real. That she really was leaving him.

Would that be such a bad thing? If she left, everyone would forget about the whole thing, and he could go back to just being himself, without all of the questions and accusations.

But he had said in the dream that he didn't want her to leave, and it was the truth. He didn't want her to go away, because he would miss her. She had become a friend in the time that she had been there. Maybe they couldn't be close anymore because of the difference in their ages. But they could still be friends, couldn't they? Parker had plenty of friends who were older than he was. There was nothing that said that you could only have friends your age, even when you were a kid and it was normal to only associate with kids in the same grade as you.

I'll have to kill myself.

What if that was how Dakota felt? What if she felt like it wasn't any use anymore? She couldn't go on if she had to act her age, and

Saul would just keep following her around and exposing her. What was there left to do but just to end it?

But that wasn't what she had meant. She had only meant that she would have to kill off that identity. Dakota Phillips. She still had those other names she was using online. She still had other ladies that she could depend on to help take care of her. She had only to pick which one was next.

Parker turned over onto his back and wriggled his phone out of his pocket. It was still turned off. He had charged it, but he had not turned it on all day. Not even to send one text. How long had it been since he had gone a whole day without using his phone?

But he was worried about Dakota. What if she had been trying to get ahold of him? What if she had been trying to get hold of the one person in that classroom who had looked her in the eyes instead of shunning her? What if she had reached out… and his phone had been off?

He powered it on, and went immediately to the fake account to check Dakota's timeline. If she had posted anything relevant, she might have blocked it from him. But he'd be able to see it with the fake account.

And it was there. A post pinned to the top of her account so that it couldn't get buried in the moving timeline with all of the questions and nasty remarks that people were posting to her.

I am going to shut down this account. I don't know where I'm going to go or what I'm going to do. I don't have very many options. This is goodbye.

She didn't say she was going to kill herself. Not in so many words. Was she that desperate? Or was it just a prelude to abandoning that identity and picking up another?

Parker read it through again. There were a number of comments on the post, but Parker didn't bother to read them. He knew that the majority of them would not be the kind and supportive remarks of friends. *(Hugs) Please reconsider. We're here 4 you.* No, far more likely they would be the nasty posts. The ones encouraging her to do something drastic. The ones that said the world would be better off without her. And he couldn't bear to read those. He didn't think Dakota would want to read them either.

There was no point in commenting under that post. She would never see it there. He needed to find her somewhere else. Somewhere she would be reading.

He started to check her other accounts as systematically as possible. It seemed that she had jumped around quite a bit, going from one account to another, as frantic as a squirrel in the snow. Knowing that she had to make her decision. What was it going to be?

Parker settled on the account that he thought was the most promising. A pastor's wife had said that if Dakota could get herself there, she would provide safe shelter until they could find something more permanent. They expected her to take care of all of the travel arrangements. And with the money she had fundraised, she had enough to buy a bus ticket to get her wherever she needed to go.

He logged out, and back in to his real account. He wasn't sure whether he would be able to message her from it, because he hadn't used it to friend her new identity. He wasn't even connected to her through the fake account, she was just posting everything publicly where anyone could see it. Maybe not the brightest idea if you were trying to maintain multiple secret identities. If he tried to message her, would she see it? Would she open it, or would she be spooked by his writing to one of her alternate egos?

There wasn't anything for him to do but try. He composed a short message to her, obsessing over the wording and whether she would even look at it. What was he going to do if she shut down that identity and moved on to one of the others? Or used one that Parker hadn't found yet. Maybe she had still more identities with privacy settings, ones that didn't post for all the world to read.

Dakota. Don't want to c u go. DM me?

He didn't bother to sign, she could see who it was from. No emoticon or funny gif. Just the bare words. Could he convince her to stay?

Parker knew that it could be hours before Dakota saw the message or bothered to answer, if she would answer. She might just shut down that account too. Did it matter to her that he didn't want her to leave? He didn't exactly have anything to offer her. No incentive to stay. He didn't even know if he'd be able to see her face-to-face. How long his grounding would last. How long he would be banned from having anything to do with her. She obviously couldn't keep going to school once they verified how old she was. Then he'd have no way to see her.

He switched over to a game and played for a few minutes, but he was too distracted and kept getting killed, so he gave up. He hadn't been beeped that Dakota had messaged him back, but he switched back to the app anyway, just to have a look.

As he double-checked to make sure that she hadn't answered him, a private message came in. The thread became bolded and there was a beep. Parker swallowed. He tapped the bolded thread. Was there any point? Would she just tell him to get lost? To leave her alone and let her live her own life however she wanted to?

Parkinson, I don't want to leave u either. Sry.

Sorry. She had to go. She couldn't see any other way. Parker tapped his phone restlessly. He wanted so badly to come up with a solution. He was a good problem solver. He was good at helping people. But his knotted stomach told him there was no other way. If she wanted to keep living as a teen, she would have to do it somewhere else. Best for her to get the hell outta Dodge, before she was lynched.

Y u have to go?

I just can't stay. Too many mean ppl.

They'll get over it.

Nah. :-(

Please please please

There was no response. Parker sat looking at the screen. There was no response. He tried messaging her again.

Where r u? Jade's?

Yes. Want to stay with my new mom 1 more day.

She might disobey and badmouth Jade, but she knew that the older woman cared for her and was trying to take care of her. Even now, when Jade probably knew the truth, she was still trying to help. Still providing shelter for at least one more night.

Jade won't kick you out.

She says I lied. She can't trust me if I won't tell truth.

Is she kicking u out?

Probly.

Parker stared up at the ceiling just a couple of feet over his bed. What could he do? He couldn't find Dakota another home. She could go to a homeless shelter, but Dakota didn't want a homeless shelter. She wanted a home. Another mom. Someone to take care of her, because being an adult and all of the responsibilities it entailed were just too much.

What r u doing tnight?

Watching ponies. Eating junk food.

Parker smiled. That sounded like Dakota. When everyone expected her to be older, she regressed even further. Acting like one of Parker's little sisters instead of someone his age or older. Watching her ponies, pretending she was a little girl, safe and secure. Someone who didn't have any responsibilities. Not even homework.

He had fallen asleep with his phone in his hand. When Mona went through the house waking everyone up, he plugged it in to charge the battery, which was dangerously low, and closed his eyes again.

"Parker. Time to get up," Mona insisted.

"I can't."

"What's wrong?"

"Just... don't feel good."

"What's wrong with you?" Her voice was concerned, not accusatory. It wasn't like he had stayed up late watching TV and was trying to play sick when she knew he was just tired. He'd been in bed as soon as he walked in the door. And to her, that meant he was sick. Teenagers didn't go to sleep in the afternoon for no reason. Especially not Parker.

"Don't know. Just don't feel good."

"Is it your stomach? Your head still? I can get you a Tylenol for your head. Do you need a doctor?"

"No. Nothing. Just want to sleep."

"You're tired? Are you fighting a bug?"

"I guess."

Mona paced across the room and back. "Should I stay home? I don't like to leave you alone if you're sick."

"No. Just gonna sleep. You can go to work."

"And you're not going to be up the minute I leave, doing something you're not supposed to? You're still grounded."

Parker pulled the pillow over his head. "Just leave me alone. I don't want to talk."

"Parker, answer me. You promise me that you're not going out anywhere?"

"Yes. Maybe the bathroom. That's as far as I'm going."

"Give me your phone."

Parker poked his head out from under the pillow. "What?"

"I want to see your phone. Make sure that you weren't up all night talking or texting."

He unplugged his phone slowly. Did it really matter if she saw the conversation with Dakota? He hadn't disobeyed Mona by messaging with her. He had said he didn't want her to go, that was all.

"Dang, my battery is dead!"

He opened the list of running apps, and swiped to get rid of the messaging app. No point in making it easy for her. She would check his call list and his texts, and probably wouldn't even think of any social apps.

"Let me see it."

Parker handed it down to her. He put his head back under his pillow and waited.

"Why is the battery dead?" she demanded.

"Must not have had it plugged in all the way. I wasn't using it."

There was a bloodcurdling shriek from the direction of the girls' room. Some mornings the girls just could not get along together. The scream sounded like Leslie. She was a bear in the morning, and had a scream that could—and sometimes did—wake the neighbors. Mona pushed the phone back onto Parker's bunk and hurried out to take care of it before the neighbors could start making complaints. Parker didn't know why they got so upset about a little bit of noise first thing in the morning. It was just kids being kids.

It could have been much worse.

Something really bad.

Mona was kept running the rest of the early morning, and made it back to Parker's room only briefly as she prepared to go to work.

"You're charging your phone now?"

"Uh-huh."

"You call me if you need me, then. I don't like to have to leave work, but I can if you really need me. I'll call you later to check in on you. You won't go anywhere else?"

"I'm staying in bed."

"Okay… love you, sweetie." She patted him on the shoulder. Then she was gone. He heard the door a couple of minutes later.

Then it was just Link getting the little kids out the door in time for school. Link also checked in on him before leaving the house.

"You okay, Parker?"

"Yeah."

"You need anything? I could make you a piece of toast…"

"No. Not hungry."

"Is it because of *her?*" Link ventured.

"No."

Of course they both knew he was lying. But at least Link hadn't snitched to Mona. He knew enough to mind his own business.

"If you need something, don't call Mom. I don't want her getting in trouble at work. Just text me. I can be home faster anyway."

"Okay."

Link stood there for a moment, looking for something to say. Then he shrugged and left the room. Parker heard the front door close and he was finally alone.

He drew in a shaky, shuddering breath, and sobbed into his pillow.

237

Chapter Twenty

W AKE UP! PARKER, YOU need to wake up right now!"
Parker was disoriented. He was sure that not enough time had passed for Mona to be home. And he hadn't called her. So what was she doing home? Why was she waking him up, pulling him back into the real world where he had to think about Dakota and how he didn't know how to help her and make her stay? Had she decided that he was just faking sick and had returned to force him to go back to school? He didn't know how he could face them all again. He couldn't focus on the work, so what was the point in going to school and sitting in his desk like a brain-dead zombie?

"Mom… what is it?"

"Come down from there right now. Come on. I want to talk to you. Face-to-face, not like this."

Parker rubbed his eyes. "Mom… I'm tired. What… what's wrong?"

"You have some nerve asking me what's wrong. Now, Parker Andrew Jurek! You get out of that bed and down here right now!"

Her voice was shrill. A rising tone that cut right through him. Not just anger, but fear. Panic. Had something happened to one of the other children? Parker tried to shake off his lethargy. If something had happened to one of the others, he needed to act. Get his mind back together and do something to help.

"What is it?" Parker forced himself to move. To crawl down the ladder, blinking and pausing to rub his eyes and trying to clear them of sleep.

Once he had his feet on the floor, Mona was pulling on him. Dragging him out to the living room, where she pushed him down on the couch. Her eyes were blazing. But her face was drawn and pale. He hadn't seen her look like that in years. Not for four years. The memory of it was branded into his mind.

"Mom…?"

If something had happened to one of the children, she had to tell him. Miranda getting bullied? Jessup? It had been two years since Jessup had had a seizure, out of nowhere. The doctors said it would probably never happen again, but Parker and Mona lived in fear that they were wrong, and that deep within the boy's brain, a tumor was growing. Or something worse.

She pulled the ottoman over and sat on it, right in front of him, so that their knees were nearly touching. "Why didn't you tell me about Dakota?" she demanded. "Why am I hearing this from the school instead of from you?"

So for all her talk about confidentiality, Mrs. Strauss had still seen fit to blab to Mona the rumors about Dakota.

"About what?" he said irritably. "It's just rumors."

"She's an adult? With a grown child? That's not just a rumor."

"You don't know it's true," Parker argued. "We don't have any proof."

"Proof? I knew there was something wrong about that girl from the start! I knew it!"

"You hated her for no reason. You're just attacking her now like everybody else, without any proof of anything."

"That's not true. I wanted to protect you. I wanted to keep my son safe. How would you feel if she had gone after Link? Or Jessup?"

Parker stared at her, baffled. Why would she go after Link or Jessup? They were little kids.

"Gone after them?" he repeated.

"You go get showered and dressed. I don't know whether they will come here, or we have to go in, but you'll need to be presentable."

"What?"

She glared at him. "Go get showered. And dressed." Her over-enunciated words left no room for argument. Just like if she'd used his full name again. There was no getting away from whatever it was Mona wanted. Was she going to call Jade and Dakota? Ask them to come to the house to discuss the whole mess?

Who was going to come to the house?

Parker got to his feet and headed for the bathroom. He felt like he was sleepwalking. Maybe it was all just another dream. His muddled brain trying to process a problem that was way too big for him to solve. One of those dreams where he could never get his clothes off and get into the shower to get ready for school. There were always weird roadblocks in his dreams. He couldn't get his clothes off. He kept getting interrupted by people who didn't belong there wandering through the house. Lights burned out or the power went out. The water wouldn't come on. Or there would be water all over the bathroom. Or he couldn't find the bathroom.

But it wasn't a dream. He did find the bathroom, and stripped down without having figured out what Mona was planning to do, and got under the soothing pulse of the warm water in the shower. He even remembered to slide a plastic bag over his cast to protect it. It felt almost as good as being back in bed. He could close his eyes and just enjoy the warmth and pretend that there wasn't a real world out there that expected people to grow up and leave their childhoods behind forever. Mona banged on the door for him to get out, but he didn't. Not until he had emptied the hot water tank and the water abruptly turned cold. Then he shut the water off in a hurry and jumped out of the tub, colder than ever. He grabbed a towel and wrapped it around himself.

He hadn't brought any clothes into the bathroom and had only his pajamas to change back into. Since Mona seemed to think that his bedtime t-shirt and sweats were not appropriate attire, he didn't put them back on, but went back to his room, clad in the towel, to find something else.

"Get dressed," Mona said, walking by the room and seeing him stopped, looking at his bed. "No going back to bed. I want you dressed. Socks too."

He shut the door in her face, but he didn't get back into bed. He obeyed and dragged clean clothes on over his damp skin. Just that was exhausting. He wanted more than anything to climb back into bed.

When he opened the door, Mona was standing on the other side of it. Probably listening through the door for the squeak of his bedsprings.

"Good boy. They're sending someone out. Come back into the living room."

Parker followed her. He sat on the couch, uncomfortable in the growing silence. He waited for Jade and Dakota to get there. It was good that they were going to come. Maybe they could get the whole thing straightened out. Dakota would have to answer his questions straight out, for once.

"Can I turn on the TV?"

Mona looked impatiently at her watch, and out the living room window. She sighed. "Yes, go ahead."

There wasn't much on that was good. Parker was just getting into a daytime talk show when he heard the footsteps on their front steps. Mona was already up and hurrying toward the door when the doorbell rang. She opened the door to let them in.

But it wasn't Jade and Dakota, like Parker had expected. It was a couple of dark-uniformed police officers.

Parker looked at them blankly. His whirling brain couldn't come up with an explanation. His first thought, ridiculous as it was, was that Mona was having him arrested for skipping school.

The officers introduced themselves. Parker grasped at the names, trying to retain them. An older man, experienced-looking, with a frosting of gray around his temples like Mr. Bonne. Costa. And a blond woman, rosy-cheeked, like a kid on a ride-along. Read.

Costa and Read. He tried to imprint their names on his memory, even though he had no idea why they were there.

Everybody sat down comfortably. Parker rubbed his eyes, trying to focus on what was going on. Everyone looked grim. Parker realized he was in trouble, but he still wasn't sure why.

It was Costa, the male cop, who spoke first. "According to your report on the phone, you are concerned that your son has been molested by a woman in the neighborhood."

Parker's heart thudded so hard it hurt and took away his breath. He looked at Mona, eyes wide, black splotches popping before his eyes like he was going to faint. "Mom!"

"I *know* he has been," Mona said in a flat, even voice, not looking at Parker. No embarrassment. No apology. She was going to sit there and tell them lies and half-truths about Dakota, impaling Parker with the same sword.

"Who is this woman? Is she at teacher at his school?"

"No. Her name is Dakota Phillips. Or that's what she's been going by. She pretends to be a teenager and goes to school with him, but she's really a grown woman. Her son has shown up to expose what she's been doing. Her twenty-year-old son!"

The officers looked at Parker, and looked back at Mona with an air of disbelief.

"You're telling us that a woman in her late thirties or early forties has been passing herself off as a teenager?" Costa asked.

"You put twenty- and thirty-year-olds in schools as undercover agents, don't you?" Mona demanded. "Some people can pass for younger. Your partner, she could pass as a teenager."

Rosy-cheeked Read turned even pinker at the observation. Officer Costa looked at her, and back at Mona. "She's in her early twenties. That's a little easier to believe than a forty-year-old."

"It may be strange, but it's true. You look into it, you'll find out."

"You said that's the name she's going by," Costa observed, making a note in his notepad. "You don't believe it's her real name?"

"I don't know what to believe. I just found out today how old she is. Parker has already been banned from seeing her. I talked to my friend Jade—that's who Dakota is living with—and she says that Dakota goes by all different names. So I don't know which one is really her legal name."

"Do you have Jade's full name and address?"

Mona gave it to them.

"Mom," Parker protested. "You can't do this to Dakota! Having her arrested? She didn't… I mean…"

There was a look exchanged between the officers, and it was Read who looked at Parker, a reassuring smile on her face. "Parker, this must all be very confusing to you. You thought this woman was a girl your own age too?"

"Yes. I mean, she is. We don't know for sure how old she is. Saul could be lying. I think he's just an ex-boyfriend, and he made this up to make her look bad. I don't think she's really that old. And she didn't… she didn't do anything to me."

"We will look into it and find out how old she really is. Don't worry, we don't just go by what people say. We'll investigate it and get proof of her age. If she is just a teenager… well, depending on how much older than you she might be…" she trailed off.

He sensed that even if Dakota turned out to be sixteen, they might still press charges against her.

"Dakota never did anything to me," he insisted. He looked at Mona. "She didn't! You can't say she did."

Officer Read's eyes flicked back and forth between Parker and Mona, considering.

"Why don't you tell me what you think happened?" she said to Mona. "And we'll go from there."

Mona covered both of her eyes for a moment, preparing herself. Then she held her hands in her lap and spoke in careful, measured tones.

"I got a call from the school saying that Parker was not in attendance. So I knew he was cutting classes. Probably with Dakota, because they'd been sneaking around together. I called Jade. We tried to track them down. Jade was out of town, but she came back, and she found the two of them…" Mona's eyes went to Parker. He felt his face flushing.

"Mom…"

"She found them together, both… passed out and only half-dressed. My son doesn't drink, officer. I know every mother tells you that, but he doesn't. She's the one who got him drunk, so she could take advantage of him."

"No," Parker protested. "No, that's not what happened!"

"We want to hear your side of the story too," Read assured Parker. "Why don't you tell us how it really happened?"

"That's not why she wanted—that wasn't why I had something to drink! She just… she was feeling down, and she didn't want to drink alone. So… I had a little… to keep her company."

"A little? And you just fell asleep?"

"I… I guess it was more than I thought. But that's not Dakota's fault. I just didn't know how it would affect me."

Officer Read nodded and wrote in her notepad. Parker hoped she was writing down his side of the story, not just Mona's.

"And how were you dressed when Jade discovered the two of you passed out?"

"I was dressed! I just had… I wasn't wearing a shirt. That's all."

"And his pants—" Mona started.

"I had pants on! They were just undone. They…" Parker searched for an explanation. But he could see there wasn't any innocent reason for him to be in that state. He swallowed hard. "So we were messing around a little. But not because of Dakota. Because *I* wanted to!"

He couldn't look at his mother. He could feel her looking at him, feel the disappointment rolling off of her. But what he said was the truth. They couldn't put that all on Dakota, say that everything that had happened between them was her fault. Parker had been eager for the physical intimacy. He had been the one pushing it, not Dakota. Mona made it sound like Dakota had gotten him drunk because she wanted to molest him, to go further than he was willing. But that wasn't the way it had been. She'd been the one putting the brakes on.

Mona made a little suppressed squawk, like she wanted very much to say something and was trying hard to keep quiet. Officer Read kept her eyes on Parker, nodding reassuringly.

"You like Dakota, Parker? How do you feel about her?"

"Yes, I like her. She's my friend."

"That's good. It's important to have friends. Do you have a lot of friends at school?"

Parker breathed out, glad to have a segue away from Mona's accusations. "Yes. I mean, a couple of close friends. And then… kids in my grade… kids in the neighborhood that I've gone to school with for years."

"Any other girls?"

"I know lots of girls… I've gone out with a couple of them…"

"But no current girlfriend?"

"No…" Parker trailed off, frowning. He didn't like that she'd circled back around to relationship stuff.

"Would you consider Dakota your girlfriend?"

Parker glanced over at his mother. He didn't want to say yes in front of her. But he didn't want to say no, to deny what he really felt for Dakota. In spite of all the nonsense about her being older, or maybe because of it, he was feeling very protective toward her. He wished that instead of sitting there talking to the cops, he were with her. The two of them giving each other comfort, helping each other through a tough time.

"There's nothing wrong with it," Parker asserted. "I'm old enough to have a girlfriend."

"You might be old enough to have those feelings toward her," Read said slowly. "But you are not at an age where you can give consent for her to have intimate contact with you. Especially with her being older."

"She's not, though. Maybe a couple of years. Maybe. But she's not…" He looked at Mona again. "It's not like they're saying. I'd know if she was that old."

"We will look into it. We're not going to assume anything until we have talked with Dakota and looked into the matter further. We're not out to damage anyone's reputation."

Parker stared down at his feet. He had put on socks, but his toe was peeking out of the end of one of them. Link was always cutting through the ends of socks with his razor-sharp toenails. It was a challenge to find a pair of socks in the house that would fit Parker that didn't have holes in the ends.

"We would like to have Parker come down to the station to make a statement," Officer Read told Mona. "This is something that needs to be carefully handled and documented. There is enough here to be of concern. We need to investigate further."

Mona nodded stiffly. "Okay. You want me to take him? Where do I go and who do I talk to?"

"We'll get the ball rolling," Costa said. "Before we go, I'll give you a file number. We'll find out who will be interviewing him, so you don't have to wait around or be shuffled around. It will be a long day, but I think you'll both feel a lot better when it's done."

After the officers left, Parker was left alone in the house with Mona. He wished he had been able to leave with the police. They could have just taken him to the police station. Or maybe given him a lift to the nearest bus station so he could clear out of town.

The walls seemed suddenly closer together. Though their house was small and filled to the brim with people, Parker had never felt claustrophobic. But it was suddenly much too small for the two of them. He didn't want to look at Mona. He didn't want to talk to her. Her calling the police to report Dakota was a betrayal of Parker. All of the trust they had built over the years was gone. He wouldn't ever be able to trust her again.

"Do you want a bite to eat before we go?" Mona asked finally.

"No."

"You didn't have anything last night and you've only been sleeping today. You need something to eat."

Parker shook his head. He was hungry, and if she hadn't suggested it, he would have gone to the kitchen to get himself something without prompting. But he wasn't going to eat, because she had suggested it. She would offer to make him something, and he didn't want anything from her. He wanted to make it as clear as possible how much her betrayal had hurt him.

"I'll take something along with us. You're bound to get hungry while we're there. Some granola bars and fruit, or some trail mix. How does that sound? Then you can have something to munch on…" She was attempting to talk in a normal, everyday voice, but there was a break at the end of the sentence. Just a little catch that told him how much she was fighting to stay in control.

But Parker didn't feel sorry for her. It was all her fault. She was the one who had called the police. If she were upset about it and regretting it now, that was her own doing. If she were crying about Parker pushing her away, that was too bad. She was going to have to deal with the consequences of her own choices. That was what she had always told him. She had to know that by reporting Dakota, she was ruining any chance at ever having a good relationship with Parker. That was over. He would leave as soon as he was able. He couldn't stay around someone who treated him like that.

"Parker…"

He didn't look at her.

"You know I had to do it. You know I couldn't just let my child be abused like that. When it happened, I was furious. But I figured… you were both children. Both experimenting. I could keep you away from her and it would blow over. But she's an adult! I will not let any woman hurt my son!"

"She never hurt me," Parker said tightly. "You're the one who is hurting me. By keeping me away from her. By reporting her to the police. You're trying to embarrass and humiliate her. And me. How is that being a good mom?"

She tried to get close and put her hand on his shoulder, but Parker jerked away from her and wouldn't let her touch him.

"Parker, I'm trying to protect you. I know you don't understand that now, but it's true. Imagine if it was Link or Jessup. Or imagine if it was a man and one of the little girls. You would feel the same way."

"It isn't the same. It's me and Dakota. I wanted to be with her. She wasn't doing anything I didn't want. And she's not some perv or weirdo. Just… just Dakota." He shook his head, frustrated at his inability to express himself clearly. "I just want to be with… the person I like, Mom. That's all." He tried to swallow the big lump in his throat.

Mona's eyes were shiny. Parker couldn't look at her anymore. He couldn't talk about it anymore. He turned around abruptly and dashed into the bathroom. He shut and locked the door, and sat there in the one place in the house where she couldn't follow him or disturb him.

To say that she couldn't disturb him there turned out to be wrong. While she left him alone for long enough to get his composure back, after ten minutes she was knocking tentatively on the door.

"Parker? Are you okay? We should be heading over there now…"

"I don't feel good. I don't think I can go right now."

That got rid of her for a few more minutes, but not for long. She was knocking again, harder. "Parker. We need to go now. The detective is waiting for us and it's rude not to go right away like we promised to, when he's there waiting for us."

"I never said I wanted to talk to anyone about it. I don't want to. I don't want to go there."

"They're waiting on us, Parker."

"Then you go. I'm not going."

"I need you to come. They're going to need to talk to you about what happened. You want to tell your side of the story, don't you?"

"I already did, to Costa and Read. I don't need to talk to anyone else."

"If you don't come out, I'm going to have to unlock the door and come in and get you."

Parker eyed the door. He stood his ground. He didn't think she would really do it. But in a couple of minutes, he heard the lock pop, and Mona opened the door.

"Come. Now," she ordered grimly.

Parker shook his head. "I'm not coming."

"You are coming. I'll take you, or I'll have the police come get you. One way or the other, you're going to the police station."

"They wouldn't come get me."

Mona stepped into the bathroom. It was small and narrow, and she didn't have to go in very far to be able to reach him. She grabbed his ear and gave it a sharp pull. Parker yelped and pulled away, but she hung on.

"You want a belt on your backside too?" she demanded. "If you don't get your butt out to the car, I will drag you out there. Do you really want to make a scene in front of the whole neighborhood?"

Parker eased toward the door of the bathroom, not liking it, but not able to do much by way of protest.

"Everybody's at work anyway," he grumbled.

"So we're going for the scene?"

"No!" Parker tried to pull his ear away again, but couldn't do it without hurting himself. "Mom! Let go, I'll get in the car."

"No more nonsense?"

"No!"

She released him. Parker rubbed his ear tenderly, especially right at the back where it connected with his head. It felt like she'd been trying to twist it right off. Parker pulled off the socks with holes in them, and slid on Link's flip flops. Mona scowled at them, and he waited for the lecture that flip flops were not appropriate footwear for a trip to the police station. He'd heard it enough times about school. But Mona held her tongue and just waited for him to head out the door.

Parker got into the car without another word, but he made it clear that he wasn't happy with the whole business. Obedience wasn't the same as agreement.

If the detective was waiting for them when they got to the police station, that wasn't obvious. Mona gave them Detective Bray's name and their new case number at the front desk, and the uniformed woman looked like she'd never heard of him before and wouldn't know what to do with a case number. Parker wondered for a minute if they had come to the wrong place. Was there a different police station they were supposed to be at? Had they gotten the name or department wrong?

"Please have a seat," the police receptionist instructed them.

Mona found a couple of seats together. There were plenty of other people sitting around waiting, looking bored or tired or angry. Parker didn't sit beside Mona. He crossed the room and found another seat. He folded his arms stubbornly across his chest and refused to look at Mona.

Parker was really getting hungry. He wondered whether she had followed through on the snack idea, or if that had been abandoned when he had refused to get out of the bathroom. He shouldn't have distracted her. But he wouldn't have taken one of her snacks anyway. Refusing her food was the only way he could think of to gain some control over the situation and to express his displeasure to her. Mona was a nurturer. Feeding the family was one of the most important things to her. Food was a way of showing her love. Refusing to eat it was a personal affront.

Parker hadn't thought to bring anything to do while they waited. He had thought from what Mona had said that the police investigator would be waiting impatiently, and Parker wouldn't have to do any waiting. That had obviously been a mistake. Parker pulled out his phone. He was worried that if anyone saw him using it, they would think that he was communicating with Dakota, and they would take it from him as part of the investigation.

That made him think about what he had already posted to Dakota or to other people about Dakota in the days and weeks since she had first arrived. What could they use against her? What might they have said to each other that could be misinterpreted? Parker woke up his phone and went first to the social networks, logging out of each of his accounts and then deleting the apps. He went to his texts and started marking and swiping like a demon, getting rid of every message that had anything to do with Dakota. He went to his recent phone calls list, and marked all of them for deletion as well. He removed every trace that he could think of. Anything that might have something to do with Dakota.

"Parker Jurek?"

Parker looked up, and saw the tall policeman standing in front of him. Bray was not wearing a police uniform, but it was obvious that he was one of them. The way he held himself. The air of authority. And they were, after all, in the police station.

"Uh… yeah."

"Would you come with me, please?"

Parker looked at Mona. He had been shunning her all the time they had been there, but suddenly he needed her. He didn't want to go anywhere with Bray. He didn't want to talk to anyone. But most of all, he didn't want to do it alone.

Mona stood up and came quickly over. "I'm Parker's mom."

The man nodded. "Nice to meet you. I need Parker to come with me now."

"Of course. I'll come too."

"No, ma'am. We need to talk to him alone."

"He's a juvenile. He needs me to be there with him."

"You don't need to worry. He'll be talking to the psychologist rather than to me. She is very skilled. She's been working with juveniles for many years."

"I am coming with him."

Detective Bray looked around the waiting room. It was too public for him to speak openly. "Ma'am… if you'll come with me. We'll go somewhere we can talk."

Parker and Mona both went with him. Parker breathed a sigh of relief. As angry as he was with his mom, he was too nervous to go through the interview all by himself.

Bray took them to a meeting room and shut the door. He didn't take one of the seats around the table and didn't invite either of them to sit.

"Mrs. Jurek. We need to follow up on the allegations that you have made about this woman interfering with your son. The psychologist is going to need to ask him very… delicate questions, and he's going to need to answer them fully. He really can't do that with his mother in the room."

"He can talk in front of me. When the officers spoke to him at the house, he talked in front of me. It's not a big deal, is it, Parker?"

Parker turned his face to look at her. He was torn, wanting her moral support in the room, but wanting to do it on his own too. Wanting her to protect him from their questions, and not wanting to talk about it in front of her.

"Parker," Detective Bray said. "The psychologist is going to have to know the specific details of anything that you and Miss Phillips might have done together. This is not something you are going to want your mother to hear."

Parker nodded.

Mona held his arm. "Parker. You want me to be there, don't you? You want me to help you."

"No, Mom. You'd better not."

She looked at him, her eyes wide with alarm. "Parker."

"No, Mom. It's okay. I'll be fine. You go get a coffee somewhere. You need to eat."

"Oh, the snacks!" Mona dug around in her purse. Bray looked on, bemused. Mona pressed a granola bar and a sausage stick into Parker's hand. "You must be starving. Or you will be. Take that with you."

This time, he accepted them. Mona kissed Parker on the cheek. "I'll be right here waiting, honey. It will be okay."

Parker nodded. The lump was back in his throat, and his eyes stung. As angry as he was with her for forcing him to be there, he didn't want to have to leave her behind, waiting for him and wondering if he were okay. She was just trying to do the right thing for him.

Chapter Twenty-One

T HIS WAY." DETECTIVE BRAY led Parker through what seemed like a rat's maze, eventually stopping in front of a light-colored wooden door, which he knocked on. It seemed all at once to be normal and bizarre.

"Come in."

The woman's voice from within was pleasant and inviting. Bray opened the door, and then motioned Parker in.

It wasn't a bare little meeting room like the one Parker had just been in with Mona. It was a comfortable office or waiting area. A couple of comfy chairs and a couch, grouped together for an intimate discussion. Carpeted floor. Abstract paintings on the walls. Shelves filled with books. Children's books on the lower shelves, and heavier tomes above. There was a toy box and a child-sized table with chairs.

The woman was sitting in one of the comfy chairs. She smiled at Parker as he poked his head in. "Come in, Parker. Don't worry, I don't bite."

He took a couple of steps into the room. Bray did not follow, but shut the door behind Parker. The small room did not feel claustrophobic with the door shut. Just private and cozy.

"Sit wherever you like," the woman said.

Parker chose the other comfy chair and settled into it. It was soft and warm and hugged his body.

"My name is Dr. Anya Bayez. Please just call me Anya. You go by Parker?"

He nodded. "Yes."

"Can I get you anything, Parker? A drink? Soft drink or glass of water?" She smiled at the snacks he still held in his hand. "I see you came otherwise provisioned."

He looked down at the food, a little embarrassed. "My mom didn't want me to go hungry."

"She must love you very much. I expect this is just as hard for her as it is for you."

Parker wasn't going to get onside with that one. He just shrugged and didn't comment. Dr. Bayez gave him a smile. "So… a drink?"

He would normally decline. But his mouth felt like it was filled with cotton. So Parker nodded.

"Yeah, just water."

She got up and went over to one of the bookshelves, where there was a tiny beverage refrigerator almost hidden from view. She opened it and got out two bottles of water, passing one to Parker before she sat back down.

"How would you be most comfortable doing this? Would you like me to ask you some questions, or would you like to tell me your story without being interrupted? We can do whatever you are most comfortable with. Of course, we can talk about other things too, and I can help break the ice with some other topics, but you understand that eventually this is going to get back to your relationship with Dakota Phillips."

Parker nodded. He unscrewed the cap of the water bottle and took a few gulps. He held a mouthful of cold water in his mouth for a few minutes, trying to absorb all of the moisture so that his mouth wouldn't be instantly dry again the moment he swallowed. It was anyway.

"Still a nice day out there?" Dr. Bayez asked. "I don't have a window and I can go all day without knowing that the weather has changed."

"Yeah. It's nice. Sunny and warm."

"That's good. It was a bit cloudy this morning, I wasn't sure if it was going to clear up."

Parker nodded. He looked around the room. He hadn't realized there weren't any windows. Not even an observation window. No big mirror on one wall like on TV. Nor a narrow one cut into the door. Parker looked slowly around the ceiling, realizing there were several cameras surveilling the room from various angles.

Dr. Bayez nodded. "Everything that happens in this room is recorded. You're safe here."

"It feels safe," Parker agreed. He didn't want her thinking that he was afraid she was going to take advantage of him after his experience with Dakota. He didn't feel threatened by being alone with her. But then, he hadn't been taken advantage of by Dakota, either.

"She was my girlfriend," he told Dr. Bayez. "Or I wanted her to be. Maybe she didn't think of me as her boyfriend, but that's how I thought of her. What I wanted her to be."

"So the two of you were dating? Going out together?"

Parker hesitated. "Yes… I went to a party with her. We went to each other's houses. To the park. Out for ice cream. Studied together at the library. All that kind of stuff."

"What did Dakota like to do the most?"

"Just hang out at home, watching TV. Kid's movies, maybe. She liked little kid shows."

"Why do you think that is?"

"It's not because she's pretending to be younger than she is. She really does like them."

Dr. Bayez nodded. "I'm not making any judgment. Just asking a question. What did you like to do best?"

"Go out for a walk in the park. Spend some time there… in the trees… where we could be alone."

"You didn't feel like you could be alone other places?"

"No, not really privately. Even if the house was empty, someone could come home any time…"

"And you were worried about that because…"

"I wanted time alone with her."

A thoughtful nod. "So she likes TV and you like nature. Who got their way most often?"

"I don't know… neither one. Sometimes we did one, sometimes the other."

"What happened at the party?"

Parker was startled at the subject change. "What?"

"You mentioned that you had gone to a party together. Tell me about that. Was it a party thrown by one of your classmates? You didn't say you threw a party, so I assume it wasn't your party."

"No… I don't really know whose party it was. There weren't a lot of kids our age there. Older high school and college kids, mostly."

"So was there alcohol?"

"Yes."

"And you both drank?"

"Well… a little. I just had a couple of swallows. Dakota… had… more."

Dr. Bayez analyzed Parker's words and tone. "Were you concerned with the amount that she had to drink?"

"She had too much. She was drunk. Throwing up. Being stupid."

"So that didn't end up being a very good date."

Parker looked down at the cast on his arm. It hadn't been his finest hour.

"That's where you broke your arm?" Dr. Bayez guessed.

"And my nose. Got in a fight with a guy who was trying to pick Dakota up."

"That didn't make it into the initial report the officers took today."

"No… my mom doesn't know that."

"She must know you broke your arm."

"I said I fell out of bed. I have a bunk bed."

"Oh. So she didn't even know you were out of the house."

"No."

"Dakota invited you to this party?"

"Yeah. How do you know that? It could have been someone at school."

"Teenagers who are into this kind of party… don't just have a few swallows of alcohol. They go to get a buzz on."

The way she said it almost made Parker laugh. A buzz on.

"So it makes sense that it was Dakota's idea, not yours. You preferred privacy. Somewhere you could be alone together, just the two of you."

Parker nodded. "She wasn't pushing me to be alone together," he said. "I was the one that wanted that."

"The report I received *did* say that Dakota got you drunk, though. Not at the party."

"At her house. I wasn't that drunk. I just… fell asleep."

"It sounds like there was more to it than just nodding off in front of the TV."

"That's all it was. We were watching a show. And we had something to drink. We fell asleep. That's all."

Bayez said nothing. Parker got warm. He pulled his shirt collar away from his neck and held the cold water bottle up to his skin.

"That's not all," he admitted.

"No. Thank you for being honest about that. You were making out. You were partially unclothed."

"But not completely," Parker pointed out. "And Dakota wasn't pushing me to kiss her, I wanted that."

"Of course you did."

Parker's face must have shown his surprise. Dr. Bayez laughed.

"There are few teenage boys who wouldn't have wanted to kiss, alone in the house with a girl and a little bit of alcohol in their system. Even without alcohol."

"So you understand. It wasn't Dakota pushing me. She didn't do anything wrong."

"Let's leave the judgments out of it. Just looking for the truth about what happened. Not to cast it in a good or bad light."

Parker was a bit irritated by this, wanting her to say that Dakota hadn't done anything wrong. But at least she wasn't calling Dakota a child molester.

"Were there other times when you and Dakota made out?"

"Yeah."

"And how far did it go?"

Parker tried to breathe around the knot in his stomach. He was glad that he hadn't eaten the snacks. Even just the water seemed to have turned into something volatile in his stomach. He shifted around.

Dr. Bayez laid a laminated picture on the coffee table close to Parker. There was a physical intimacy scale on it, with different levels of intimacy clearly labeled. It was colorful, Parker thought, but he couldn't differentiate all of the colors. Green for okay and red for bad? He couldn't tell if they were random colors or in a meaningful spectrum. Bayez sat watching him. He knew what the question was. She didn't have to repeat it. He read through the descriptions and looked at the pictograms slowly, as if he might make a mistake if he weren't careful. He put his finger down on one of the squares. Dr. Bayez nodded and noted something in her notebook.

"Did the two of you use any kind of protection?"

Parker swallowed. "No."

"Did you discuss it?"

"No."

"Why not? You didn't consider the consequences?"

He shook his head slowly. He knew what Mona would have to say about that kind of behavior. It was a good thing that she hadn't come to the interview. That she couldn't see and hear what Parker had to say. She thought the worst of it had been drinking and making out at Jade's. If she'd known how far they had really gone, she would be choked.

"How many separate occasions?"

Parker held up his fingers.

"Where? At your park?"

He nodded. "Not close to anyone. There are places you can go that are far away from the paved pathways. No one was close by."

"And the park was where you wanted to go. Your idea."

"Yes. Not Dakota's. She didn't even like to hold hands in public. She said that we couldn't let people think that we were a couple. It wasn't her that was pushing for this," Parker tapped the chart again. He wanted Dr. Bayez to understand that it wasn't Dakota preying on him. He liked her, and she liked him, and one thing had naturally led to another.

"What do you know about Dakota?" Dr. Bayez inquired.

It was an open-ended question. Parker wasn't sure what she was looking for. "I dunno… she was homeless when I first met her. I helped her to get a home, with Jade, and for Mr. Bonne to get her registered for school. We went to school, and she's really smart. Especially with math. She helped me with my work. We hung out." He flicked a hand toward the laminated chart. "Did stuff."

"Do you feel like you have a lot in common?"

Parker tried to think of one thing that they had in common, and couldn't come up with anything. "Well… no. I dunno. There are… things…"

"So other than the fact that you go to school together, there isn't really anything?"

"School, yeah. Same school, same grade, same neighborhood, all that."

"But no similar interests? Backgrounds? Cultures?"

"No…"

"What did you talk about other than school?"

"I don't know."

"Do you know where she came from before she moved here? When her birthday is?"

Parker shook his head. "No. She didn't want to talk about her past. I asked sometimes, but… she didn't want to talk about it."

He bit his lip, trying to figure out how to explain to her that even if he didn't know everything about Dakota, they still had a special relationship.

Parker sat in another waiting area. It was more comfortable than the one he had been in at the beginning with Mona, out in the front, which had been more like an emergency room. The one they had put him in after he was finished talking with Dr. Bayez was just a small grouping of soft, dark, leather-like chairs. Mona wasn't there. Parker sank down into one of the chairs, wondering how long he was going to have to wait. He was tired in spite of the extended length of time that he had slept. The talk with Dr. Bayez had wrung him out and left him feeling empty and hopeless. As much as he had tried to tell her that Dakota had done nothing wrong, he knew he had not helped his own case. Dr. Bayez had teased out the details and assembled them into something she could make sound evil and sinister. When it had just been two kids enjoying each other's company.

Once he was away from everyone else, Parker was hungry. Starving. He looked around and unwrapped the granola bar, trying to keep the wrapper from crinkling. There were police officers coming and going, but no one was specifically guarding Parker. No one paid any attention to him or seemed to be disturbed by the fact that he was eating. He was careful not to get crumbs in the chair.

"What did she have to say for herself?"

There were two policemen talking back behind Parker. Neither paid any attention to the skinny kid waiting in the chairs. Parker had sunk into the chair so far that only the top of his head was visible. He had been thinking that he might catch a nap, but the officer's voice was nasal and grated on his frayed nerves. Couldn't they go somewhere else to talk?

"Kept denying it," the shorter of the two said. His voice, at least, was not so irritating. He had a bit of an accent that Parker tried to analyze. Boston, maybe?

"What, her fingerprints were lying?" The first snorted. "We've got the wrong person?"

"The records were messed up. A computer error. Couldn't I tell just looking at her that they were wrong?" Boston shook his head.

"She does look good for her age. But sixteen? No way. One good long look under bright light will tell you that."

Parker swallowed. Were they talking about Dakota? Right there behind him? He swiveled his head again to look at them surreptitiously. Were they just that stupid, or did they not even see him? He thought maybe they were trying to get a reaction from him, but neither was looking in his direction.

"Not now, maybe, straight out of bed and no makeup. But have you seen some of the selfies she's posted of herself? Cute as a button. Doesn't look any older than my daughter."

So Boston had a daughter. Parker wondered how old she was. Eighteen? Twenty? How old did he think Dakota looked?

The nasal voice wormed into Parker's brain. "ID puts her at thirty-seven. That's a bit older than your daughter. Almost as old as you!"

"She's scared," Boston said. "I don't know why she was still sitting around waiting for us. She was spooked. Bags were packed. She was ready to run, but she didn't."

"Guess she was hoping it would all blow over."

"Stupid. Looking at her record, she usually runs. She doesn't wait around for the police to come knocking at her door."

"She done this before? Messing with a kid?"

Boston shifted his stance and blew out his breath. "If she has, it's gone unreported. No previous sexual assault charges or obvious pedo red flags. Previous investigations have only been into her identity. And generally, once suspicions are raised, she's out of there. Hops the bus to a new city. Starts over again."

"And her son? She ever touch him?"

"She says she's hardly even seen him since he was five. He said no in his initial interview. She didn't mess with him and he was disgusted when he found out she had a fourteen-year-old boyfriend. That wasn't why he set out to find her."

"Poor sap. Wants to find his mom, be reconciled. Maybe have something to do with her life. He's willing to forget the fact that she abandoned him. He finds a trail of pseudonyms and folks she's defrauded. That's bad enough." The voice climbed up in tone, making Parker grind his teeth. It was worse than fingernails on a blackboard. "He figures if he makes his peace with her, maybe she'll stop running. And then he finds out she's a freakin' pedophile!"

"Best thing she probably ever did was leave him." Boston sighed. "Now she admits her age. But she's saying she never lied to folks about it until her police interview. Then she just panicked.

Says she never told anyone around here she was a teenager. They all just assumed. If we can't get her for misrepresenting herself, we're going to have to find a way to make sure the sex charges stick. Get her off the streets for a good long time. At least until she can't hide her age anymore."

"She never lied to anyone about her age?" The nasal voice was incredulous. "She went to junior high school. Flipped burgers. She never lied?"

"She used her own social for her job. On their computer records, her birth year is flipped. No one has the original paperwork to check whether she filled it in with the year fudged, or if the person entering it in on the computer reversed it, thinking it was wrong. The school hadn't put her into the computer yet. We've got the registration paperwork she filled out in her handwriting, and the year is illegible. The person who is transcribing it onto the computer is going to interpret her writing differently if they know they're entering information for a student than they would if they knew she was an adult."

"Well, none of that matters. She lied to the police about her identity. I'd rather get her on the sex charges than identity charges anyway."

Boston grunted his agreement.

"Where's the kid?"

"In with Bayez."

"Kid's going to be in therapy for years. What a sicko."

Parker sat silently in the car on the way home. Mona looked over at him. "Are you okay, honey?"

"Just let me be."

He wondered how much they had told her. Did she know all of the details of his relationship with Dakota? All those things that he couldn't even say out loud to Dr. Bayez? Had they filled her in, or had they respected Parker's right to privacy?

"I'm sorry," she said. "I don't think you'll ever understand how sorry I am that I let this happen to you. I have always done everything I could to protect you children."

He felt a stab of guilt even in the middle of his self-pity. She had always been a mama bear, jealously protecting her young. She had gone above and beyond what most mothers would ever be forced to do. She had done what it took to keep them safe. And now she was feeling bad because of what Parker had allowed to happen. What he had *wanted* to happen.

"I'm okay, Mom. I really am."

"You can never get back what she took away from you. You'll never be that innocent boy again."

He flushed, turning away from her to hide his pink cheeks. Though she'd still be able to see his ear, its brilliant red giving him away.

"I wasn't that innocent," he pointed out. Who could be with everything that was in the media, available with a few clicks on the internet? He and his friends had grown up knowing far more than their parents have ever imagined.

Mona was quiet for a while. Her lips were twitching, and he knew she was composing a speech in her head. Trying to get the words all right. Something that he would listen to and understand.

"When you have a relationship with someone," Mona said slowly, carefully laying the words out in the way she had planned, "I want it to be with a person that you love. Someone who is similar to you. Someone that you can share intimacy with on an equal footing. Can you understand that?"

"Mom… Dakota *was* all that. I never felt like there was a big gap between us. Or like I had to do what she said. It was just… we were friends. I… really liked her and wanted to be with her."

Mona nodded and stared straight out the window. Her stare was so fixed that he didn't know how she was even able to monitor the traffic and what was going on around her. She must have been seeing it all with her peripheral vision, because her gaze didn't vary one degree.

"She didn't hurt me," Parker repeated. "And I didn't hurt her. It wasn't like… you know… internet stuff. It was just…" He wanted to say, 'two people in love,' but he knew she wouldn't accept that. She wouldn't acknowledge that their feelings for each other were that strong. That he loved her, maybe even more than Mona had loved Parker's dad before he had lost his job and everything had gone sour.

But instead of his memories bringing back the good feelings he'd had with Dakota, the feelings of happiness and satisfaction and optimism, he just felt guilty and dark. What had been something tender and treasured had been turned into something evil and awkward. He hated Saul for that. Saul, and the police, and Mona, even though he knew she had thought she was doing the right thing. Instead of protecting him, she made him feel dirty and shameful. He hadn't just lost his relationship with Dakota, but with Mona too. He would never trust her and look up to her like a little child again.

He stared out the window.

Everything had changed.

Nothing would ever be the same again.

By the time they got home from the police station, all of the kids were home from school and were scattered through the house pursuing their various activities. Parker headed for his room without a word, but Mona grabbed him by the arm, a little tighter than necessary, steel in her grip.

"Stay out and spend some time with the family," she ordered.

"I'm tired," Parker protested.

"I'm tired too. But you've spent the last two days in bed, you need to spend some time with your brothers and sisters now."

Parker looked for an argument. But Miranda and Leslie grabbed his hands, trying to pull him back to the couch, begging him to sit with them. He ruffled Leslie's hair. "You don't want your big, boring brother in here, do you? I'm just tired and want to go to bed."

"No!" she squealed. She hung onto his hand more tightly. "Stay! Come sit with us! Watch TV."

"I don't feel like watching TV."

But they forced him anyway, pushing him over to the couch, toppling him into it, and then jumping on top of him. Parker couldn't help but smile, even in his bad mood. They were so sweet to him, and he'd been having such a crappy few days. It wasn't the end of the world if he had to cuddle with them on the couch for a little while.

Link was standing in the doorway of the kitchen.

"How'd it go?" he asked Mona. Since he didn't ask where they had been or what was going on, Parker had to assume that she had been in touch with him earlier, texting or calling him to let him know what they were doing.

Parker scowled.

"We're tired," Mona said. "It's been a long day. But… we're all home safe and sound." She looked over the children. "Where's Jess? In his room?"

Link nodded. "Doing homework," he informed her. "I confiscated that." He nodded toward Jessup's handheld game, lying forlornly on the counter.

Mona smiled. "Then I'm sure he'll be done his homework soon. Sophie?"

Sophie was on the couch with the rest of the tumble of children. She looked over at her mother.

"What about you? Do you have any homework?"

"Just reading. I already did it."

"You read in your room, or you read in front of the TV?"

Sophie's eyes were already back on the TV. "I read… in my room."

"What did you read?"

"Umm… *The Hobbit.*"

"The movie or the book?" Mona demanded. "Sophie…!"

Sophie dragged her eyes away from the TV again. "The book! I read the book, okay? Well, not the whole thing, just what we were assigned. About the trolls. I read the part we were supposed to."

"Do you have questions you need to answer about it?"

"No. We're talking about it in class tomorrow."

"Well, you'd better be prepared for it. You know the teacher will know the differences between the book and the movie. She'll try to catch anyone who tried to get around reading the book."

Mona waited. Sophie shrugged. "I read the book," she repeated.

Her eyes stayed steady and none of the other kids jumped in to say that she was lying, so Parker assumed it was the truth. Mona nodded, satisfied.

"You want to take a break?" she asked Link. "I'll take over on dinner?"

"No. You're more tired. You go put your feet up."

Mona smiled gratefully. "That sounds really good." She disappeared into her room for a moment to pick up her laptop, and then settled into her easy chair in the living room. She looked at the girls sitting on Parker's lap and cuddling close to him and gave him a smile.

Parker looked away from her. He was still mad. She wasn't getting out of it that easily.

By the time the girls had watched one more inane cartoon, Parker had had enough. "This is boring. If you want me to stay with you, we have to watch something I like now."

"Oooh," Miranda complained. "I wanted to watch…"

"No more stupid little-kid cartoons."

He pulled the remote away from Sophie, and started cursoring through the on-screen guide for something that looked acceptable. It would have to be something that wasn't too offensive or Mona wouldn't let him keep it on with the girls around. But anything would be better than more sugar-coated rainbow crap. Parker switched channels while he looked for something good, not wanting them to start watching another cartoon while he was looking for something. All it would take was twenty seconds, and they'd be wrapped up in it and wouldn't let him start something else for another half hour. As he looked for something better to watch, the evening news came on. Parker was focused on what he was doing and wasn't listening to it at first. Then it started to penetrate his consciousness.

'Thirty-seven-year-old Dakota Washington, going by the alias Dakota Phillips, was arrested today for statutory rape in the case of a fourteen-year-old boy who cannot be named publicly, with whom she went to school. In a bizarre twist, this is not another case of a teacher becoming involved with one of her students. It turns out that Washington was actually masquerading as a seventeen-year-old registered in ninth grade…'

Sophie looked at Parker, her eyes wide. She pointed at the picture on the reduced-size screen beside the programming guide.

"That's Dakota! That's your friend!"

Parker swallowed. He nodded, thumb over the channel change button. A carousel of pictures was moving across the screen. Some selfies of Dakota. Then mug shots, a pixelated newspaper photograph, and some grainy family photos where the faces of the other people in the pictures had been blurred out.

"But *that's* not Dakota," Miranda said.

"Yes, it is, they're all Dakota, stupid," Sophie shot back.

"No!"

"Shh," Mona admonished. "Turn the channel, Parker. How about that sci-fi station? They might have one of the Star Treks on."

Parker numbly keyed in the digits for the science channel and it switched over to a scene from *Next Generation*. The girls didn't immediately turn their attention to the show.

"I wanted to hear what they were saying about Dakota," Miranda complained. "Is she in trouble? What did she do?"

"She didn't do anything," Parker told her.

"They arrested her," Sophie disagreed. "They said so."

"What did she do?" Miranda repeated.

"Miranda, watch the show or find something else to do," Mona said. "Parker doesn't want to talk about it."

Miranda looked up at Parker's face. She gave him a hug, stretching her thin arms around him as far as they would go.

"Are you sad, Parker?"

He nodded, swallowing. A lump in his throat again.

"Is it because of Dakota?"

Parker rubbed his burning eyes.

"I don't want to talk about it, monkey."

She gave him another squeeze. "Okay."

Parker didn't look at Mona. He sank back into the couch, cuddling with the girls and closing his eyes. Trying again to get back to that place in his brain where he didn't have to think anymore.

Mona made it clear that Parker was going to school in the morning. She sent him off to bed at the usual time, reminding him that he needed to get enough sleep so he would be able to get up and wouldn't be too tired for school the next day. Parker obeyed, because sleep was the only thing he wanted to do, the only place he had to hide.

But his brain rebelled.

Back to school?

When Dakota had been arrested?

He was still trying to process her arrest. It seemed so unbelievable, he couldn't really comprehend it. It was like it was all just an act. A play that was being acted out in front of him, and then it would end. Everyone would have a little laugh that anyone had believed it. And life would go on as normal.

"Don't forget to brush your teeth."

Parker rolled his eyes and didn't answer his mom. He wasn't going to brush them. Just because she had told him to and he was mad at her. Like she was the one who would suffer the consequences of Parker not brushing his teeth. He knew it was petty, but there was so little that he actually had control over. He went to the bathroom and he changed for bed. He didn't look at any of his schoolwork that had been assigned before the whole fiasco began. He didn't reload any of his social apps onto his phone or check his messages. He just plugged in his phone and shut his eyes, shutting out the world the best he could.

As much as he wanted to lose consciousness, sleep eluded him. He lay for a long time, staring up at the dark ceiling and waiting for sleep to come. His chest hurt and he kept seeing Dakota in his mind. Arguing with the police and telling them that they had it all wrong. Locked up in a jail cell somewhere, being treated like the vilest of criminals, when all that she had done was try to retain her childhood.

All I want is for someone to take care of me.

I want to be a kid forever.

Life had been cruel to her and ripped away her chance at a happy childhood. She was still trying to get it back. As much as he tried to picture her as a grown woman, the mother of someone Saul's age, he just couldn't see it. He only saw teenage Dakota, a sparkle in her eye, smooth cheeks, shimmery lipstick, and hot pink hair. Whatever trick life had played on her, that was the Dakota that he knew and loved.

It was a long night.

Chapter Twenty-Two

I DON'T FEEL GOOD," Parker insisted when Mona woke him in the morning. "I didn't sleep good. I'm sick."

"You are getting out of that bed and getting ready for school, Parker. If I have to come up there and pull you down. You know I'll do it!"

Parker rubbed his eyes. "I'm sick," he repeated.

"You've missed enough school over this. I don't feel good either. But we have to face life. Running away from school or from my work isn't going to get us anywhere. Running away from problems isn't what makes you strong enough to handle them."

He didn't really care that she didn't feel good. She couldn't feel anywhere near as bad as Parker did. It wasn't happening to her.

Parker unplugged his phone and dragged his body over to the ladder to climb down. Mona withdrew, seeing that Parker was getting up. He stood there rubbing his eyes, trying to wake himself up.

"Will you be okay?" Link asked. "At school today?"

Link was sitting up in bed. Not quite ready to go yet himself. His brows were drawn down as he watched Parker.

"What's going to happen?" Parker asked with a shrug. He really didn't want to think about what might happen. He preferred to just avoid it. If he didn't think about it, nothing would happen.

He knew what he wasn't going to do. He wasn't going to go talk to Mrs. Strauss again. If they sent him down, he would just go home. No one would know he was absent, because they would all think that he was just talking for a long time with Mrs. Strauss. And why wouldn't he? He obviously needed to talk to someone.

But he wasn't going to. He would go to his classes. He would sit at his desk and pretend that he was following what was going on. And he would go home. That wouldn't be so hard.

When he went to the bathroom, he considered what Mona would do if he threw up. She couldn't very well insist that he wasn't sick and couldn't stay home. She'd have to let him stay and go back to bed. Though bed hadn't turned out so well the night before. Maybe the couch in front of the TV. Wrapped up in a blanket, bingeing on his favorite TV shows.

But when he tried to stick his finger down his throat, he chickened out, gagging but not able to bring anything up, and too scared and freaked out to stick it down far enough to make himself puke. He thought about the alcohol he had consumed with Dakota. It hadn't tasted so bad. And it took the edge off. Took away the stress and strain and made him feel more relaxed. He threw up when he'd had too much, but if he had just had one cup, just enough to bring the numbness that would help him get through his day...

It was all just academic, of course. Since there was no alcohol in the house even if Mona had let him stay home, and no way for him to get it at school either. He didn't have friends who had access to alcohol, and he was too shy to approach any of the wilder students who might.

"Parker!" There was pounding on the door. "I have to pee! Get out of there!"

Parker quickly flushed the toilet and ran the tap, then let Leslie in. The girl had a last-minute bladder; she never knew when she had to go until she had to go immediately. She couldn't wait for five minutes while someone brushed their teeth or combed their hair. She couldn't wait a minute. Ten or fifteen seconds was about her limit, and then there was a waterfall to clean up after.

Leslie shoved past him and didn't even stop to shut the door, yanking down her pants on the run and aiming to land on the toilet before she had an accident. Parker shut the door for her and went to get his book bag.

"Breakfast," Mona admonished. "And maybe you could help get the lunches ready with me."

Parker stopped and considered.

Normally, he wouldn't think of disobeying when she asked for help. He was the oldest, the man of the house, and it was his job to help take care of the other kids. Mona worked herself to the bone and rarely asked any of them for help. They had learned to help when they could without being asked, worried she would be sick or have a breakdown. If she couldn't take care of them, they would all be out on the street. Separated.

Parker was mad at Mona, but not at his younger siblings, most of whom had no idea what was going on and were certainly not the reason Mona had called the police. That had been the school's fault. So much for students having any right to privacy.

Parker went into the kitchen and started with the sandwiches. Dealing the slices of bread out on the counter like a practiced card shark. Four pieces each for himself, Link, and Sophie was twelve pieces. Two slices each for Jessup, Miranda, and Leslie was six more. One and a half loaves of bread. Peanut butter wasn't allowed at the elementary school, so PBJ was out for the youngest kids, and Parker wouldn't want to contaminate their sandwiches by using the same knife to cut or spread peanut butter on the big kid sandwiches. He worked quickly, spreading mayo on the right-hand slice of each pair, then mustard or ketchup on the left-hand slice. He would try to remember which kids got mustard and which got ketchup, but it wasn't the end of the world if he messed some of them up. They would still eat them.

By the time Mona finished going through the younger kids' bags to make sure they had all of their homework and permission slips and hadn't left anything in there to rot, Parker was putting the meat in the sandwiches and pulling out the plastic to wrap them up. They had the industrial-sized rolls of plastic wrap like caterers used. The serrated knife edge used to cut the plastic wrap was wicked sharp and he had cut his hand on it more than once before, moving too quickly in a rush to wrap the sandwiches up. So he slowed down and moved deliberately, wrapping each sandwich. Link had finished getting ready, and he stood beside Parker as he wrapped, taking the finished sandwiches from him. Parker announced each sandwich as he handed it to Link.

"Ketchup, ketchup, mustard…"

Link divided them among the appropriate lunch bags, sitting open in the tops of their backpacks.

"Thanks," Parker acknowledged. He picked up his backpack and headed for the door.

"Breakfast!" Mona reminded him.

Parker shrugged. "I have to go. I'll need to talk to Mr. Bonne before class."

"Mr. Bonne knows what's going on. Sit down, have a bowl of cereal."

Parker shook his head. "Gotta go. Bye."

"Grab a banana. A granola bar."

"Not hungry."

Parker pushed by, not giving her a goodbye hug or letting her kiss him on the cheek. He hoped that she understood clearly that he was still mad at her.

Parker ran his thumbs between the backpack straps and his body, settling the backpack comfortably onto his back. He mounted his bike and was off.

There were no kids gathered around the doors of the school smoking. It was too early for the smokers to be there yet. The kids who arrived early for school were there for sports, clubs, tutoring, or special projects. They weren't the rebels who slacked off and smoked.

Parker went into the cafeteria and looked around to see if Mr. Bonne were there supervising. He hadn't intended to go in for anything to eat, but despite what he had said to Mona, he was starting to feel hungry and the smells in the cafeteria were enticing.

Mr. Bonne wasn't there, and Parker wasn't sure if any of the other teachers would let him have food from the free breakfast program when he wasn't signed up for it. He didn't have the money to buy anything, and he hadn't heeded Mona and grabbed a banana or granola bar on the way out of the house. Parker bit his lip and left the cafeteria, going upstairs to Mr. Bonne's classroom.

Mr. Bonne was there at his desk, working away on papers. He had a big travel mug of coffee and half a muffin on a napkin on his desk. He didn't notice Parker immediately, and Parker didn't want to startle him by just showing up at his elbow. He knocked softly on one of the desks.

"Uh… Mr. Bonne?"

Mr. Bonne still startled, but he looked up at Parker and smiled, not upset over it.

"Parker. Come on in. I wasn't really expecting to see you today."

"My mom told me I had to come."

"Tough moms," Mr. Bonne said with a smile, shaking his head. "They're the ones who force us to grow, aren't they?"

"She said we don't learn by running away."

"She's right about that. We get stronger by fighting our way through the tough times." Mr. Bonne took a sip of his coffee. "So… how are you holding up?"

"I dunno yet. I just want to crawl back into bed. Or for everything to be normal again. Just like this never happened."

Mr. Bonne nodded. "It's tough. I'm sorry that you've had to go through this. I know things can't be easy for you right now."

"Yeah."

"What can I do for you, Parker?" Mr. Bonne took a bite of the muffin and looked at him expectantly.

Parker had told Mona that he needed to go to school early to talk to Mr. Bonne, and he had been operating under that vague claim, but the fact was, he didn't really know why he was there. He had wanted to get out of the house, and seeing Mr. Bonne had been a good reason. But now that he was there, he wasn't at all sure why.

"I guess… Just show me what I missed. I'll try to get caught up."

"Okay." Mr. Bonne wiped his fingers on the napkin before opening his books. He started to show Parker the material they had covered during his absence. Parker's stomach growled loudly. The sweet, vanilla smell of the muffin made him salivate. Mr. Bonne stopped talking and looked at him.

"Hungry?"

"No, it's okay."

"Did you have breakfast this morning?"

"Well, no… I left the house early. I didn't get a chance."

"You didn't bring anything to eat on the way?"

"No. I was kind of mad at my mom."

Mr. Bonne's mouth quirked up. "Well, you showed her, didn't you?"

Parker laughed. He covered his mouth and pressed down the muscles that pushed his mouth up into a smile. He felt like it was a betrayal, laughing while Dakota was in jail. Having any kind of pleasure while she was gone.

Mr. Bonne's expression sobered and he touched Parker on the side of the head for a moment, a fleeting gesture of comfort and communion.

"Let me see what I can dig up for you," he said briskly. "Or do you want to go downstairs and pick something up?"

"I… I'm not signed up for the breakfast program."

"No, but sometimes these things happen. No one is going to give you any trouble for participating in the breakfast one day."

Parker shrugged uncomfortably. Mr. Bonne didn't press him. "I'll have something around here," he promised. Parker waited while Mr. Bonne went through his cupboards and file drawers and pulled out some crackers, peanut butter, and dried fruit bars. He indicated the peanut butter. "You're not allergic, are you? I'm not really supposed to have this stuff around. But it sticks with you better than just crackers, and keeps better than cheese."

Parker imagined cheese secreted away in Mr. Bonne's desk, getting gradually moldier and smellier. He nodded. "I'm not allergic. We eat it all the time at home."

"Good. Have at it, then." Mr. Bonne handed him the crackers and peanut butter and a plastic knife. The fruit bars were within reach. While Parker made himself a scant breakfast, Mr. Bonne reviewed the material they had covered in Parker's absence.

During his early-morning hour with Mr. Bonne, everything had seemed pretty normal, and Parker's anxiety had gone down a notch. Maybe everything was going to be okay, and he could just go on with life as he had before, as if nothing had happened to change him.

But when other students started trickling into the room, Parker knew he was only fantasizing. There was no way things were going to be the same again. Chris and Adrian were not on duty; they probably had no idea that Parker was at the school. Without them there to run interference, Parker had to face the questions and abuse from his fellow students on his own. There were hoots and jeers from the other boys. Dirty comments about Dakota whispered so that Parker was the only one who could hear them. Punches in the shoulder, one by Bobby Clarence that was so hard Parker nearly fell right out of his seat.

"Cut it out!" he complained in a low growl, not wanting to attract the attention of any other bullies or of Mr. Bonne. Bobby just looked at him with a huge grin, and after making sure that Mr. Bonne was occupied, looking the other direction, he made an obscene gesture at Parker.

Parker sat at his desk, arranging his books, papers, and writing implements, trying to avoid looking at anyone else. He didn't want to see or hear what they were saying to him. He just wanted to be invisible.

He couldn't understand why Mona had been so adamant about going to school so soon. She must have known how hard it would be. How stupid the students were going to act toward him. When their father had died, it had warranted a week off school. He thought that losing Dakota should get him at least half that. Three days off school didn't seem so outrageous. But he was sure the comments and the bullying weren't going to stop in that length of time. Not unless there was something like a school shooting to distract everyone's attention.

Mr. Bonne called for the class to settle down, and started in with the day's announcements, followed by the lesson. Parker did his best to focus, but it seemed like Mr. Bonne and his lesson and the board were getting farther and farther away, smaller and smaller, fading quickly out of his view.

"Wake up, loser!"

A punch in the shoulder startled Parker out of his sleep, and just about out of his seat. There were giggles from a few of the nearby students. Parker realized that the lunch bell must have rung, and he had pretty much slept through all of his morning classes. They didn't have to move from one classroom to another for every lesson, and it was one of the rare mornings where, with double Social Studies, he didn't have to leave his desk all morning.

"Kerouac!" Mr. Bonne snapped.

The boy who had punched Parker moved a step away, the vicious expression on his face changing to something deferential. "I was just waking him up, Mr. Bonne. He was sleeping during your lesson…"

"Leave him alone, Kerouac, or you'll be sitting there after school."

"I'm just trying to help…" Kerouac moved away, flashing Parker one final evil look that Mr. Bonne could not see.

Most of the class had filed out.

"You okay, Parker?" Mr. Bonne asked.

"Sorry about falling asleep… I dunno, I didn't sleep much last night. Seems like all day I want to sleep, and then when night comes around… I can't."

"You're going through a lot," Mr. Bonne said understandingly. "Don't worry about it. Give yourself some time to adjust."

Parker nodded. He got up and stretched his sore muscles. He felt like he'd been folded up and crammed into a little box. All of his muscles and joints hurt. His shoulder most of all. He massaged it the best he could as he went out to his locker to pick up his lunch.

Lockers gave the illusion of security. That Parker had a safe place to put his things and no one else could access them. But when he opened his locker, he found, as he had a couple of times before, that things had been rifled, and his locker had been decorated with a few pieces of paper that hadn't been there before.

There were pictures of Dakota, selfies, with obscenities scribbled across them in black marker. And someone had dug up pictures Parker hadn't seen of her before, provocative poses showing off her ample cleavage or other suggestive angles. And there were a few pictures, close-ups of body parts that probably weren't even Dakota, pulled off of some porn site somewhere. Parker tore them all down, his eyes burning. He had been hungry, but after seeing the pictures, he felt like throwing up. There was nothing in his stomach, but he felt sick anyway. He felt guilty and shameful and dirty, as if he'd been the one to dig the filthy pictures up and arrange them there.

"Mr. Jurek—"

Parker whirled around and found Mrs. Strauss behind him, leaning in to make an inquiry. But he wasn't going to talk to her anymore. He'd had enough of talk. She had caused him enough trouble, blabbing to Mona and getting the police involved in something that wasn't any of their business. Nobody needed to poke their noses into Parker's relationships. It wasn't any of their business.

Parker thrust the pile of crumpled-up pictures into her hands, grabbed his lunch, and strode away. He didn't even bother to close and lock his locker. What was the point, when anyone who wanted to could get in there?

He didn't eat in the cafeteria. He didn't want to have to look at Chris and Adrian, to have to answer their questions about how he as doing, and what it had been like, going to the police station and having to talk to them about Dakota. He didn't need to hear their speculations about what was going to happen to her, or why she had done what she did. He went out, instead, and sat on a grassy hill near the school, looking down on the fields of the nearby elementary school. He pretended to be enthralled by watching the little kids playing, but he wasn't. He watched to see if he could identify any of his siblings, but he wasn't really that interested in what they were doing.

Someone approached and sat beside him. Parker turned to look, frowning. He didn't need anyone else teasing him about his girlfriend being an old lady.

It was Charity. And she didn't tease him or make fun of him. She just sat there, not saying anything, pulling out a cigarette and lighting it up. Parker ate one sandwich, but couldn't force the other one down. He held it in his lap, staring at the kids playing without actually seeing them.

"I really miss her," Charity said finally.

Parker swallowed. He looked at her face. She wasn't teasing him. She wasn't just trying to pull him in and then make fun of her. She really was missing Dakota.

"Yeah," he agreed.

"She was a lot of fun. I never thought… I mean, I figured she was older. But, like, nineteen or something. Not *that* old."

Parker nodded his agreement.

"Man, I hope I still look that good when I'm old. Damn. I gotta know her secret."

Parker forced out a bark of laughter. But it didn't sound good, and it hurt worse. It wasn't about looking young. She was young. She was like a female Peter Pan. The girl who never grew up. But it wasn't funny or happy or silly like Peter Pan. It was really sad.

"You didn't know?" Charity asked. "She never told you?"

"No. I asked her, but she'd never say."

Charity put her hand on Parker's knee for a brief moment, then removed it.

"She said we couldn't act like a couple. That people wouldn't understand." Parker hadn't told anyone this. "She said there was more to it than just black and white. That people wouldn't like it and wouldn't understand."

"Well, she got that one right, didn't she? Just forgot to mention the fact that it was illegal."

They sat for a while longer in silence. Charity offered her cigarette to Parker. He shook his head.

"I don't know what I would have done if I had known," Parker confided. He'd thought about it. A lot. What if he had known how old she really was? Would it have changed anything? He'd never know, because she'd never given him the opportunity.

"Really? You think you would have been okay with it?"

"I don't know."

Charity nodded and sighed. "Yeah."

Parker gathered his lunch together. Pretty soon the bell would ring and it would be time to head back to class. He didn't know if he'd be able to stay awake through it. The world just seemed like it was way too big to handle. Too big and loud and intrusive. He'd never felt like that before. He'd always been able to center himself by taking a walk in the park, or slowing his breathing, just stopping and counting.

Mona would have laughed at the thought. As far as she was concerned, Parker was way too daring and impulsive, never considering the consequences. But that was different. He could always find himself. He could always push the world back a little, and find the part that was him, the part he wanted to be in, and he could just be himself.

Maybe that was what scared Mona the most, that he could just be himself and not care about the consequences.

Charity stood up as Parker did. "Listen… Parker…"

He had been staring at his feet. He lifted his gaze to her face. "Yeah?"

"I'm… I'm sorry if I ever made fun of you, you know? I… I think you're pretty cool."

It was a nice thought, on the surface. Parker nodded and politely thanked her, and then walked away. She knew very well that she had made fun of him. That was the only interaction she had had with him for years, probably since first grade. She'd always been strong and popular, two attributes that made her the perfect bully. She could beat Parker up physically, and could verbally lambaste him with impunity. There was nothing he could do to fight back.

"I mean it," Charity said, trailing along beside him. "All the stuff that happened with your dad… you were so strong. And I've never heard you put anyone else down."

Parker nodded. What was he going to say? That she had been a jerk and a bully the last seven or eight years and he couldn't forgive her? Or that she had hurt him, but it was okay?

He walked back to his locker without saying anything.

Parker stopped at the convenience store on the way home to spend some of his hard-earned change on what little junk food he could afford. He took it up to the counter and threw a few coins down to pay for it. The clerk didn't pick up the change, and Parker looked up at him to see if he was talking on his phone or otherwise distracted. But the man wasn't messing around with his Bluetooth receiver or distracted by the football game or the CCTV surveillance camera. He was staring Parker straight in the eye. Parker shifted his stance anxiously. Did the clerk think that he had been shoplifting? Had he miscalculated and put down the wrong amount of money?

"Uh… is something wrong?"

He could run if the man thought he was shoplifting and called the police. He could get out of there and be gone on his bike before the police were even close. As long as the man didn't grab him over the counter. Parker took a small step back, distancing himself.

"You are that boy," the man said. "On TV."

Parker shook his head, not understanding. "I haven't been on TV."

"No. They were talking about you. You're the one. With that woman. I've seen you with her."

Parker bit his lip and tried to think of how to respond. What was the appropriate response to someone who recognized you as the victim of a crime? Someone who had been promised privacy and anonymity? How was he supposed to respond to that?

Parker put his fingers on the coins and slid them over the counter, closer to the man.

"You're the one she molested, aren't you?"

Parker suddenly couldn't even breathe. He turned around and dashed for the door. He ignored the man trying to call him back. Ignored the fact that he had paid for the candy and had left both his money and the merchandise behind. He got on his bike and pedaled hard, leaving everything behind.

If only he could.

Chapter Twenty-Three

H E RODE FOR A long time. He ignored his phone buzzing as texts and calls came in. He rode until the muscles in his legs burned and begged him to stop. Then, even though he had ridden out of the neighborhood and into parts unknown, he found himself again in the park.

His park.

His and Dakota's park.

He had gone in a circle, and must have entered it from the opposite side. Attracted by the neat pathways that ventured into the greens of the park, he found himself back on the familiar pathways again.

He propped his bike against a tree and chained it there. Not the most secure thing to do, but he didn't think anyone was going to steal it. Then he walked through the animal trails, many of which had now been significantly enlarged by people pushing their way through the brush. Parker walked silently, not even stepping on any dry sticks that would pop and announce his approach. If Dakota had been with him, she would be crashing through the brush like a buffalo.

But she wasn't.

So he went silently on his own.

Eventually, he found their clearing. He lay down in the soft green grass and closed his eyes and thought.

The glade was just the same as it had always been. It was green and smelled of moss and leaves. The sun was getting low, dusk approaching. But Dakota wasn't there. Her absence was palpable. A living thing.

The question, he realized, was not what he would have done if he had known how old she was.

The question was what he was going to do now that he did.

Was he going to abandon her to her fate, standing back and acting like he didn't know what was happening? Like he didn't have any influence over it? Or was he going to act? See what he could do. Talk to her lawyer, if she had one.

Dakota was still Dakota. And he needed to act instead of letting everyone just kick him around.

Parker walked in the door. Mona hurried out from the hallway to get after him for being late. Parker knew that his phone had been vibrating, but hadn't even taken it out to look at the caller IDs or texts. Mona's eyes were rimmed in red.

"Where have you been? I've been so worried!"

Parker held up his hand, stopping her from getting any closer to him. He didn't want a hug as she expressed her relief that he was safe. He didn't want the lecture about how he couldn't just disappear and not answer her calls.

"I'm going to my room."

"Parker! I'm trying to talk to you."

"I know, I know. I didn't call. I didn't answer my phone. Why don't you ground me?"

He tried to move past her in the small space. She didn't move out of his way. When he looked at her face, she had a hurt expression. It made him feel both glad and guilty. He moved determinedly around her, trying to get by without shoving, so close that his clothing brushed hers as he squeezed through.

Parker went to his room. He shut the door and threw his backpack on the floor. He didn't even know why he'd brought any work home from school. He certainly had no intention of doing it.

The door opened behind him. He whirled around to confront Mona again. To insist that he needed privacy. He needed somewhere he could go and have space to himself. Maybe he wouldn't bother to go home at all if he couldn't have that.

But it was Link, not Mona.

"She really was worried," Link said, shutting the door behind himself. "Not just, 'where *is* that boy?' Really scared. She was talking about calling the police."

Parker looked at Link. "I don't care. I needed space."

Link frowned, his eyebrows pushing close together. "You always care if she's really worried. What if she was calling you because one of the kids was hurt, or she really needed you home for something?"

"Then you'd have to take care of it. You're almost as old as I am. I was looking after you guys since I was ten, you're old enough to do it now."

Which wasn't really fair, because he knew Link always stepped up and took the responsibility if Parker wasn't there. He wasn't one to whine or shirk his duties. But Parker wasn't concerned about fairness. He was tired of having to be responsible for everyone else, and tired of trying to keep up with Mona's expectations and the pressures of growing up. More responsibilities kept getting added, and he wanted to just be free of them.

Link gave Parker a hurt look.

Parker was hurting a lot of people lately.

Parker held up his phone. "I need to figure something out. So leave me alone now."

Link stood there for a minute, then he shook his head and retreated. Parker climbed up onto his bed and stretched out. He swiped open his browser and started to search for information on Dakota's case. He had been avoiding the news and social networks, not wanting to hear what they had to say about him. Not wanting to hear what they had to say about Dakota. But if he were going to do anything to help her, he had to know what was going on. He steeled himself and dove in.

In spite of the number of stories, there really wasn't much information there that he didn't know already. Everything he was reading was just a repetition. Maybe one more tiny detail, dressed up to sound like it was an entirely new story, but there was nothing there.

Parker took a break from searching to glance through his texts. Mostly Mona or his school friends wanting to know where he was or what he was doing. But some of them were from people he barely knew, or numbers he didn't know at all, saying nasty things about Dakota or asking questions that weirded him out. Like his school locker decorator, there were people sending him pictures, too. Not just of Dakota, but of random sleazy women. Parker went into the operating system settings and wiped his texts completely. He closed his eyes and thought for a while, almost asleep, but still on the edge of consciousness, aware of his surroundings and everything that was tumbling through his mind.

It was late when Parker got up and wandered into the kitchen. The little girls were already in bed. The others were sprawled around the living room, doing their own things. Separate, but together. Mona was on her computer, but she looked up when Parker walked by. She followed him into the kitchen.

"I'm sorry you're going through such a hard time with this," she said. "I wish I could make it easier on you."

"I want to go see Dakota," Parker told her.

Mona's eyes widened. Her face was white and waxen. "You want to…? You can't go see her. She's in jail!"

"They allow visitors, don't they?"

"Not… not minors, I'm sure. And certainly not her… victim. You need to stay away from her."

"I want to go see her. I want to talk to her. And know how she's doing."

"Parker, that's not a good idea."

"You think this is hard on me? Think of how hard it is on her! She didn't do anything wrong, and now she's sitting in a jail cell, all alone, and everyone has turned on her. She doesn't have a friend in the world. Except for me. And I want to go see her."

"No, Parker. Absolutely not. I won't allow it."

"I'll find a way to go see her," he said stubbornly.

He found some cold spaghetti in the fridge. He pulled a fork out of the cutlery drawer and shut the drawer so hard that everything clanged together, loud in the evening quietness of the house.

"I don't understand why you would want to," Mona said in a more conciliatory tone. "Explain to me why you want to go there."

Parker stood for a moment, trying to decide whether to eat the spaghetti at the table, or retreat to his lair. But he had to have it out with Mona sooner or later. Maybe if he sorted it all out before bed, he'd be able to sleep, instead of tossing and turning on the edge of nightmares, his thoughts too restless and wild to settle into rest.

"You think Dakota did something wrong," he said. He sat down at the table, and Mona took the seat opposite him. "But she didn't. She didn't do anything wrong. Anything I didn't want. I… really like her, Mom. I mean I *really* like her. As more than a friend."

Mona shook her head in bewilderment. "I know you like her. And it's okay to like someone. And to make friends that are older or younger than you. But there are certain things… that are not allowed."

Parker ate his spaghetti.

"I know you're growing up," Mona tried. "You're not just a naive little boy…"

Parker nodded his agreement. And while she had said it, he wasn't sure that she really believed it. He was the oldest, the first of her children to grow up, and she didn't know how to handle the fact that he was almost an adult. In a few years, he would be out of her home. Starting his own family.

"You know I don't want you… being with a girl that way. It's too early. You might be ready for a girlfriend, but one that you can take to movies, ice cream or pizza. Some nice, sweet girl your age. Holding hands, kissing, but not…" She swallowed hard. "You're not ready for the full meal deal yet, Parker. It's not just me saying that. It's the law."

Parker wiped tomato sauce from his cheek with the back of his hand, then licked it off. He looked her in the face. "You can't stop me."

Mona licked her lips. Her face was white. She stood up, got the Kool-aid out of the fridge, and splashed some in two glasses. She put one in front of Parker and sat down with the other. She took a couple of swallows.

"I'll do everything I can to keep you safe," she said. "You can't go see her. You can't have anything else to do with her."

It was not a peaceful night. Parker felt so wrecked in the morning, he might as well have drunk a full bottle of wine all by himself. His head hurt. His eyes were swollen and had dark pouches under them.

Once again, he wrestled with his feelings. He knew how Mona had raised him. What she believed. He had always been on-board with her before. The fact that he was going against her and disagreed with her so strongly made him awkward and embarrassed. And made him question himself again, to reexamine his feelings about Dakota and all that had happened.

"You're up!" Mona observed, when Parker got out of the bathroom. She hadn't started to wake the other children yet. "Hot shower if you want it!"

In a houseful of people, a hot shower was a rare luxury. Parker supposed that he should take advantage of it, but he didn't. Instead, he returned to the bathroom to run cold water over a cloth and held it over his eyes for a few minutes, hoping to take down the swelling and ease his headache. To clear his brain so he could think straight.

Mona was looking at him when he lowered the cloth. "You look a mess. Are you okay?"

He squeezed the cloth out and hung it over the rail. "Yeah. I'm fine."

"I'm sorry—"

"Quit saying you're sorry for what I'm going through," he snapped. "It's your fault and you're determined to keep it up, so just quit apologizing."

She stood there and looked at him.

"Are you going to let me see her?" Parker demanded.

"No."

"Are you going to drop the charges against her?"

"Even if I wanted to, I couldn't. It really doesn't have anything to do with me. It isn't a civil charge. It's criminal."

"But if you could, would you drop them?"

Mona folded her arms. She looked smaller than Parker ever remembered her being. Frail and defenseless instead of the iron lady he knew her to be.

"No. I wouldn't."

"Yeah." Parker nodded, resting his point. "So quit saying sorry."

She unfolded one arm to hold her thin hand out toward him, to touch him comfortingly. "I'm just so sad that you're upset and hurting."

"Don't act like you care what I'm feeling."

He brushed by her and went into the kitchen to get a quick breakfast and lunch together for himself. Mona went to wake the other children and get them moving, shuffling her feet along like an old lady. By the time she got back, whether to check on Parker or to continue the discussion, he had his breakfast and lunch tucked into his backpack and was pulling it over his shoulders.

"It's too early to go to school! Even to see your teacher early."

"See you later," Parker said brusquely. He headed for the door and she didn't try to physically detain him. Parker hopped on his bike and pedaled away.

Chapter Twenty-Four

P ARKER DIDN'T GO TO school. Mona was right. The doors wouldn't even be open yet. Any teachers that were there were laboring away behind locked doors, getting their lessons prepared or papers marked while they had a little peace and quiet.

He went back to the park.

He didn't go back to their glade. It was empty and he would miss Dakota too much there. There was no point in torturing himself. But he rode slowly through the pathways between the trees. The morning air was cool and the birds were cheeping loudly. He was surrounded by green, alone but for the occasional runner or walker. It normally soothed his soul, but it just pricked him now. Reminded him that Dakota was somewhere behind bars and concrete walls, with no fresh air except maybe the occasional walk in the yard or on some kind of highway cleanup detail. She was languishing in jail and he was out walking free. She was judged to be a criminal, and he was told he was the victim, when what they had done had been consensual. It made no sense, and he alternated between feeling guilty for his part and angry for the way she was being unfairly treated.

He didn't need Mona to tell him what was okay and what was not. He was old enough to decide for himself.

Parker rode away from the park and back to the police station.

The officer at the counter didn't quite know what to do about Parker asking to see Dakota. She looked him over, frowning and biting the end of her pen. She pushed her glasses up on her forehead and looked at the computer screen in front of her, clicking through various screens and tapping in her queries. Eventually, she shook her head.

"Miss Washington has already been transported to the women's facility. She is no longer being held here."

"Where is that?"

"What?"

"The women's facility. How do I get there?"

She looked at him again, blinking. "You want to go there?"

"Well, I want to see her. How else am I going to get to see her? If that's where she is, that's where I have to go."

She took more time to think about this, and finally pulled out a pad of sticky notes and wrote down an address on it. "That's the address. You'll need to get your mom to take you out there. You should call first about visiting hours and procedures."

Parker looked down at the address. It sounded completely foreign. "Where is this?"

She started to repeat the address, and Parker shook his head, stopping her. "I mean, what part of the city is it in? I don't know the street."

"It's east of the city. Outside of city limits. You'll need to get your mom to take you there."

"Okay, thanks."

Parker walked back out of the police station and toward his bike.

"Parker! Is that you, Parker?"

He turned around and saw Dr. Bayez striding down the sidewalk toward him. Her hair was awry, a little disheveled by the wind. Parker stopped.

"What are you doing here?" Dr. Bayez asked with a smile, sweeping her hair back with one hand. "Did you need to talk to the investigators again?"

Parker swallowed and looked for words. "Uh... no."

"Do you want to come in and talk to me again? I could make some time for you."

"No. I don't need to talk to anyone, thanks."

"Then what are you doing here?" She said it with a cheerful, friendly smile, but Parker heard the steel behind it. Maybe he had been stupid to think he could just walk into and out of the police station without anyone asking questions. But it was a free country, wasn't it? He was entitled to walk into a public place and didn't need to give anyone an explanation.

"Sorry," Parker said, looking at the time on the face of his phone. "I need to be getting to school."

Dr. Bayez looked at her own wrist. "I think school has already started," she countered.

"Then I'd better get going."

She held his gaze. "Are you sure you won't come talk to me, Parker? You seem a little agitated."

"I don't need to talk to anyone." Except Dakota. He needed to talk to Dakota. And he wasn't going to be deterred by Mona, or a desk clerk, or Dr. Bayez. He was going to go see Dakota. That was certain.

"Let me give you my card. You can call me or come by to talk to me anytime. I know this is a very difficult time for you, Parker. You have a lot of feelings to work through. What happened to you is very confusing."

"I never told you she raped me," Parker said, his voice low. He took a glance around to make sure that no one was listening in on their conversation. "I don't know why you told the cops that, because I never said that! I told you that it was my idea. It was what I wanted. Why did you tell them that?"

Dr. Bayez tried to lay a calming hand on Parker's arm, but he pulled back and didn't let her touch him. "Parker… that's just the wording under the law. It doesn't mean she forced you. It means that you're too young to consent."

"I knew what I was doing."

She nodded reassuringly. "We have to have these laws in place to protect minors. I understand how confused you are about it, and that's partly why those laws are in place. You aren't mature enough to understand all of the consequences of having a physical relationship with Miss Washington. Or to understand the power that she held over you by being so much older than you. It's an unequal relationship."

"It wasn't," Parker told her. "I didn't do anything because I thought I had to. She didn't talk me into it or force me into it. We were friends. We *are* friends. You can't say who I can or can't be friends with."

It was his fight with Mona all over again. They were the women who were trying to control his life. Who were trying to force him into the kind of life that he didn't want. They were the ones trying to force the kind of relationship Parker didn't want. A platonic relationship. A loveless relationship. They were the ones who were doing what they said Dakota shouldn't.

"I have to go now," Parker told her. "I have to get to school."

Of course, he should have known that Dr. Bayez wouldn't just take Parker's word for it that he was on his way back to school. Before long, Parker's phone was buzzing like an angry bee in his pocket. He pulled over to the side and pulled it out to look at it.

Mona.

Wanting to know where he was and why he had been at the police station. As if she didn't know.

Telling him that he was supposed to be at school. Which he knew.

His first thought was just to slide his phone back away into his pocket, but he didn't. He was supposed to be grown up and mature now. He was supposed to be responsible and not worry his mother. If he wanted to show her that he was a man now, no matter what she thought, then he needed to act more like one.

So he stopped for a moment to text her back.

I'm safe. Talk to you later.

His phone started to ring almost immediately, but he didn't answer it. She would just demand to know where he was and yell at him to get to school. He had done his duty and told her that he was fine. He would check in with her again later. When he had done what else he had to do.

He put the phone back away and got on his bike. He didn't have a very good idea of where the women's prison was, but east of the city he could understand, and it would take him a couple of hours at least to bike to the city limits. He didn't know how much farther it was beyond that.

It was a good thing that he had a couple of meals with him. He would need them.

His phone eventually went quiet. He was glad, because if she kept calling him and making his phone vibrate constantly, it was going to run down the battery much faster. And he was going to need it once he got to the edge of the city.

He went through all kinds of neighborhoods he had never seen before. Houses, industrial areas, malls, office buildings… he barely knew anything outside of his own neighborhood. A few miles around his home, that was all he was familiar with.

He stopped to eat his breakfast, stomach feeling like it was ready to consume itself. He took that time to put the address of the prison into his maps app and see how he was going to get there and how long it would take him. He still had a good long way to go.

There was little traffic on the road that led up to the prison. He supposed that the long highway approach was intentional, making it easy to see any vehicles coming and going, and to spot any escapees if there ever were a prison break. He rode up to the guard booth on his bike. The woman guard there, her hair smoothed into a severe bun, looked like she had never seen a boy on a bike before.

"What are you doing here?"

Parker put on his friendliest smile for her. He tried to look as if he were expected there. Like it was all planned out and approved. If he were confident, she would believe him.

"I'm here to see Dakota Phillips," he said. "I mean… Dakota Washington."

"Who is that?"

"She's a new prisoner here. I was told that she was transferred here… last night."

"You're here to visit a prisoner."

Well, what else would he be there for? Did she think that he had just lost his way and was looking for directions?

"Dakota Washington," he repeated. Then he looked at the red and white gate arm pointedly, waiting for her to raise it.

"And who are you?"

"Parker Jurek."

"But who are you?"

Parker shifted. He was getting saddle-sore, and if he had to sit still for too long while he was visiting with Dakota, he was going to get pretty stiff.

"What do you mean? Parker Jurek. That's who I am."

"Are you related to the prisoner?"

Parker wondered if he could get away with it. But he decided not, and shook his head. "I'm a friend."

"Are you on her visitor list?"

"I… don't know. Does she even have a visitor list if she just got here yesterday?"

That made the guard think. She tapped a query into her computer, and waited for it to bring up the records she wanted. She shook her head.

"No, she doesn't have a visitor list."

"Well, I'm her friend. If you ask her, she'll want to see me."

"Since she doesn't have a visitor list, the only people who are allowed to see her are her lawyer and her immediate family. Or other police or court officers."

Parker's stomach roiled. They were just going to turn him down at the door because Dakota hadn't had a chance to make up a list of the people she wanted to see?

"I just biked for three hours to get here," he said. "I'm not going to leave. Have someone talk to her. I'll wait while she writes up a visitor list. Please."

The guard looked at him, uncertain. It was obviously a breach of protocol. Something that was just not done. But she wasn't used to dealing with fourteen-year-old boys who showed up on their bikes after riding for three hours. Parker flexed and released his leg muscles, trying to work out the stiffness that was setting in.

Eventually, the guard picked up her phone. She turned away from Parker while she talked, keeping her voice low so that he couldn't hear what she was saying. Her eyes flicked back to Parker a couple of times. They were asking her more information about him. Who he was, why he was there.

"Somebody is going to come out for you," the guard finally said, hanging up the phone. "You can leave your bike here." She motioned to the front of the guard booth, the side that was beyond the gate arm. Parker got off of his bike and walked it around the booth, leaning it against the front. There was nothing to lock it to, but there was a guard right there to make sure that no one interfered with it. He wondered if he should leave his backpack there as well.

A pick-up truck with prison seals on the doors drove slowly up to the other side of the gate. Another woman in uniform got out. She had dark curly hair, speckled with gray. She was dressed in pants that were man-cut and a dark uniform shirt that did not compliment her mature figure.

"You are Parker?" she asked briskly.

Parker nodded. The woman gave a little wave to the guard booth, and motioned for Parker to follow her back to the truck. "Get in."

They were letting him in. Parker's heart thumped harder. He was going to get to see Dakota. To talk to her and see how she was doing and let him know how much he had missed her. They could talk about strategy, what he could do to help her case. There had to be something he could do. Some way to help her by saying that he had made conscious decisions to do all the things that he had done and it didn't have anything to do with Dakota's age, pretended or real.

The woman clicked her seatbelt into place and Parker followed suit, sitting with his backpack balanced on his knees.

"What made you come out here to visit the prisoner?" She asked.

Parker took a surreptitious look at her, looking for a name tag. She had an ID badge with her picture on it clipped to her lapel, and over her breast a name bar in block letters. Julia Fox.

"She's my friend and I wanted to visit her."

Fox shot him a look. "I think there's more of a story here than that."

Parker shrugged. He didn't feel like divulging any details. His private life was already splashed all over the newspaper. He couldn't walk by anyone at school without them whispering about him and what might have happened between him and Dakota. Why should he have to tell the story to everyone he knew?

"I want to be able to talk to her," he said. "Everything happened really fast, and I didn't get a chance to talk to her. I want to make sure she's okay. I just… want to talk to her."

"Where's your mother?"

"She… didn't come."

"You biked all the way out here. Three hours, Mel said. Why would you do that when you don't even know if you're on Washington's visitor list?"

"I didn't know there was a visitor list. I thought anyone could visit."

"No. There is a strictly controlled list."

"Well, can she write hers up now, and I'll wait, so that I can see her?"

Fox didn't answer. She drove through parking lots and past various blocky buildings, pulling up in front of one and coming to a stop.

"In here."

Parker followed her clipped command. She led the way into the building. There was a reception desk there, with a guard standing there, but Fox didn't take him up to it. She led him past, into a small meeting room with a table and two chairs, all bolted to the floor. Parker sat down. He wanted to inch his chair a bit closer to the table, but of course he couldn't. He felt uncomfortable sitting too far back from it. Exposed.

"Do you have identification?"

Parker dug into his backpack for his wallet. He pulled out his student ID card and his learner's license, passing them across to her. Fox barely glanced at them.

"You're a minor."

"Well… yeah."

"Where is your guardian?"

"Not here. I just came by myself. My mom has to work."

"We can't let a minor in here. Let them just walk around without accompaniment."

"My mom has to work. She couldn't come."

"Do you have a permission form?"

"A permission form… from who?"

"From your guardian," Fox said, as if Parker were being incredibly dense. And he supposed he was. Mona had said he wouldn't be able to visit Dakota, and he had thought that he could get around it. If he just showed up and told his sob story, they would give in and let him in. But they apparently were not going to cave so easily.

"No… why can't I just visit her?"

"Because as a minor, you need permission."

Parker sat there in the rigid plastic chair, his muscles stiffening up. He wanted to be at home in bed, where he could just go back to sleep and shut it all off again. His brilliant plan to go and see Dakota and help her out had failed.

"Can I… talk to her on the phone or write her a note?"

Fox leaned back, making her chair creak in protest. "I can't give you any direct contact with the prisoner. If you want to write a letter, send it through the regular channels. Post it by mail. It will go through our censors here, and provided it passes inspection, she'll get it."

Parker scratched his chin, thinking about that. All that effort for nothing. He had to figure out a way to get in to see Dakota, but it wasn't going to happen right away. He sighed.

"Can you get your mom to come out and pick you up?" Fox asked. "Sounds like it's a long ride back home for you."

"No… that probably wouldn't be a good idea." If he were going to have any chance of getting her permission, he couldn't ask her to do anything like that. In fact, he'd have to make up with her. If he didn't start doing what he was told and fly straight, and stop arguing with her and showing her how angry he was, there was no way she would even consider changing her mind.

Parker stood up. He rubbed the muscles in his legs. He was used to riding around a few blocks at a time in the city. He'd never gone on a three-hour trek before. And now he had another to do back. His legs already felt like jelly. Fox gave him a sympathetic look, but didn't offer to have someone drive him back into town. She led him back out to the front desk, and had him sit down there for a minute while she followed up on a phone call that needed her attention. Parker stretched and rubbed his muscles, hoping to somehow be ready for the return trip by the time she drove him out to his bike. He had only eaten one of his sandwiches, so he ate the other while he sat there waiting.

Fox returned.

"Can I use a bathroom and refill my water before I go?" Parker asked.

She nodded. He followed her to a locked restroom, and she waited outside the door while he used it. They walked back out to the truck and got in.

"You know, if you were my son, I wouldn't want you having anything to do with her either," Fox said.

Parker stared out the side window. "Maybe you two can start a club."

"I know what that woman has been charged with. There's no way I would want my kids anywhere near her. It doesn't matter whether it is a man or a woman, a pedophile is a pedophile."

"She's not a pedophile."

"According to the law she is."

"No, she isn't. She's innocent until proven guilty."

Fox couldn't argue with that one. She nodded, but seemed unconvinced. Parker supposed she was jaded, seeing the nasty women who were incarcerated there every day. She saw everyone through that filter, and thought that everyone was guilty, whether they were convicted of something or not.

She stopped at the gate. "Call ahead. You can't see her if your name isn't on the list, and you need proper accompaniment and permission from your mom. Visiting hours are limited. You can't just show up and expect to see someone."

Parker collected his bike and started on the long trip home.

Chapter Twenty-Five

PARKER HAD BEEN DELETING messages from any numbers he didn't recognize. It was weird and sort of sad that the people who were calling Dakota or Parker nasty names were the same ones who were sending pictures of Dakota or other women. He tried not to see them as he went through and deleted them.

One number that was texting him hadn't sent any pictures, and he realized after glancing at the messages, had not been sending anything mean or disgusting. He paused with his thumb over the most recent message, then pulled away again.

I'm sorry for what my mom did to you.

I'm sorry for making a mess of your life by outing her.

It was Saul. Parker had no idea how Saul had gotten his number, but it didn't look like a scam. It looked like it really was from him and he really was sorry. Parker wondered whether he should answer Saul, or just ignore the messages.

He went back to deleting the rest of his messages, thinking about it. Eventually, he went back to Saul's number and added Saul into his contacts list. He read through the messages again. They were all in pretty much the same vein. Apologies. Extending an olive branch.

Don't worry abt it.

U did what u did

It didn't feel like much of an answer, but he didn't know what else to say. He couldn't say that it wasn't Saul's fault, because it was. Dakota would have continued to pass as a teenager if he hadn't said anything. She wouldn't be in jail and Parker wouldn't be trapped in a life where he was every bully's new favorite victim and couldn't focus on schoolwork or sleep at night.

He sat staring at the screen for a while, not really seeing anything. His head in the clouds, not focused on anything. His phone chimed.

I'd like to apologize face-to-face.

Parker shook his head.

You apologz already. No need.

And Saul's answer was back almost instantly.

Please. I want to talk.

Parker sat on a stool in the food court of the mall, scanning the crowds for any sign of the tall black boy he had once thought of as Dakota's stalker. Now her son. He still didn't quite believe that it was true, that Dakota was old enough to have a son, let alone a son Parker's age. When he pictured Dakota, he saw the Dakota he knew. A cheeky, bright-eyed teenager. He couldn't see her as anything else. He had seen pictures of her that made her look older. But they didn't have any more effect on him than bad tabloid pictures, or app-generated aged photos. He could use a photo app to make her into a zombie too, but that didn't mean that he thought she was one.

He saw Saul looking around and raised his hand to get Saul's attention. The older boy nodded and drifted over. He sat on the stool next to Parker's. His face was impassive. He looked older than Dakota did, if that were possible. Nineteen or twenty, he looked twenty-five or older. Angular features. Worry lines. He looked like he had lived a hard life.

"Hey, Parker. Thanks for meeting me."

He hadn't really given Parker the opportunity to say no. He'd continued to argue and cajole until Parker had finally agreed. Saul put down a large cup of coffee.

"Can I get you anything?"

Parker shook his head. He couldn't afford to get himself anything, and he didn't want Saul paying for it. He didn't want to owe Saul for anything, not even a soft drink.

"I guess…" Saul was having difficulty figuring out where to start. Finding words for what it was he wanted to say. "Things must be pretty rough on you right now."

"I'm okay," Parker returned quickly. He didn't need Saul's pity. He didn't want Saul looking at him as some victim. Because he wasn't.

"I know the kind of email and phone harassment I'm getting," Saul said. "Yours has got to be ten times worse. And I'm not part of this community, so people don't really say anything to me or know who I am. But you…"

"Is that what you want to talk about? How stupid people are being?" Parker demanded.

"No… partly, I guess. Because I feel bad about the way this whole thing has affected your life."

"You already apologized. It's fine. I'll live."

"But I haven't apologized face-to-face. And I really wanted to. So… I'm sorry. I wanted to put a stop to my mom's lies. That's why I came here. Followed her."

"Yeah." Parker stared out at the crowds of people instead of looking at Saul. "Well, you did it. So good for you."

"And when I found out about you… that my mom had a fourteen-year-old boyfriend, I had to warn you. And I couldn't let her run away and abuse someone else."

"It's not abuse. Don't call it that."

Parker could feel Saul's eyes on him.

"That's what it is," Saul insisted. "She's not allowed to touch you like that." He gave a shudder that Parker still saw out of the corner of his eye. "That's sick."

"We were friends," Parker insisted. "Are friends. She never did anything that made me feel bad. *You* made everyone think that there was something wrong, but there wasn't."

Saul shifted in his seat. He was sitting at an angle, facing toward Parker, as if trying to make up for the distance Parker was putting between them. He took a sip of the strong-smelling coffee.

"Parker… Is it okay if I call you that? I don't know any other name…"

"Yeah, Parker is fine."

"I know what it's like."

Parker was startled enough to turn his head and look at Saul. "You know what *what's* like?"

"I went through a lot of different families. Placements with my own extended family, foster care, group homes. Lots of different places. And I…" Saul's Adam's apple bobbed down and up as he swallowed hard. He looked at his coffee but didn't take another sip, trying to force the words out. "I have been abused myself. So I know… how confusing it is. How hard it is to accept it for what it is, and to talk about it."

"It's not the same."

"I've had someone I loved and trusted do that to me. I understand what you're going through."

Parker was angry. "You don't understand!" he insisted. "I lost someone I loved because of what you did! I wasn't being hurt or abused. I was in a relationship! It wasn't some scuzzy foster father forcing me to do stuff. I was just… I just loved her."

"You're in denial," Saul said in an understanding tone. "But at some point, you'll understand what I'm talking about."

Parker wished he had something to throw. Instead he just sat there and seethed.

"I think it would be good for you to go see her," Saul said. "To get a chance to talk to her and see her for what she really is."

That made Parker take notice. He looked at Saul. "Tell that to my mom. She won't let me see Dakota. The prison won't let me in without a permission form. And an escort."

Saul tilted his head slightly, considering this. "You want to see her?"

"Yes! If my mom would let me."

"Did you ever forge her name on a permission slip for school?"

Parker shook his head. "She always let me go to whatever school stuff I wanted. I know other kids who did, and didn't get caught."

"It can be hard to do it for school, because the office might have other copies of her signature on file. But the prison doesn't. They don't know what her signature looks like."

"You don't think they'd call her?"

"Why would they? If you've got the signed form, and an adult to escort you…"

"Who, you?"

"Yeah. I'd take you. If you wanted to go see her. I think it would be good for you. Help you to see her for what she really is."

"Why do you hate her so much?"

"I don't hate her. I can't say I love her," Saul admitted, "but considering she hasn't been a part of my life since I was five, you wouldn't expect me to, would you? I just… I wanted her to have a place in my life. Or to be able to say that I had tried, and just say goodbye to her. So that I wasn't always waiting for her to come back and share something with me."

Parker thought about his father. He had been ten, not five, when his dad had been killed. If he had just gone away, and weren't dead, would Parker have wanted the same thing? Just to go see him, and to say goodbye if the man didn't want anything to do with him? Closure, the therapists called it. They had encouraged him to write letters or dictate a message to his dead father.

"I still might not be able to see her," he told Saul. "There's a visitor list. If I'm not on the list, they won't let me see her."

"Leave that to me. I'll make sure you're on it."

"How can you do that?"

"I can. Just tell me you'll do it. Get them to send you the form. Print it off and sign it. Don't try to make the signature legible, just make a scribble. They'll always catch you if it looks like a kid trying to write a name. Just scribble. It doesn't have to look like anything."

"But my mom's signature—"

"They don't know what your mom's signature looks like. Don't try to copy it. Just scribble."

Parker nodded. "Okay. Okay. I'll just scribble."

"You get that. I'll make sure you're on her list and I'll find out what time you can go visit."

"Do you drive?" Parker asked. "I'm not going to bike out there again. I can hardly sit down."

Saul chuckled. "You biked out there? There is a bus that will take you, you know."

"No, I didn't know anything. I just had the address, so I went."

"Ouch. I have a car. I'll drive you. Deal?"

"Yeah, deal," Parker agreed. His hopes rose. He could see Dakota. Talk to her and discuss the case with her. Find out how he could help her. If they still had a chance at a future together.

He couldn't believe that Saul was actually going to help him do it.

It was so much faster to get to the prison by car than by bike, Parker couldn't believe that they had already reached the guard post. Saul spoke with the guard, showed his ID, and the arm went up, letting them in. Saul found the appropriate parking lot for the section that Dakota was being kept in, and Saul and Parker went in together.

Things were moving so quickly that he thought it would only be a few minutes until he saw Dakota. But of course, nothing in the legal system ever moved that quickly, and just like at the hospital or police station, he had to wait while they went through all of the red tape to get him in. There were several levels of security, walking through x-rays and metal detectors, showing his ID and his permission form, having to leave his wallet and phone and everything in his pockets in a little tiny locker so that he was walking into the visit with nothing other than his clothes. They even had him remove his shoes and put on little paper booties, as if they were afraid he was going to get the industrial tile dirty.

There was a bit of a disagreement when they were ready to go into the visiting room, and Parker expected Saul to hang back and let him go in alone.

"I'm your escort, Parker. I'm supposed to go in with you," Saul pointed out.

"I want to talk to her by myself."

"You can't go in by yourself. I have to go in with you."

Parker looked at the guard who was accompanying them. "I can go in by myself, can't I? I want to talk privately."

The guard looked at Saul, and back at Parker.

"Washington is in the sex offender unit," he said.

They both nodded.

"Sex offenders are not allowed to meet in the public visitor room. There will be a booth to sit in, and a phone to talk with, with barriers between you. You've seen that kind of thing on TV."

"Yeah," Parker agreed. He was disappointed by the fact that they would not be able to touch, even to hold hands, but a barrier between them meant that they didn't have to worry about Dakota doing anything to hurt Parker, so he could talk to her alone. "So he doesn't have to be right there, listening in. He can be back farther, so I can have a private conversation."

"That's up to your escort," the guard said. "He can be as close as he likes."

Parker glared at Saul, daring him to say that Parker couldn't have a private conversation with Dakota. "You said the reason you wanted me to meet with her was so that I could see what she's really like. So let me see. Just her and me."

"All right," Saul agreed.

The guard indicated that they should go on, taking them into a visitor room like he had described. "You can just sit in the back," he told Saul. Then he took Parker up to the little cubicle marked 'B' and pointed at the chair. "Have a seat, please. You must stay in your chair. If you get up, the interview is over, no exceptions. The prisoner is not forced to stay, she can also end the interview at any time she chooses. Understood?"

Parker nodded.

The guard then pointed to a sign mounted to the front of the barrier glass. "All conversations are recorded and are subject to review by the warden. Anything that is said during the interview that could involve the commission of a future crime is not subject to privacy laws and will be turned over to the police department or other authorities. Got it?"

Parker nodded again. The guard stood there silently, but made a motion to the guard patrolling the other side of the glass barrier. That guard shouted something out, and Dakota came shuffling into the narrow room. She was in restraints; handcuffs and leg shackles that were joined to a waist chain. She had on an orange prison jumpsuit. Parker wondered if it really was as ugly as it seemed to him, or if it was a more attractive color to someone who was not so color-blind. Dakota walked to the cubicle opposite Parker's and sat down in the chair. The guard gave her a warning or instruction on her side, and she nodded. He stepped back to give her space. Dakota picked up the phone receiver in the cubicle and Parker did the same.

"Parker…" her voice crackled a little over the phone. "I really didn't want you to come here. I don't want you to see me like this."

Parker studied her closely. Everything seemed a little bit off. Like the difference between seeing your favorite movie character on-screen, and then seeing a candid picture of them taken at the beach with pasty skin and a paunch. Dakota had no makeup on. No shimmery lipstick. No concealer to hide the bags under her eyes. He could see faint worry lines across her forehead. Most startling was her hair. Instead of falling around her face, framing it in the style she usually wore it, she had a severe hairstyle, everything pulled back into a ponytail. The roots that were normally camouflaged by her hairstyle were instead emphasized. And the roots were not pink like the rest of her hair or black because they hadn't yet been bleached and dyed, but gray.

Parker stared at the gray roots at her hairline all the way around her face.

The overall effect was to age her by ten years or more. She looked tired and worried and old.

Parker swallowed. She was still waiting for some kind of response from him.

"I had to see you," he said. "I wanted to make sure you were okay."

Her eyes closed halfway. "It isn't exactly the Ritz," she sighed. "But it's a roof over my head. I guess I don't have to worry about getting kicked out of here."

"I hate seeing you here."

"Then I guess you shouldn't have come here to see me."

Parker gazed at her. He wasn't sure what he wanted to say to her. What he wanted to ask. He didn't really want her to admit to him what her age was. He preferred the illusion. Or at least, the illusion he had had before seeing her under the harsh lights of the prison, with no makeup or pretense.

"Do you think… that they're going to convict you?" he asked tentatively.

"They pretty much have to, don't you think?" she countered. "I knew you'd tell them the truth. What am I going to do? Say that you lied? I won't do that to you."

"But then you'll go to prison."

She shrugged. Her expression was flat, showing nothing.

"Is it really bad?" Parker asked. "I know they say… accused sex offenders are treated really bad…"

"It's not where I'd recommend for a vacation."

He didn't ask her why she had pretended to be a teenager. He already knew why. Because she wanted that childhood. She had to get back what she had lost. She needed to be taken care of.

She wanted to be a kid forever, without the responsibilities of an adult.

And he didn't ask her why she had carried on a relationship with him. He had wanted it. He had asked her, had pursued her. If she had some of those feelings for him and succumbed to the pressure, how did that make her an evil person?

Instead, he asked, "What can I do? I want to help."

Dakota sighed. "You can leave money for me for commissary. That means I can get cigarettes."

"I mean… for your case. What can I do to help… fix it?"

"There's nothing anyone will do. We're hoping that they'll offer a deal. A plea to a reduced sentence, so they don't have to go to all of the expense of a big trial. We keep waiting. But right now, they're not making any offers. I think they know there would be too much of a backlash. Your mom and the other ladies in the neighborhood. They're all going to think that I was after all of their boys. I wasn't after anyone. I was just… lonely. I just wanted a friend."

"I know," Parker asserted. "It was me. I was the one who was always pushing. You told me no to start with. You said we couldn't have a relationship. People couldn't know about it."

"I shouldn't have given in. I could have stayed around and no one would have found out, if it wasn't for Saul. If he hadn't been jealous of you."

She could see him at the back of the room, off behind Parker, and shot him an angry look. "Saul just couldn't leave well enough alone!" she sneered. "He decided that just because I was with you, he was going to tell everyone and not let me live my life. What business is it of his who I am involved with?"

Parker shifted and looked for a way to salvage the conversation. "So if they won't offer you a plea… what can I do? Can I write them a letter? Tell them you didn't do anything. That it was all my own idea…?"

"No. It's not going to make any difference. They say I seduced you. Tempted you into falling for me. That with your hormones and you not having any experience, I was controlling you, and you didn't even know it."

"It wasn't you," Parker insisted again.

"You may as well go on with your life. I'm going to be stuck in here until I go to trial. I don't have the money for bail. You should have your life. Date girls your own age. There's some really cute ones in class."

"Who, like Charity?"

"Yeah, she's fun. Why not?"

"She'd never look at me twice. And I don't want any other girl. I want to be with *you*."

"That can't happen. I'm going to be here for a long time."

Parker shook his head, overwhelmed with anger and disbelief. "What about bail?" he asked, grasping at her previous words. "You could get bail? You could be out?"

"While I was waiting for trial, yeah. But bail is way too high. I don't have any way to raise money. And once I go to trial, I'm done. I'll be right back here."

"It's not fair. What if I can raise the bail? You have money in some of your online accounts, don't you? You were raising money for other things."

She gave him a narrow look and didn't ask him how he had known about that. Different personas with different sob stories. He shouldn't have known about them.

"A little. But not enough." She told him how much she was going to need to get bail.

Parker closed his eyes. "Do they ever lower it? They reduce bail sometimes, don't they?"

"I don't think they're going to reduce mine. They're trying to keep me away from contact with teenagers, so they don't want me leaving here."

"Then what if I can raise that? If I can raise that, I can bail you out? And then you could go back to stay with Jade again, and I could see you?"

"You think your mom or Jade would let you see me again? I don't think Jade would let me stay there again. She was all ready to kick me out before I got arrested."

"Dakota…?"

"Yes," she agreed finally. "If you raised that much money, I could get out on bail."

Parker nodded. "Okay. I'll see what I can do, then."

Dakota smiled and gave a little laugh. "That's what I love about you, Parker. You always want to rescue me."

Parker didn't have much to say to Saul on the way back home. So Saul tried to get a conversation going.

"You see what she's like?" he asked. "You see that I'm not lying, she really is as old as I said she is. And she really was taking advantage of you. Of your youth."

"It doesn't matter if she looks old or young," Parker insisted. Though if he were to be honest with himself, he was a little freaked out by her gray hair and the creeping understanding that she was so much older than he. "That's not why I like her. I like her for who she is. Not for her age. And that's what she likes about me, too. She isn't a pedophile. She isn't just out to get boys. She likes me for who I am."

Saul's mouth twisted, and he shook his head. "You can see her right in front of you like that, and still defend her? Still say that you don't think she intended to molest you."

"That's right," Parker agreed stiffly. It was a good summary. He would never believe that Dakota had entered into the friendship only for a physical relationship. She could have sought that anywhere. She could have gone to any man she were interested in. But she had loved Parker. Not anyone else.

Parker reinstalled all of his social networking apps and a few extras as well. He made sure that Mona was not in any of his audience or friend lists, and started to work. He set up a fundraising campaign to raise money for Dakota's bail. He wasn't going to say that it was for some fake cause and then use it for her bail. He was going to be right up front that that was what it was for. She had friends online. Lots of friends under lots of different profiles.

He wrote a description of what Dakota meant to him and why he wanted to get her out on bail. He recorded a video plea. The fundraising website said that campaigns with videos always raised more money than those without. So he made the best video plea he could. Young love. Injustice. Homelessness. He hit all the hot buttons he could and started sending it out to everyone. All of the friends on all of the networks. His friends, Dakota's timeline, the timelines of her other sock-puppet accounts. He posted it on Saul's timeline too, smiling grimly to himself. The post was taken down within a couple of hours, but in the meantime Dakota's family had seen it. Maybe some of them would contribute, even if Saul himself wouldn't. It seemed to Parker that they might feel guilty for the way they had treated Dakota and Saul in the past and want to soothe their consciences by throwing a little cash in Dakota's direction.

He sent it to the local radio and TV stations. Let them write sensational stories about it. Fourteen-year-old raises money to get thirty-seven-year-old girlfriend out on bail. The more outrageous, the more it would be shared, and the more it would bring in.

For once, Parker slept soundly.

Chapter Twenty-Six

M ONA COULD GROUND PARKER, but she couldn't prevent him from continuing the fundraising campaign, and from transferring the money from the campaign to Dakota's lawyer so that he could arrange for the bail to be paid. It had taken forty-eight hours to raise the amount needed to get Dakota out of jail, and money was still trickling in after the goal had been reached. There was nothing that Mona could do about the reporters who camped out on the sidewalk in front of their house, hoping to get a few choice quotes from her or from Parker.

Parker was still grounded, and under threat that she would send him to his grandparents until the whole thing was resolved. But he still had to leave the house to go to school, and with her job, she couldn't be there to drop him off and pick him up every day to make sure that he didn't cut school. Even if she could, she still couldn't be there the whole time to make sure that he didn't take off partway through the day.

He watched his phone, checking it every minute or two for a text notification. He didn't know how long it would take after the bail was paid for Dakota to actually get out of jail, or what she would do once she did. She was put on electronic monitoring so she couldn't flee the jurisdiction. She had to stay in town.

Parker had asked the lawyer to have Dakota text him once she was out. But the hours passed and his classes all blurred together and he still hadn't heard anything. It wasn't until the end of the school day he finally got the message he had been waiting for.

Bail paid and am out. Meet me u no where.

You know where.

Parker knew where she wasn't. She wasn't going to be at his house or Jade's house. She wasn't going to be anywhere out in the open where people walking or driving by might see them together and raise a big stink. She didn't want to be filmed by reporters or sent straight back to jail because she had breached her bail conditions by being within 300 yards of Parker.

He got on his bike and headed over to the park. He rode the trails for a while at random, watching for reporters or anyone else suspicious before finally heading toward their place, his heart thumping way harder than it should riding on a flat trail with little effort. Parker locked his bike up and went to find her.

She was there waiting for him. Looking like herself again, pretty and cute. Sitting in the grass tapping away on her phone, waiting for him to arrive. She looked up and grinned as Parker made his way over to her.

"Hey, handsome," she said in a low, hoarse whisper. "Long time, no see."

Parker knelt beside her and gave her the whisper of a kiss, his emotions raw and tender. "It's only a few days since I saw you at the prison," he reminded her.

"But that wasn't me." Dakota closed her eyes, and he kissed her again. "That wasn't me," Dakota repeated. "I couldn't be me in that place."

"No," he agreed.

"You're a genius," she murmured. "You're hopeless at algebra, but are you ever great with a fundraising campaign!"

Parker was embarrassed. "I'm getting better at the algebra," he insisted. "You know I am."

"Oh, I don't care about the algebra. When are you ever going to use it? I never used it in any of my jobs."

"I want to get a scholarship. So I can go to university. If I want to be a vet or something, I need math and science."

"Why would you want to do that? Why don't we both just stay teenagers forever?" She pulled him in this time, pressing her body against his while she kissed him.

Parker smiled at her, trying to catch his breath again before speaking. "I don't want to be a teenager forever. I want to be a vet. Or something else like that. A biologist, or a person who watches animal behavior, like Jane Goodall."

"You sound like Saul," Dakota complained. She stuck out her lip in a pout. "Scholarships and university and getting ahead in life. Making a difference in the world. You know who makes a difference in the world? Nobody. In the end, you leave the world just as crappy as it was when you were born. You and Saul aren't going to change the world. Neither am I."

Parker frowned and shook his head. He couldn't figure out why she was so down on him. Why was she comparing him to Saul, when Parker had helped to get her out of jail? Saul had put her in there, but Parker had gotten her out. Temporarily, at least.

"Maybe I'll have to find another guy who will stay with me," Dakota said. "Someone like me, who wants to stay a kid, instead of growing up and having a career that doesn't mean anything anyway."

"Have you been drinking?" Parker asked. It would explain her annoyed, emotional behavior. But he couldn't smell anything on her. Maybe she had taken some other pill or drug that was making her agitated. Or maybe it was just the stress of being in prison, and she was just letting it all out now that she was free.

"How about Link?" Dakota suggested. "Think he'd like to stay a kid forever? Or is he an overachiever like you?"

Parker went cold. He let go of her hands and just stared at her.

"It's a joke, Parker," Dakota said, laughing at his reaction. "I'm just teasing you."

But in his mind, Parker saw her and Link together. He saw, not Dakota the way she looked now, but the Dakota he had seen at the prison, tired and gray, together with Parker's little brother. Calling him handsome, plying him with alcohol, cuddling up with him under a blanket in front of the TV, all alone in the house.

"Parker? Come on, what's wrong? I'm just joking about Link. He's just a little kid."

"He's a year younger than me," Parker told her. "Eleven months."

She shrugged and frowned. She caught Parker's arm and tried to pull him closer again. "I'm not interested in Link. Only in you."

Parker shoved her away. She hung on to him for a minute, her grip like iron. Much stronger than she looked. Her face was angry and desperate as she tried to hold on to Parker, to pull him to her. Then she let go, laughing and shaking her head.

"I thought you wanted to get together," she said. "I guess I was wrong. They all got to you. Your mom and the cops and the news and everyone. They all got to you and convinced you that it's wrong, and I'm some kind of monster for being friends with you."

"No." Parker shook his head. He stayed well back out of her reach. "I never believed any of them."

"Stay with me, Parker," she coaxed. "Don't be in such a hurry to leave. I don't have anyone else. I don't even know where I'm going to stay now that I'm out. A motel, I guess. No one will take me in now."

"Or a shelter," Parker said, not feeling pity for her. "You could always try a shelter."

"I don't want to be homeless again. Being homeless is so hard. Will you help me to find a motel? Somewhere private, where the TV reporters couldn't find us? You're the one with the money. We can put it in a fake name so no one can track us down." She laughed, one hard bitter syllable. "The cops would have a field day with that one."

"Yeah. So I'd better not go anywhere like that with you. I think I'd better head for home. My mom will be wondering where I am. I'm supposed to be grounded. Straight home from school."

"She won't know. She won't be home yet."

"I have to go," Parker insisted. "I'll see you later."

Parker got on his bike and pedaled for home. He wasn't going at a relaxed pace like he had on the way there. Link would already be home and Parker felt suddenly guilty for having let all of his responsibilities fall on Link lately. The kid was only thirteen. He didn't need to be solely responsible for his four younger siblings because Parker was out with Dakota, or pouting or angry at Mona. Parker was supposed to be at home.

Sweat was running down his face when he got home and his heart was racing. He stashed his bike by the house and hurried in the door, making it bang against the inside of the wall in his hurry. Link, sitting on the couch with Leslie, his schoolbooks nestled in his lap, jumped at the bang. His head swiveled around and he looked at Parker, his eyes wide.

"Sheesh, what's your hurry?" His eyes went over Parker. "What's wrong? You look like you ran all the way here."

Parker shook his head. He hooked his thumb toward where he'd parked his bike. "Just biked."

"Were you being chased by a cougar?" Link blew out his breath. He looked over at Leslie, making sure she was engrossed in the TV, before speaking again, his voice low. "I thought Dakota got out today. Didn't think you'd be coming home."

"Course I came home." Parker toed off his sneakers and wiped sweat from his face with both hands. "Link…"

Link's eyes had wandered over to the TV. "Yeah?"

"Link," Parker said more firmly, demanding his attention.

Link turned back to look at him. "Yeah? What is it?"

"I just wanted to know…" The words stuck in Parker's throat. He cleared his throat and moved farther into the room, trying to frame them. Link continued to stare at him, one eyebrow raised, waiting for him to say what he wanted to know. "I mean… I'm just wondering…" He swallowed and forced himself to go on. "If Dakota ever came on to you."

"On to me?" Link held up both hands and made a 'stop' motion. "She's your girlfriend, Parker, I'd never touch her. No way."

"No, I'm not accusing you. I'm wondering if she ever did anything."

Link frowned and bit his lip. "Like what?"

The chill Parker had experienced in the clearing returned, in spite of the fact that he was sweating profusely.

"I don't know. Did she ever… make you uncomfortable? Ever kiss you on the cheek or hug you or something. Act too friendly. Or invite you… to anything."

Link shook his head slowly. "She was your girl, Parker."

Parker waited, silent.

"Sure, she's touched me on the shoulder. Joked around with me. *Teased* me about going out with her. But… none of it was serious." He cocked his head. "Was it?"

Parker sighed and shook his head. "No," he agreed. "I… hope not."

Link looked back down at his schoolwork, a crease between his eyebrows.

Mona worked late. She had picked up an extra shift, needing to make up for the time she had missed recently dealing with Parker's escapades. Link had told her that Parker was home, but she still looked surprised when she walked in the door and saw him sitting in the living room. The house was quiet.

"Kids are all in bed?" she asked. Her face was lined with fatigue, and when she bent to put her purse down and to remove her shoes, she acted like it was a long way to the floor. Parker felt a pain in his chest, thinking about how much he had put her through lately. How many of those lines were a direct result of his recent choices.

"Link is still up. I think Jessup's playing a game under the blankets."

She nodded and eased into the couch beside Parker. "How are you?"

Parker let his shoulders rise and fall in a shrug. "I dunno. Okay." He shook his head slightly. "Confused."

"Uh-huh." She looked at the TV playing. Parker didn't even know what was on. "I guess Dakota is out on bail today, thanks to you."

"Yeah."

"But you're here, where you should be."

"She's not allowed to see me. That's part of her bail conditions."

Mona snorted. She knew only too well how likely Parker and Dakota were to pay any attention to the bail conditions. Parker had completely disregarded his grounding. Dakota had broken the law. How could either of them be expected to abide by bail terms?

"Was it all just… pretend…?" Parker asked.

"Was what pretend? Dakota was pretending to be a teenager, yes. I can't explain why she would do that. Maybe she's mentally ill. Who knows how much of the rest of her story was true. I have a feeling that some of it was and some of it wasn't."

"But our feelings for each other? Did she… not care about me?" Parker bit his lip to keep it from quivering and to hold off the tears that threatened. He tried to swallow the hot lump in his throat.

"I don't know what her feelings were. I'm sure she was grateful to you for helping her. You're a kind, friendly boy, and I'm sure she appreciated your friendship toward her. But she took advantage of you. Something she very well knew she wasn't supposed to do. That's not… showing love. That's just physical gratification."

"I love her."

He hadn't said the words before. The look on Mona's face was one of incredible sadness. She didn't get angry at him. She didn't argue and say that he couldn't love Dakota, as he had expected her to. She reached an arm around him and pulled him against her, putting her head against his shoulder, since his no longer nestled against hers like it had when he was smaller. She stroked his hair and reached up to kiss his cheek.

"I know you feel very strongly toward her," Mona said softly. "I'm so sorry that this happened and you got hurt." She sighed. "And I'm sorry for apologizing again. You said you didn't want to hear it anymore."

"It's okay."

She held him tightly and rubbed his shoulder. For a long time, she didn't say anything. Parker wasn't sure if she saw the single tear that escaped his eye and ran down his cheek.

"Do you know that I love you, Parker?"

"Yes!" He was shocked that she asked. He might not be the best kid in the world, and had fought against her and rebelled because he didn't think she could understand what he was going through, but he had never doubted her love for him. "Of course, I know that."

"Not just a little bit. And not just when you're 'being good.' I love you more than anything. No matter what."

Parker laid his head on top of hers. "I love you too, Mom."

"You'd better get off to bed, or you're going to have a hard time getting up for school in the morning."

Chapter Twenty-Seven

FOR A FEW DAYS, Parker didn't see Dakota. He went to school and he went home, and he didn't go to the park or any of the places that Dakota might be hanging around. He worried a little about running into her by accident, but that wasn't too likely if he only traveled between the school and home, two places that Dakota was not allowed to be without breaking her bail conditions.

"Parker. Parker, hey!"

Parker blinked away the cobwebs and turned his head to look in the direction of the whisper. He was sitting at his desk and Charity was looking at him, exasperated. He made a little shrugging motion with his hands. "What?"

She tossed a small, folded-up piece of paper onto his desk. Parker looked at the note, then at Mr. Bonne to make sure he hadn't seen or heard anything, then back over at Charity.

"Open it!" Charity mouthed.

Parker unfolded the note carefully, trying not to let it crinkle and attract the teacher's attention. There was a flap folded over and tucked in, like some origami design. He spread it out on his desk and smoothed the folds.

She had, at least, remembered not to write in cursive. Taking the letter home to Mona to get her to read it for him might have been a problem.

Parker wasn't sure why she hadn't texted or messaged him. He supposed she didn't want to leave an electronic trail that showed she was not complying with her bail terms. Or maybe she felt the letter was too long or too emotional for a text message.

Parkinson,

I'm sorry I upset you when I said that about Link. It was just supposed to be a joke, but I guess you didn't see it that way. I waited for a long time for you to come back. I've waited for you every day after school. Are you really that mad at me?

Please come see me. You know I can't come to you, but I want to see you again. We have to talk.

Dakota

The O in Dakota was a little heart.

Parker shook his head, trying to take it in. Dakota's voice begged in his head. The images he had of her fought for priority. Homeless Dakota. Teen Dakota wildly happy over the gift of a toy pony. Dakota with him in the glade. But also Dakota drunk. In prison. Teasing him she may as well get together with Link instead of him.

"Parker. Parker Jurek!"

Even Mr. Bonne's voice didn't immediately pull him out of his reverie. Parker looked up at the teacher standing right beside his desk. He swallowed.

"Uh... hi."

Mr. Bonne gave him a look of disbelief. "Are you... under the weather, Mr. Jurek?"

Code for, 'Are you drunk? What's the matter with you?'

"No. Sorry. I just... I guess I'm tired."

Parker looked down at the unfolded note. Mr. Bonne reached over and picked it up. His eyes flicked over the page and then at Parker's face. Parker got hot, the rush of blood turning him into a tomato. A couple of students giggled nervously. Parker shook his head pleadingly.

Mr. Bonne didn't read the note out loud to the class. He had never been one of the teachers who would try to humiliate students by reading their text messages to each other out loud. Sometimes with silly voices and intentional mispronunciations where students had used abbreviations or shorthanded by leaving out vowels.

Mr. Bonne walked over to his desk and put the note down right in the middle of it. Then he walked back up to the front of the class and continued his lecture. A few students strained to see the note, but Mr. Bonne's desk was too far away from any of the student desks for them to get a clear look at it. It still wasn't safe on Mr. Bonne's desk. A student could get up to, say, throw something in the garbage, and get a cell picture of it to circulate throughout the school.

Mr. Bonne was talking, and Charity was trying to catch Parker's eye. Parker looked up at Mr. Bonne to make sure he wasn't still being monitored, and then turned his face toward Charity. She mouthed a swear at him, and he shrugged. What was he supposed to do about it? The paper was on Mr. Bonne's desk. Parker didn't have any control over it anymore. Charity gave Parker an angry scowl and he saw her hand hidden just under the lip of her desk, tapping out a message. His phone vibrated a minute later, and Charity lifted her eyebrow at him, demanding that he read it. Parker stretched. He rearranged himself. He pulled his phone out of his pocket and hid it between two pages in his notebook, then pretended to be leafing through his notes as he looked down to see what it said.

You idiot!!! He'll report her to the cops 4 contacting u!

Parker swallowed, then looked at Charity again. She gave him a look that hammered the message home. As soon as Mr. Bonne had the chance, he was going to contact the authorities. And then Dakota would be rearrested and thrown back in prison, with no chance to make bail again. Because Parker had screwed up.

Parker slid out of his seat and was almost to the door before Mr. Bonne noticed what was going on.

"Parker—"

"Restroom," Parker gasped. "Sick!"

"Adrian," Mr. Bonne said, "would you—"

"I'll check on him!" a girl's voice interrupted.

Parker turned slightly once in the hallway to see who was coming after him, grasping for an explanation. But it was Charity. She dashed after him.

"Go, go, go!" she insisted. "I'll wait a few minutes. I'll tell Mr. Bonne you went into the bathroom and I could hear you throwing up. Delay him for as long as I can, but it might only be a few minutes. Run! You've got to tell her!"

"Tell her what?" Parker asked. "What do I say?"

"Tell her that they're coming for her. If she doesn't run, she's going to prison for ten years! What do you think?"

"Okay," Parker agreed. "Okay, okay."

She swore as he tore away from her. "Why do boys have to be such morons?"

Parker got out of the school and to his bike without being stopped. He pedaled away furiously, and then a couple of blocks away from the school, pulled to the side and stopped. He had no idea where Dakota was staying. No idea where she would be during the middle of the school day. He looked down at his phone, expecting to see a message from her, but only saw Charity's warning text.

He scrolled through the texts to Dakota's name, and tapped for a new message.

Where u now?

He had only a minute to wait and she had sent him back a smiley face.

Ice cream shop. U hungry?

Parker growled angrily at this. She had no idea what danger she was in.

Go to underpass. Where met first day.

Minutes ticked by without a response. Was he too late? Had they already apprehended her?

OK

Parker breathed out. He slid his phone back away and jumped back onto his pedals. In a couple of minutes he was at the underpass where he had found Dakota panhandling before taking her to Jade.

She didn't move as quickly as he did on foot, and she didn't seem to be in any particular hurry to get to the rendezvous point.

Once Parker spotted her, he rode the rest of the way down the block to meet her.

Dakota gave him a cheerful smile.

"Hi! I thought you were giving me the cold shoulder. We all okay now?"

Parker spluttered as he tried to get the words out in a way that made sense, so that she wouldn't delay.

"Charity gave me your note at school—"

"I knew that would work—"

"Work? It didn't work! Mr. Bonne got it. Now he knows you're in contact with me, and he's going to call the cops. You're going right back to jail for breach of bail conditions!"

"Crap!" Dakota's voice had lost all of its girlish breathiness. "What the *hell* did you let that happen for?"

It was like a slap in the face. Parker stared at her, shocked at her tone.

"I'm… sorry… I didn't mean to…"

"What did she do it in class for? Stupid cow! Couldn't you open it between periods? Or hide it in your book or something? Mr. Bonne has it? He took it away from you?"

"Yes."

She swore, staring at him.

"I screwed up," Parker said. "I'm sorry. I didn't mean to make things worse."

"Well… they're not worse yet. No cops in sight. I've still got time to run."

"What about your monitor?" Parker pointed at Dakota's ankle. "If you run, they're just going to track you down."

"I'm not stupid. I'm not going to run with it *on*."

"How are you going to get it off?"

"I've done my research. I know what to do."

Parker swallowed and nodded. He stood there, not sure what else to do or say. He wiped a stream of sweat from his temples.

"Ice cream?" Dakota held her cone out to him.

Parker was confused, and not knowing what else to do, took a couple of licks. "Don't you have to go?" he said. "What are you waiting for?"

"This isn't the movies, Parker. Things don't move that quickly in real life. It will take Mr. Bonne time to call the cops. Maybe he'll wait until noon or after school. Then it will take him time to get through to the right department and the right person. They're not going to send someone out right away. It's not a big panic. I'm tagged, so they know they can track me down." She took a long, sensuous lick of the ice cream. "Don't you worry about me. The wheels of justice turn slowly."

"Oh." Parker hadn't realized how naive he was being. And Charity too. Thinking that he had to run, that the cops would be on Dakota in minutes. "I get it."

She offered him another lick of the cone. Parker wiped a bit of ice cream from the corner of his mouth.

"You're coming with me, right?"

Parker stared at Dakota. "What?"

"You're coming with me. When I run. You're going to come along with me. Right?"

"No." Parker shook his head. "I… I can't go with you."

"Sure you can. Why not?"

"I need to stay here… to take care of my family. Finish my education."

"Your mom will look after your family. She's done it until now, hasn't she? And you can get your education anywhere. We'll just start somewhere new." She gave him a sly smile. "As long as you have an address, you can get registered. Or so I hear."

She chuckled as Parker's face blossomed red.

"Come on, Parker. You have to come with me. I don't want to be by myself. I need my friend. My buddy." She hooked a finger over the collar of his t-shirt, pulling him toward her. "My lover."

Parker pulled back, wrenching free. Dakota stepped forward, closing the space between them again. Parker put up his hands defensively.

"Don't touch me," he warned. "Don't do that."

"Don't touch you? That's not what you've been saying until now. What's gotten into you? I was sure you'd come with me."

"Because that's always the way it's been before?" Parker challenged. "Whatever boy you pick out, he's always followed you before? You just keep doing it? Picking them up, and using them until you don't want them anymore?"

Dakota's eyes widened. "What the hell are you talking about? I've never done that!"

"You run from one place to another…"

"Yeah, I do. Never stay in one place more than a few months or a couple years. Always on the run for the next one. But always alone. I never took anyone with me." She shook her head. "Not even Saul." She stared at him, her eyes hurt. "I never had anyone to take with me before."

He felt the prickle of guilt. All the years. All that running, and she'd finally found what she was looking for. She'd finally found the one guy who was kind to her, even knowing her secret. Parker was going to take away the one thing she'd been looking for all those years.

But he couldn't leave his family behind, without even a word. He wasn't going to abdicate his responsibilities and let everything fall on Link. He couldn't leave his family, the people he really loved, and who had always loved him, to go with Dakota.

How long would it be until she got tired of him? Decided to run from the next place but to leave him behind? How long would it be until she decided he was too old and might blow her cover? Maybe she hadn't been with a string of young men. Maybe he had been the first to fulfill her needs. But she wouldn't stay with him forever. She hadn't even stayed with her own baby until he started school.

His eyes burned, but he shook his head. "I'm sorry, Dakota. I just can't."

"You said you love me."

"I do."

"No, you don't. If you loved me, you would go with me."

"You gotta fly free. On your own." His throat hurt. He swallowed hard.

"So I'm just another hurt animal. I never meant anything to you."

"You do. But you have to go. And I have to stay."

Her eyes looked tired. Not with rings under her eyes. If there were any, she had concealed them well. But they seemed strained. Her whole posture said that she was tired of the business of living. The pretty pink hair was suddenly just a wig to him. The makeup was just a mask. She wasn't a teenager or an old woman. She was just Dakota, pretending to be something she wasn't.

She would never know the joy of raising a family or retiring from a successful career.

She would always shirk responsibility and run away when faced with the realities of life. She would never get the same satisfaction out of life as Parker would, taking on new responsibilities and growing and facing challenges as they came up. That only came with growing up.

The whine of a siren in the distance awoke them from their tableau. Dakota tossed her ice cream cone on the sidewalk. She opened her shoulder bag and dug through it, pulling out some kind of cutting shears. Parker watched in fascination as she bent down and pulled the ankle monitor away from her leg, slipped the shears into place, and cut it off. She watched the traffic go by, and after half a minute or so, flicked the ankle cuff into the back of a passing truck. She smiled at Parker.

"That will give them something to chase."

"Yeah."

"You won't come? Really?"

"No."

She shrugged. "Okay. Well... I'll be in touch, okay?"

"You better not. They'll be looking for you. They'll be watching me."

"Ah, speaking of which..."

Dakota pulled out her phone. She ejected the tiny SIM card from it and snapped it in half. She tossed the phone into the road, where it was quickly flattened by several vehicles in succession.

"Goodbye, Parkinson." She leaned toward him and brushed his lips with a kiss. "I know you said not to, but…" She wrapped her strong arms around him and pulled him close, giving him a deep, passionate kiss, their bodies thrumming together. Parker didn't fight her, and when she released him, didn't know what to do with himself.

Dakota laughed at his cherry-red face and walked away from him.

Parker stood there, watching long after she had disappeared.

He bent over and picked up the discarded ice cream cone and tossed it into the garbage can.

Epilogue

Forget them all. Come with me where you'll never, never have to worry about grown up things again.

PARKER LOOKED UP FROM his English lit class copy of *Peter Pan and Wendy* at the TV as they announced the upcoming exposé about Carolina Craig, a forty-year-old black woman accused of submitting scholarship papers that falsified her age. The face on the screen was older than he remembered. No longer able to pass for a teenager, she had applied at a Christian college as a twenty-year-old, but the scholarship and loan papers she had filled out to support herself while at school had been discovered to be false.

Her face had changed, but she was still trying to recapture her childhood; refusing to grow up and take on grown-up responsibilities.

"Do you miss her?"

Parker glanced over at Miranda, who was looking up from her schoolbooks at the screen. He wasn't sure what to say.

"You… remember?" he asked tentatively.

"I remember Dakota," she confirmed. "She was nice."

"She was fun," Parker agreed. "You girls liked her."

"So did *you,*" Miranda countered, drawing the word out teasingly into two syllables.

"Yeah."

"Do you wish she hadn't left?"

Parker shook his head.

He looked down at Sophie, watching TV on the floor, leaning back against the couch. Leslie had fallen asleep with her head in Sophie's lap. Link had gone to the school to watch Jessup's tournament. Parker thumbed the pages of his book.

In a couple of weeks, Parker was scheduled to take his SATs. The local college offered veterinary medicine, so he could continue to live at home and help with the kids while studying. Leslie was now nine, so by the time he had finished four years of post-secondary schooling, she would be thirteen. Old enough that the Jureks would no longer need a babysitter.

Parker patted the couch beside him. "Come over here."

Miranda left her books where they were and moved over to sit close to him. Parker put his arm around her to give her a squeeze and kissed the top of her head.

"I liked Dakota," he told her. "She was… someone special. But she wasn't happy."

"You could have made her happy."

"I thought I could. I thought I could fix everything for her. But she was hurt deep down inside… so she didn't want the things that would make her happy."

Miranda's brow furrowed. Parker could tell that Sophie was watching him as well, though she pretended she was still engrossed by the TV.

"Dakota wanted to be happy," Miranda disagreed.

Parker thought about how to explain it. "You know when you won that creative writing contest at school…?"

"Yeah!" Miranda lit up at the memory.

"And they gave you a coupon for a free pizza to celebrate?"

"Yeah," Miranda enthused. "That was the best!"

"Was the pizza the best part?"

Miranda looked confused. She looked at Parker, then at Sophie, who was watching them openly now.

"No… the pizza was good, though."

"But it wasn't anything special. It was the same as any other pizza."

"It's better when it's free." Miranda snuggled against Parker, wrapping his arm around her again. "But the best part was when they told me I won. And showing everyone the certificate. Especially Mom." Miranda's face shone. Mona had been so proud of her.

"You worked really hard on that story."

Miranda nodded vigorously.

"You didn't have to. You could have just whipped something up during class and handed it in. Instead of putting all those extra hours into it."

"But it was good. The best thing I ever wrote."

"And you were really proud of it even before you won."

"Uh-huh."

"Even before you got the pizza."

She rolled her eyes. "Yeah. I get it. I felt good because I worked so hard."

"Well… Dakota, she just wanted the pizza."

Miranda traced a scar down Parker's arm. The one he'd gotten falling through the branches of a tree after putting a baby robin back into its nest. When he was nine; the first time he'd broken that arm. "She didn't want to do the work?"

"No." Parker looked down at Miranda. "She didn't get that the good stuff comes from staying around and working at it. Being responsible and taking care of each other."

"Like you did?" Miranda asked. "After Daddy got shot…?"

"Yeah." He gave her one more squeeze and let out a long breath. "Like that."

Parker looked back down at *Peter Pan* and finished reading the passage.

Forget them all. Come with me where you'll never, never have to worry about grown up things again.

Never is an awfully long time.

Did you enjoy this book? Reviews and recommendations
are vital to making a book successful.
Please leave a review at your favorite book store or review
site and share it with your friends.

Don't miss the following bonus material:
Sign up for mailing list to get a free ebook
Other books by P.D. Workman
Read a sneak preview chapter
Learn more about the author

Preview of
She Wore Mourning

Zachary Goldman stared down the telephoto lens at the subjects before him. It was one of those days that left tourists gaping over the gorgeous scenery. Dark trees against crisp white snow, with the mountains as a backdrop. Like the picture on a Christmas card.

The thought made Zachary feel sick.

But he wasn't looking at the scenery. He was looking at the man and the woman in a passionate embrace. The pretty young woman's cheeks were flushed pink, more likely with her excitement than the cold, since she had barely stepped out of her car to greet the man. He had a swarthier complexion and a thin black beard, and was currently turned away from Zachary's camera.

He waited patiently for them to move, to look around at their surroundings so that he could get a good picture of their faces.

They thought they were alone. That no one could see them without being seen. But they hadn't counted on the fact that Zachary had been surveilling them for a couple of weeks and had known where they would go. They gave him lots of warning so that he could park his car out of sight, camouflage himself in the trees, and settle in to wait for their appearance. He was no amateur; he'd been a private investigator since she had been choosing wedding dresses for her Barbie dolls.

He held down the shutter button to take a series of shots as they came up for air and looked around at the magnificent surroundings, smiling at each other, eyes shining.

All the while, he was trying to keep the negative thoughts at bay. Why had he fallen into private detection? It was one of the few ways he could make a living using his skill with a camera. But he could have chosen another profession. He didn't need to spend his whole life following other people, taking pictures of their most private moments. What was the real point of his job? He destroyed lives; something he'd had his fill of long ago. When was the last time he'd brought a smile to a client's face? A real, genuine smile? He had wanted to make a difference in people's lives. To exonerate the innocent.

Zachary's phone started to buzz in his pocket. He lowered the camera and turned around, walking further into the grove of trees. He had the pictures he needed. Anything else would be overkill.

He pulled out his phone and looked at it. Not recognizing the number, he swiped the screen to answer the call.

"Goldman Investigations."

"Uh… yes… Is this Mr. Goldman?" a voice inquired. Older, female, with a tentative quaver.

"Yes, this is Zachary," he confirmed, subtly nudging her away from the 'mister.'

"Mr. Goldman, my name is Molly Hildebrandt."

He hoped she wasn't calling her about her sixty-something-year-old husband and his renewed interest in sex. If it was another infidelity case, he was going to have to turn it down for his own sanity. He would even take a lost dog or wedding ring. As long as the ring wasn't on someone else's finger now.

"Mrs. Hildebrandt. How can Goldman Investigations help you?"

Of course, she had probably already guessed that Goldman Investigations consisted of only one employee. Most people seemed to sense that from the size of his advertisements. From the fact that he listed a post office box number instead of a business suite downtown or in one of the newer commercial areas. It wasn't really a secret.

"I don't know whether you have been following the news at all about Declan Bond, the little boy who drowned…?"

Zachary frowned. He trudged back toward his car.

"I'm familiar with the basics," he hedged. A four- or five-year-old boy whose round face and feathery dark hair had been pasted all over the news after a search for a missing child had ended tragically.

"They announced a few weeks ago that it was determined to be an accident."

Zachary ground his teeth. "Yes…?"

"Mr. Goldman, I was Declan's grandma." Her voice cracked. Zachary waited, listening to her sniffles and sobs as she tried to get herself under control. "I'm sorry. This has been very difficult for me. For everyone."

"Yes."

"Mr. Goldman, I don't believe that it was an accident. I'm looking for someone who would investigate the matter privately."

Zachary breathed out. A homicide investigation? Of a child? He'd told himself that he would take anything that wasn't infidelity. But if there was one thing that was more depressing than couples cheating on each other, it was the death of a child.

"I'm sure there are private investigators that would be more qualified for a homicide case than I am, Mrs. Hildebrandt. My schedule is pretty full right now."

Which, of course, was a lie. He had the usual infidelities, insurance investigations, liabilities, and odd requests. The dregs of the private investigation business. Nothing substantial like a homicide. It was a high-profile case. A lot of volunteers had shown up to help, expecting to find a child who had wandered out of his own yard, expecting to find him dirty and crying, not floating face down in a pond. A lot of people had mourned the death of a child they hadn't even known existed before his disappearance.

"I need your help, Mr. Goldman. Zachary. I can't afford a big name. But you've got good references. You've investigated deaths before. Can't you help me?"

He wondered who she had talked to. It wasn't like there were a lot of people who would give him a bad reference. He was competent and usually got the job done. But he wasn't a big name.

"I could meet with you," he finally conceded. "The first consultation is free. We'll see what kind of a case you have and whether I want to take it. I'm not making any promises at this point. Like I said, my schedule is pretty full already."

She gave a little half-sob. "Thank you. When are you able to come?"

After he had hung up, Zachary climbed into his car, putting his camera down on the floor in front of the passenger seat where it couldn't fall, and started the car. For a while, he sat there, staring out the front windshield at the magical, sparkling, Christmas-card scene. Every year, he told himself it would be better. He would get over it and be able to move on. To enjoy the holiday season like everyone else. Who cared about his crappy childhood experiences? People moved on.

And when he had married Bridget, he had thought he was going to achieve it. They would have a fairy-tale Christmas. They would have hot chocolate after skating at the public rink. They would wander down main street looking at the lights and the crèche in front of the church. They would open special, meaningful presents from each other.

But they'd fought over Christmas. Maybe it was Zachary's fault. Maybe he had sabotaged it with his gloom. But the season brought with it so much baggage. There had been no skating rink. No hot chocolate, only hot tempers. No walks looking at the lights or the nativity. They had practically thrown their gifts at each other, flouncing off to their respective corners to lick their wounds and pout away the holiday.

He'd still cherished the thought that perhaps the next year there would be a baby. What could be more perfect than Christmas with a baby? It would unite them. Make them a real family. Just like Zachary had longed for since he'd lost his own family. He and Bridget and a baby. Maybe even twins. Their own little family in their own little happy bubble.

But despite a positive pregnancy test, things had gone horribly wrong.

Zachary stared at the bright white scenery and blinked hard, trying to shake off the shadows of the past. The past was past. Over and done. This year he was back to baching it for Christmas. Just him and a beer and *It's a Wonderful Life* on TV.

He put the car in reverse and didn't look into the rear-view mirror as he backed up, even knowing about the precipice behind him. He'd deliberately parked where he'd have to back up toward the cliff when he was done. There was a guardrail, but if he backed up too quickly, the car would go right through it, and who could say whether it had been accidental or deliberate? He had been cold-stone sober and had been out on a job. Mrs. Hildebrandt could testify that he had been calm and sober during their call. It would be ruled an accident.

But his bumper didn't even touch the guardrail before he shifted into drive and pulled forward onto the road.

He'd meet with the grandmother. Then, assuming he did not take the case, there would always be another opportunity.

Life was full of opportunities.

~ ~ ~

She Wore Mourning, A Zachary Goldman Mystery by P.D. Workman is coming soon!

About the Author

FOR AS LONG AS P.D. Workman can remember, the blank page has held an incredible allure. After a number of false starts, she finally wrote her first complete novel at the age of twelve. It was full of fantastic ideas. It was the spring board for many stories over the next few years. Then, forty-some novels later, P.D. Workman finally decided to start publishing. Lots more are on the way!

P.D. Workman is a devout wife and a mother of one, born and raised in Alberta, Canada. She is a homeschooler and an Executive Assistant. She has a passion for art and nature, creative cooking for special diets, and running. She loves to read, to listen to audio books, and to share books out loud with her family. She is a technology geek with a love for all kinds of gadgets and tools to make her writing and work easier and more fun. In person, she is far less well-spoken than on the written page and tends to be shy and reserved with all but those closest to her.

~ ~ ~

Please visit P.D. Workman at pdworkman.com to see what else she is working on, to join her mailing list, and to link to her social networks.

~ ~ ~

If you enjoyed this book, please take the time to recommend it to other purchasers with a review or star rating and share it with your friends!